SPLASHBACK

JAMES TARR

BOOKS

Vinci Books

vinci-books.com

Published by Vinci Books Ltd in 2025

1

Copyright © James Tarr 2019

The author has asserted their moral right to be identified as the author of this work in accordance with the Copyright, Designs and Patents Act 1988. This work is a work of fiction. Names, characters, places and incidents are the product of the author's imagination or are used fictitiously. Any resemblance to actual persons, living or dead, places and incidents is entirely coincidental.

All rights reserved. No part of this publication may be copied, reproduced, distributed, stored in any retrieval system, or transmitted in any form or by any means, including photocopying, recording, or other electronic or mechanical methods, nor used as a source for any form of machine learning including AI datasets, without the prior written permission of the publisher.

The publisher and the author have made every effort to obtain permissions for any third party material used in this book and to comply with copyright law. Any queries in this respect should be brought to the attention of the publisher and any omissions will be corrected in future editions.

A CIP catalogue record for this book is available from the British Library.

Paperback ISBN: 9781036701093

Printed and bound in Great Britain by Clays Ltd, Elcograf S.p.A.

By James Tarr

James Tarr Conspiracy Thrillers

Failure Drill

Splashback

Splits and Transitions

Whorl

Waiting for the Kick

Ghosts and Madmen

The Subsection

Greater love hath no man than this, that a man lay down his life for his friends.

John 15:13

Greater love hath no man than this, that a man lay down his life for his friends.

John 15:13

DECEMBER 2002

ONE

Friday

7:41 a.m.

She kissed me passionately, breath hot on my cheeks, her lips pressed firmly against mine. She was insistent, demanding, her tongue fighting to get into my mouth. When that didn't work she nuzzled my ear, licked the earlobe once to get my attention, then came back to my mouth once more. Her tongue was relentless, and she pressed against my chest, holding me down. I felt myself begin to respond finally, and her tongue found its way into my mouth.

I opened my eyes to see two beautiful brown eyes staring lovingly at me. She licked my lips playfully.

"Aaack!" I spat, and brought up a hand to block the tongue as it snaked out again. "Get off me! Leave me alone, dog." She wagged her tail enthusiastically and bounded off the bed, looking for a chew toy to bring back to me so I could throw it for her.

"What the hell is going on over there?" I heard sleepily

from the other side of the bed. I rolled my head over and saw my wife. She lay on her side, turned away from me.

"Guess," I said, wiping dog spit from my face with the sheet. My wife turned her head and looked at me over her shoulder.

"Just think how many other guys would like to be sleeping with two women at once," she told me. I heard sounds of approaching dog and looked up to see her appear in the doorway, red rubber barbell in mouth. She looked at me expectantly, tail wagging fiercely.

"She probably licked her butt before she kissed me, too," I said. "Jesus, what time is it? The sun's not even all the way up yet."

"Stop your bitching. You're the one that wanted a dog," she told me. "Get up and let her outside, that's probably why she's hyper, she has to go to the bathroom." I groaned theatrically and struggled to right myself.

"Jeez, am I sure I want kids?" I said after I made it unsteadily to my feet. Kelly rolled onto her back and I saw the bedcovers pushed upward by her distended pregnant belly. It looked like two Cub Scouts had pitched a tent on her stomach.

"You back out now and I'll disembowel you," she told me sweetly.

1:13 p.m.

Jerry Phillips walked into my office without a word and dropped into the chair I leave in front of my desk for clients. I checked my desk calendar and shook my head slowly.

"No wonder this country's going to hell in a handbasket," I said to him. "December ninth, and you're off for Christmas vacation already. You don't have to be back until what, the third or fourth?" Jerry shot me a wide smile, with no hint of guilt whatsoever. In another six months he'd be graduating with a Criminal Justice degree from MSU, with Honors no less, but he still hadn't started sending out job applications. I think he just didn't know exactly where he wanted to go – uniformed or plainclothes, local, state, or federal.

"Tough life, ain't it?" he said. "And Ron got done with his finals before me, he's been home for a day and a half already. So," he said, changing the subject, "we still on for tomorrow?"

"Is it tomorrow already?" I said, and checked my calendar again.

"Oh no, don't start that shit with me," he said, leaning forward in the chair to stick a finger at me. "You knew it was tomorrow, and you're going. Don't *even* try to pull some lame excuse out of your butt." He crossed his arms and sat back. I grinned at him.

I was a private investigator, a former Special Agent with the Drug Enforcement Administration, and before that I was in the Army. Married, with a baby on the way. Jerry and his friends, who had become my friends—Ron Kelly, Bob Grinnand, and Steve Reath—were fifteen years my junior. All of them but Bob still in college. Even I had to admit the five of us made an odd group.

Everyone knows the phrase "politics makes for strange bedfellows". The original quote, as so many do, comes from Shakespeare, *The Tempest*: "Misery acquaints a man with strange bedfellows." I had definitely shared misery with these young men, and we'd bonded in a way that most people will never experience. That transcended our ages or position in the world. Even if we could tell the story, I doubt anyone would believe it. In truth, I was still amazed we hadn't found ourselves the semi-permanent guests of the Michigan Department of Corrections.

"You lose weight or something?" I asked him. "You look different." He was a little over six foot and slender, with brown hair in a slightly long brushcut.

"I've been working out a lot lately," he told me. "Seems like I always get into this workout thing from around the start of school until Christmas vacation. I've replaced about eight pounds of fat with five pounds of muscle. Me and Jodi've been working out a lot together, giving each other moral support." Jodi was his girlfriend, also attending Michigan State. She was barely old enough to drink, gorgeous, and had a naturally abundant physique my old college roommate would have described as 'topheavy'. Imagining her jogging, or maybe doing aerobics…oof. Anyway, moving on, nothing to see here, happily married man.

"Sounds like me," I told him. "Except for me it started when I hit thirty. I get into these six-month cycles. Work out hard for six months, get in good shape, then slack off for about six months until guilt drives me back to the gym."

"Where are you now?" he asked.

"About four months into the working out part. Kelly can't work out 'cause she's pregnant, so I feel obligated to be working out for the both of us. Because I can, don't have any excuses. Are you going to be working over the break?" I asked him.

"Yeah. Selling Christmas trees over at Champion again. This'll make it five years in a row I'm dumb enough to stand outside in December freezing my ass off and getting frostbite on my fingers. So, what kind of holster are you going to be using?" Jerry asked me, getting back to the subject at hand.

I'd agreed to go to a shooting match with him and put my money where my mouth was. He'd been doing a lot of competitive shooting lately and kept browbeating me to come along and use the pistol he and the guys had given me for my thirty-fifth birthday a few months back. That 'misery' we'd shared had involved a kidnapping attempt and several gunfights with members of Detroit organized crime, so a gift of a gun wasn't as weird as you might think. Besides, the guns we'd used were still in the evidence lockup at the Oakland County Sheriff's Department, and likely to remain there forever.

The match was a monthly event put on by a local sportsmen's club. It was an I.P.S.C. event, a "combat" pistol match that wasn't quite realistic and yet was better than anything else around for practicing defensive pistol skills. I'd never competed in one but had read up on them and felt confident I could kick Jerry's butt. After all, I'd been through the DEA Academy at Quantico, which is where the FBI has their Academy. The FBI Academy is several weeks longer than ours, because those courses teaching them how to be egotistical officious pricks add a lot of classroom hours.

"I was gonna work from a Safariland paddle holster," I told him. "It's what they gave us in the DEA, I never had any problems with 'em."

"Good, that's good," he said. "Secure, no snaps or flaps to slow you down, rides a little high but it's a real-world holster, not one of those erector sets some of these gamers strap onto their hips. You talk to Bob recently?" he asked me.

"Yeah, I just talked to him yesterday," I said. "He's looking forward to coming home, but I don't know how they talked him into taking a vacation."

I'd met Bob about the same time I ran across Jerry. They'd graduated high school together, then Bob'd joined the 82nd Airborne. Since then he'd moved on and had spent most of the last year romping through the world with a green beret atop his head. It was barely more than a year since Nine-Eleven, and everyone in the U.S. military seemed to be overseas or en route. Bob had been out of contact for months at a time. Blond and built like Mike Tyson in fighting trim, but more skilled with his hands, Bob'd told me over the phone that he was back at Fort Bragg on leave, which seemed odd, as the smart money was on us jumping into Iraq inside of a month or two. Then again, maybe this was the calm before the storm for him. "He sounded a bit weird on the phone," I commented to Jerry.

"Yeah, I noticed that too, last time I talked to him. I don't know what's up but I'm sure we'll find out when he gets here. He was in gunfights before he ever deployed for the Army, but God only knows where he's been or what kind of *Heart of Darkness* shit he's seen. Does he need anybody to pick him up at the airport? I haven't been able to get ahold of him lately, they're not real big on leaving messages down there."

"Naw, he's driving, he's not flying. I guess he's leaving early Sunday and will be pulling in late that night. Helluva drive from Bragg."

"Driving? Why the hell is he driving? Between the five of us we can spare a car for him to use on leave."

"He said he bought a new truck he wanted to show everyone," I explained.

"So bring a goddamn picture and save yourself a sore butt and a hundred bucks each way in gas money," Jerry said.

"Set off fewer airport metal detectors this way," I speculated.

Jerry slapped a hand to his forehead.

"Christ, what was I thinking?" he said.

4:45 p.m.

My office mail was in a pile on the corner of my desk and I decided to go through it just to kill time until five o'clock. Nothing much, just a few bills and a lot of junk mail aimed more at corporate-type enterprises than me and my little one-man company. I looked blearily around the office to see if anything else needed to be done, found nothing, and started to pack it in. I'd just grabbed my coat off the chair and was heading toward the door when the phone rang. With a short but choice word I strode across my office and snagged the receiver just before the machine picked up.

"John Phault, Security and Investigations," I said.

"Hey."

"Yeah, what do you want?" I said tiredly.

"My, we're in a good mood, aren't we? Your dog bite you or something?"

"Just a long day." Lieutenant Scott Copley, Oakland County Sheriff's Department, a long-time friend and general pain-in-the-ass, a workaholic with no home life to speak of and not many friends at or outside of work besides me. "So what's all the big buzz I've been hearing coming from the County about the new Prosecutor? He seems to be on TV an awful lot."

"Same shit, different day, that's all. Hendricks, the old Oakland County Prosecutor, decided to retire in mid-term, and now we have Mr. Steve Shields to deal with. Smart as a whip, sly as a fox, compassion of the Terminator. Will not deviate from the letter of the law for anyone. That is, unless they're someone that can do him a favor. He's the new kid on the block and looking to make a name for himself, and boy did he hit the ground running. Too bad Kevorkian's in jail, he could go after him next, that seems to go with the position."

"Hendricks retired, huh? Too bad. At least he knew his ass from a hole in the ground."

"Shields knows from asses. He spends half the day kissing them and half the day kicking them. Hey, how's Kelly? She like being fat?"

"Tell you what. You ask my wife that, face to face, without changing the wording, and see how she replies. I promise I'll send flowers."

"When is she due anyway?"

"February third. But I think she'll be early, 'cause that's still almost two months away and she's huge. She decided to take off work early. She's got a lot of leave saved up, and it's getting hard for her to get in and out of chairs. Friday was her last day."

"Are you sure it's not twins? I saw her two weeks ago and she couldn't fit through doorways." I knew Scott well enough to hear the barely contained laughter just beneath his words.

"It's not twins. We've had ultrasounds done and amniocentesis and they all say one kid. I even have an ultrasound picture of it, though the damn thing could be a moonscape for all I can make of it."

"I can't relate to that," Scott said, "being a father-to-be. I can't even imagine what that's like."

"Me neither. I'm making it up as I go along. This is the easy part, though. All I have to do is make Kelly feel wanted and loved and attractive, to help minimize those hairy hormonal fits. Once the kid arrives, though, all bets are off. A puppy was a pain in the ass but I have a feeling it was nothing compared to what this kid's gonna be like."

"I bet."

"Now all that's left is getting you hitched," I said to him. "Settle you down. Soothe the savage beast of bachelorhood."

"No way. I'm planning to be in the delivery room when Kelly's in labor. Seeing her screaming and spitting, speaking in tongues and levitating shit will stifle any paternal feelings I might be developing."

"God, what an image you just put into my head."

"It's not too late," he told me. "We could still run away and become porn stars. How 'bout it?"

"It's waaaay too late," I told him. Realizing I was still holding my coat in my arm I asked him, "Did you call me for any particular reason?"

"No, not really," he said. "Just working late, stuck in the office and bored."

"What I figured," I said. "I'm late leaving for home, and you know how I've been dancing around Kelly lately to keep her on an even keel, so I gotta go. Bye."

5:19 p.m.

Kelly had her back turned toward me as she stirred something in a pot on top of the stove. The dog sat at attention behind Kelly, every atom of her being focused on the pot Kelly was fiddling with. The dog took the time to make sure I wasn't a burglar lunging for her mother and then glued her attention back onto the stove lest she miss a chance to eat some tasty People Food. I nuzzled Kelly's ear and hugged her. It took some effort to get my arms all the way around her.

"Hi baby," I said. "What are you making?"

"It's my mother's recipe for spaghetti sauce," she told me.

"I take it that we're having spaghetti for dinner, then," I said.

"I feel vindicated. I kept telling everyone that you weren't as stupid as you looked," she commented, still stirring the contents of the pot.

"Thanks," I said. She kept stirring awhile, with my arms around her and my chin on her shoulder.

"Is there something else that you wanted?" she asked finally.

"Would you like to go upstairs with me and make a baby?" I asked her. She looked at me out of the corner of her eye.

"We already did that," she replied.

"Well, maybe we could just practice for the next one, then." I looked at her and wiggled my eyebrows up and down. It's a patented technique, known to make women around the world swoon. She turned her body slightly towards me.

"Are you doing this just to make me feel like I'm still attractive and not just one big house-sized blob?" she asked suspiciously.

"You forget who you're talking to," I said. "Since when have I done anything just to make someone other than myself feel better?" She looked at me for a few seconds. I was trying hard not to stare at her chest, which had grown remarkably over the past few weeks, but I can't exactly say I was successful. Kelly looked at me, looked down at her chest, then back up at me, rolling her eyes.

"Do you even know what subtle means?" she asked, then leaned backward and kissed me. I could taste the spaghetti sauce on her lips. She reached over and shut the burner off, then took me by the hand.

"Just be gentle," I said as she led me toward the stairs. "Remember, I have a weak constitution." The dog stayed rooted to her spot, looking at the stove, then us, then back at the stove in case the pot of sauce tried to make a break for it.

"Shut up or I'll sit on you," my wife told me sweetly.

"Actually…" I began.

TWO

Saturday

8:32 a.m.

"I can't believe I'm up this early on a Saturday," I said to no one in particular.

"This is gonna be fun, so shut up," Jerry told me.

We were standing with a small group of people at the rear of a large indoor range, gearing up for the match. Jerry was beside me buckling on a holster and magazine pouches, but we weren't in a designated "Safe" area so no one was touching any pistols. The match safety rules were very strict; the gun I normally carried everywhere I'd left in the car. As strange as it sounds bringing a loaded gun to a shooting match was Number 1 on the no-no list and would've gotten me ejected.

"Too bad it's so cold out, this is a lot more fun when it's outside," Jerry was telling me. "If you like this, you should come to some more matches with me. It'll keep your shooting skills sharp."

"If I remember, my shooting skills were sharp enough two years ago to save your pimpled butt," I told him, feeling a bit intimidated by the unfamiliar surroundings. I hadn't been around this many heavily armed and presumably skilled shooters since Quantico. One of the guys near us gave me a curious glance but said nothing.

Jerry and I moved to a side table and began loading magazines for the match. A lot of magazines. Jerry'd said most of the matches had a lot higher shot count than the real world gunfight average of 4 rounds, although the shooting was divided up into several different stages. Besides, he'd said to me on the way over, who'd want to drive twenty or thirty minutes each way to only shoot half a dozen rounds?

"Remind me again of how this is supposed to work," I told Jerry, looking at the array of targets downrange.

"It's simple," he told me. He pointed to the cardboard silhouettes with square heads that were the standard targets of the International Practical Shooting Confederation. "The tan targets with no visible aiming point, no bullseye, just like real people, get two rounds each unless stated otherwise. The closer to the center the better, because there *are* scoring rings on 'em, you just can't see 'em from here. The white silhouettes are hostages, or innocent bystanders, what-have-you. Don't shoot them, they're just there to make your job harder. Where the tan silhouettes are painted black it's considered hard cover, like the person is standing behind a brick wall or something. A hole in the black won't get you any points, and you get points deducted for the miss. Some days we have falling steel plates to shoot at, Pepper Poppers, but it doesn't look like we'll have any today." He peered at the shooting course laid out on the range. "Stage three looks like fun, shoot and move, shoot and move, duck under the table and shoot again. All at close targets. You practice at all to get ready for today, Mr. Hot Shot?" he asked me.

"A little," I said. What a lie. I'd gone to the range by my house three times in the past two weeks in preparation for the match. I wasn't about to let myself get beat by a snot-nosed kid not even out of college.

"You like this, I'll have to take you to one of the 3-gun matches a club out in Livingston puts on," he told me.

"A 3-gun match?" I said.

"Yeah. Pistol, shotgun, and rifle. I don't know if I like 'em any better, but they're a change of pace and real good to keep your skills sharp on the long guns. Not many other places around where you can shoot shotgun or rifle in combat scenarios. I took Ron a couple of times to those matches, he likes playing around with his new shotgun."

"I haven't shot a rifle in years," I said. "Maybe not since the DEA Academy. Shotgun, yeah, but not rifle."

We moved to the Safe area and uncased our weapons. The pistol Jerry and his friends had presented to me on my birthday was a customized Colt 1911 .45 ACP Government Model, first choice of the FBI's Hostage Rescue Team, LAPD SWAT, 'Delta' Force; pretty much everybody who took their job seriously. Not to mention most of the people milling around me, although a lot of the people I'd be competing against had accessories on their guns like electronic red-dot scopes and recoil compensators, things not suitable for actual day to day use but rather designed specifically for high-speed competition. Jerry'd said the real world guns were scored in a different class from what he called the 'race' guns, so I shouldn't worry. Something like handicapping in golf, I supposed.

The 1911 had become the weapon of choice due more to its ease of customization and mode of operation than anything else—it had the best trigger pull by far, and could be made amazingly accurate. It was also meant to be carried with the hammer cocked and the safety on, which meant someone familiar with its use could get a quicker, more controlled first shot off with a Colt, or its copies, than with any other type of pistol.

I practiced a few draws from my holster and then left the Colt in it, empty, hammer down, reassured once more with my reasonable competence in gunhandling. Over the past two weeks I'd fired close to six hundred rounds through the Colt. I'd draw it, fire one, two, or three rounds at a silhouette, sometimes close, sometimes far, and then do my best to reholster while still looking downrange like they'd taught me all those years ago at Quantico. I watched Jerry practice a few draws of his own and he almost looked like he might be quicker than me from the holster, but the real test would be whether or not he could hit the target.

"Line's going hot!" The range officer yelled out, and everybody made sure their ear and eye protection was in place. The first competitor of the day stepped into the designated shooting box, a four foot square on the floor made of two-by-twos. She'd have to stand inside the box while shooting the first part of the stage. She blew on her hands and wiped her palms on her thighs, then nodded to the R.O. when he asked if she understood the course of fire.

"Load and make ready," he told her. After staring at her for a few seconds I realized that she reminded me of one of my aunts. However, I couldn't picture my aunt Josie ever picking up a gun unless someone trampled her prize rose garden. The female shootist confidently drew and loaded her pistol, then set it in her barely there competition holster, cocked and locked, eyes focused downrange.

"Shooter ready?" the R.O. asked her. As she nodded he held up an electronic timer close behind her head that

Jerry'd told me "heard" the gunshots and recorded the shooter's time down to the hundredth of a second. "Stand by!" he called out, and a second later pressed a button on the timer, which emitted an electronic beep.

The woman's hands were a blur as she scooped up her gun and brought it to bear on the leftmost target. The very second she was on target she began firing, loud staccato blasts that were so close together I'd have thought she was using a submachinegun if I hadn't seen her pistol with my own eyes. She dropped her empty mag and sprinted through her still-airborne empty cases to the next shooting box, reloading on the run, the R.O. glued to her heels with the timer held high. No sooner had her feet crossed into the second box than she opened up on the remaining targets, her empty brass pelting the crowd to her right rear. Done firing, she stood there, panting just a bit, and scanned the targets. No misses.

"If the shooter is finished, unload and show clear," the R.O. told her. "Hammer down, and holster." When she had done so and holstered her now empty gun, the two of them walked downrange with a scorer to check the targets.

As the scorer began recording the mostly A-zone hits that the R.O. was calling out Jerry nodded his head in admiration.

"Damn," he said. "I'm gonna have to watch myself. She gets any better and she'll get bumped up into my class and that'll be one more person I'll have to beat. So," he said, turning to me, "what do you think so far?"

"Jesus Christ," was all I could think to say.

"Goddamnit," I heard someone beside me curse. A middle-aged man was rubbing his cheek just below his impact-resistant shooting glasses. A divot the diameter of a pencil lead was welling blood. "Fucking splashback." He pulled his hand away from his smarting cheek and looked at his fingertips. "Hey, I'm bleeding!"

Angled steel louvers at the end of the range directed the flying bullets down into a sand bank. Occasionally a bullet would hit the front edge of a louver and shrapnel would fly backwards, sometimes all the way to the shooter. It was an uncommon occurrence, but not so rare I hadn't seen it happen before. That's why everyone always wore eye protection.

"Oh, quit your whining, Frank," one of the other shooters said. "You want to participate in something that's inherently dangerous, don't complain if you get bit."

1:18 p.m.

"Well?" Kelly asked as we walked through the front door. She was half sitting, half lying on the couch in the living room, a paperback book open on her stomach.

"I am humbled," I told her. "Truly, deeply, humbled." The dog came running and slid to a stop on the linoleum in the doorway to the kitchen. She saw that indeed her daddy was home and began darting around, looking for a toy so I could play fetch with her.

"That bad, huh?"

"Oh, he did pretty good," Jerry said to her as I tossed my gear bag onto the couch. "He just forgot one basic fact, namely that the average shooter is a lot better shot than the average cop. Cops do paperwork, shooters shoot. And competitive shooters shoot a *hell* of a lot."

My dog came running up with her red rubber barbell in her mouth. I was her first intended target but when she got close she veered toward Jerry and performed her basic attention-getting trick—she ran nose and barbell first right into his crotch. Jerry recoiled more in surprise than pain and I saw the dog's chew toy had left a big wet drool spot on Jerry's jeans. Both Kelly and I laughed while Jerry stared at the spot on his pants and shook his head.

"Story of my life," he said, and reached for the offered barbell. At which point the dog darted back a half dozen steps and readied herself for a high-speed pursuit, tail wagging enthusiastically.

"No, I'm not chasing you," Jerry told her.

"Oscar, go lay down," I scolded her. The dog dropped the toy dejectedly and jumped up next to my wife on the couch and curled into a ball.

"Explain to me again how you ended up naming a female dog 'Oscar'," Jerry said.

"Don't look at me," I said, raising my hands.

"I've always wanted a dog named Oscar," my wife explained. "Didn't matter what breed of dog, I just liked the name. Any dog named Oscar has got to be a good dog. We went to the Humane Society last year with every intention of getting a male, but when I saw this little girl here I knew I had to get her." She patted the dog, whose ears kept perking up every time she heard her name.

"You've warped that poor dog for life by giving her a boy's name," Jerry said. We all looked at Oscar who decided at that moment there was nothing she would rather do than lick her own butt.

"Yeah, she really looks warped, doesn't she," I remarked. "Never seen a dog do that before."

"All right, now quit evading the question," my wife demanded. "Just how badly did you do?"

"I shot respectably," I said honestly. "I didn't do anything stupid and embarrass myself, or anything dangerous and get disqualified. But I thought that would mean I'd be one of the top shots there, not just in the middle of the pack." Actually, deep down I'd thought there'd been a pretty good chance I'd win the match, but I wasn't about to admit it, especially after how things had turned out. I dropped onto the couch while Jer took space on a chair across the room.

"John shot at maybe a B-class level," Jerry told my wife. "I just got bumped up to A-class myself. B-class ain't too bad, especially for his first match. It's actually better than I thought he'd do."

"Thanks a lot. I really like that Colt," I told both of them. "I think I'm going to start carrying it instead of the Smith." My normal daily carry gun was a Smith & Wesson .45 automatic, a nice piece, but it couldn't compare to the customized Colt.

"How do these 'classes' relate to real-world competency with a gun?" my wife asked Jerry. I took her shooting frequently and she was probably wondering where she'd be in the ratings. If the ladies she worked with knew she was bringing a gun to the office every day they'd probably have aneurisms…but I'd bet none of them had been nearly murdered in their own home.

"Well, my own personal opinion is that you ought to be shooting a real high D-class score to be considered competent enough to handle a gun adequately in a life-or-death confrontation. That skill level should be the bare minimum for cops. Preferably C class. However, the sad fact is that most cops are shitty shots. Most people don't know that, or would hate to believe it, that they're trusting their lives to people that . . . well here, let me put it this way. The average distance of your typical gunfight, per the F.B.I., is between six and eight feet. Current police hit percentage, that is, the number of rounds fired by cops at that distance that actually hit their intended target, is running at about twenty-three percent. Twenty-three! Yeah, a few cops are avid shooters and a lot better than that, but they're bringing the average up to that level. When people see the uniform and the gun they assume the guy must be a pretty good shot to be allowed to wear it. And that ain't the case. If cops were all running at high D-class level their hit percentage would probably double. At least." He was a college kid who didn't know anything, and I was a former federal law enforcement agent, so my instinctive reaction was to tell him he didn't know what the hell he was talking about…except I knew from my own experience that everything he said was true. It still hurt to hear, though.

"How good is Ron?" I asked Jerry. He said he'd taken Ron to a couple matches, but I still had some faint hope that I was a better shot than *someone*.

"Well, Ron's an okay shot with a pistol, maybe not quite as good as you, but when we go to those 3-gun matches you should see him on a rifle or his shotgun. He just smokes the whole course." I wasn't surprised, Ron had spent his freshman year of college at Virginia Military Institute – the cadets practically slept with their rifles. "And you know how you saw those gamesmen at the match today with their tricked-out pistols? At the 3-gun matches those same guys have tricked-out rifles and shotguns, compensators, extended mags, the whole works, and Ron still beats most of 'em, mostly using my M4."

"M4?" I said.

"Yeah, you know, you were in the Army." He frowned at me. "Oh, wait, that was back in the dark ages, wasn't it." I ignored my wife's smile at his comment.

"The M4 is the current carbine version of the military's M16 rifle," he told me. "Shorter, fourteen and a half inch barrel, collapsible stock. I've got a permanently attached muzzle brake on mine to bring it up to the 16-inch minimum legal barrel length, and I've got an Aimpoint on it."

"One of those red-dot sights they were using at the match? I thought you didn't like those."

"On pistols they're too big for use in the real world. On rifles they're not, and the Aimpoint's been around for a while, the Army's even using them now."

"How good of a shot is Bob?" Kelly asked. Our homegrown Green Beret was usually the standard against which the rest of us judged ourselves. Kelly began rubbing Oscar's belly, and the dog squirmed over onto her back, eyes closed in ecstasy.

"The last time I shot with Bob was . . . hell, two years ago?," Jerry said. "At the time he was a lot better than me."

"That was before you started shooting competition though, wasn't it?"

"Yeah. I've gone to at least two matches a month the past year, shot about eight thousand rounds."

"You think you're as good as him now?" I asked him. *Eight* thousand *rounds? Jesus*. No wonder he'd practically embarrassed me at the match. Oscar rolled onto her stomach and crawled snakelike over the couch cushions to me, laying her head in my lap and groaning pitifully because no one was paying attention to her. I scratched her ears absently.

"You on drugs?" Jerry said, laughing. "I've been screwing around for a year, having fun, while Bob's been training eight days a week with the green beanies doing room clearing, knife fighting, CQB, sniping, demolitions, seventeen ways to kill someone with a plastic straw, you name it. Plus, Uncle Sam's been providing free ammo to him the whole time, too. He hasn't exactly had my budget restrictions when it comes to the amount of lead he can send downrange. And it hasn't all been training, either. Hell, maybe not much training at all, I don't think the military is holding any of the elite troops in reserve, I think they're all kicking ass. Worldwide, it's not just in Afghanistan. Although I doubt he'll be able to tell us anything about it."

"Shit, you know how driven Bob is. He won't be satisfied until he's the best shot he knows, and remember where he's based. Fort Bragg is home to a lot of interesting and talented folks, number one on the name recognition list probably being Delta Force. Let me tell you, you weren't around in junior high when Bob decided wrestling and football, while great exercise and a nice way to pick up hotties, weren't doing anything for his hand-to-hand combat skills. So, since school sports weren't improving his proficiency in the art of interpersonal conflict, he dropped out and devoted all his spare time to martial arts."

"Karate, right?" my wife asked. "That's what his black belt's in."

"That's what his first black belt is in," Jerry told her, "and I'm sure his fellow green beanies have been teaching him all sorts of off-the-books dirty tricks. Like his instincts and freakish reflexes weren't good enough already."

"You ever seen him sparring with me or Ron?" Jer asked. I shook my head. "Jesus Christ, we're like third graders trying to explain long division to Albert Einstein. It's not even a challenge for him. I hope I get the chance to spar with him when he comes into town this time, it's a lot of fun."

"I'll bet," I said.

Jerry looked at my wife with a smile. "My God you're huge," he said with the amount of tact you'd expect from a college-age male. "You sure we're just talking about one baby?" I cringed and braced for impact but relaxed when I saw Kelly's smile.

"God, don't *do* that, man!" I pleaded with him. "She's riding the hormone rollercoaster from hell. If we don't have this kid soon I'm gonna say the wrong thing one day and she's gonna snap. Our neighbors'll be finding parts of my body all over the subdivision."

"Since when have you ever said the *right* thing?" Kelly asked me with a smile. With help from Jerry and me she struggled to her feet. From her perch on the couch Oscar looked at all of us grunting and straining and tried to figure out what was going on.

"You want lunch?" my wife asked us, looking at Jerry. He looked at her silently for a moment, a soft gleam in his eyes, then gave her a shy, fond smile.

"You sit your impregnated butt down and relax," he told her. "Me and Mr. Mom here'll make you lunch. That is, if he can locate the stove for me."

"Sure I can," I told him. "It's somewhere near where she's always standing when I come into the kitchen and ask her what's for dinner. *Ouch!*"

Later that afternoon I cleaned my pistol and took a leisurely four mile jog. My wife had the courtesy to wonder aloud if my new interest in working out had anything to do with my recent birthday. In response I politely told her to shut up. After the run I took a shower. Then, feeling energized, I changed into some old clothes and began the tiresome job that I'd put off for more than two months—stripping the wallpaper from the upstairs bathroom. It was going to be the baby's room. When I was done with that I'd be able to get out the belt sander and work over the walls in preparation for painting. I figured the entire task, including repainting, would take me at least twenty hours of hard work. I'd never understood how my father could spend so much time repairing things around the house and never get *done* until I bought my first house.

I peeled the first long strip of vintage 1970's textured orange and yellow stripe wallpaper off the wall, releasing a dense cloud of dust that sparkled in the light shining through the bathroom window. As I fought back a sneeze, swearing, trying not to suck in the dust, I consoled myself with the thought that I ought to be happy I had such a calm, normal life. If only I'd known how right I was.

THREE

Sunday

11:16 a.m.

The pull chain on the light fixture in the storage area underneath my basement stairs had snapped a few days before when I came down to look for some old paperwork. The chain didn't have the decency to break off halfway down its length, where it would be easy to fix, instead it had separated inside the ceramic housing. All of which explained why I was covered in dirt and grime and cobwebs early on a Sunday morning instead of planted in front of my TV watching football. I'm really more of a baseball fan, but that's not the point.

I'd never realized how intricate a simple light bulb pull-chain switch could be until I tried to repair one. In my toolbox I'd found a replacement beaded metal chain that I intended to install, figuring it'd be a ten-minute task, tops. Forty-five minutes into the "simple" repair I realized that it would have been easier for me to replace the entire light fixture. But a small part of me, perhaps something I inherited from my miser father's side of the family, rebelled at the idea of buying something I really didn't need just to save myself a little work.

The pull chain was attached to a coil spring inside the housing and it was trying to take that apart that was causing me so much trouble. Whoever had put it together originally must have had three hands or prehensile toes, because that was the only way I was going to get it back together. I had the spring under pressure in my left hand, a small screwdriver I was using as a prybar in my right, and the new pull chain between my teeth when the phone rang. I paused for a second, waiting, then remembered Kelly was out being walked by the dog. Muttering a few choice words, I released the spring with a snap, backed out of my cramped workspace, and shuffled, as fast as my halfway asleep leg allowed, in hopes of getting to the phone above my workbench before the machine answered.

"Yeah?" I said none too gently, massaging my thigh.

"John, it's Ron." It took me a beat and a half before I figured out that this Ron was Ron Kelly, Jerry's college buddy. Within the year he'd be completing his dual degree in Bio-Chemistry and Forensic Science; that is, if he ever stopped hunting everything that ran, swam, or flew and instead went to class. Ron sure didn't sound happy to be home on break.

"Hey Ron, what's up?" I could hear some loud voices in the background. Didn't sound like the TV or his parents. Maybe he'd had another one of his famous parties last night.

"I've got a bit of a situation over here," he told me evenly. Just the way he said it sent up red flags all over my mental terrain. Something was wrong. Probably something big, or he wouldn't be calling me, he'd have handled it himself.

"Uh, what's the matter, Ron?" I asked warily. The voices in the background didn't sound like partygoers anymore. And Ron definitely sounded worried.

I heard Ron sigh. "I'd rather not get into it over the phone." There was quite a lengthy pause, then he said, "I've got a bit of a situation over here." That was how he put it, and that was all he said. He wouldn't come right out and ask me for help, and it wasn't because he thought I might turn him down. He was just one of those people that hated to ask for help, hated to be put into a position where he was obligated to someone, even a friend. Ours wasn't just a casual relationship, though. He'd saved Kelly. Taken bullets that could have hit me. I owed Ron. Big time. I owed all of Jerry's friends, Bob probably most of all, and knew I'd never really be able to pay my debt. But I could try.

"I'm there," I told him, never a question in my mind. "What should I do?"

"Can you come over here?" he asked me, strain and a bit of relief in his voice.

"I can be there in twelve minutes or I can wash up and put on some good clothes and be there in about half an hour," I told him. There was a short pause and I could imagine him looking around.

"Go ahead and wash up," he told me. "No need for you to hurry. Won't do either of us any good if you show up here dirty and out of breath. Get cleaned up and we'll all see you when you get here." I said good-bye and hung up the phone, wondering just who the other part of "we" was.

11:58 a.m.

Half a mile away, I could sense something was awry, but it wasn't until I was nearly in front of the sprawling ranch house that I could see the patrol cars of the Sheriff's Department pulled into the circular gravel driveway. Three marked units, parked mostly off the grass near the front door. I pulled over to the side of the dirt road and stared at the house. Ron's car was just visible, parked on the driveway spur that led to the barn a hundred feet from the house. Except for a couple of barn swallows chasing each other across the meadow behind the house the whole area seemed devoid of activity, as usual. I could feel the acid chewing at my stomach.

I stared ignorantly at the house, not getting any answers to my unspoken questions. *Was I making the right decision, getting involved?* Then I pushed that thought aside, ashamed at myself for even thinking it. Ron, or any one of his friends for that matter, would come to my aid unblinkingly.

I left my car in front of the house on the road, figuring if I pulled into the driveway I'd get blocked in. The leafless trees across the road stood silent and unmoving, no breeze to rattle their gray branches. They clustered together and towered over me. It seemed like they were leaving me, backing away, but really it was just the clouds above us, heading east.

I could just make out the intersection at the end of the street almost a mile ahead. As I stared into the distance yet another police car turned the corner and headed my way. Close behind it was a Chevy Suburban, sporting the blue and silver logo of Channel 7, identifiable even at that distance. The Suburban had a double pronged broadcasting boom mounted precariously on its roof and its driver seemed determined to beat the squad car to Ron's door or die trying. I quickly shut my car door, locked it, and headed up the drive to the house.

Just before I reached the front door it opened and an

older man wearing Sheriff's Department browns with Sergeant stripes on the sleeves stepped out onto the porch. He gave my hands a quick onceover for weapons. Seeing none, he was about to give me the third degree when he realized he knew me. We stood there staring at each other for a few seconds, trying to remember why we knew each other. I had an advantage -- he had a nametag.

"*Sergeant* Randolph," I said, "congratulations on the promotion. Been a while."

He snapped his fingers and pointed at me. "The P.I., right? Phault? How's your wife?"

I didn't try to shake his hand, not when he was on duty. Cops shy away from handshaking, because it gives the impression that they've taken sides. Just because he knew me didn't mean he was my friend.

"Better than the last time I saw you," I told him. He rolled his eyes.

"I went through everything that happened to you, I'm not sure I'd ever leave the house again," he admitted.

"I finally stopped taking a gun with me into the bathroom," I said. I made it sound like I was joking.

Randolph nodded solemnly and crossed his arms over his chest. "So, what're you here for?" he asked me.

"Ron Kelly called me about half an hour ago, asked me to come over." Randolph's eyebrows went up.

"He hired a P.I.? That's different. What, you got a law practice on the side?"

"He didn't hire anybody," I explained, "I'm a friend."

Randolph's face went blank. "A friend? A friend like…" he snapped his fingers, trying to remember.

"Bob," I said.

Randolph pointed at me. "That's him. Grinnand, right? What happened to him?"

"Special Forces."

"No shit? Well, best place for him, especially with a war on." His eyes narrowed. "This isn't related, is it?"

"I don't even know what *this* is," I told him. "But no, it's not. That's all over." Randolph's eyes left mine and looked over my shoulder. I heard the growing roar of engines as the squad car and the TV truck approached and briefly turned around to see them heading toward us, clouds of dust blooming as they sped down the dirt road. I turned back to Randolph.

"Just what the hell *is* going on here?" I asked him. He gave me a strange look.

"Fuck if I know," he said. He turned around and opened the front door. "Hey Charlie!" he called out. "Got one coming in. Don't shoot him." He gave me a wink and held the screen door open. I stepped through the doorway and then turned and followed his gaze to the Suburban just skidding to a stop in the driveway.

"And the circus has come to town," I heard him mutter. "Looks like somebody was actually listening to their scanner for once." Then he strode determinedly off the porch toward the grungy cameramen piling out of the Suburban.

"Don't even think about parking that thing there," was the last thing I heard him shout as I stepped into the house.

Just inside the front door was a large sitting room to the right, small loveseats with flowered print facing each other across a glass-topped coffee table. The front hall was about six feet wide and ran straight back into the house past stairs which led to the second floor. The hallway ended in a T-intersection. From in front of a small bathroom the hallway ran right and left. To the left was George Kelly's study which had a window that looked out onto the front lawn.

Past the study was a large spare bedroom and a back stairway leading to the garage underneath the bedroom.

If you turned right the hallway led into the large kitchen and the dining area. Sliding glass doors led from the dining room out onto a large wooden deck in the backyard. On the far side of the dining room was the family room where Ron and his family usually ate dinner in front of the TV. Stairs in the kitchen led to the walk-out basement and the garage. Also down there was an expensive pool table George had bought for the well-equipped game room.

Once inside the house I could hear voices from the back and headed in that direction. I stopped in the kitchen doorway where I was visible to the two deputies. They were talking to Ron at the dining room table.

"And who are you?" one of the deputies shot at me. He seemed irritated, perfectly understandable if he'd been talking to Ron for any length of time.

"John!" Ron said, sounding relieved. "This is the guy I called," he told the deputies. From the expressions on their faces they didn't seem too happy to see me.

"What the hell is the Sarge doing letting this guy in here?" the second deputy said. "Hasn't he ever heard of contaminating the scene?" His partner shook his head.

"What's up?" I said, looking directly into Ron's uneasy face.

"Sir, you're gonna have to—" began the one deputy. I didn't let him finish.

"Sergeant Randolph knows me," I told them. "He seemed more concerned with the news crew from Channel 7 that pulled in behind me."

"Jesus Christ!" the talkative deputy exclaimed, exasperated. "The fucking news people are here and still no sign of an ID tech." He grabbed his prep radio from his belt and spoke into it. "809 Dispatch," he said. The radio crackled.

"Go ahead, 809."

"Can you give me an ETA on the ID unit we requested?" he asked.

"411 to 809, I'm about five minutes out," a deeper voice informed us.

"What, is he driving here in reverse?" the deputy asked the heavens. "Ten-four," he said into his radio and then replaced it in his belt.

"Relax, Charlie," the other deputy told him, but got only a scowl in return.

"Dispatch is ten-four on that also," the radio proclaimed. The deputy looked around and seemed surprised when he saw me still standing in the doorway. It was obvious that they wished I'd just disappear, but I wasn't going anywhere until Ron gave me the green light.

"What do you need from me?" I asked Ron.

"I need to ask you a couple of questions as soon as they're done asking me questions," he said.

"What do you need to ask him?" one of the deputies asked Ron. Most cops are by nature if not occupation control freaks, and my intrusion was not, by any means, welcome.

"He's a friend, and he used to be a cop, and I've never had anything like this happen before, okay?" Ron's voice got louder and louder until at the end he was nearly shouting.

"Mr. Kelly, there's no need to get upset," the deputies tried to soothe him. "When did you say your mother would be getting home?" Ron rolled his eyes at me.

"I'll be in the front room," I told him, "whenever you get done." He gave me a nod.

"The Sarge wants you in here, I'm not gonna countermand him," the first deputy said. "He's the rank on the scene, it's his baby. But I'm telling you, stay in that sitting room and don't fucking touch nothing."

I held up my hands in mock surrender. "Hey, I'm just happy to be here," I told him, pushed away from the door jamb and walked off.

From the sitting room window I had a good view of the front yard. Channel 4 had joined 7, and stocky, disheveled guys with beards were scurrying about, pointing minicams at the house, the cop cars, the street, and each other. Randolph had found more uniforms to restrain the journalistic vultures from scurrying inside the house, but he didn't have enough manpower yet to keep them off the lawn entirely. I knew if I opened the front door all those cameras would swing toward me like gun turrets, but I didn't think they were able to see me through the window since it was darker inside the house. I'd been the subject of a few news reports in my time and recognized some of the faces outside, but I was under no illusions that those people were my friends. Most of them would skin their mother if they thought it would get ratings.

I watched the cameramen move about for a few more minutes before I got bored and sat down in one of the loveseats. It bugged the living bejeezus out of me that I didn't know what was going on, but I figured I'd find out soon enough.

12:29 p.m.

The two Sheriff's Department's ID techs had finally arrived in their minivan. They'd walked in the front door and spotted me sitting on a loveseat, looking like a high school kid waiting for his date to come downstairs at her parent's house. Before they could say anything I stuck a thumb over my shoulder and they headed toward the kitchen and the other deputies, bemused expressions on their faces. Since then I'd heard them moving about somewhere in the rear of the house. I couldn't tell what was occupying their attention and didn't want to walk back there to see. Whatever Ron wanted me there for, it wouldn't help him at all if I started out by pissing off the cops. The excitement of being "On The Scene" had faded and the TV news crews were just standing around waiting for something to happen. Randolph had parked himself on the porch and was glaring down anyone who even looked like they wanted to talk to him. The talent huddled like curs in their Suburbans while the cameramen braved the cold and stood by their equipment.

Ron sat down on the loveseat opposite me and rubbed his face vigorously with the palms of both hands. Then he slouched down on the loveseat and looked at me. His blond hair was in its usual brushcut and he had on a sweatshirt and jeans over brown hiking boots. He had a lot of muscle on him from lifting weights, but other than the amazingly huge calves inherited from his father he looked deceptively like ten thousand other college kids. I leaned back on the cushions and waited for him to start. The cops in the house were moving around and talking, but I couldn't hear them well enough to discern any words.

"I suppose you're wondering why I've called you all here," Ron said.

"We figured it was about our Christmas bonuses, boss," I told him.

"My dad's been kidnapped," he told me. I blinked twice, slowly, then sat up. For several moments I digested that information, its implications.

"Tell me," I said.

"I went out this morning," he told me, "around nine-thirty. My dad was home, working in his study on the computer."

"Where was your mom?" I interrupted to ask him.

"Out also. When I left I told Dad I'd be gone about an hour."

"Where'd you go?"

"Meijer." He gave me a tired look. "You're asking me all the same questions the cops were asking."

"Let me tell you right now," I said, "before I know anything. If your dad was kidnapped, or anything else happened to him, you're gonna be number one on the list of suspects. Don't take it personal, that's just the way it is."

"Yeah, I figured that out quick enough. I showed 'em my receipt from Meijer and everything. I think they still have it."

"Where's your mom?" I asked him.

"Out at a horse show in Canton," he told me. "She left about seven. Should be home pretty soon, the cops got ahold of her by phone. And no, she and my dad haven't had any fights recently, the cops asked me that too."

"Family and friends are the first suspects in any investigation of foul play, just remember that. There's a reason for it—they're the ones that're usually guilty." We sat and looked at each other for a while.

"So what are you telling me?" he said, a little heat in his voice. I stood up and took two steps and got right in his face.

"I'm telling you you'd better get your temper under control and remember I'm the only one here who knows that you *didn't* do it," I growled, pointing a finger at him, "because until the rest of these assholes figure out what the fuck's going on you're the number one bunny. All right?" He nodded, chagrined, and I sat back down.

"So you went to Meijer," I began for him. He sighed.

"So I went to Meijers and bought some stuff, and got home about an hour later. About ten-thirty, ten-forty at the very latest. I came in, put the stuff on the kitchen table, called out for my dad. He doesn't answer, so I head to his study. He's not there, but I see his chair tipped over." I knew which chair he was talking about, it was a large leather affair on wheels, totally unsuited to the room but just big enough for George's bulk. "That God-awful ugly Tiffany floor lamp that he likes, the one that stood in the corner near the door, that's got its shade busted into a bazillion pieces of glass all over the floor, some of 'em ground into the carpet like they were stepped on.

"I see all this and I can't figure out what I'm looking at. For some reason I think he must've had a heart attack and had to run from the room. I start calling his name, checking the bathroom and the bedroom and running all over the house like a fucking idiot." Ron shook his head at himself. "Like a fucking idiot," he repeated.

"When I get to the side door," he told me, "you know, the one past my dad's study that goes down to the garage and outside?" I nodded my head. "Well, I'm about to grab it and head down the stairs when I notice some shit all over the knob and the door, right above where the knob is. It took me about five seconds to figure out that it's *blood*. Then I finally get my head outta my ass and see drops of blood all along the carpet from the study to the door. I go back into the study and look a little closer. The carpet's darker there but I can see a couple drops of blood anyway." He scowled, then looked over his shoulder toward the kitchen. When it seemed like there wasn't anyone close enough to hear him he leaned forward.

"I didn't tell the cops this," he said quietly, "because I wasn't sure how they'd react. But I went upstairs into my room and got my pistol and did a house-clearing. For all I knew there could be people still in the house. Didn't find anything, or anybody, and nothing seemed to be stolen, so I stuck my gun back upstairs and called the cops. After they got here and started grilling me I thought I'd better call you."

"Nothing taken," I said.

"Not that I could see."

"You have no idea why anyone would have wanted to kidnap your father." He shook his head. "Any sign of forced entry?"

"No. I reset our alarm system when I left the house 'cause Dad likes it that way and it never went off. Which means that Dad shut it off when he let whoever in. And then went back to his study with whoever it was." I eyed the alarm system keypad on the wall in the entryway. It was a decent system, not the best, but someone would've had to break into the house before they'd be able to disable it.

"You came in the front door?" I asked him. He nodded. "Was the door locked?" Another nod.

"So," I thought out loud, "whoever showed up here probably came in the front door. No doorbell on the side door and your dad probably wouldn't hear anybody knocking on it. He knows 'em, maybe, or at least is unsuspecting enough to let them in the house and—I'm guessing here—locks the door behind them out of habit. But doesn't reset the alarm. Then BAM!, something happens and somebody starts bleeding and whoever rushes out the nearest door, the side door, bleeding the whole way." *But whose blood?* I thought. I was going to want to see the study, but I knew I'd have to wait until the cops got done. However many hours that took.

"Maybe your dad just cut himself and rushed off to the ER," I said, trying out another, more likely situation.

"His car's in the garage. And the cops called all the hospitals, they've got no one by his name or description."

I nodded. The cops would be calling George's workplace just to double-check he wasn't there, hadn't headed in to finish up some work. They'd call the State Police to see if he'd been a passenger in any car accidents. This seemed like it could be a kidnapping—*something* had happened in this house—but they'd want to cover all their bases before calling in the F.B.I. Be embarrassing as hell to call the feds in on a kidnapping and have the supposed victim come home from a hard day's shopping at the mall. Once Ron's mother arrived home the deputies would talk to her too, just to make sure Ron wasn't a lunatic with an overactive imagination.

I tried to imagine who would want to kidnap Ron's father, and why. And, if that's what actually happened, I'd like to meet the man that pulled it off. George Kelly was one of the most imposing humans I'd ever met. The first time I saw him I wondered who'd lost the bet and had to shave the gorilla. George was just under five-ten and ran nearly three hundred pounds, most of it still muscle even with him approaching fifty-five. He was built like a fifty-five-gallon drum set on two stumps, and, when he bothered to work out, started with three hundred pounds on the bench press.

George wasn't just all muscle and no backbone, either. I wondered how anyone would've been able to kidnap him out of his own house without having to kill him or lose a limb in the altercation. I couldn't see George going without a fight, and him enraged in the close confines of the study would put Bugs Bunny's Tasmanian Devil to shame.

"Well, I'm glad you called me, Ron," I told him, "but I don't know what I'll be able to do for you. As soon as the cops have established to their own satisfaction that your father was indeed likely kidnapped, they'll be on the phone to the FBI. They're probably in the kitchen on the phone talking to 'em now. The FBI'll be able to do anything I can do for you, only twice as fast. And then a lot more. They've got a whole network in place for this sort of thing. Besides, once the feds get in on this they won't even let me get close. They'd call it interfering in an ongoing federal investigation. They get real territorial on this shit. You've got no idea whatsoever why someone would want to grab your dad?"

Ron looked at me, checked over his shoulder for anyone listening, then leaned close.

"That's sort of what I called you about," he said.

My expression remained unchanged. Inwardly I curled up into a little ball and began whimpering "Mommy!". I should've kicked myself for thinking that Ron would ever get me involved in something simple. No, it had to be something weird, complicated. He was one of those people—and I seemed to be one of them as well—cursed with having an "interesting" life. *His dad's been kidnapped, though*, I thought. *How much worse could it get?*

"What," I said.

"This is gonna sound stupid," he told me.

"Since when has that ever stopped you?" I replied. That got a little smile.

"I think my dad works for the CIA," he said to me. I blinked, not sure I had heard him correctly.

"What?" I said again.

"Well, I know he did," Ron said. "Does. I'm pretty sure.

I just don't know if it's relevant, if I should've told the cops."

"The CIA?" I said, a bit too loudly. I lowered my voice and continued in a hiss. "The CIA? As in the Central Intelligence Agency. You're serious?" He nodded soberly at me.

I reached up and ran a hand through my hair, then set my chin in my palm. "You are not joking," I said flatly.

He shook his head.

"Ron," I said to him, after a pause, "I've known you long enough to know you wouldn't joke about something like this to me, not this way. But," I continued with a small smile and tiny shake of my head, "I'm having a real hard time swallowing this. This is Detroit, you know. Not New York, or D.C., or even L.A. Hell, it's not even Detroit, it's Rochester Hills, the end of the yuppie yellow brick road."

"I know where we are," Ron told me. I scratched my head and thought hard for a couple minutes.

"I can see your dad doing that," I said, more to myself than to him. "With his temperament, and what little I know of his background, I can see him working for the spooks." The one time I'd asked George what he did for a living, he made a point of not answering the question.

"But," Ron said for me.

"Yeah. Big time 'But'," I said. "He *told* you he worked for the CIA? No, wait, that's not what you said."

"He never told me he worked for them," Ron said to me. He held up a hand as I opened my mouth. "Hold on. You know I'm not some half-assed idiot. Dad never came out and told me he worked for them when I asked, but he as much as did."

"Whoa, whoa, whoa," I said, giving him the time-out signal with my hands. "Let's start with the easy questions.

Your Dad, I'm assuming, was getting paid by somebody. What was the name on the top of his paychecks?"

"Consolidated Systems, Inc." he told me. "A computerized research firm in Dearborn. They've got office space—I've been there—and about a dozen other employees." I looked at him and pulled on my ear. He looked down at the carpet and then back at me. I gave another little laugh, then crossed my arms and looked at my legs stretched out in front of me. I smiled again, then sat up and leaned forward. I looked at Ron's face, then at the painting on the wall behind him. It was a landscape, rolling hills and trees in the distance just starting to bloom with fall colors. I thought about all the stunts Ron had pulled in the two years that I'd known him, then looked out the front window at all the news crews still standing around.

Out of sight, around the side of the house, was a large two-story horse barn. Two years before, Ron and Bob Grinnand had shown up at my house when I wasn't there and walked into two mob soldiers setting up an ambush for me. Actually, they hadn't quite got to that part yet, one of them was about to rape my unconscious wife while the other watched. Bob killed one of them, and the boys had dragged the other one to barn behind Ron's house.

Where, together, we'd tortured the man for information. Then killed him. Like I'd said, shared misery.

I'm not the same person I was before that day. But I don't regret what I did. And I'd do it again.

The point is, Ron's father had walked in right in the middle of the whole thing. Gun in his hand, no expression on his face. When the situation was explained to him, George Kelly hadn't yelled or attempted to intervene. He told us to be quick about it and then get the man the hell off his property.

"You know," I told Ron, "I always wondered what your Dad did for a living. I asked him, once. He basically told me to fuck off. Politely."

"Think about how it was for me," he said. "All those years…I was thirteen before I began to get the idea that something might be up. It took me a year and a half before I got up the nerve to ask my mom. You know what she said? '*Don't ask,*' and gave me one of those looks. You know the look I'm talking about." I nodded. "I suppose I should be complimented that they didn't lie to me. That they felt I was mature enough to handle the truth. Sort of. After that I hinted around the subject a few times with my father but got nowhere, so I just dropped it."

I leaned forward and kneaded my skull between my palms. "The main problem I have here," I told Ron, "is not what you might expect. Thousands of people work for the CIA, and there's no reason why your dad can't be one of them. I've met a few, when I was with the DEA. Your Dad may or may not work for the CIA, I don't know. But you obviously think he does, and from what you told me your mother said I can't see that I've got any choice but to believe you. But this problem, maybe you can help me with it. You've had a lot more time to think about this stuff than I have, so you tell me. What the hell kind of work could your Dad be doing for an intelligence agency? He's obviously not a field agent, so why would he need a cover?"

"His office is in Dearborn," Ron said. "Dearborn is known for two things. It's got one of the largest population of Arabs in the world outside of the Middle East, and it's also the site of the Ford Motor Company's World Headquarters. You're talking a hell of a lot of potential intelligence sources with either of those."

"Not to mention GM and Chrysler Headquarters, all

three within an hour's drive of each other," I said. "Hell, the Chrysler Tech Center is ten minutes from here. And as for a cover," I answered my own question, "the CIA is not, officially, allowed to operate inside the US, not on their own." I sat back and thought for a moment. "The NSA, however, has no such restrictions on it. National Security Agency," I told Ron. "You think the CIA's tight-lipped, nobody even knew the NSA existed for I don't know how many years. NSA—No Such Agency."

"I think I've heard of them," Ron said.

"Mostly they intercept sigint—signals intelligence," I told him. "E-mails, cell calls, you name it. And those are just two. There's also the Defense Intelligence Agency, National Reconnaissance Office, National Geospatial-Intelligence Agency, probably another dozen smaller uber secret agencies neither of us have ever heard of. The government loves their secret agencies."

Ron frowned, then sat back in the loveseat and crossed his arms. "But does any of it matter?" he asked me. "I mean, does it have anything to do with what happened today? And," here he lowered his voice, "should I say anything to the cops?"

"Ron," I said quietly, "it's too early to know anything for sure. I mean, we don't even know that your Dad's been kidnapped. Yeah, it sure looks that way, something happened here, but I'm not about to start making snap judgments. Not until I know more. The cops don't even have a type yet on the blood back there, I'll bet. And as for telling the cops?" I crinkled my forehead in doubt. "Let them do their job, start investigating. Let them first eliminate you as a suspect, or at least move beyond you. Then they'll start talking to your Dad's coworkers and supervisors and whoever else they find at Consolidated Systems. If they don't find anything hinky, anything weird, if it just seems like a regular computer place to them, anything you say about the CIA will make you sound like a nut. If that place *is* a cover for the CIA or the NSA or whoever, and passes a quick onceover, it'll pass any sort of detailed investigation the county'll be able to muster. That business has a cover identity for a reason."

"But if I don't tell these guys about my suspicions, about what I suspect, they won't be able to do a complete investigation, will they?"

I sat and thought. "Well, if he does work for the feds, they'll damn well hear about this pretty quick. They won't wait for the locals to come to them."

"Yeah, but what if he was working on something secret, and they can't—"

"Ron," I asked him, "do you know for a fact that your Dad worked for anyone other than Consolidated Systems, Inc.?"

"No," he said petulantly.

"Do you think, when those nice earnest white boys from the FBI show up, half of them probably not much older than you, do you think that when they get nowhere asking you questions that they might start asking questions around your father's office?"

"Yeah."

"You bet they will. They'll run background checks on everybody in that office if this thing lasts more than a day and a half. Run your phone records. Subpoena your financials. Then, if they come back to you and your mom and start asking you off-the-wall questions about what your Dad did for a living, did he ever go out of the country, did he ever get phone calls from Uzbekistan, *then* maybe it'll be time for you and your mom to talk."

"But what if that's too late?"

I didn't get a chance to answer. We both turned at the loud exclamation of surprise from the rear of the house, then heard one of the techs yell, "Hey Charlie, come take a look at this!"

Both Ron and I got up and started down the hallway. We saw the deputy that had been summoned cross in front of us, heading for the study. Trying not to stick out so much that I'd be noticed and sent away, I sidled up to the study doorway. Ron stayed in the background, maybe afraid of bad news.

Charlie the deputy was a couple steps inside the study, looking at the left wall, nearly opposite George's desk and overturned chair. He was watching as the ID Techs fiddled with something on the wall five feet off the floor. The busted lamp glass Ron had mentioned was gone, probably tagged and bagged by the techs hoping to get a good print. The desk and bookcase were totally covered with different colors of fingerprint powder, bare rectangles here and there where they'd used tape to lift a promising print.

I watched them for about thirty seconds before my eyes could interpret exactly what I was seeing. The walls in the study were covered in an off-white wallpaper that had some sort of dark green leafy vine motif. While the end result was more attractive than you might think, the pattern confused my eyes for a few seconds. Then I realized the techs were digging something out of the wall, digging around a hole in the drywall that the pattern had concealed.

"D'you photo it already?" Charlie asked. Both techs nodded their heads and continued their scraping.

"It's a bullethole," one of the techs said, nodding.

"How can you be so sure?" Charlie asked him.

"'Cause I can see the fucking bullet," the tech replied.

"It went in through the drywall and stopped just against a two-by-four stud. Went in at a slightly upward angle, but the hole's so shallow we'll never be able to trace its path backward. Not accurately."

"Came from inside the room. Look at this," the other tech said. "I can't believe it only went in this far. What is that, three quarters of an inch? We're talking drywall, and it barely went into the wood. And it's not a tiny bullet. This ain't no .25 Auto here."

"Nine-millimeter?" the other tech pondered aloud. He stopped his burrowing and dug a small evidence baggie out of his pocket, then held it under the hole they'd made. His partner gave one more flick with the plastic dental pick he was using and the bullet dropped out of the wall into the bag. The tech held the bag up and he and his partner looked at the spent slug.

"Hollowpoint," the one said. "Not much deformation, either. Cavity's all plugged up with something, can't tell if it's drywall or what, yet."

"That's a .380," his partner said. "It's gotta be. Right diameter, too short for a nine. Look at that nose profile, five bucks says its a Federal, 90 grainer."

"I've been burned too many times to ever bet bullets with you again," the other tech said. "But five'll get you ten the reason it was so shallow was because it went through something or someone before it hit the wall." Charlie the deputy turned around and saw me standing just outside the doorway. An unpleasant expression crossed his face, then his eyes shifted left.

"You own a .380?" he asked Ron. Ron took a few steps forward to stand beside me.

"No," he said defiantly, something new in his eyes. "But my Dad does. He keeps it in his top right desk drawer." Ron pointed, and one of the gloved techs walked over and opened up the drawer. It was empty.

"If I remember correctly," the tech said slowly, "that's the drawer that wasn't closed all the way, right?" He looked to his partner for confirmation.

"Don't remember," the second tech said. "It'll be in the pictures, though. Remind me to look for that when I develop 'em."

"You find a spent shell casing?" I asked the techs. Unless they were complete idiots, part of their job would have been to scour the carpet for trace evidence. They both looked slightly puzzled.

"No," one said.

"Better start looking," Charlie told them. "Check on top of the bookcases and shit. Cases end up in weird places." He looked around the small room, obviously trying to visualize how an ejected cartridge case might carom off the walls. Both the techs gave him the same look, not liking anyone to tell them their job.

"You know your Dad's blood type?" a tech asked of Ron.

"B Positive, same as mine," Ron told him. The tech looked around the study again, this time appraising it with different eyes.

"All the blood we've found so far and field-typed has been AB Negative," he said absently. He turned abruptly to Charlie.

"Are the dicks ever going to show up or do they want us to mail them our reports?" he asked.

"Supposedly on their way," Charlie told him. "They better show up soon. We find anything else and it'll take an hour to get 'em up to speed."

"The feds been called yet?"

"Not my call," Charlie told him. I heard footsteps and looked over my shoulder to see Charlie's partner approaching. "That's up to the Sarge. Maybe not even him, the lieutenant might have to make the call."

"Well, you better get Randolph in here then, get him up to speed," the tech told Charlie. "Get the feebies in motion. 'Cause this looks like something." Charlie looked to his partner who grumbled and headed toward the front of the house. One of the techs began looking over the bookcase, trying to find the spent case that went with the bullet he'd just pulled out of the wall. Ron and I watched from the doorway, trying to see around Deputy Charlie who stood just inside the room, looking like he was deep in thought.

"Got it," the tech said with only a hint of excitement in his voice, cheek pressed against the wall as he peered behind the bookcase. "Bring that camera over here," he told his partner. The partner snagged the camera off the top of one of their tool kits and brought it over. The other tech took it and smashed his face against the wall as he tried to get a good sight picture through the camera's viewfinder. Suddenly he twitched in surprise.

"Hey, wait a minute," he said. He lowered the camera and used his naked eyes to look, then raised the camera again and looked through it.

"What?" his partner asked. "Don't tell me that thing's broken again."

"Nope," was the response. The tech with the camera took a picture, readjusted his position, and took another picture. "Help me pull this thing out for another picture, a close-up." he told his coworker. The two of them together struggled with the ungainly bookcase, finally moving it out from the wall a foot or so. When the tech without the camera straightened up, his back to us, he raised a hand to scratch his head.

"Whoever said this job wasn't interesting?" he asked nobody in particular. He turned around to look at Deputy Charlie. "There's two. Two cases back here. We got us a second shell casing," he told him. "They both look like three-eighties?" he asked his partner.

"Sure do," was the response. "Why don't you start looking for another hole in the wall. Floor too, although with this carpeting…"

There was pressure on my leg and I looked to my left. Ron jerked his head toward the kitchen and then started that direction. I followed, wondering what he wanted now.

Ron leaned his butt against the dishwasher and looked at me with a thoughtful expression on his face. I looked back over my shoulder to double-check that we were alone.

"My Dad kept all of his computer disks in a plastic box file folder kind of thing. Green, about eight by four by four. He always kept it on the bookcase shelf just to the right of his desk."

"And it ain't there," I finished for him, guessing the punch line.

"Standing in the doorway just now, that's the first time I got a real good calm look inside the study," he told me. "I didn't see the box anywhere."

"It could be inside the desk," I told him. "He could've put it in a drawer. You look in the desk?"

"Haven't had a reason to, but he never kept it in the desk. As soon as these yahoos clear out I'll check the desk, but I bet it's gone."

"What kind of disks are we talking about?" I asked.

"He had about ten disks in there that were just personal stuff. A couple CD's, too. Financial software and money management programs, mostly. Taxes. I used the computer once in a while and looked through all that. But there were other disks in there, too. I'm not sure if he brought them home from work or just worked on them at home. Not all the time, but pretty regularly I'd see either an unmarked disk or a disk with CSI logo on it."

"You ever stick them in the drive, see what was on 'em?"

"I stuck 'em in the drive every once in a while, even though I knew Dad would kill me if he saw me doing it. Ninety percent of 'em, most of the ones with CSI labels, had boring lists of all sorts of things. Stock tables, agricultural reports, New York Times bestseller lists, congressional voting records. I never could figure out those, most of that stuff seemed like it would be public record. But the other disks, when I tried to boot them up, all had some sort of encryption code or something. I never got anywhere, never was able to get the screen to display anything other than gobbledygook."

"Get the cops looking for those disks," I told him. "At the very least it'll give them something to do, maybe it'll send them looking in the right direction, talking to his employer. Motive, maybe? You've got no idea what might have been on them, if anything, so it shouldn't do any harm. Maybe it'll get them asking tougher questions of your father's coworkers." He didn't seem too sold on the idea but pushed himself off the counter and went back to the study. I glanced at my watch. It was later than I'd thought. Kelly had gotten back from walking the dog before I'd left home, so she knew where I was, but I was surprised that she hadn't called wondering just what the hell I was doing.

12:14 p.m.

I heard a clatter and voices approaching from the front door. Charlie's partner and Sergeant Randolph appeared in the kitchen doorway with another uniformed officer.

"Well, let me use a land-line to call a Lieutenant," Randolph was saying. "I can call the feds myself but I'm sure as hell not gonna do it without letting someone upstairs know about it first. You still here?" he said to me when he saw me.

"Moral support," I told him. He nodded and looked around for a phone. He saw it and quickly grabbed it off the wall.

"I just hope a Lieutenant's in," he said, punching buttons. "Otherwise it'll have to be the Undersheriff, and he'll want to come down here and re-interview everybody 'fore we do anything." The two deputies smiled and looked down at their shoes. "Yeah, Radio," Randolph said. "Who is this, Lori? This is Randolph. Are there any lieutenants in the building?" He paused for a reply. "Thank God," he said with relief. "Can you put him on the line for me?" He listened for a couple seconds. "You think it's bad now, just wait," he told her. "This is gonna be a clusterfuck of astronomical proportions. And where the hell are the dicks? I could've walked here from there by now." A few more seconds of silence as he held the receiver to his ear and shook his head. "What the hell is Dubrowski doing? That's what, the fourth flat tire he's had this month? The guys at the garage look up 'job security' in the dictionary, there's his picture." I'd taken two steps toward the kitchen doorway and the sitting room out front when I heard the front door slam and someone began stomping loudly my way.

"Goddammit! Who the hell's in charge around here, anyway? Where the hell is everybody?" I moved to a better viewpoint as Deputy Charlie quickstepped from the study to intercept and contain this new disturbance. He stopped in front of the newcomer and attempted to control the scene, just like he'd been taught in the academy.

"Mrs. Kelly? I'm Deputy Brock, the first officer on the scene, and—"

"Pardon me son if I cut through the bullshit for you," she told him. Carla Kelly was in her fifties, with frosted dark blonde hair and a jawbone large enough to park a truck on. She radiated such a force of personality and determination that the deputy almost took a step back when she pointed her finger at him. Today she was in cowboy boots, and stood all of four foot eleven. "From what I hear, my son was the first person on the scene, and this is *my* house to begin with, so don't start telling me the way it is like you're Mr. Jesus H. Christ. My day was shitty to start with, and now I've got you and that bunch of halfwits tearing up my lawn outside. What was your name?" Charlie was caught staring at her, mouth open, and it took him half a beat to get his mouth in gear.

"Uh, ah, I'm Brock, Deputy Brock ma'am, and we're gonna have to ask you—"

"Who's the ranking officer on the scene?" Carla asked him, obviously not paying much attention to what he was saying. "You got a sergeant or somebody around here yet?" She looked around.

Brock stopped talking and blinked twice. This was not going the way he had envisioned. "Sergeant Randolph's here, he should be—"

"Well," she told him, "better get him on down here, then. Y'all are gonna ask me a bunch of questions and I have no intention of repeating myself. I've got a few of my own to ask, while we're at it. If we're gonna do it let's do it, I say, no use beating around the bush." She wasted half a second staring at him. "Well, young man," she admonished him, "I'm working on a migraine, I've got a husband that's still missing, could be facedown in the Detroit River with a bullet in his brain for all I know, and none of us are getting any younger while you're standing there gawking, so what say you get your ass in gear and find your Sergeant?" Brock stood there for a second and a half, mouth hanging open. Then, without saying a word, he turned on his heel and headed past me into the kitchen, making a beeline toward Randolph who was still talking on the phone.

I swiveled my head back to Ron's mother, who was shaking her head and muttering to herself. She held back, didn't move for nearly ten seconds. Then she was in motion again, marching straight for the kitchen doorway.

"...better not have to deal with a bunch of bumblefuck Barney Fifes," I heard her mutter as she strode purposefully at the clump of deputies, giving me a quick nod of recognition as she passed. I joined Ron outside his father's study and watched through the kitchen doorway as the voices began to increase in volume. I turned to Ron as he watched his mother at work.

"That was beautiful," I told him.

"You ain't seen nothin'," he replied. "We call her 'The General' for a reason."

"You better get with your mom," I told him. "Decide just what the hell you're going to tell these guys about your father's employer. She may have a dissenting opinion on the subject."

"Yeah, you're probably right."

"You got a phone I can use away from this circus?"

He nodded and led me upstairs to his bedroom, then headed back down to talk to his mother. Ron returned just as I was hanging up the phone.

"What'd your mom say about spilling the beans?" I asked him.

"We don't know nuthin' until they bring it up," he told me. "Who'd you call?"

"Scott Copley," I told him.

"Will he be able to help?" Ron asked me. He knew Scott slightly, mostly because of me. Scott had helped me and Ron and the rest of Jerry Phillips' crew when we'd run slightly astray of the law during the search for Jerry.

"Help with what?" I said. "We don't even know what the fuck we've got. That was his voicemail. I just wanted to let him know what's going on and that I'm involved. Again."

I was staring out the front window about an hour later at the news people who seemed immensely bored. There'd been some excitement a while back when the two FBI Agents pulled up in their gray Ford, everyone recognizing them for what they were, but that had been short-lived. Special Agents Harris and Griffin, I wasn't sure which one was which. Seemed competent enough, but so far it was just the two of them. They were about my age, dressed in conservative suits, and seemed a bit confused as to exactly why I was hanging around. So was I. I figured the only reason I hadn't been interrogated by someone yet was that the whole situation was so odd for the suburbs—kidnapping, bloodstains, bullet holes, etc.—that they hadn't gotten their footing yet. The Special Agents were in back, interviewing Ron and his mother separately to see if there were any inconsistencies in their stories.

Scott Copley had returned my call ten minutes after I'd left him the message. He'd been out doing some early

Christmas shopping for his nieces and nephews and had been grateful for the interruption. When the phone rang a zealous deputy had snagged it quickly. He'd asked who had called Lieutenant Copley, visibly disappointed that it wasn't the kidnappers on the phone. I got some queer stares when I announced that *I* had called one of their Lieutenants. They probably thought there was a reason I'd gone over their heads, when in reality I'd only called the one contact I had on the Sheriff's Department. Scott just happened to be a Lieutenant.

When I told him where I was, what had happened so far, and why I was there (minus the small item of possible CIA/NSA involvement), I got thirty seconds of silence in response.

"You're shitting me," he said finally.

"I shit you not," I replied. I was treated to another long silence.

"You know, you must be loaded with some natural disaster chemical or something," he told me. "Everywhere you go, bad things happen. I've been in one gunfight in my life and it happened while I was having lunch with you. You take on a missing persons case and it turns into the biggest mob-involved double-digit bodycount this town has seen since the '67 riots. I'm surprised anyone still returns your calls. I'm surprised I do. Who all is there?"

"Two ID techs, half a dozen uniforms, Sergeant Randolph. Two Dep dicks should be here any time. They're running late because of a flat tire or something. Feds are probably on their way here by now, too. Randolph got hold of one of your fellow Lieutenants in Pontiac and apprised him. He might be on the way down here, I'm not sure."

"Probably Lewis, he was on call."

"Most of the uniforms are pulling duty out on the front

lawn. Someone in the newsrooms was actually listening to their scanners today. 7, 4, and 50 are here already. With all the cops around, they know something big is up, but no one's come out of the house so they don't have anything yet. If this wasn't Sunday they'd be parachuting people onto the roof in hopes of getting some video for the six o'clock."

"Swell." He then paused, and I could hear him breathing over the phone line. "You know," he said, "I've got enough clout around here to get assigned to this. I mean, assuming the feds don't claim jurisdiction and get the Sheriff to completely hand it over. I can't do it, though, because I know the people involved."

"I know that," I told him. I hoped he didn't think that was why I'd called him. "I was just hoping you could keep me up to date on the investigation."

"If this is being treated as a kidnapping, the feebies are gonna be in charge by default," he told me. "Possible interstate transportation, all that jazz. The Sheriff is doing his best to play nice with them."

"I know that, but they'll be sharing most if not all of what they get with your guys who're assigned as liaisons. I'm not looking for complete and total access, I'd just like a line on anything unusual they turn up. You know, stuff they might not tell the family."

"This whole thing is unusual," he told me. "I can't remember the last adult male kidnapping we had in this county. We might not've ever had one. Well, Hoffa, but that doesn't really count."

I told him about the bullet the techs had pulled out of the wall. So far, it had been the only one they'd found. They'd gone over the entire study twice, walls, floor, ceiling, and furniture, but no second bullet. They were betting that bullet had left the house in somebody.

"Man," he said, "I wish I didn't know any of you guys. This sounds interesting as hell, I'd love to be working on it." He paused. "Then again, Ron's dad shows up dead somewhere, it makes anybody working the case look bad."

"Can you get the word out to whoever you know in other departments or M.E. offices to notify you in case they find a body, living or dead, in the next couple days with a bullet wound in it?"

"Unless they've suffered major head trauma that'll be the first thing the assigned detectives do. Same goes for the extra special FBI agents. Shit," he told me, "chances are the feds'll have the body autopsied, dissected, and sewn back together before I find out about it, but I'll try." Scott paused and fell silent, and I could just picture it as he fought with himself. He was dying to ask me a lot of heated, pointed questions about why I was involved in this thing, about why a Rochester Hills businessman who I just happened to know had been kidnapped. And did I know something that he didn't but should? But Scott and I had known each other for almost twenty years, almost since junior high school, and he wasn't going to ask me any of those questions. He didn't want me to have to lie to him, or refuse to answer, so he bit his tongue. He promised to do what he could for me, and then we hung up. Twenty minutes later the feds had shown up, and I migrated into the front room to be alone so I could think.

One of the things I hated about winter, besides the snow and cold weather, was the damnably short days. The shadows of the cameramen and their equipment stretched ominously across the faded green of the front lawn, still bare of snow. The light hadn't yet begun to fade, but that was, perhaps, only a matter of an hour or less. So far the winter had been mild, with no snow to speak of and moderate temperatures. Today it was in the high twenties, with no wind, and the deputies were standing around outside in their jackets, talking, instead of huddled inside their cars with the heaters roaring. The media seemed well behaved so far, due more to the lack of activity than anything else. The cameramen stayed outside with their equipment like loyal soldiers, stamping their feet occasionally. The high-priced talent took refuge in the vans and Suburbans, not willing to brave the elements or risk mussing their hair until it was time to do their live on-camera lead-ins for the six o'clock news. Randolph was back outside, standing with his men, awaiting the arrival of some department brass. He didn't look happy.

The cameramen all sprang to life at once, like a single being, as a maroon Lumina pulled into the gravel driveway. Two men whom I assumed were the long lost OCSD detectives climbed languidly out of the car and ambled toward the house, ignoring the videocameras swinging to follow their progress like so many gun turrets. I saw their mouths move as they spoke to Randolph and the clump of deputies. Whatever they said got quite a few chuckles out of the deputies. Randolph's mouth remained clamped shut, and he glared at their backs as they headed toward me. A couple of the news people had exited their vehicles and I could see their breath in the cold air as they shouted questions at the detectives, who ignored them. The large window I was looking out of was double-paned and looked new, which explained why I couldn't hear a damned thing that was going on outside.

"...and I told him we were going to keep getting flats until we got a newer car," one of the dicks was saying with a grin as they came through the front door. "He just grunted like he didn't give a shit. Probably try to write me up for it."

The detective's partner grunted. They closed the front door and stood in the foyer, looking at me in the front room.

"FBI?" the one that had been speaking asked me.

Great, I thought. These guys were going to be the Sheriff's Department's lead investigators, and they were a couple of flaming assholes. I shook my head and jerked a thumb down the hallway toward the back of the house. They started that direction, then the other dick stopped and looked quizzically at me.

"Who are you?" he asked.

"Friend of the family," I told him. That didn't seem to satisfy him, but his partner pulled him along and they disappeared down the hallway.

Ron was going to be busy for a long time answering questions, and it was doubtful I'd get to see much of him. The FBI would probably camp out at the house round the clock until they found George or made an arrest.

Abruptly I turned on my heel and headed toward the back of the house. I wasn't going to be able to do anything else, and my presence might in fact hurt Ron, make him look guiltier in the eyes of some. So much for hindsight. He was in the kitchen surrounded by half a dozen people, all wanting something. He looked more than a bit harried. When he saw me his eyes lit up with relief. I felt guilty about leaving, but there wasn't anything else I could do for him. I heard his mother somewhere in the house, sounding like she was reading someone the riot act. "Horseshit," I heard her say. Several voices rose in protest. I did my best not to grin.

"I'm taking off," I told him. As I expected, he did not greet this news with joy. He opened his mouth to object, both of us ignoring all the cops trying to ask him questions.

"You can't stay?" he asked plaintively.

"Nothing for me to do here," I told him. "I'm going

home, gonna make a few phone calls. If anything new pops up," I gave him a look, "give me a call there." He wasn't happy about it, but he nodded.

"I was supposed to go to the movies with Steve tonight," he told me. "Can you call—" I held up a hand.

"Don't worry about it," I told him. "I'll call everybody and let them know what's going on. I *will* talk to you later," I told him as I headed toward the door. I paused before going outside and looked out the window, trying to plot the shortest route to my car that wouldn't take me through the center of the news crews. There didn't seem to be one.

Squaring my shoulders, I opened the front door and stepped outside. All the camera guys snapped to attention and swiveled their lenses my way as the talent climbed hastily out of their vehicles. My stride was quick and steady as I made a beeline down the driveway toward my car, giving a nod to Randolph as I passed by him and the clump of deputies still standing around.

The media types thought I was one of the County dicks. They kept yelling "Detective!, Detective!" at me, trying to get me to look their way, but kept to the far side of the circular driveway, away from the uniforms. Randolph must have laid down the law, normally they'd have rushed me like an offensive line.

"Any comment on rumors that the homeowner here has been kidnapped?" a few of the reporters yelled at me.

"He ain't one a our dicks," an annoyed deputy told the gathered flock of newsmen. This got a short period of silence, then dozens of questions flew at me and the uniforms as to my identity and affiliation. Most assumed I was FBI. Perhaps filled with a renewed sense of purpose, one of the reporters started following me down the driveway, his cameraman in tow.

"Hey buddy," Randolph called to the reporter, whose trench coat looked like it cost as much as my car, "you know what a hematoma is?" The reporter paused and glanced back at Randolph, which gave me enough time to reach my car, unlock the door, and jump inside. Past experience with the media hadn't left me a fan, and I lost no time getting my car into gear. The only depressing thought was I knew at least one of the vultures was copying down my license number, and while it didn't come back to my home address, it was registered in my name.

2:48 p.m.

When I got home I could tell Kelly was upset, and this time it wasn't her hormones. She was slouched in a chair at the kitchen table, not doing much of anything other than idly scratching the dog's head with a trailing hand.

"What's the matter, honey?" I asked her, sitting beside her on one of the kitchen chairs.

"You were gone so long I got worried and turned on the radio and the TV to see if I could find out anything," she said listlessly. "The guy on the radio said something about a possible abduction in Rochester Hills. That was where you were, wasn't it?" *Wonderful*, I thought. *No facts to report but they still put it out over the air anyway.*

"It was George Kelly," I told her. "It looks like he might've been kidnapped. Ron called me because he wasn't sure what else to do." Kelly's face turned pink and scrunched up as tears began rolling down her cheeks.

"Aw, babe, what's the matter?" I got up and moved next to her, putting my hands on her shoulders and looking in her eyes. She brought her hands up to touch mine.

"I'm scared," she said, trying to fight back the sobs with only partial success.

"Scared of what? About what?"

She sniffled and wiped ineffectively at the tears on her face. "I'm afraid you're going to get hurt. I'm scared for the baby."

Oh Christ. "Why are you scared?" I asked her. "I'm not gonna get hurt, and the baby'll be just fine."

"This is gonna turn out bad again, just like the last time," she told me.

"What are you talking about?"

"Ron Kelly's father being kidnapped, what the hell do you think I'm talking about!" she exploded at me. "Jerry Phillips was missing, same as this, and when you start to look for him two guys come into my house and try to rape me!" The dog got up and beat a stealthy retreat into the living room. The kids don't like it when Mom and Dad fight. "I had cops guarding me for a week because people kept trying to kill you and those damn kids. This is the same thing all over again."

"Honey," I told her, "those kids saved both our lives, you know that as well as I do. And this isn't going to be anything like that. Ron's scared half out of his mind, that's why he called me. Nobody knows yet what the hell's going on, he just called me for moral support. There's nothing to be worried about." My wife didn't look convinced. Maybe because I had no idea if what I was saying was true. If only I'd known then what I know now…

"Look," I told her, "he called me because he wanted someone on the inside to give him information on what was happening with the case, that's all. Ron knows I know Scott. The FBI's there already, they're the ones that are going to be running the investigation. Them and the Sheriff's

Department detectives are going to be doing everything. They've already started an investigation. With all those people working the case, what the hell good am I gonna do Ron?"

"The FBI?" she said, dabbing at her eyes.

"Yeah, the FBI, they handle kidnappings. Which they're still not sure this is. Whatever they find out they're gonna tell the Sheriff's Department people, one of which is Scott Copley, and then he's going to tell me, and I'm going to tell Ron. That's all."

"Won't the FBI tell Ron? It's his dad."

"The first people the cops suspect in any kind of person crime is family," I told her. "You know that. And even if they don't suspect him, there's some things they might find out that they won't think the family should know about."

"Like what?"

"I don't know," I told her. "Maybe they find out George spent every Thursday afternoon with a hooker, and so now she's a possible, but unlikely, suspect. The feds sure aren't going to say anything to the family about her until they've got evidence, but Ron would sure want to know about any leads, any progress. That's all I'm gonna be doing, feeding him information."

"You promise?" she asked me, already looking to be in better spirits. The fiercer the storm, the quicker it blew over.

"I promise."

A sour look remained on her face. She'd heard promises from me before. "I want to go shooting again," she announced. "I haven't gone shooting in over a month."

After the last bit of trouble we'd had, Kelly had been adamant about me buying her a gun and teaching her how to shoot proficiently. She'd been taught how to shoot by her father, but her skills were rudimentary at best, only a loose grasp of the fundamentals. I'd bought her a revolver, and for six months we'd gone shooting together two or three times a month, until she'd felt confident in her skills. And had stopped having nightmares about the near rape/murder. Since she'd gotten pregnant, however, Kelly's interest in shooting had fallen off. Her gun stayed in the drawer of a small table in our living room, loaded, for those occasions when strangers knocked on our door. After all the bad things that had happened to both of us, I'd made a pledge to never open the door to somebody I didn't know unless I had a gun in my hand. Paranoid? Yes, but our living room wall had already been repainted once due to bloodstains. Somebody had been out to get me and I'd been blissfully unaware of that fact until it was almost too late. If it happened again I didn't want to die for lack of shooting back.

"Okay," I told her. "We'll go to the range in the next couple of days. But I don't want you to worry. Whatever this is, everything'll work out fine."

With a slightly teary smile she held out her hand and I helped her up out of the chair. It was amazing to me how much her belly had grown. The idea that there was a little human being inside her, right there on the other side of her belly button, was just so weird. I kept thinking of the movie *Alien*, although I didn't dare mention it to Kelly. Maybe that was because I was male, and would always be just a spectator in this game. Well, the growing the baby part of the equation. I had definitely been involved in making the baby.

"The whole day's shot, now," she said, sounding a little down. "You want me to start making dinner?"

"Sure," I told her. "I'll even do the sensitive guy thing and help." The phone rang and I grabbed it as she began poking around in the cupboard.

"Hello?" I said.

"Yeah, John?" It was either a bad connection, a cellular phone, or a pay phone, I couldn't tell which.

"Yes?" I said politely. I didn't recognize the voice.

"It's Bob. Bob Grinnand." Now I recognized his voice, although it was still real staticky.

"Oh, yeah, hey, I didn't recognize your voice. Where are you calling from? You in town already, at your parents' house?"

"No," he said slowly. "I'm at a pay phone in Rochester Hills. I just drove by Ron's house, and I was wondering if you could tell me why his yard is full of cops and reporters? Or why when I called his house two minutes ago the FBI answered?"

"Not before your quarter runs out," I told him. "Uh, you gonna be at your parents' later?"

"Well, they're not going to be home 'til late," he said. "I was gonna hang at Ron's."

"Oh," I said.

"Why don't you invite him over for dinner," my wife called out to me from the kitchen, where she was busy pulling ingredients from the cupboards and piling them on the counter.

"You want to come over here for dinner?" I asked him. "I can fill you in on what's going on while we eat." I could see him standing there, curiosity and worry eating him up as he thought about Ron and what he'd seen at Ron's house. He was probably going nuts, but was too self-contained to let it show.

"Is Ron okay?" he asked finally, sounding like he didn't want to hear an answer.

"Ron's fine," I told him gently.

"Okay," he said, sounding very relieved. "Um, should I come straight over or what?"

"Yeah, why not," I decided. "I haven't seen your ugly face in a while, it'll give us a chance to talk. Unless you've got stuff to do first?"

"Nah," he said. "I'll be over. I wait around here any longer I'm gonna put on my cammies and facepaint and head into the woods behind Ron's house, see what I can find out."

"No no no," I said quickly. "Don't do that. Pleeease." I heard him chuckle, then we hung up.

"Well, he's coming over," I told Kelly. "You think I should call Jerry and Steve, invite them over too? We've got enough food, would you mind the extra work?"

"No, I don't mind," she said. "It's not much more work cooking for five than for three. I was going to make a big dish of lasagna, anyway. We'll have enough, even for those eating machines." I smiled and began dialing. Steve agreed to come over for dinner immediately, even before I told him why he'd been invited. Jerry didn't want to come, saying he was just sitting down to dinner with his parents, although he appreciated the offer.

"Kelly's making lasagna, though," I told him. "She makes *great* lasagna. And while we're eating, I can explain to you guys why the Oakland County Sheriff's Department and the FBI are over at Ron's house."

After a second's pause, he said, "I'll be right over." His parents wouldn't be pleased about him skipping out on dinner, but his relationship with them had…changed?…matured? since they'd learned he'd knifed to death two mob enforcers on a school playground. They were just glad he was alive, and didn't worry about the small stuff anymore.

"You need any help?" I asked Kelly. She had bowls and

measuring cups and cans and opened packages of noodles strewn all over the kitchen counters. I was, once again, amazed. She could get half of our pots and pans dirty just making a peanut butter and jelly sandwich.

"No, that's okay," she told me, waddling around inside the 'U' of our counters. "I'll make dinner, you guys can clean up afterwards." She blew a stray lock of hair off her forehead. "You realize, of course, that after our little bundle of joy arrives you can kiss meals like this goodbye. I won't have the energy."

"Yeah, but by then the Milk Fairy will have arrived," I said with a wicked grin. "Everything always balances out."

Kelly gave me a dirty look. "You are a pervert. That's for the baby."

I tried to reason with her, using simple math. "He can only use one at a time."

The bing-bong of the doorbell echoed through the house. Oscar began barking and scrambled toward the front of the house as I headed for the door. I looked out the peephole in my door and saw Bob staring back at me, a black bag slung over his shoulder, although his appearance made me do a double-take. Behind him, in my driveway, was a big black truck with knobby tires and black metal tubing sprouting from its grill. I pulled open the door with a grin.

"Robert," I said.

"How-dee," he replied, shaking my hand. A huge smile creased his face. "*Whoa whoa whoa*! Ooof!" he exclaimed as Oscar buried her nose in his crotch at full gallop. He rubbed her head affectionately as she snuffled at him, nose still buried in his fly. "Hiya doin, Oscar?" She wagged her tail fiercely.

"What the hell is that on your face?" I asked him.

He smiled sheepishly, which was almost charming. He

reached a hand up to stroke his jaw, which was covered with a thick beard. A thick red beard. It changed the shape of his face so much he looked like a different person, especially with his hair grown out. He looked like a lumberjack.

"We've been told facial hair is going to be part of our standard kit for the next few years. I haven't needed it where I've been working, but…"

"But you're probably going to a new job site in short order," I finished for him. What few photos had appeared in the media of the Special Forces troops working in Afghanistan had showed them all sporting beards, as that culture apparently looked down on clean-shaven men, and Green Berets were usually tasked with working with the locals. "So that's the new truck, huh?" I said, stepping out on the porch so I could get a better look at it. It was a full-size Chevy Blazer, a few years old but in perfect shape, with oversize off-road tires and dark tint on the rear windows.

"I don't know," I told him. "Don't you think people will question your masculinity driving that thing?"

"It's a chance I'm willing to take," he said with a grin. He pointed. "Thirty-three inch BFG Mud-Terrains, with a two-inch lift kit. Factory tint on the rear windows, brush guard I installed myself, running boards so climbing in isn't a chore, golden brown interior." His voice was filled with pride. "Plus a hell of a V-8 under the hood, factory, but with a couple modifications Ron told me about to give me almost fifty more horses."

"All you need now is a Confederate flag in the rear window," I told him. "Some of those mudflaps the truckers have with the chrome naked ladies on 'em. Maybe a squirrel tail hanging from the antenna."

"That sure sounds like me," he said sarcastically. He

looked down at Oscar. "Boy, I can't believe how big she's gotten," he said to me.

"Sixty-five pounds," I said proudly.

"Still hasn't learned any manners, though."

"You should talk." He patted her head and we headed toward the kitchen. Oscar roared away in search of a toy.

"Bob!" my wife exclaimed, happy to see him. She came out from behind the counter and gave him a hug.

"Hiya doin, Kelly," he said as she hugged him. His eyes went wide at the sight of her stomach, but he didn't say anything. He caught me watching him and I gave him a smile, trying not to laugh.

"You're so handsome with that beard, it looks good on you," she told him, stepping back to get a better look at it. "You want something to drink?"

"Beer," he said. She nodded her head and moved toward the fridge. His eyes followed my wife's belly as it moved across the room.

"What kind?" Kelly asked him, her head stuck inside the refrigerator.

"Cold," Bob told her.

"Spoken like a true connoisseur," I said. "You look tan," I observed.

"We haven't had a war in a cold climate since Korea," he pointed out. Oscar reappeared, her teddy bear hanging by one leg from her mouth.

"No, you go lay down on your bed," I told her. "We'll play with you later." She pouted at me and laid down on her small padded bed in the corner of the kitchen. She dropped her teddy bear and rested her head on it as she watched the three of us.

Kelly brought Bob the can of beer and he quickly downed half of it. "You got a bathroom around here where

I can clean up? I've been in the car all day." I turned him around and showed him where the bathroom was. He set his bag on the sink, leaving the door open, and proceeded to crank viciously on his neck until it popped. I winced in pain just watching him.

"One of these days you're gonna do that and your head's going to pop off and go spinning across the room. You look thinner," I remarked after he'd taken off his jacket. Of course, his arms were still nearly as big around as my thighs.

"Yeah, I've lost a few pounds," he said. After draining the rest of the beer from the can he pulled his shirt over his head and dropped it on the floor. A Browning Hi-Power in an inside-the-pants holster was tucked behind his right hip. I didn't even bat an eye when I saw it, even though I knew he didn't have a Michigan concealed weapons permit. The hammer on it was cocked.

"Wow," I said, looking at his back. "What the hell happened to you?" Most of the skin to the left of his spine, from the curve of his neck all the way down to just above his hipbone, was red and angry and puckered. There were dimples and divots in his skin too, about half a dozen small gouges scattered about his back.

"Bad luck," he said.

"Youch." I looked closer at the red flesh on his back. "What is that, a burn?" And a relatively fresh one, too from the looks of it. Second degree, maybe third. Not completely healed. Bob had a dark tan on his neck, face, and arms, a farmer's tan, but the rest of his torso was lily white. It made the scars and splotches on his skin seem even more ugly.

"Yeah." He bent over and began splashing water on his face.

"Care to tell me about the tattoo?" I asked him. Seeing

it was even more of a surprise than the scar. Bob had, on numerous occasions, loudly expressed his distaste for skin art. The tattoo covered his left shoulder and I looked close. In the center was the shield-like symbol of Special Forces, and above that was their motto, "De Opresso Liber", which I assumed meant something like "Free the Oppressed". Below the shield was some more Latin that I couldn't decipher -- "Si vis pacem, para bellum".

"'If you want peace, prepare for war'," Bob explained to me. "All the guys in my team got one."

"I thought you didn't care for tattoos."

"I don't. This was a special occasion." I thought about that for a second. Bob normally wasn't very nostalgic.

"Can I assume there was some alcohol involved in your decision making?"

"Large quantities."

I looked back at the scar. "What caught on fire? I mean, besides you."

"Kerosene."

"I bet that hurt."

"You have no fucking idea," he said slowly, wetting his hands and rubbing his armpits.

"What caused those pockmarks?" I asked, pointing. He looked up into the mirror to see where I was pointing.

"Shrapnel," he said. *Shrapnel?*

"Shrapnel from what?" I asked.

"A grenade."

"A grenade?" Now I was sounding like a parrot. "I didn't think grenades threw shrapnel pieces that big. At least, the grenades we had when I was in the service didn't."

"They don't. The wounds got infected because I couldn't get to a hospital for almost a week."

"A week? Where the hell were you?" He turned around

and gave me one of his looks. "Right. Top secret. If you told me you'd have to kill me."

After drying himself off with a towel, he unzipped his bag and pulled out a T-shirt. He looked at it, cocking his head, then shook the shirt a few times in an attempt to eliminate wrinkles. On the front of the shirt was emblazoned a slogan. I looked closer to read it.

WAR
The <u>Original</u> Team Sport

"You ever been across the Pacific?" he asked as he pulled the T-shirt over his head and stuck his hands through the armholes.

"Japan, once," I said. "Stopover. Did a little shopping."

"Shopping," he said, and snorted. I knew we had quite a few Special Forces advisors over in the Philippines, helping their military deal with the Marxist guerrillas that had been causing problems for decades, but Bob volunteered nothing else and I knew better to ask. But I knew it hadn't been an idle question. And if he was running around the jungle I wasn't surprised he'd lost a few pounds.

"I hope everything worked out all right."

"I'm here, ain't I?"

Wow, I thought. *Talk about essence of character.* That *statement was pure distilled Bob.*

He flexed his left hand, then massaged his ring finger. "Hairline fracture," he told me. "Probably should still have it in a splint, but it's almost healed."

"That explains the leave," I said, nodding. "Let you get healed up. I'm betting you're going to be real busy here the next year or so." It was no secret, we were heading into Iraq, sooner rather than later.

He looked at me a little dubiously. "I've *been* busy."

We headed back out to the kitchen where Kelly was busy chopping some sort of vegetable. Oscar was watching her intently in case something fell to the floor. The dog didn't even like vegetables, but she had her principles.

"You want another beer?"

"Sure. You trying to get me drunk, take advantage of me in a weakened condition?" he asked with a grin. I pulled a can of beer off the shelf in the refrigerator door and handed it to him. He cracked the top and took a sip.

"Sheeeeit," I said. "Since when did you ever need alcohol?"

"If you're that easy, Bob," my wife told him, "finish that beer and we can head upstairs right now." When she winked his eyes widened and he jerked his arm involuntarily. He shook his head at himself as he tried to cough and hack the beer out of his nose. I snorted and grabbed a Diet Coke out of the refrigerator while he wiped at the beer running down his chin.

"She's serious, too," I told him, enjoying his discomfiture. "If she didn't have the good sense to be married to me she'd be all over you like a cheap suit." Bob coughed once more and shook his head at the two of us.

"There'd be no future in it for us because of you being so young and in the Army," my wife said, trying to appear serious but cracking a smile despite her attempts. "But at least I could use you for sex." She caught Bob with his head tilted back, in the middle of a gulp of beer, and as he choked and snorted foam sprayed all over his beard and shirt. Kelly laughed and laughed and handed him a kitchen towel to dry himself off with. Oscar licked the droplets of beer off the floor.

"Well damn," he said laughing, a mischievous smile on his face, "I guess it's a good thing I'm engaged then, huh?"

"Oh Bob, that's so wonderful!" Kelly exclaimed, and hugged him. He turned bright red and a huge bashful grin crept across his face. "What's her name? Where'd you two meet?" My wife began peppering him with questions, while I could only stand there, blinking, mouth open and a stupid look on my face. Bob, getting *married*? He couldn't have shocked me more if he'd said he was quitting Special Forces to work for the Democrat National Committee.

"When the hell did this happen?" I sputtered, finally coming out of my shock enough to speak. Bob's neck and cheeks were crimson, and he kept looking down at his shoes. He reminded me of an eight-year-old boy caught by his friends kissing a girl.

"We got engaged last month," he told us, unable to keep the gigantic smile off his lips. "I met her last February. Her name's Cathy. Catherine."

"Hey now," I said cautioningly, "that's pretty fast. She know what you do for a living?"

"Yes she knows what I do," Bob said, giving me a disdaining look. "Like I wouldn't tell her?"

"What does she have to say about your being gone for weeks or months at a time to places you can't tell her about?" I couldn't make Bob's decisions for him, much as I'd like to, but I sure as hell was going to make sure he looked at marriage from every angle. He was my friend, and old for his years, but he was still only twenty-two and therefore full of hormones and the idiocy of youth. When he got married, I wanted it to last. I'd seen too many people get married that shouldn't have, and although I trusted Bob's judgment completely in matters of life and death, love was something else entirely.

"She doesn't necessarily like it," Bob answered, "but she knows it's part of the job. Her father's a career Army man, so she's lived it, and she's got no illusions about the life."

"It must be love," I said.

"When's the big day?" Kelly asked. "Do you have a picture of her?"

"June 20th?" Bob said uncertainly. "Somewhere around there." He dug out his wallet and removed a small photograph which he handed to my wife.

"She's very cute," Kelly said admiringly, then passed the picture to me. The girl was in a bikini on a beach somewhere. She was gorgeous, and blond, and had all the right curves in all the right places. I handed the photo back to Bob.

"I still can't believe you're getting married," I said. "Of all the guys, I figured you'd be the last to get hitched. Well, except for Ron." Ron hadn't quite realized that women were good for things other than sex, so his relationships tended to be rather short-lived. "I figured Jerry would be first, he and Jodi've been going out for three years."

Bob smiled. "Yeah, I'm gonna catch a bunch of shit about it, too."

"Well, do you love her?" Kelly asked him.

"More than I would've thought possible," he said. "She's so smart, and funny, and she doesn't take shit from anybody, not even me." As he reeled off her innumerable good points I watched his face and could see he was a goner. The boy was in love, big time. I could only hope she treated him right. "And she's gorgeous," he finished up, staring off into the distance, the beer in his hand forgotten.

"Well, as long as you love her, and she loves you, that's all you need," Kelly told him. "Anything else, any other problems, you can work out, if you're willing to stay together and stick it out. She does love you, doesn't she?" she asked with a small smile.

"Yeah. Hell if I know why, but she's crazy about me."

"How does her father feel about you?" I asked.

"I don't know," Bob said. "I haven't met him yet. She lives down in North Carolina with her mom," he explained. "Her parents got divorced about ten years ago. Her father's in D.C., he's some sort of desk jockey, pushing papers. She doesn't talk much about him, I think it's because she's afraid I'll try kissing his ass, or start treating her differently. He's got to be at least a lieutenant colonel at his age if he's in Washington. Her mom likes me, though. Hell, I think her mom'd want to marry me herself if Cathy wasn't around."

"When are we going to get to meet her?" Kelly asked. She finished assembling the lasagna and flipped a piece of meat toward Oscar, who snatched it out of the air. "Good catch." After sticking the dish in the oven she set the timer, then turned and surveyed with dismay the huge mess she had made.

"Cathy's coming into town the day after tomorrow. She'll meet my parents and all that stuff. Then, the day after that, her father's flying in and I'll finally get to meet him. My parents are planning a big evening out. I don't know, none of us have met the guy, I hope it goes okay."

"Doesn't she get along with her dad?" I asked.

"I'm not sure. I think it's just that they're not very close. The first couple times I asked about him she got all weird on me, so I don't know what the deal is. I guess I'll find out when I meet him."

"Don't worry about it," I told him. "Even if he doesn't like you at first. A father's first reaction to someone dating his daughter usually isn't pleasant. And marriage is a hell of a lot more permanent than a date." Bob shrugged, resigned to the outcome, whatever it was.

"Listen," I asked him quietly, turning slightly away from Kelly. "I've got a question for you." As Kelly began stacking the dirty bowls and measuring spoons in the sink I led Bob a few steps away from her. He picked up on my serious tone and put on his blank work face. It was almost scary how quick he could wipe all emotion from his expression.

"I don't care what you know, or can prove, I want you to tell me what you *believe*," I told him. His eyes followed me as he stood there silently. "I'm asking you because I know you'll give me a no-bullshit answer." It was true. He was barely old enough to buy beer, and yet I trusted his judgment more than anyone else I'd ever met. "And I'm not asking out of idle curiosity, either." He took another swallow of beer, nodded, and waited expectantly.

"This have something to do with the cops at Ron's?" he asked. I waved the question away with my hand and asked what I had to ask.

"Who does George Kelly work for?" I asked him.

"That's easy," he said. "He's a spook."

At that my tense body relaxed and I let out a big sigh.

"I don't know exactly what he does, but it's something in the intelligence field. CIA, NSA, or someone else in the alphabet soup, I don't know."

I nodded my head a couple times. "That's what I wanted to hear," I said out loud to myself. Even though Ron was a good friend, and usually solid as a rock, his story was so off the wall that it was good to have a second concurring opinion.

"You gonna tell me what the fuck's going on?" Bob said, sounding a little annoyed.

"Jerry and Steve are on their way over here," I told him.

"I'll fill you all in at dinner. I have no desire to have to tell this thing more than once."

"What about Ron?"

"Ron's otherwise engaged," I told him. Just then the doorbell sounded and Oscar sprang to her feet and charged from the room, barking.

"Speak of the devils," Bob said as we headed toward the front door. Oscar was standing in the living room looking out the bay window, barking ferociously and wagging her tail.

"That's a hell of a burglar alarm," Bob remarked.

"Best kind you can buy," I said. "Works even when the power goes out, shuts off by voice command, and you can't forget to turn it on when you leave the house."

"Would she bite an intruder?" he asked as I looked out the spyhole in the door. Jerry and Steve were on the porch making faces at the dog.

"Hell if I know," I told him as I pulled open the door. "Gentlemen," I greeted them.

"You're only saying that 'cause Ron's not here," Jerry said with a grin. He stepped around me and stopped so short Steve bumped into him.

"Jesus, dude," Jerry said, staring at Bob's face. His eyes ran down and then back up. "You look like a Viking with that beard. You should have a double-bladed axe in your hands, beard like that."

"Don't go all homo on me," Bob told him, deadpan.

Jerry laughed out loud and threw a bear hug around Bob. "Hey ugly, how the fuck you doin'?" he said with a smile. As Jerry let Bob loose Steve patted him on the back heartily.

"Welcome home, hippie," Steve said. Bob had four inches of blonde hair atop his head, which was three inches more than I'd ever seen before. Between that and the beard he was almost unrecognizable. Steve eyed his friend. "Why's it red? You're blonde. You dyeing it?"

Bob shook his head. "Yeah, the red was a surprise to me too. I guess it comes from my mom's side of the family. Howya doin', boneheads."

Both Jerry and Steve were a bit taller than Bob, but with his muscle he outweighed them both. Steve stood just under six feet, with a medium build and brown hair cut short over a wide, plain face. His hair didn't look good short, but then it didn't really look good any length.

The dog danced around them, wagging her tail and nudging them with her nose in hopes of garnering some attention. Jerry took off his coat and hung it and Steve's in my front hall closet, then turned to me.

"You mentioned something about getting me a pop?" Jerry said, eyebrows raised.

"I mentioned something about kicking your ass, too," I told him. I stuck a thumb toward the kitchen and off he went through the doorway, smiling.

"Watch it, watch it, SHE'S GONNA BLOW!" I heard him start shouting. Oscar ran into the room to see what was going on.

"You're treading on thin ice, you little shit," I heard Kelly scold him.

"Jesus John, she's huge!" Bob said to me, his voice low and eyes wide.

"She's also getting big hormonal mood swings," I told him and Steve. "Between that and what happened today she's pretty upset, so try not to irritate her, okay?"

"What the hell *did* happen today?" Jerry asked, standing in the doorway with a can of Diet Coke in his hand.

I craned my neck and looked into the kitchen. "I

suppose we've got time before dinner. Honey, I'm gonna be talking to the guys out here," I called to her. She was banging around again out of sight beneath the counter. "You going to need help getting up from back there?" Her eyes appeared above the countertop.

"I can hold onto the counter to get myself back up," she said. "I'm not completely disabled you know, I'm just pregnant. I'm gonna make a salad, go ahead and talk to them." I waved the guys into the living room where they sprawled on the furniture.

"Ron kill somebody again or what?" Jerry asked. Anyone ignorant of our shared history might have thought he was joking, especially since he was grinning when he said it.

"I don't think that's it," Bob told him slowly, looking at me.

"It ain't," I said, and told them everything that I'd seen and heard, from the time Ron called me to our good-byes in his kitchen. With all of their shouting and questions it took me over twenty-five minutes to tell my tale. When I finished they sat still for a few seconds, digesting the information.

2:56 p.m.

"You know, somebody Mr. Kelly works with is involved," Jerry said. "Has to be."

"If that's true," Bob said thoughtfully, "that whoever responsible for all this was after a disk, then it's a good assumption that they didn't get it. If they'd got it, they wouldn't have needed to kidnap him."

"That's a whole hell of a lot of assumptions there," Steve said, "with absolutely no evidence to back any of them up."

"The kidnapping could be totally unrelated to the missing disks," I pointed out. "If they are missing. Right now we don't have enough information to even start coming up with theories. Right now we're still assuming he was kidnapped, nobody knows for sure. Unless there have been some developments in the last few hours."

"Either way, we need to start talking to the people he worked with," Jerry said. "Somebody knows something."

"Whoawhoawhoa, back the fuck up," I told him. Kids, I swear to God. "*We* are not doing anything. *You* are going to sit on your asses and let the FBI do their job. This is out of my league, which means it's *waaaay* the fuck out of your league. This isn't a shitty little divorce or some workman's comp case. I don't have the background or the resources to even try to work on this, and you know it. And if I did try to stick my nose in it, it wouldn't help."

"But the FBI—" Jerry began.

"Listen," I cut him off. "I've told you guys before, and I'm gonna tell you again right now, that the first person the cops suspect in a crime like this is the family. Until George shows up they're always going to be looking at Ron like a suspect, and if you or even I come around and start making a nuisance of ourselves it's not going to help him."

"We can't just sit around," Steve complained.

"Okay, so don't," I told him. "Ron's all torqued up, and the longer this thing goes on the more weirded out he's going to get. You guys need to go over there and try to keep his mind off of it, if you can. Keep him occupied. Try to imagine how *you'd* feel if it was your father missing and the cops kept treating you like a suspect. Go over there, help him keep his mind off his father, make sure he doesn't do anything stupid. With him all cranked up, somebody over there is going to say something that'll set him off and I want at least one of you over there when it happens, jump on him and stop him from doing anything dumb." They all nodded—Ron's temper had proven itself many times. "And don't carry any guns over there when you go," I pleaded with them. That was one more bad habit they'd developed after Jerry's troubles. I carried a gun everywhere too, but **I** had a permit. "The feds will lock you up. Any plans you had to go into law enforcement will end. Scott Copley is going to feed me whatever info he gets, so we'll be in the loop. I hate the fact that there's nothing I can do just as much as you guys do, but those are just the facts of life."

"We can carry at Ron's house, it's private property," Jerry said in protest.

"Not the point," Bob told him out of the corner of his mouth.

"So we sit and wait," Steve said, frowning.

"Yeah. We wait and see what the FBI turns up, especially from George's workplace. In short order they'll have interviewed everybody he worked with, and once we find out what they had to say, I think we'll have a good idea where the investigation will be going." They did not look pleased at all, but I believed I'd convinced them to do things my way, at least for the moment. We all noticed about the same time how Steve was shaking his head violently, an ugly look on his face.

"What?" Jerry asked him.

Steve looked up at him, then at the rest of us. "'What?' What do you mean, *what?* You're kidding me, right? This isn't freaking you out?"

"What are you so worried about?" Jerry asked him, his forehead creased in confusion.

"Am I the only person in this room who remembers what happened two years ago?" Steve demanded, his voice going up an octave. I glanced at the kitchen doorway, wondering if Kelly could hear. "The last time one of us went missing we got into, what, three fucking gunfights and a car chase? And Ron caught four bullets! We all sat in jail for how long?"

"I was wearing a vest," Ron felt obliged to point out.

"Not on your leg," Jerry reminded him.

"That's got nothing to do with this," Bob said.

Steve's mouth opened, but he didn't even know how to respond. His neck turned red as he fought for the words.

"I understand what you're trying to say, but don't use what happened then as a guide," I told Steve. "You don't have a normal frame of reference. You're expecting lightning to strike the same spot twice. That doesn't happen."

Steve gave me a dirty look. "Unless you're a lightning rod," he told me pointedly. "And aren't we having this conversation because lightning did strike twice? Somebody's missing. Again. Bullet holes. Blood. I mean, fucking come *on*."

"Well, what the hell, aren't you getting a degree in Criminal Justice?" Jerry asked him.

"Yeah, so?"

"Didn't you expect to see any more shit in your life? Isn't that why you want to get into law enforcement? If you were interested in money, you'd be getting an MBA. Or a law degree. What's got your panties in a bunch?"

Both Jerry and Steve were getting degrees in Criminal Justice, and were leaning toward federal law enforcement when they graduated. Although, after Nine-Eleven, they were both considering joining the military as well. I'd talked to them at length about that, as I'm sure their parents had, and they'd decided to put off any decision on military service until they'd completed their bachelor's degrees.

Steve jabbed a finger at him. "Fuck you. Don't you dare tell me you think Ron's dad is just going to walk through the door, that this was all just a big misunderstanding." They glanced at each other, and it was obvious none of them believed George's disappearance was innocent. Steve jabbed his finger at Bob. "You think you could get Mr. Kelly out of that house with only one broken lamp to show for it, he didn't want to go?"

Bob didn't answer the question. "How is Ron holding up?" he asked me, trying to diffuse the tension in the room.

I scratched my ear and shook my head. "So far so good. Not a lot to know, yet, so right now it's the not knowing that's the worst. His mom's there, kicking ass and taking names, so at least he's not alone with all the badges."

"I hope she doesn't piss off the feebies too much," Steve said.

"She's domineering and overbearing, but she's not stupid," Bob told him. "She'll just keep those boys jumping, get 'em working harder."

"You know," I said to them, "I've got a bone to pick with you guys. I've known you assholes for two years, saved your life," I pointed at Jerry, "and until now thought I was one of your friends."

"You are," Jerry said. "What's the problem?"

"What's the problem? Two years, and nobody tells me George Kelly works for the CIA, NSA, DIA, whoever? What is this shit?" Bob looked surprised, and Steve seemed upset that I was angry with them.

Jerry looked confused. "You never asked," he said defensively

"I never asked?" I nearly shouted. "I sure as hell did! And you know what you told me? 'Don't ask.' You didn't think it might be good for me to know this little tidbit of information? Hmmmm?"

"It wasn't our place to tell you," Bob said. "Besides, even Ron doesn't know for sure, and it's not exactly something that comes up in everyday conversation."

Jerry got a funny look on his face. "DIA?" he said to me. "The Detroit Institute of Arts?"

"Defense Intelligence Agency," I snapped. Kids these days, Christ. "You sure you didn't pay someone to take your SATs for you?"

Kelly came into the room and leaned an arm on my chair. When I looked up at her I could tell she was tired, but she didn't seem upset. She liked to cook, and was good at it, for which I was eternally grateful to her mother. She also didn't mention the raised voices.

"Okay, so which of you strong young men wants to help set the table?" she asked the room. "Dinner's going to be ready in about ten minutes. Set the table and we can sit down and start on the salad."

The boys and I climbed out of our chairs and headed into the dining room without further prodding. Whatever else I could say about them, they'd all been raised right. Steve came with me and I pointed out the cupboard containing the glasses. As I distributed the napkins around the table Kelly sank carefully onto the living room couch. She heaved a big sigh, then blew at a lock of stray hair hanging over her forehead.

"So what's up with you?" Jerry asked Bob. He laid silverware next to the dishes Bob was setting on the table, the two of them working the table counterclockwise. "Why the hell are you carrying that Browning Half-Power?"

"I carry what I carry in the field," Bob told him. "I like the .45 better, but if I take a pistol with me I want to be able to reload from any local ammo dumps. And the only other country in the world where I've got a halfway decent chance of finding .45's is Argentina. Nine millimeter is worldwide, and the Beretta is too big for my hand."

"You going to take us for a spin in your truck or what?" Jerry asked Bob just as the timer on the oven went off. I stepped over and gave Kelly a hoist up and followed her into the kitchen. A large bowl of salad was sitting on the counter, waiting to be served.

"Can I eat dinner first?"

"So, anything new with you?" Steve asked Bob.

"I'm getting married in June," Bob replied. As I walked into the dining room with the salad I saw Jerry and Steve both staring at Bob.

"Yeah, right," Jerry said a little uncertainly.

"He is," I told them, enjoying the looks that news got. I set the salad on the table just as Kelly came into the room carrying the lasagna. Her hands were encased in oven mitts to protect them from the glass dish's heat.

I caught Steve's eye and jerked my head. We talked in the living room away from everybody else. "Are you doing okay?" I asked him.

He seemed nonplussed. "You think I'm crazy for thinking this is crazy?" he said to me, his eyebrows high and together.

I made a face. "No, but..."

His frown got deeper. "Kidnappings and missing persons and gunfights are not normal," he said defensively. He threw a glance toward the dining room. "Even if you're a Green Beret. And I'm not the only one of us who had nightmares after the last time."

"No, I know," I assured him. "I just worry. I'm supposed

to be the adult here." We'd all had PTSD to one degree or another. One triple-digit-speed car chase, a brief kidnapping, and indeed three gunfights as Steve had said would be enough to give anybody but the most combat hardened veterans pause. None of us had talked to psychologists—in my experience shrinks are crazy people who get into the business to figure out why they're so messed up—but I'd had my wife to talk to, and they'd had each other. We'd all had a shared experience and, on more than one occasion, stayed up very late at night drinking and talking about everything that had happened, and what could have happened. Thinking about the 'what ifs' was worse.

"*Dinnahh* is *saaaahved*," my wife called out in a horrible British accent. "Drinks are self service, 'cause I'm sitting down, my feet are killing me. So's my back."

Steve and I traded a look, then headed into the dining room. He started back in on Bob. "You're getting married?" he asked incredulously, once we were all in chairs. "You're messing with us, right?" Oscar wandered into the dining room and sat in the corner. She got as close to the table as she could without being in the way, but made sure to never look at any of us directly so we couldn't accuse her of begging. Dog logic.

"I bought her a ring and everything," Bob said. "I be officially engaged."

"Is that why you've been so squirrelly on the phone?" Jerry took the salad from Steve and filled his bowl.

"Have I?" Bob asked.

"Yeah. We were wondering what was up. I figured you'd had a mission that went poorly."

Bob blinked, and his face went dead for a second. Just a second, and then he covered it up, but they'd seen it.

"He's got a hell of a scar on his back," I told them around a mouthful of salad, pretending not to notice the moment. I could see the lasagna bubbling in its dish as it sat on the table. The whole room filled with its delicious aroma.

"You lose anybody on your team?" Steve asked quietly.

Bob's gaze became distant, and the golf ball-sized muscles on the corners of his jawbone popped out. "Sometimes bad things happen to good people," he said finally.

"Aw, shit. That sucks." Suddenly the lasagna I'd just dished out onto my plate didn't seem so appetizing.

"That's the biz, sweetheart," Bob said tonelessly, sounding like he didn't believe his own words. He stared at his own plate with something less than enthusiasm.

"So what's this girl like?" Jerry asked, trying to lighten up the mood in the room. "You got any naked pictures?"

"You wish. I'm still waiting to see those Polaroids of Jodi you've been promising to show me for two years."

"Jerry, you didn't!" my wife exclaimed. "What a horrible thing to even think about doing." Jerry looked like he wanted to climb under the table while staring daggers at Bob. Bob just smiled pleasantly and began serving himself some lasagna.

"Did Jodi get the baby shower invitation yet?" my wife asked Jerry.

"I don't know."

"I saw Carla Kelly's sitting on their kitchen counter," I told her around a mouthful of food.

"How long have you been dating?" Steve said.

"Since February," Bob responded.

"That's pretty quick to already be engaged," I said. "And haven't you been deployed for a lot of that? How much time have you even spent together?"

"Enough," Bob said flatly.

"What I want to know is when are you getting married?" Kelly asked Jerry.

"Not until after I graduate," Jerry told her around a mouthful of lasagna. "One thing at a time. College, career, marriage, and then, someday, probably, kids."

I nodded. "Best way to do it," I told him. "Play it smart, no need to rush into anything." I said it while staring at Bob. My wife frowned at me, but I pretended not to notice.

"All we gotta do now is get Steve laid and we'll be all set," Bob remarked with a smirk.

"Oh, up yours," Steve shot back. "You and Jerry and Ron, all you do is think with your zippers. Just because I don't go cruising the bars at State with Ron, pick up God knows what diseases, doesn't make me a eunuch."

"Well, we know he's not gay," Jerry said. He looked to Bob. "You remember sophomore year Spring Break down in Daytona? When I walked into that room—"

"Don't you even say it," Steve warned, flicking his eyes quickly at my wife. "I swear to God I'll climb over this table and stick this fucking fork in your neck, you better just shut your mouth while you're ahead." He held the fork up and shook it while Bob and Jerry laughed and snickered.

"I haven't heard this story," I commented.

"And you're never going to," Steve told me, "so forget it." He glared at Jerry, who ignored him.

After that the conversation died off as we shoveled lasagna into our hungry mouths. My wife and I are both healthy eaters, but the three of them made us look like we were fasting. Nobody spoke for ten minutes, except to compliment my wife on the meal.

As we ate, I looked around the table at the three of

them and my wife. An unexpected wave of emotion hit me, and I struggled to identify it. The only sensation I'd ever felt that was anything like it I'd experienced as a little kid coming home to Mom and Dad after several weeks at camp. A huge warmth in my heart and sense of comfort and relief because I knew that finally I was home. Among people who loved me. I was no kid, and my parents had been dead for a few years, but sitting at the table looking at those guys I felt the same feelings tugging at my heart. After everything we'd been through together, they were my family now. I felt very possessive of them, fatherly almost, because I'd seen them through some tough times. I cringed at the same time, because I knew how prone to trouble they were. They just loved to put themselves in harm's way, and there wasn't anything I could do to stop them. I shuddered.

God, if this pride and worry so fierce it made me ache was what awaited me when my child was born, I wasn't sure my heart could take it.

Kelly saw me gazing around the table, with God only knows what kind of expression on my face, and she gave me a radiant smile. I was able to send a quick lopsided grin her way before my breath caught in my throat and I had to look down at my plate.

3:47 p.m.

Jerry was the first to finish, sighing and setting his fork on his plate with a clank. "That was good," he groaned, holding his stomach. "I ate too much."

"I was wondering if you guys had lost the power of speech or something," my wife teased them.

"That's a hell of a lasagna," Bob said, diligently working on his third helping.

"Thank you."

"Now back to this marriage thing," Jerry said to Bob, who heaved a sigh without looking up from his plate. "You got engaged and everything, right?"

"Last month."

"That whole thing is a big rip-off if you ask me. Something invented by women to get a free present out of guys. You did buy her a ring, didn't you?"

"Cathy, her name's Cathy. Yeah, of course I got her an engagement ring, what do you think?"

"Exactly," Jerry said, throwing his hands up, his point made. "The women always get the engagement ring, and what do we get? Zip, zilch, nada."

"I got an engagement present," Bob said defensively.

"Yeah? What, a shirt? A nice dress belt?" Jerry said derisively. Steve snickered. Bob gave them a dirty look and held up a finger, signaling them to wait, then left the table.

"You want to spar with him while he's here, but then you keep pissing him off," Steve said, shaking his head. Bob returned carrying something in his hand which he held out for Jerry to take.

"You'll appreciate this better'n anyone," he said. It was a large fixed-blade knife with a black handle in a brown leather sheath. It was obvious the knife was new, I could smell the leather sheath where I was sitting, and a hint of some sort of oil.

Jerry popped the snap holding the knife in place and slid the blade from the leather. He looked at one side of the blade, then the other. "Randall!" he exclaimed, surprised. He set the sheath down and inspected the knife with renewed interest, touching the blade with his fingers. The steel was covered with a thin film of oil.

"This is the one you wanted," Jerry marveled. "The

custom handled Model 1." He moved the knife around, performing a few slashes and thrusts above the table.

"Yep."

"She got you this?"

"You got it."

"How?"

"She asked me what I wanted for an engagement present. I said hell if I know. Then she asked if there was anything that I wanted, period. So I said I'd wanted that knife for a while. I knew she couldn't get it for me. I was wrong."

"This is the custom handle you wanted, though, isn't it?" Jerry said. "Black linen micarta, single finger groove, hole through the pommel for a thong." Bob nodded.

Steve slid his chair away from Jerry as the blade weaved through the air beside his head. "Van Gogh I'm not," he scolded.

"There's still a three-year wait on orders, though, isn't there?" Jerry asked. "And this handle is a special order, it's not a regular item."

"As far as I know," Bob replied.

"So how the hell'd she get it?"

"Beats me," he said with a smile.

Jerry shook his head admiringly. "Man, this is nice," he cooed. "I gotta approve of this marriage. Any girl that'd buy you this is all right in my book."

"She'll be so glad to hear that," Bob said sarcastically.

"That's a custom knife?" I asked. Jerry grudgingly held it out to me, handle first, and I took it. The knife had a good heft to it, and the handle fit my palm nicely.

"It's a Randall Model 1," Bob told me. "Often imitated, never equaled. The guy that started the company began hand-making knives right about the start of World War

Two. The Model 1 was the first thing he came out with, and the GI's couldn't get enough of 'em."

"Seems real nice," I said, sliding it into the sheath and handing it back to Bob. "But I'm afraid it's sort of wasted on me, I don't know much about knives." He took the knife in its sheath and set it beside his plate while he eyed the remains of his third piece of lasagna. Deciding it was too much for even him to handle, he set his fork down with a sigh. All three of them were more or less motionless now, stunned by the force of their appetites.

"Food coma," Steve mumbled, eyes glazed.

"Isn't this the point where the gentlemen retire into the parlor to smoke cigars and sip cognac?" Jerry asked.

"Who can move?" Bob asked.

"Have you ever tasted cognac?" I asked Jerry. "That's why they needed the cigars, to get the taste of the cognac out of their mouth."

"So when do you think we're hitting Iraq?" Steve asked Bob.

Bob looked down at his plate, his lips pursed. I think he was trying to decide how much of what he knew was suitable for public consumption. Even though we were his friends, he took his job—and his Top Secret clearance—seriously.

"Don't you mean *if*?" my wife said.

"Oh please." Jerry laughed. "We don't hit 'em we'll have absolutely no credibility with the rest of the world. Maybe if Clinton was still President…"

Bob massaged his fractured finger, right where his wedding ring would sit. He squinted at Steve. "I can't tell you anything you don't already know," he said apologetically. "Best I can say is between the end of Ramadan and February, unless diplomacy rears its ugly head again." He paused, and looked at his finger again. "Soon enough," he said quietly.

After a few more minutes, I decided I should make the first move and got up. Kelly was still sitting beside me, sipping her water and looking tired. "Grab your plates," I told them. "Nobody gets dessert until these dishes are done."

"Dessert?" Steve asked with a pained expression on his face.

Once the kitchen was cleaned up we headed out to the family room to talk. We hadn't spent nearly enough time together lately, and with Bob in town I didn't want to pass up the opportunity. Kelly sat next to me on the couch, mostly just listening as they harassed each other as only old friends could. Oscar wedged herself between Bob and Jerry on the loveseat and they both patted her affectionately. Ron should have been there, and everyone noticed his absence—he had what could be referred to as an abundance of personality—but we did our best to keep the mood upbeat. Whatever had happened to his father, they were confident that it would all work out fine in the end. I wished I was still that young.

7:03 p.m.

Finally talked out, the boys scattered to find their coats. Kelly joined me at the bottom of the stairs as the guys congregated near the door. She'd put on some sweatpants and hugely thick socks, sure sign she was tired and ready to hit the sack. To keep them from sliding down her belly she had to pull the sweatpants up so far they were in her armpits.

"You'll let us know as soon as you hear anything," Jerry as much as told me.

"You hang around Ron and keep him distracted, like I told you," I said. "If I learn anything worth passing on that he doesn't already know, he will, soon enough."

"Do you think we should head over there tonight?" Steve asked me. I looked at my watch.

"After a day with the FBI I'm sure he would love to see a few friendly faces," I said, "but it's a little late. Better save it for tomorrow morning. Call first, though. And don't be surprised if the feds aren't ecstatic to see you, even if you do get Ron out of their hair. You're just another distraction to them. Remember to stay on your best behavior. And keep him on his."

"Okay, Pa," Jerry told me with a grin.

"See you later, guys," Kelly said with a big smile on her face, and gave a small wave. They piled out my door, and I locked it behind them. I watched through the window as they climbed into their vehicles and drove off. Oscar stood at the window beside me, wagging her tail and whining as she watched them leave.

"You shouldn't have made such a big dinner," I told her. "They'd eat Spam and used coffee filters."

"I know," she told me. "I wanted to."

She was tired after spending so much time on her feet, and we ended up on opposite ends of the couch, reading. Twenty minutes later I threw the paperback across the room accompanied by a choice piece of profanity and a sigh. Oscar lifted her head, looked at the book, then cocked her head at me.

"What now?" my wife asked, not even looking up from her novel.

"I'm done," I told her. I'd tried toughing it out but after four books about a Chicago PI with an unpronounceable last name I couldn't take any more. "Four books," I told my wife. "Four books and she's never eaten a bite of food, all she does is drink whiskey. She's ruder to her friends than I am the people I hate. And she almost never carries a gun and yet somehow anytime she needs a gun is when she magically happens to be carrying it." As a private investigator I felt I had a duty to read novels about them, but I had yet to find a series that accurately represented the job even a little bit. Still, I kept trying.

"You get so worked up about the dumbest things," my wife told me, frowning. She levered herself up off the couch. "I'm exhausted, I'm going to bed."

"Hey, you want some coffee? I feel like coffee."

She groaned, shook her head, and began trudging upstairs.

"You know I can't have any caffeine when I'm pregnant. It's not enough that I already have to pee every thirty seconds, you want to get him doing backflips and karate in there."

Hoping for some sort of edible treat, Oscar stayed on my heels as I headed into the kitchen, then sat and stared at me adoringly as I pulled out a cup. I was scooping heaping tablespoons of coffee into the filter when the phone rang. Past dark we rarely got calls, especially on Sunday, so I glanced at the Caller ID readout before grabbing the receiver.

"You're ugly but you smell bad," I said cordially.

There was a second-long pause, then Scott Copley spoke. "I hate that damn Caller ID," he bitched. "I'm gonna get a block on my phone just so you can't do that to me."

I smiled. "What's up?"

"You remember Jack Russell Terrier?" he asked me. It took me a second before I realized he wasn't referring to a dog but a guy he'd gone through the police academy with.

"Yeah. He still with DPD?" Jack, a middle-class white guy from the suburbs, had wanted to be a cop in Detroit for reasons known only to him. Working in Detroit was exciting, but the DPD contract had a residency requirement. All cops—and fireman for that matter—had to live in the city. That's where I, and a lot of potential applicants, drew the line. There were nice areas of Detroit in which to live, but none of them was more than a quarter mile from a war zone, and I refused to live anywhere I had to put bars on my doors and windows. As a PI I'd turned down residency cases that called for me to spy on Detroit cops and firefighters to prove they'd actually moved out of the city. Most of the time it was so they could get their kids into better school districts. One famous case that hit the Free Press was eight firefighters sharing one address in the city...which turned out to be a one-bedroom apartment.

"Yep. Jack's a Sergeant now," Scott told me. "He's one of the people I put a call in to after you called me today. Him and Steve DeKerk in Bloomfield, Wally in Southfield. Also Doc Rogers with the Macomb County M.E.'s office."

"Doc Rogers is still around, huh?"

"Yeah. He says he hasn't found an assistant yet he'd trust to do an autopsy on *him*, so he's not ready to retire. Anyway, I just got off the phone with Jack, he said they pulled a guy out of the Detroit River not two hours ago, been shot in the throat." My ears perked up, but only a little. Detroit had been reporting a homicide a day for the past several years, so one more body wasn't that big a deal.

"White guy, in a suit," Scott went on. "He hadn't been

in the water too long, either. Fluke he was found, I guess he got tangled in some lines or something."

"Oh really?" I set down the coffee filter. "Any ID on the guy? Or a description?"

"No ID on the stiff, I guess, when they checked his pockets. I asked what he looked like, though, to see if it could be George Kelly." My body tensed as he paused briefly. "It wasn't. Jack said this guy maybe weighed two hundred pounds, max, no way that could be Kelly." I let out the breath I hadn't realized I'd been holding in. "The floater's at the Wayne County Morgue, now."

I checked my watch. "Are you driving or am I?" I asked.

"Hours are from eight to four, Monday through Friday," he told me. "After four, nobody can get in, not even Detroit Homicide. Besides, it's not Kelly."

"So is Jack meeting us there or what?"

"Aren't you being a little presumptuous? Who says I'm going anywhere? I'm nice and relaxed in my recliner, got a good movie on the DVD, why the hell would I want to go down to Detroit at night just to look at a floater?"

"Because you live for the job," I told him. "It's why you don't have a wife or any friends, except me."

"Jack called one of his buddies who's an investigator for the M.E.'s office. He'll be expecting us. He wondered what the big hurry was. So do I." I didn't respond, and after a couple seconds I heard Scott sigh. "I might as well drive. It'd be out of the way for you to come up here just to drive back down."

"Sounds good."

"I'll be there in ten or so," he told me, then we hung up. After putting the coffee and filter away I headed upstairs with the dog and found Kelly in the bathroom, washing her face.

"That was Scott," I told her. "Detroit fished a guy out of the river a little while ago with a bullet hole in his throat."

"It's not George, is it?" she asked worriedly, still bent over with water dripping from her nose into the sink.

"No, but it's a white guy in a suit," I explained. "There's a chance that he's the guy we're assuming George shot." I'd briefed her on what little details we knew. She definitely wasn't happy to hear that there'd been gunfire at the house.

"But you don't know."

"Life is a mystery," I said expansively, spreading my arms.

"Don't make me hurt you," my wife told me, grabbing her toothbrush and pointing it at me like a knife.

"No, we don't know," I admitted. "But a small chance is more than no chance at all. I guess the guy didn't have any ID on him. His wallet's probably at the bottom of the river, next to Hoffa. Scott's coming by to pick me up and we're gonna go down there, have a look at this guy."

"If he doesn't have any ID, what's the use of going?" she asked plaintively, not too pleased at being left alone on a Sunday night.

"Never know til you get there." She dried her face on a towel and gave me a look that left me in no confusion as to her feelings about me heading to Detroit with Scott. Then she put some toothpaste on her toothbrush and started scrubbing her teeth. Oscar heard the sound and pushed past my legs into the bathroom. Kelly sat down on the toilet seat lid and let Oscar lick some of the minty toothpaste froth off her lips.

"I don't know who's worse, you or the dog," I told her, shaking my head.

"E wikes how eh ace," Kelly told me, mouth full of brush and foam.

"So what if she likes how it tastes, you're going to give her worms or something." My wife pulled the brush out of her mouth and leaned over to spit in the sink. She looked up at me and smiled, her lips covered in white, while Oscar tried to get at her face with a wildly flailing tongue.

"Mad dog, grrrr," she said with a twinkle in her eye.

"I'm getting out of here. You two nutballs can entertain each other," I told her as she pursed her lips, pushing them out for the dog to lick. Downstairs on the kitchen counter near the phone was where I usually stuck my holstered gun and spare mags when I came home, so that's where I headed. I never went out of the house anymore without a gun, and I sure as hell wasn't going into Detroit at night without one.

I was carrying the new custom 1911 that I'd shot at the match, together with two spare magazines. If I ever needed more than 25 rounds of premium .45 caliber hollowpoints to stop a fight, I was either doing something wrong or should have started the fight with a rifle in my hands.

7:52 p.m.

"I can't believe I'm spending a perfectly good Sunday evening going to Detroit to look at a dead body," was how Scott greeted me after I shut the car door.

"Stop with all the negative waves, Moriarty," I admonished him. He looked sideways at me as he drove.

I told Scott about my meeting, if that's what you wanted to call it, with the boys earlier that day. I caught him shaking his head in the glare of passing streetlights.

"What?"

He made a face I couldn't read. "Grinnand's back in town?"

"Yeah, on leave."

"And he says he's a Green Beret now?"

I turned in the seat and regarded him. "Just what is that supposed to mean?"

He shifted uneasily in his seat, because he knew how close I was to the boys. "It's just—" he began. He took a breath. "Well, I've been doing a lot of reading about Afghanistan. Special Forces are doing all the heavy lifting over there. Is Grinnand the same age as the rest of them?"

"Who, his friends? Yeah. In fact, Bob, Jerry, and Ron all have birthdays within a couple weeks of each other. Why?"

"They're what, twenty, twenty-one?"

"Twenty-two. What are you getting at?"

"Navy will let anyone apply to SEAL school. Youngest SEAL I've heard of was nineteen. The average Green Beret, U.S. Army Special Forces, on the other hand, has been in the Army for something like eight or ten years. A lot of them go in as Sergeants. After they're selected, the actual training course itself, including language school and all that, takes one and a half or two years. How the fuck could Grinnand be a Green Beret already? He's got less than four years in."

I had to laugh. "You think he's lying?"

Scott relaxed a little when I didn't blow my top, but all he could do was shrug. "I know back during Vietnam when they were short on bodies they were taking recruits straight into the training course, but they don't do that anymore. I admit, Grinnand doesn't seem the type to make something like that up, but…."

I leaned back in my seat, smiling. After a while the smile faded. "You know by the time Bob graduated from high school with a near perfect grade point he had two black belts and was fluent in Spanish?"

"I didn't know about the Spanish, but it doesn't surprise me." Scott kept staring out the windshield. "And I'm not saying it's not impressive. But you know as well as I do that as far as the military's concerned none of that means shit."

I nodded. "You're right," I said. "In the grand scheme of things, the Army only cares about what you've done since you've been in. But I'm hearing that things changed after Nine-Eleven. At least for a few months there the people who pull triggers had carte blanche to do whatever they thought they had to to get the job done. If you've been reading about Afghanistan then you know that about two hundred Green Berets won that war in two months, something the entire Soviet Union couldn't do, period. War is changing, now every action's going to be lousy with spec-ops guys. The SF guys know it, but not many other people do. My guess is they decided they wanted him, and nobody could think of a good reason to say no. So not long after he made it through Ranger school he was invited to attend the Special Forces qualification course. I think they call it the Q Course." A wry smile creased my face. "And, honestly, I doubt he's been through all the training, once he passed the Q Course I'm guessing they threw him on a plane for a faraway land. That's something you'll have to ask him. He's made Sergeant now."

"In four years? That's pretty fucking quick. That's way too quick, unless they're handing out battlefield promotions like they did in World War II."

I shrugged. "I get the skepticism. But I think you're forgetting one important detail."

"What?"

"When Kelly and I went to Disney?"

Scott smacked himself on the forehead. "You went and stopped at Bragg on your way back. To visit him."

"Yeah."

"He wearing a green beanie around the base?"

"The day we showed up, he had some sort of function. Met us at the gate in full dress, beret and everything. Sergeant stripes on his sleeve. And they don't have him stuck in training, he showed up at my house with a barely-healed burn across half his back, shrapnel wounds, and a broken finger, and he can't say how or where or how it happened."

"Forget I said anything," Scott said, and shook his head for a while. Finally he added with sudden force, staring out the windshield, "Glad he's out there, killing those motherfuckers. I hope he gets every single fucking one of them. I knew someone who was in the North Tower."

"You and me both, buddy."

He glanced at me. "Where were you on Nine-Eleven?"

"Serving a Summons in Troy at some law firm. The secretary was staring at a TV on her desk, hands over her mouth, lawyers in two rows behind her, all of them on phones. By the time I got home both towers and the Pentagon had been hit." I eyed him. "Whether you were working or not I know they had to've called you in."

He nodded. "Nobody knew what the fuck was going on, who was responsible, whether or not we'd see parachutes in the sky like Red Dawn. I don't think I slept for a week." He shook his head, and we both stared out the windshield for a while at the passing scenery, remembering.

Scott had acquired a reckless disdain for posted speed limits at about the same time he'd gotten his badge, which meant we were in the heart of the Motor City in less than twenty minutes.

"Shit!" I exclaimed as the tower of the Fisher Building came into view. "I was going to bring my Polaroid to take a picture of the stiff's face for Ron, but I forgot it at home. Damn it. Good thing my head's on tight, I'd lose that in a day."

"This is my work car. I've got one in the trunk we can use," Scott said.

We zipped up the Lafayette Street exit, and Scott hooked a quick right onto Macomb. The Detroit Police Department's headquarters on Beaubien was two blocks up, with the Sheriff's Department, County Jail, and the Murphy Hall of Justice all within spitting distance. During the week all the streets within a two-block radius were choked with cops and visitor cars, like Manhattan during rush hour.

"Oh, man," Scott exclaimed, looking at me. "Talk about your head not being screwed on tight. I don't even know where the morgue is. I haven't been down here in a while."

"It's right up there," I said, pointing.

"That's where it used to be," he told me. "They built a new building last year, I forgot all about it until we got down here."

"So pull over here and I'll ask," I told him. The female deputy manning the desk in the lobby of the Wayne County jail was a bit curious why I was looking for the morgue on a Sunday night, but since I looked halfway respectable she gave me directions.

"It's on Brush Street," I told Scott as I climbed back into the car.

"Brush and what?"

"Warren, she thought." Scott threw a U-turn and headed back toward I-75, grumbling.

"She *thinks*? Great. While we're at it, why don't we just

take of tour of Greater Detroit? Hit all the hot spots. We could stop at the Malice Green memorial, say a few words, then cruise through the Cass Corridor, get our knobs polished by a transtesticle for ten bucks each. Drive by that house on St. Aubin where all those people got whacked." Two Detroit Police officers had been convicted of beating Malice Green to death with their flashlights, and the Cass Corridor was Detroit's version of Cabrini Green. Who says Detroit is a cultural wasteland?

After five minutes of weaving through the one-way streets, with no signs indicating where the morgue might be, I convinced Scott to stop at the front entrance to Detroit Receiving Hospital.

"It's probably in the basement of one of these buildings," I told him reassuringly. He just looked at me, a sour expression on his face. I was back out in less than a minute.

"Okay, so the deputy was wrong. But I got good directions this time."

"Grrrr."

The morgue was a modern but plain building constructed of four-by-four light brown bricks and huge square windows. In front of it was a cheap-looking white sign with green lettering: **Wayne County Medical Examiner**. Scott pulled into the small lot in front and we climbed out of the car. He grabbed the Polaroid out of the trunk and we headed up the walk.

"You're getting mellow in your old age," I told him. "In the car forty-five minutes and I don't think you were up on two wheels once."

"Hey, you're the one with the fast car now."

"Yeah, but I've never been so pissy and irritable that I outran a State Police cruiser just because I was late for an appointment. You know your badge'll get you out of a speeding ticket ninety-nine times out of a hundred, even with the staties."

Near the round vestibule outside the main door was either a piece of modern sculpture or a circular stairway that hadn't been finished yet. There were lights on inside, but the glass was tinted so I couldn't see too far. Scott tried the door and then banged on the glass.

"Oh, screw that ramp rooster," Scott spat out in response. "If he'd been a halfway decent driver he wouldn't have lost me and I'dve stopped." Even though the trooper had never gotten close enough to see Scott's license plate, somehow the story had gotten out. There were a few people around Scott's department who suspected that was why he had been picked for a Lieutenant's slot over more senior officers. The Sheriff's hatred of the State Police was legendary.

As we peered through the glass someone walked into view and opened the door. "Copley?" the man asked, looking from me to Scott. He was an older black man, thin and tired looking, wearing a white shirt and black tie loosened at the neck.

"That's me," Scott said. The man held out his hand and Scott shook it, then we stepped inside.

"I'm Bill," he told us, and I shook his hand. The lobby of the Medical Examiner's office was done in pale wood that looked sanded and unfinished. The walls were covered in it, and weird circular…couches—for lack of a better word—used the same wood slatting for their backs. It felt like a nature center. I was half expecting to hear our tour guide start on a lecture about the spotted owl.

"C'mon back," he told us. We headed through another similarly decorated room, where people who'd just identified a loved one could grieve away from prying eyes. It seemed as cold inside the building as it had been outside, but I figured that was just my brain doing some preliminary shudders at the thought of having to look at a dead body.

"Jack said you liked this guy we pulled out of the river for some RAs up north?"

"I don't know, we're probably just here on a wild goose chase," Scott told him. "But we got a tip that sounded good, so here we are."

"Thought you fellas weren't going to show," Bill said to us.

"I forgot you moved to a new location," Scott told him. "Got bad directions, took us a while to find you."

"Damn building's not even a year old yet and it's falling down around us," he said. "This week it's the furnace that's gone out. Most of the time the whole building's as cold as the cooler." We strolled through a couple more rooms and then down a hallway. Bill opened a door and we entered a small room with counters on both sides full of medical paraphernalia. Below the counters were cabinets with locks. I saw plastic bottles and a "sharps" container, and a sink where the handles on the faucet were huge so the doctors could operate them with their elbows. A poster with the unofficial motto of the DPD's Homicide Squad was on one of the cupboard doors: **Our Day Begins When Yours Ends**. The far wall of the room was mostly just one big metal door that Bill pushed open. He flipped a switch and the room exploded with light as cold air rolled over my legs.

"Aw, I was expecting some of those small metal doors where the drawers that hold the body slide out," I told him.

"Everybody says that. Only place I've seen those is TV, same as you. Here we go for quantity, not quality." The room was filled with utilitarian metal shelves which held half a dozen corpses, some of which were still in body bags.

Each shelf looked like it slid out for easy loading. The sheer number of shelves was frightening.

"That one's yours," Bill said, pointing. "The lucky stiff." A black body bag rested on a wheeled table in the corner. "He looks like a lawyer. In a suit and everything. Some banger probably carjacked his sorry white ass near the RenCen and when the stiff complained, POW!"

"Never can tell," Scott observed.

No way, I thought. *No way would a gang kid take the trouble to dump a body in the river. Middle of the street works just as well for corpse disposal in this town.*

"Ain't that the truth," Bill was saying. "I wish he'd had ID. Gonna make my job a pain in the ass. There was this one guy—" he was interrupted by a persistent buzzing noise and looked down to his belt where his beeper hung. "Shit. You know what that means." He looked up at us. "The population of the city just dropped by one. And I was hoping to get some sleep tonight. My partner's already out on one on the East Side, some teenage crackhead dropped her baby on its head and killed it."

Scott shook his head. "I don't know how you guys do it. Day after day, like an assembly line."

"Hey," Bill said with a small smile, "sometimes I go a whole week without a body dropping." He stuck the beeper back on his belt. "Most of the time it doesn't bother me, but some days... Excuse me a second, I gotta go make this call." He headed into the small room outside the cooler where I could hear him using the phone.

Scott and I moseyed over to the body on the cart and looked down at the smooth black bag. Only a zipper and an identifying tag in a slot marred its surface.

"Shall I?" Scott asked me, pointing at the body bag's zipper.

"Knock yourself out," I told him. He pulled the zipper at the top of the bag down toward the corpse's feet with a loud "Brrrrippp". When the human Ziploc was halfway open Scott grabbed the sides of the bag and pulled them apart.

"Well if he was a lawyer, you can't blame a guy for wanting to shoot him," Scott observed as we looked down at the body.

Every time I saw a corpse I got the same creepy feeling. A corpse looked like a person, but didn't. There was the hair, the clothes, and the sheer physical presence, but everything seemed fake. Like an ultra-realistic mannequin. I think it was the stillness. The unnatural, disconcerting stillness. My brain told me that this object in front of me was a person. They should be moving, walking, talking. Blinking. Instead there was nothing. Even asleep, a living being moved. It breathed, or twitched, or scratched. Corpses didn't. It wasn't just creepy, it was scary. My pulse always raced, looking at a dead person, waiting for the surprise. Outwardly my face was expressionless.

This John Doe had the flat, pale face I was expecting, although he was a little paler than I expected for such a fresh corpse. The small, rough-edged hole in his Adam's apple just above the knot of his tie seemed fairly innocuous, but accounted for his unnatural whiteness -- a good portion of his blood had gone fishin' and probably been replaced with Detroit River water. That alone would've killed him.

Bill came back into the room, pulling on a winter coat. "I gotta hit it," he told us. "I'm not supposed to leave you guys here alone, but then again I wasn't supposed to let you in in the first place."

"We appreciate it," I said. He dug a card out of his wallet and handed it to Scott.

"Don't figure you're gonna steal any bodies. When you're done just head out the way you came in, the door'll lock behind you. God knows how long I'll be gone."

"Thanks a lot for going out of your way for us," Scott told him.

"Well, Jack says you're cool, and I was on duty 'til midnight anyway. It ain't any trouble. That your man?" Scott turned and looked at the stiff.

"Hard to tell," I said. "Everybody looks so different when they're dead."

"Yeah. Weird, ain't it? And listen, if a black lady shows up when you're still here, claims to work for us, don't let her in. Last time I saw her she had blonde dreads, but who knows what she's done with herself since then. Used to be a receptionist here but got fired 'cause somebody caught her sneaking in at night and getting' freaky with the bodies. I think she's out of the nuthouse again, that's why I'm warning you."

"Probably get elected to Detroit City Council next," I said. "Talk about screwing a corpse."

"Clinton?" Scott said dubiously. "Bill Clinton?" He was looking down at the business card Bill had handed him.

"Yeah. How's that for dumb luck?" With a wave and a smile he was gone. Scott stuck the card in a pocket and we returned to the stiff. It was always hard to tell with dead people, but this guy appeared about my age. He was still damp, and his light brown hair was swirled around messily. Scott took a picture of his face, the flash reflecting off the man's one open eye.

"What do you think?" Scott asked me. He handed me the developing picture and we waited to see if it had turned out properly. "You ever seen him before?"

"No." I took a pen out of my pocket and pushed the

corpse's head to the side. No exit wound. "Whatever he was shot with, the bullet's probably lodged in his vertebra. Or maybe it angled up and bounced around inside his skull. No way to tell if it's a .380 without cutting him open." The entry wound in his throat was rather small, but no matter what the TV cop shows tell you there's no way to determine caliber of the weapon used by looking at the entrance wound. Flesh is elastic and acts in unpredictable ways.

"I can show the picture to Ron, see if he or his mother knows the guy. The feds'll hear about him within a day and do the same, but I promised him I'd keep on top of things. That's about all I can do, I guess."

"That's it?" He gave me a look.

"Why, what else can I do? Am I forgetting something?"

"When you were with DEA, what'd you do when you picked up a prisoner somewhere for transport?"

I frowned, unsure of what he was trying to get at. "I'd search him, switch my handcuffs for theirs, sign for him and his property, and then toss him into my car. Then I informed the guy what would happen to him in the way of hideous injuries if he gave me any trouble."

"What if the guys you were picking him up from told you that they'd already searched him?"

"So what? You know as well as I do that there's no such thing as the Easter Bunny, Santa Claus, or someone that's already been searched. Both of us have seen too many weapons pulled off people that supposedly were clean."

"We sure have."

"And?" I pestered him.

"You gonna take the word of Mr. Bill Clinton or Jack Russell Terrier of the DPD that this guy has already been searched properly?"

"Jesus," I said, "I'm getting rusty." I took hold of the

zipper and pulled it down the rest of the way. The dead man was wearing a navy blue suit over a white button down shirt and tie.

"Nice tie," I said. "You think anyone'd notice if I stole it?" That got no response, so I asked him another, more relevant, question. "You see any rubber gloves around here? Although I doubt this guy's got much more that a quart of blood left in him."

"I think I saw a box of them in the room outside," Scott replied, heading toward the door Bill had pulled most of the way shut. Twenty seconds later he returned with a wad of latex gloves in his hand. We both pulled on a pair and began picking through the stiff's pockets from either side of the table.

I got a push-button ball point pen from his right inside jacket pocket, as well as a small wet piece of white paper from his right front pants pocket. If anything had been written on the paper it was unreadable now.

"Nothing. Shit," Scott said, letting the corpse's soaked jacket fall back to the table.

"Hey, did you see this?" I asked him. I pulled the body bag open a little further and grabbed a corner of the black wool topcoat bunched under the dead man's waist.

"Well, he sure went out dressed like a million bucks," Scott said as we wrestled the body for possession of the coat. Scott disentangled the coat's sleeve from the corpse's left arm and we spread it out on top of him. The thick wool was soaked with water, and the coat felt like it weighed forty pounds.

I dug through the side pocket, then opened the coat up and stuck my fingers in the inside pocket. Nothing. Scott finished checking the other pockets and then looked up at me. We scowled dispiritedly at each other for a few seconds, then Scott lifted up his side of the coat to check underneath and make sure he hadn't skipped a pocket.

"Hey hey, what's that?" I exclaimed, grabbing at the coat. Farther down from the inside left pocket I'd spied what looked like an opening. I explored it with my fingers and discovered it was a pocket, about a foot from the bottom. The pocket would be about thigh level when wearing the coat. I stuck my fingers into it and rummaged around, Scott watching me expectantly. With a flourish and a smile I pulled out a wallet.

The wallet was brown leather and dripped water as I held it up. I set it down on the wool and pried it open as Scott came around to my side of the table.

"All right, let's see how badly the water fucked things up," Scott said. I opened the long compartment and pulled out everything inside. Eighty-four bucks in cash, plus a Lotto ticket for Wednesday night's drawing.

Scott removed the clear plastic credit card holder and began thumbing through it.

"Ops," he announced, and tossed a driver's license onto the coat. Officially they were "Operator", not "Driver" licenses, but only cops seemed to care about the distinction. I picked it up. Frank Hohimer, birthdate May 30, 1962. A resident of Troy, Michigan. I looked at the back of the license and saw Mr. Hohimer had opted not to donate any organs or tissues in the event of his death. Little Timmy isn't going to get a liver after all.

"This ID look kosher to you?" I asked Scott.

"It's been a while since I worked the road, but yeah, it looks good. Whether or not the address is real I couldn't tell you." He continued digging through what he had while I wrote down the information on the license.

"I got a Visa and an Amoco card in the same name," he

told me as I went through the remaining papers in the wallet. There were some scraps of white paper, all of which were unreadable from the water. Also present were half a dozen business cards, none of which were in his name. One was in a woman's name, so I doubted he'd been using them to scam people.

"He's a AAA member," Scott informed me. "Everything I've got is in the same name and looks real, if that means anything. We get back out to my car I can use the radio, call dispatch if the Ops is real." He handed me an ID card/badge with a magnetic stripe on the back. I turned it over and saw Frank's name printed right below the logo for Consolidated Systems, Inc., George Kelly's employer.

"Isn't that...?"

"It sure is," I told him.

"Damn I wish I was on this case," Scott complained. "This is like *Bullitt* or something."

"It seems to me you are on this case," I shot back, waving a hand around the morgue. We began stuffing everything back into Frank's wallet, including his driver's license.

"How about this?" Scott held up the CSI ID card.

After a pause I said, "Better put it back. We have to leave the feds something to do." I stuck the wallet back into the coat, this time in an outside pocket where it'd be easily found. We wadded up the coat and stuck it next to the body, then I zipped the bag back up.

Scott closed the cooler door behind us with a loud clank while I peeled off my latex gloves. I looked around and Scott pointed to the trash can where we both deposited our gloves. The box of fresh gloves was on the counter under some cupboards and I went over to it and grabbed a handful and stuck them in my pocket. When I turned around Scott was looking at me.

"What?" I said innocently. He sighed and shook his head.

"I thought you were going to let the feds handle this one," he bitched. He shook the camera at me. "I know you, I know exactly what's going on in that so-called mind of yours."

"I am going to let them handle it," I said defensively. "I'm just thinking of Ron, that's all. What I can do to help him."

"And I suppose you're not thinking of driving by the dead guy's house in Troy, either." He started walking toward the building's front, and I followed.

"You're the one with the car keys," I told him. "If you want to take me straight home, that's fine. I don't mind. So what if his place is on the way? Drive by, just see what it looks like, if it's a real address, see if there's any car in the driveway. Nah. Kelly will be glad to see me home so soon." He looked at me sideways as we entered the lobby. I opened the door outside for him as I kept talking. "I mean, Ron only asked me to keep him informed. The feds, they'll get around to the guy's house tomorrow afternoon, evening. Probably not any later than day after tomorrow, that's for sure. What difference could a day or two make? In a kidnapping. I mean, what are the chances of someone breaking into this guy's house and stealing a clue to George's disappearance between now and then?"

"A ***clue?***" he said incredulously. He unlocked the car.

"Yeah, that's detective lingo," I told him as I sat down. "I heard it on *Law & Order*. I mean, what are the chances of this guy having anything at his house, right? Probably the same chance as of George working for the CIA, or there being a conspiracy among his coworkers to kidnap and/or murder him for some as yet unknown reason. Ludicrous. Never happen. Besides, there's no way they'd think to go back to his place and wipe it of anything incriminating, would they? They know he wouldn't have anything there. That'd be as dumb as taking your wallet with you on a covert op. I mean, that stuff only happens in movies, right?"

"All right, ALL RIGHT, shut up! Jeez, you talk more than anybody I ever met. You're using a sledgehammer to drive in a tack. I'll drive by the place, okay? Just be quiet." Scott looked disgusted with himself for being so weak.

We hopped back on I-75 northbound and headed up to the Big Beaver Road exit. Once we were off the freeway Scott pulled into an office parking lot.

"There's a street map guide in my briefcase in the back seat," he told me. I dug it out and went to the index in the back and looked up Hohimer's street. We were there in just a few minutes.

Both sides of the street were lined with newer two-story townhouse condos with vertical tan wood siding, four residences to a building. The condos had dark red trim and were rather attractive. Driveways led around either end of each building to covered parking spots in the rear. A six-foot brick wall bordered the rear so the homeowners on the next street didn't have to look out their back windows and see a parking lot. The brick wall, at least to me, didn't seem much of an improvement.

"2402, Sergeant Friday," I told him. The address was a couple hundred yards down on the left and Scott pulled in front of it, left wheel to curb.

"Do you think this guy's buddies just dumped him in the river when he died?" Scott asked me. "Seems sort of harsh."

"Seems like a hell of a cold-blooded thing to do," I agreed. "Especially if whoever did it worked with him. Doesn't seem to be any reason for it, either. If they'd taken the trouble of digging the bullet out of his neck, they could have left the body on first base in Tiger Stadium and there wouldn't be any way to trace it back to the kidnapping."

"As far as you know."

"Yeah," I said disgustedly. "That's the problem. We don't have anything at all to go on, so any guesses I make might be totally off and we'd never know. Was George Kelly kidnapped? If he was, why? If he was grabbed, did those same people take all the computer disks out of his office? What was on the damn disks? Does or did he even work for the NSA, or CIA, or whoever? If the dead guy was involved in the kidnapping, why dump his body in the river, without any weights to hold him down or anything? If these guys are spooks," I told Scott, "you would assume they've had some sort of professional training. You would hope. There's a war on for Christ's sake."

"Jack said it was a fluke they found the guy. Some mooring lines on a freighter tied up downriver came loose and had to be redone. The ropes dropped into the drink, the freighter shifted, and when the dockworkers pulled on them, voila, up pops our guy." Unlike what the media portrayed as science on TV, dead bodies didn't float right after death unless a large amount of air got trapped in their lungs. And that wasn't at all common. It normally took several days of decomposition before the bacteria eating away at a body's tissues generated enough gases, as byproducts of digestion, to float the body to the surface. By that time the fish had usually eaten away most of the recognizable features. Nose, eyes, tongue; all the soft, tasty parts. Yecch.

"Let's head around back, see if there's a car in his slot." Of course there wasn't. We sat in the car at the rear of the building and stared at Hohimer's back door.

"I never understood the allure of condos," I said.

"What do you mean?"

"I mean they've got all the disadvantages of an apartment, and all the disadvantages of a house, and none of the advantages of either. You own it, but condos have shitty resale value. You don't have to pay rent down an unending black hole every month, but you have to pay outrageous 'condo maintenance' fees or whatever to the guys that cut the grass. I could make fifty G's a year just charging half of what these guys do to mow the lawn and trim the shrubs. Plus they're not freestanding, so you can hear your neighbors every time they flush the toilet." I shut up and looked around. "Parking back here, he probably went in the back door most of the time, huh?" I looked at Scott, who slowly turned his head to stare balefully at me. Before he could say anything I swung open the door and climbed out of the car.

No one was in sight as I casually walked up to Hohimer's back door. I could see a faint light inside, but it was so dim I took it for a night light of some sort. The exterior aluminum and Plexiglas storm door was unlocked and I swung it open, then knocked on the window of the wood door. While I waited to see if anybody was going to answer I checked out the deadbolt on the door. Child's play. One good kick and it'd go.

After two minutes with no one answering my knock I cupped my hands around my eyes and peered through the window. Even though it was rather dark I could see I was looking into the kitchen. A sink and cupboard were on the left, as well as a refrigerator. To the right were more cupboards and probably the stove, although I couldn't quite make it out. A doorway on the right led into a larger room where I could see a couch and what looked like part of a chair. I was about to pull away and head back to the car when I saw the green light on the right wall beside the doorway.

I blinked twice, thought a second, and looked at the green light a second time. It shone from the lower left-hand corner of a small rectangular box mounted on the wall. The box had squared bottom edges but the top of it was rounded. Scratching my head in thought I returned to the waiting car and got in.

"Well?"

"You got a Swiss Army knife in here, anything like that?" I asked him. "Something with scissors or clippers."

"What?"

"A Swiss Ar—"

"I heard you. Are you honestly thinking of breaking into that guy's condo right here and now? What the hell is wrong with you?"

"There's nothing wrong with me. I'm just—"

"John, I've known you since we were both fifteen years old, and I've seen you do a lot of stupid things, but this doesn't even make any sense. The feds are gonna be here tomorrow with a search warrant, wait to see what they dig up. If they get anything I'll hear about it in an hour or two, and pass it on to you." He was practically pleading with me. "I can't believe you're seriously considering this."

"I gotta do it, Scott," I told him. "I owe this kid my life. Between getting nailed in the back at Wendy's and that firefight in the mall parking lot he got shot four times. Shit, maybe it was five, I forget. The only reason he's not dead is he was wearing that vest I got for him from the feds. I never even got nicked. Now somebody's kidnapped his father, his fucking Dad for Christ's sake, and I'm the only person he knows to turn to for help. What the hell would you be doing if it was your dad?"

"The feds'll be here tomorrow. Day after at the latest." He watched me to see if his words were having any effect. "Besides, what makes you think you can even get away with it? Someone will hear you, or see you, and the Troy cops will show up and stick your ass in jail. And I'm sure as hell not hanging around to save your worthless butt." He waited for the logic center in my brain to kick in.

"Nail clippers, anything like that?"

Scott began to swear, and kept it up for a good thirty seconds. When he finally had exhausted his vocabulary he grabbed the steering wheel and shook it so hard the car rocked on its springs. Fingers white around the wheel, he spoke through clenched teeth.

"In the briefcase."

I dug around and found a Leatherman multi-tool. It was about twice the size of a Swiss army knife and sported a plethora of useful tools, including a good-sized pair of pliers, with a convenient set of wire cutters underneath.

"Excellent. Just what the doctor ordered." I slipped on a pair of latex gloves filched from the coroner's office before I pulled the tool from its leather case and used my shirt to wipe off any of Scott's prints still hanging around. In case I dropped it making a hasty exit.

"John, I've known you for almost twenty years. As a friend, I'm asking you: Do you really know what the hell you're doing?"

"No, why? You got any helpful hints?"

He closed his eyes and banged his head gently a few times on the steering wheel.

"Yeah," he said when he stopped. "Don't get caught. I'll

be around front. The cops'll have to come in off Golfview. If I see a cruiser turn the corner I'll pull around back and honk, then keep driving. You head out this door and over the back wall here and I'll pick you up on the next street over."

I got out of the car and walked back up to the back door of the condo, looking around to see if there was anybody around. No one. Scott put the car in gear and pulled away.

When I reached the condo I nonchalantly pulled open the storm door once again and looked around. No one in sight, no shapes moving around in the windows of the adjoining condos. Now was as good a time as any. Trying to remember what I'd learned in my three years of karate in college I pulled my right knee up to my chest and drove my heel against the door next to the deadbolt. With a loud crunching crack the wood jamb split and the door opened six inches. I shouldered the door open the rest of the way against the protests of the splintered wood still wrapped around the bolt. I drew my gun and quickly checked the ground floor, then hurriedly returned to the alarm control panel I'd observed through the window. The steady green light was now flashing red.

If it was a standard time delay I'd have ninety seconds to punch in the right code to deactivate the system before the alarm company got the signal that something was wrong. I pushed the back door closed as far as it would go while I checked out the alarm. I'd been right. The distinctive hump I'd thought I'd seen through the window was definitely there. That meant the alarm was a Home Guardian Model 121. Mr. Hohimer definitely hadn't done his homework when picking out his burglar alarm system. One of the benefits of professionally installing alarm systems was learning all the intricacies of their operation from the alarm manufacturers themselves. It also made me a prospective customer of the reformed B & E guys who made a living telling people how crappy their security systems really were. Not two months ago I'd watched a video where one of those guys broke into a house and disarmed a 121 in ten seconds.

I spun around and spotted what I was looking for on a back corner of the counter. The kitchen knives were in a block and I grabbed the biggest one, assuming it would have the thickest blade. I wedged the blade between the plastic alarm box and the wall and gave the knife a vicious yank. The screws holding the 121 to the drywall popped out neatly and I saw the two wires I was looking for trailing out of the back of the unit into the wall. The Leatherman Tool was in my jacket pocket and I dug it out and pried it open so I could use the wire cutters. I neatly snipped the exposed black wire in its center, then carefully used the teeth on the Leatherman's plier jaws to strip the plastic coating off both ends. When I had enough of the wire laid bare I put the tool down and twisted the wire back together. Then I lifted up the alarm unit and punched the 9 button six times. The flashing red light disappeared and the green one came back on, steady and clear.

I waited and watched the green light for about a minute, making sure it wasn't going to reset on me. When I had assured myself I'd done the job right I let the alarm box hang against the wall on its wires and listened at the back door. No raised voices, no sirens, no barking dogs. So I found the switch on the wall and flipped on the light.

Think about it. If you were coming home from work and saw a flashlight moving around inside your neighbor's house, and nobody else on the block had lost power, wouldn't you be a little suspicious? It wasn't like the homeowner was likely to come home and surprise me.

I turned on all the lights in the kitchen and living room, then closed the venetian blinds he had in the windows. Then I looked around the place. The walls were off white, and the furniture looked relatively new, but nothing unusual jumped out and grabbed my attention. If I'd been looking for something specific my job would have been a lot easier. At least I would've had an idea of where to look. But since I didn't know what the hell I was looking for, I couldn't eliminate any part of the condo.

The best way to search a house is room by room. After checking the upstairs for any other unwanted visitors, I went back into the kitchen with the idea of starting the search there. Then I saw the door that had been partially hidden behind the refrigerator. I drew my gun again and opened the door. Basement stairs, with wire racks filled with spices attached to the inside of the door. After I flipped on the light I headed down and checked the basement. Finally satisfied I was alone, I began to search.

One hour, to the minute, after I'd kicked in the back door I stepped back outside. I pulled the door shut behind me and strode away nonchalantly. The rubber gloves got peeled off and stuck in my pockets to be disposed of somewhere far far away. The night air chilled the sweat on my hands as I walked around to the front of the complex.

As I came up to the car I saw Scott bathed in the green glow of the dashboard clock, looking both nervous and bored. I smacked the window with my palm and almost gave him a heart attack.

"Well?" he asked as I climbed in. He wasted no time in getting the car in gear and started moving before I had the door all the way closed.

"It was a brilliantly conceived plan, flawlessly executed," I told him. "And the fact that I didn't find a damn thing should in no way detract from your feelings of a job well done."

"You've been listening to Rush Limbaugh again, haven't you?" He heaved a big sigh. "Home?"

"Unless you can think of someplace else I should break into tonight."

He just grumbled and shook his head.

FOUR

Monday

7:44 a.m.

My alarm clock began buzzing insistently at me far too early in the morning. How did I know it was too early? If it wasn't, I wouldn't have needed an alarm clock to wake up. Science.

I groaned and tried to burrow my head under the pillow to cut off the noise. Under the pillow the clock's annoying buzz became an almost pleasant hum, and I began to drift back to sleep. My body relaxed and I entered a beautiful dream about Acapulco, where the sunspeckled waves rolled up smooth, sandy beaches, and oiled topless women played volleyball for hours on end, hugging after every point. Everything was perfect until my wife began kicking me.

I jerked and floundered in bed, finally getting my head out from under the pillow.

"What are you kicking me for?" I complained sleepily. Kelly rolled over and fixed me with an evil glare.

"Your alarm's been going off for five minutes! If you don't want to get up at least shut the damn thing off."

"You're a horrible woman," I told her. I crawled out of bed and stepped over to my dresser where the clock was still happily buzzing. "Why did I ever marry you?"

"Because I was the first person who'd sleep with you that had an IQ above sixty," she shot back. I clicked off the alarm and went to climb back into bed. Oscar had moved from the foot of the mattress and now gazed lovingly at me, her head on my pillow as she sprawled across my entire side of the bed.

"You guys are killing me," I announced, and headed into the bathroom. After a minute getting my nerve up I did fifty pushups on the tile floor, then spent five minutes huffing and puffing like an old man until I recovered. By the time I'd taken a hot shower, shaved, and dressed, Kelly had disappeared downstairs. I found her in the kitchen in a robe, making coffee.

"Where's the dog?"

"You know exactly where the dog is," she said, scowling at me. "Outside, where else? She has to do her business every morning at the same time, but do you think you could let her out since you're already up? Noooooooo. You head into the shower and make your poor pregnant wife get up to let the dog out."

"That dog has got you wrapped around her little pinkie-toe," I told her. "She can wait an extra twenty minutes, it's not gonna kill her."

"So you're saying you'd rather torture your dog with physical discomfort than expend a tiny little bit of energy to let her out." Kelly handed me a cup of coffee with cream and sugar already added.

"Yep," I replied. I looked at my wife. Her hair was short enough that after a night tossing and turning it pretty much stood straight up. "Wow."

My wife set down her cup of coffee and headed toward the side door to let the dog in. "I may look scary, but that's nothing compared to how frightening my morning breath is, so you better be nice or I'll kiss you."

The roads were crowded with Monday morning rush-hour traffic, but I still managed to get to my office by nine a.m. After I hung up my coat and sat down behind my desk I spent an hour typing up letters to clients on my computer. While the letters were printing up I got a call from a prospective client and spent twenty minutes on the phone. I ended up scheduling an appointment with him to examine his store and new warehouse. His warehouse had been vandalized repeatedly while under construction, and he was worried that now that it was completed the vandalization would change to theft. A past client had recommended my services to him and I was more than happy to help out. For a fee, of course.

For another hour I puttered around the office, cleaning, organizing, and doing bookkeeping. Finally I couldn't stand it anymore. I threw on my coat, made sure the answering machine was turned on, and then headed out the door.

11:42 a.m.

Both Bob's Blazer and Jerry's Camaro were parked in Ron's driveway. I parked next to the Blazer in the gravel turnaround between the house and the barn. The truck towered over my car like a black wall. There was a bumper sticker on Jerry's Camaro that I hadn't noticed before—

Limbaugh/Nugent 2000

I trudged up the lawn to the front door, which opened as I stepped onto the porch.

"Can I help you?" The door opener was a white male in his thirties that I'd never seen before, wearing a nice burgundy sweater and gray slacks. He kept his body slightly angled as he faced me, with his right hip (and presumably his gun) farthest from me.

"You must be the FBI," I answered. I slowly pulled out my wallet and handed him my driver's license. "Friend of the family," I told him. "I'm more or less expected. Is Ron or his mother around?" The Special Agent raised his left hand and I suddenly noticed he had a radio in it.

"Two'll be clear," he said into the radio. "Special Agent Reilly. Mrs. Kelly's inside," he told me, handing my ID back. He waved me inside. "She said you'd be stopping by sometime today or tomorrow. Ron's in the barn with a couple of his friends." From his tone of voice it didn't sound like he approved of Ron having guests while his father's fate remained uncertain. Either that, or the guys had already done something to piss off the feds. Another guy in a suitcoat stepped out from his place of concealment down near the end of the hallway. He was waved off by the door opener and disappeared into the kitchen.

"Any word yet from the kidnappers? Ransom demands or anything?" I asked. He shook his head. "That's unusual, isn't it? I mean, he's been gone over twenty-four hours now."

He looked at me sideways. "Was it you one of the County people said used to be a fed?" he asked me.

"Yeah. I was in the DEA for six years."

"Why'd you quit?"

"I won close to four million dollars in the lottery."

"No shit?"

"Somebody has to win, better me than somebody else."

"I hear that."

I'd told him the truth, just not the whole truth. The extra money was nice. It wasn't enough to retire on, not after taxes, but it sure made life easier. I'd quit the DEA because I could afford to…and because my wife was growing increasingly worried about how dangerous my job was becoming. Ironically, I'd been in more danger, and more gunfights, since leaving the DEA.

I took a step to head into the house, but Reilly put up a hand to stop me. "How do you know the Kellys?" he asked me. He did his best to sound casual, but I could tell he was curious as hell about me. I might not've been a viable suspect in the FBI's eyes—yet—but anything unusual, like an ex-federal agent being close friends with the abductee's son, was bound to raise an eyebrow.

"Long story," I told him. "I'm a private investigator now. I met Ron and his father about two years ago on a case, and we still keep in contact. Ron called me yesterday when it happened. I'm the only person he knows with a background in law enforcement and he was hoping I could do something for him."

"What did you tell him?"

"I told him I didn't know my ass from a hole in the ground when it came to kidnappings. He's just looking for a friendly face in the crowd. This whole thing has freaked him out." When I said that, Reilly got a funny look on his face. He leaned close and lowered his voice.

"What am I missing here?" he asked me.

"What do you mean?"

"I mean something is going on and I'll be damned if I know what it is. You know the family, maybe you can tell me what the deal is."

"I'm not sure…I don't know what you're getting at," I told him. "You mean having to do with the kidnapping?"

"It's not the kidnapping," he said, shaking his head. "Well it is, but it isn't. This kidnapping is weird enough. Unknown person or persons kidnaps a white-collar nobody from a well-to-do neighborhood. Shots were fired but we're not sure by whom, and we definitely don't know why. Got blood, but no body. And we still haven't gotten a ransom demand. So we're assuming it's a kidnapping, operating as such, but we still don't know. But it's not just that." He looked back over my shoulder into the house to make sure no one had snuck up on us.

"I've dealt with eccentric families before," he told me, "and that's not what's bugging me. I mean, they're eccentric enough, don't get me wrong. Mrs. Kelly is ordering my people around like a seasoned drill sergeant—"

"That's just how she deals with stress," I tried to explain. He cut me off, jabbing a thumb over his shoulder.

"I've got her son and his friends out back behind the barn running through combat pistol drills. One of his buddies, Bob somebody, brought over a fucking sniper rifle! The only reason my guys didn't take him out when he pulled the rifle case out of his truck was because Ron was standing there talking to him like a long lost brother." *A sniper rifle? Jesus H. Christ on a popsicle stick, Bob, what were you thinking?* Mentally I slapped a palm to my forehead.

"Bob's a Green Beret," I explained, or tried to. Sometimes nobody could adequately explain Bob's actions, not even Bob. "A friend of Ron's from high school. He just started his leave yesterday, drove up from Fort Bragg." I knew they'd be checking Bob out after his breach of etiquette, but it'd be easy for them to verify he was nowhere near Michigan when it happened. "Recovering from some minor wounds, as a matter of fact."

"Afghanistan?" Reilly asked.

I shook my head. "He can't say, but it's no secret we've got Special Forces troops all over Afghanistan, so I don't think so. Most of Ron's friends are a little gung-ho, heading into law enforcement after college, but Bob's...exceptional," was all I could think to say. "Ron does a little competition shooting, they're probably just trying to get him to relax, get his mind off his father."

Reilly gave me a long, flinty stare. "I don't have enough people to run down all the weird shit I've come across in just the past twenty-four hours. Somebody's not telling me something. I don't know what it is, but I think you do, and if I find out you're withholding evidence I'll have your ass in jail, ex-DEA or not. Interfering in a federal investigation. You can tell young Mr. Kelly that, too. If anybody eats a shit sandwich on this one, it's not going to be me." He pointed the prep radio at my face. I held up my hands in surrender.

"Hey, I know what the score is, you don't have to tell me. I wish I knew what to tell you, but I really don't know what's got you all upset. Ron and Carla have been answering all your questions, haven't they? Complete cooperation? Ron told you about that box of computer disks he thought might be missing? How are you guys doing with that, anyway? You been talking to George's coworkers?"

"We've been talking to everybody," Reilly told me, for now dropping the hard-ass act. "I can't say anything more."

"Where's the press?" I glanced over my shoulder. I was expecting a street full of boom trucks.

"Nothing to look at," he said. "If they don't get video, it's not a story. America, the land of short attention spans."

He started walking down the hallway toward the kitchen and I followed in his wake. I couldn't know for sure, of course, but Reilly definitely wasn't acting like someone about to nab a bunch of kidnappers because they'd made a stupid mistake. If I had to guess, the feds hadn't developed anything substantial from the physical evidence the techs had found in the study, and were still hoping for that call from the kidnapper.

I found Ron's mother in the walk-in kitchen pantry, yelling and cursing and throwing things. Two FBI agents were sitting at the table in the small dining area off the kitchen, looking like they'd roused a rattlesnake and now weren't too sure what to do with it. A jumble of electronic equipment, and three phones, were on the table in front of them.

"Glad to see all the stress doesn't have you acting weird," I said to her back. Carla turned around, knee deep in boxes of cereal and oatmeal.

"Just what I need, another smartass," she said tiredly. "You gonna help me organize the dry goods or are you going to stand there and watch?"

"I'm gonna stand here and watch, but you just go right ahead with what you were doing." I leaned a shoulder against the door jamb. "Place is a mess, anyway. It could use a good cleaning."

I could almost feel the agents lean back as they braced for one of Carla Kelly's explosions. They weren't going to get one. I didn't take any of her flak, so she respected me. The agents obviously hadn't figured that out yet. I just let her brusque manner roll off me like raindrops. The feds apparently had strict orders to behave, so when she started bitching they stayed quiet, which only encouraged her. She had a hard time being herself around strangers at the best of times, and usually became defensive. With her husband missing and presumed kidnapped, and a house full of federal agents, Carla was on a rampage.

"What are you doing here?" she demanded of me.

"Just checking up on what's been happening."

"You want to know what's been happening? Dick, that's what. Not a fucking thing." She shook a Cheerios box, then tossed it over her shoulder. I ducked and it missed my head by an inch, bounced off the wall, and landed at my feet.

"I'd hate to see how you dust." Carla turned to me and darted her eyes over my shoulder. She was out of sight of the two agents sitting at her table, but they could see me. Reilly had disappeared. Carla raised her eyebrows questioningly. I looked at the two agents, then back at her.

"I'm gonna go talk to Ron," I told her. "See how he's holding up. This not knowing has got to be the toughest part. Maybe I can get him to relax, if only a little bit."

She looked down at the floor for a couple seconds. Then she took in a deep breath, staring at me with hurting eyes, and went back to silently tossing boxes around.

"You hang together, Carla," I said quietly, and squeezed her arm.

I backed out of the doorway and headed out the front door toward the barn. Steve's Mustang was parked next to my car and I could hear the engine ticking as it cooled down.

The ground floor of the barn contained a cement-floored two car garage, its wide door facing the house. The barn door was open partway and I could see Ron's dark blue Dodge Diplomat parked on the slab, gleaming and spotless. It had been a totaled Detroit PD scout car that he'd rebuilt from the ground up. It took him two years, but when he was done the car was in better condition than the day it had rolled off the assembly line, and was so fast it scared me. He'd tried explaining just exactly what he'd done to rebuild the engine, telling me about Holley carbs and over-boring and race cams, but he might as well have been speaking Greek for all I understood.

"Four hundred and fifty horse," he said.

"Now *that* I understand," I'd told him. "Jesus."

During the finale of our last…misadventure, I suppose, is an apt word, Ron's Diplomat caught more bullets than he did. I think seeing the holes in its body panels hurt him more than the bullet hole in his leg.

The rear of the barn contained four stables, with a large rolling door that opened out onto the fenced backyard. The Kellys owned two horses that Carla took to shows, but she boarded them in the winter so the stalls were empty. A large workshop area was in a corner on the far side away from the house.

In the center of the barn, separating the garage from the workshop area, were bare pine stairs that led up to the second floor. As I ducked under the garage door I heard loud rock 'n roll from upstairs, and voices.

When I stuck my head above floor level I saw Steve and Jerry sitting on a ratty couch, watching Bob and Ron circle each other. Bob and Ron were directly above the Diplomat, in an area cleared of furniture and other loose objects. They circled warily, knees bent, weight on the balls of their feet. There was a red spot under Ron's left eye, and they looked a little sweaty under their T-shirts, but neither of them seemed winded so I couldn't tell how long they'd been at it.

Bob moved easily, his hands up in front of his chest but relaxed, the fingers splayed. He slid sideways, letting Ron's movements guide his responses. Bob was focused entirely on

Ron, noting every shift in weight, every dart of Ron's eyes as they spun in a tight, focused orbit.

I finished climbing the stairs and headed for an empty chair while watching the action. Ron caught a glimpse of me out of the corner of his eye and made the mistake of looking at me for a second. Quicker than seemed possible, Bob's right hand darted out. There was a **CRACK!** like a bullwhip, and Ron's head jerked back from the openhanded slap to his cheek. Bob tagged him hard enough to bring tears to his eyes, and I could see the red imprint of Bob's fingers start to appear on Ron's flesh.

"Rook eye," Bob said to him in a horrible Japanese accent. He pointed at his own face. "Always rook eye!"

"Oooooh, baby, that had to hurt," Jerry said sympathetically.

"It ain't your fucking eye that's slapping me around," Ron growled, wincing.

After every war, the papers are filled with stories of incredible, almost impossible to imagine feats performed by the men who'd fought and usually died. Bakers from Pittsburgh, pig farmers from Georgia, high school dropouts, it didn't matter who they were. These stories—of men dragging their buddies out of the line of fire even though they themselves had already been hit dozens of times, soldiers whose positions had been overrun killing five, ten, fifteen enemy soldiers with their bare hands or the butt of a broken rifle—are always explained the same way. Ordinary men in placed into extraordinary circumstances. Most of these incidents never even make the news, or at least not until years later. Only the people who were there knew.

With Bob, I always felt I was in the presence of someone special. Something special. Like Michael Jordan or Tiger Woods, Bob had not just a physical gift, but more importantly he had determination and a sense of purpose so intense it was frightening. Bob had wanted to become a warrior, and so he had. If he'd wanted to play for the NFL, even at five foot ten, I believe he'd have made it in. The only thing I could imagine stopping Bob was Bob. Bob was an extraordinary person, in ordinary circumstances. Well, that wasn't quite true—he did whatever he could to make sure his life wasn't ordinary, and was usually successful. And that was before the Twin Towers had come down.

The slap had obviously pissed Ron off, but whether he was angry at himself or Bob I couldn't tell. He feinted at Bob with a foot and then lunged at him, charging in with a series of blindingly fast punches. Bob lazily floated to the side, reached out with his hands, and Ron went spinning away into his friends on the couch. I don't think he ever touched Bob.

Steve and Jerry disentangled themselves from Ron and pushed him back towards Bob.

"You've got him on the run!" Jerry broke into laughter.

Now really mad, Ron lowered his head like a bull about to charge and moved in. Bob gave him a big, beatific smile and beckoned him closer.

"Hey Bob, your shoe's untied," I called out. He shot a middle finger in my direction but refused to take his eyes off Ron, who began circling him like a shark smelling blood.

Ron lifted his left knee as if to kick, then feinted with his left hand. Bob smacked at Ron's hand, apparently taking the bait, and moved in. Ron yanked back his left hand even before his arm was fully extended and sent out his right. There was the meaty sound of an impact, a brief grapple, the blur of airborne extremities, and then Ron was on his back on the floor, looking stunned.

"Ow," he said, in what looked like an understatement.

"I knew I should have put carpet up here." He looked up at Bob, who was tentatively touching his nose. "You gonna help me up, ugly, or do you have to check your makeup in the mirror first?" Bob removed his hand and held it out to Ron. As soon as his fingers left his nostrils, Bob's nose began to bleed.

"Hey, I actually nailed you?" Ron asked, delighted, as he was yanked upright. "That's the first time I've connected in years."

"Lucky shot," Steve called out.

"I walked right into it," Bob grumbled. "Overconfident." He grabbed a rag off the floor behind the couch and walked over to a corner of the room where he began exploring his nostrils with a finger.

As a fight scene, it hadn't been that impressive to watch. No flying, spinning kicks to the head, no backflips, no bellowed *ki-yais*. Nothing that Jean-Claude Van Damme would have wanted in one of his movies. But, in the real world, half the time unarmed combat ends up a wrestling match on the ground, where eye gouging and throat crushing reign supreme. But that isn't pretty, so people get warped ideas from Hollywood about what is and isn't fair in a fight.

The only time I'd ever killed someone barehanded I'd bounced his head off a wall, hit him with an elbow, tripped him, and then while he was down kicked him so hard in the face that his skull cracked when it rebounded off the floor. Pretty? Not at all. But it worked. Forget what looks good. Forget what's *fair*. The first rule of combat is there are no rules. Not when second place means a body bag.

Ron dropped into the seat next to me and looked over.

"When you came up the stairs I thought you were that FBI guy back for more abuse."

After a brief pause, I asked, "What do you mean?"

"Oh, we were shooting earlier and one of the agents came out and asked us to stop," Jerry told me.

"So you apologized profusely and immediately ceased and desisted."

Ron gave me a dirty look. "Hey, fuck that guy. He tried telling us the kidnappers might be scared off because of the shooting, which is a bunch of horseshit. He was the one we were making nervous."

I took a deep breath, counted to five, and tried to find my Happy Place. "You don't believe what he said has any merit at all?" I asked.

"Anybody that gets up the nerve to kidnap my father isn't going to get scared off by a little target practice. Besides, we shoot here pretty regularly. If the bad guys did any preliminary surveillance at all they'd know about the shooting and it wouldn't worry 'em. Besides, what the hell would they be doing watching the house now anyway?"

"To see whether or not you called the cops. See if the FBI was here."

"Nobody told us not to. So whoever did it should have expected we'd call the cops."

"You've got a point," I admitted. "So what'd you tell him?" Ron got a huge grin on his face.

"Jerry challenged him to a shooting contest. His choice. We figured the guy's a federal agent, all that training at Quantico, he ought to be a better shot than a mere college student. We've got an electronic timer, we showed him there'd be no way for us to cheat. If he won, we'd stop. If Jerry won, we'd keep shooting." Jerry and Ron looked at each other and giggled like lunatics.

"So?"

"He wouldn't do it. I think he'd been watching out the

window of the house for a while before he came down, saw us shooting."

"He wouldn't?"

"Nope. He got all huffy and stomped off. You know a lot of these guys are control freaks, he couldn't handle the tables being turned on him and got intimidated."

A headache was beginning to form behind my left eye. I closed my eyes and shook my head slowly from side to side.

"You guys are going to give me an ulcer. No one in the history of my family has ever had an ulcer, but you guys are going to give me one. Didn't I say don't piss off anybody? Didn't I say keep a low profile? The idea was for you to be seen and not heard, so the feebies don't get distracted from their job, which is finding your dad."

"I know," Ron said, "but it is my house."

"Ron," I told him, massaging my brow, "I..." I decided I'd just be wasting my breath and shut up. Something caught my eye near the weight bench. "What is that?" I pointed.

"Gun case," Bob told me. He'd managed to stop the flow of blood and was using the rag to clean his face.

"Is that the fucking sniper rifle Agent Reilly was complaining to me about?"

"That'd be the one."

I wanted to whimper. Everything I'd told them had gone in one ear and out the other. I wondered why I even bothered. They all had brains in their heads, I just wasn't too sure if there were full-time hookups involved. Most of it could be explained by the fact that they were healthy twenty-two-year-old males, but not all. I got up and walked over to the rifle case.

"Why is this here?" I asked, not really expecting an answer I'd find acceptable.

"We were gonna shoot it," Bob told me. "Out the window of that tiny room in back you can get good line of sight on the clearings on the hill behind the house. The furthest one is nearly eight hundred yards out. It's hard as hell to find a long distance range like that, you gotta take it where you can get it."

"I've been working with my M1A out to three hundred yards," Ron called out to us. "I just wish I didn't live in a state that had six months of winter, I'd get a lot more time behind my rifle."

"Don't even start bitching," Jerry told him. "I'd love to have a backyard that I could shoot in."

"Today it's just too damn windy," Bob declared. "There are gusts up to twenty miles an hour out there. Shooting at anything out past three hundred would just be an exercise in frustration. I haven't even uncased it."

"What is it?" I asked out of morbid curiosity. Bob knelt down and flipped open the latches on the case, then opened the lid. A black bolt action rifle wearing a large scope and bipod laid in a bed of charcoal colored foam.

"Robar SR-90," he told me. Never heard of it.

"What caliber?"

".300 WinMag," he told me. "Kicks a bit, but when you have to buck crosswinds eight hundred yards out a .308 just won't cut it." A small blue button was pinned to the foam inside the lid. **Reach Out and Touch Someone**. Jerry wandered over and looked down at the rifle with lust in his eye.

"How much did that cost?"

"Thirty-five hundred."

"Dollars?" I exclaimed. "Thirty-five hundred dollars? Did it come with a car to carry it in?" Bob gave me a grin in response.

"That's an improved 700 action, right?" Jerry asked Bob. "What kind of groups can you get?"

"Half a minute of angle, on a good day. With Black Hills Match. That thing's more accurate than I am. If I stuck it in a vise I'd probably be able to cut the groups in half."

"Not bad." Jerry went on to ask him about mil-dots or duplexes, adjustable cheekpieces, pelican cases, and something called barrel fluting. I stood nearby, smiling and nodding my head, waiting to hear something I understood.

"I'm really not good enough with a rifle to need one this accurate," Bob said to Jerry. "Carlos Hathcock I ain't. But I had the money and the opportunity, so I took it." Bob swung the lid closed on the rifle case and snapped the latches shut.

"What's that?" Jerry asked. He pointed to what I'd thought was a black canvas duffle bag on the floor behind the rifle case. Bob gave him a smirk and wiggled his eyebrows. He bent down and lifted the bag onto the hard rifle case. Now I could see it wasn't a duffle bag but rather an unusual square-ended piece that looked like a soft-sided long gun case but seemed too short.

"The most powerful and effective small arm for close range interpersonal conflict that has ever been invented," Bob stated.

"A shotgun, huh?" I said. The media, for reasons I'm sure are political, would have people believe so-called 'Assault Weapons' are the most deadly weapons ever invented. The truth was that any duck hunter's twelve-gauge shotgun, loaded with buckshot or slugs, was as deadly as anything—hand-held—ever made. Inside of twenty-five yards, that is. Past that distance, the buckshot pattern begins to spread out too far to be reliably effective. It wasn't magic, just physics.

Twelve-gauge slugs are .72 caliber and travel half again as fast as most pistol bullets. The standard load of double-ought buckshot sends nine .32-caliber pellets downrange at the same velocity. Which pretty much explains why you can find a shotgun in every cop car in the country.

"Open it, monkey boy," Bob said to Jerry.

Jerry took the big zipper on the bag and ran it from one end of the case to the other, then flipped it open.

"Ooooooh," he cooed. "Oooooh." He looked up at Bob. "You get all the fun toys."

"Perks of the profession. Although the fucking IRS won't let me write it off on my taxes as a business expense, I already checked."

"May I?"

"Be my guest." As Jerry gingerly picked up the shotgun like he would a newborn I could see Steve shaking his head.

"You guys and your hardware," he said disdainfully. Jerry ignored him and *ooohed* and *aaahed* over the shotgun, clicking and snicking and snapping it up to his shoulder for a quick sight picture.

The shotgun looked a lot like the Remington 870 pump guns I'd been trained on by the DEA, but there was something different. It took me a second to realize that Bob's gun wasn't a pump, it was a semi-auto. The shotgun looked pretty traditional, with its wood buttstock and forend, but I knew Bob would never buy a firearm off the shelf without customizing it.

"Is that a Remington?" I asked him.

"Yeah, an 11-87. Customized by yours truly."

"Eighteen-inch barrel with ghost ring sights, extended magazine, oversize safety," Jerry practically panted, turning the weapon over and over in his hands. "Oversize bolt handle. Free carrier. On-gun shell holder. Non-binding magazine follower. Tritium insert in the front sight!"

"Gimmee that!" Bob wrestled the shotgun out of Jerry's hands, exasperated. Jerry immediately began to pout.

"And how much did all that cost?" I asked Bob.

"The gun was six hundred, plus about four hundred in extras." He put it away and closed up the case.

"I'll stick with my Mossberg," Ron told them. "Best damn combat shotgun on the market, period, right out of the box, and you can get them for a lot less than *that*." He nodded in the direction of the Remington.

"I don't like pumps, I short stroke 'em and jam them up," Jerry said. "Although that 590 is pretty kickass with those ghost ring sights. And a nine-round capacity."

"590 A1," Ron corrected him.

Steve walked over. "You better enjoy it while it lasts," he told Bob. "'Cause unless she's an idiot there's no way in hell your future wife'll let this kind of spending on guns continue. Especially on your salary. My *dog* makes more money than you do."

"Why do you think I'm buying all this stuff now?" Bob replied. He shivered, cold now that he was standing around instead of sparring. He walked over to the table beside the couch and pulled on a dark sweatshirt. Ron had already done the same, then disappeared downstairs.

"So where's the MP5?" Jerry asked Bob. "I know you've got to have one somewhere." The MP5, a 9-millimeter submachinegun made in West Germany, was generally considered to be the best of its type in the world. Two years ago, during the search for Jerry, Bob had produced an MP5 that he'd purchased illegally on the Fort Bragg black market. He'd used it to kill several mob soldiers who'd been shooting at us, then had to ditch it when the Justice Department showed up.

"I'm not going to bring an illegal, unregistered submachinegun to a house I know is filled with federal agents. I'm not that dumb," Bob scolded Jerry. "I left it at home. MP5*SD*," he told Jerry with a grin, wiggling his eyebrows.

"Oooooo," Jerry sighed appreciatively, then his face fell. "You left it at Bragg?"

"No, my parent's house. Mom knows by now not to look under the bed when I'm home. Or when I'm not. You don't think I'd travel without my baby, do you?"

"Yeah," I quipped, "God knows you'd be helpless without it." Ron reappeared, coming up the stairs with a six-pack of beer in his hand. He began distributing the bottles, which were nice and cold. If I hadn't been carrying a gun I would have grabbed one.

"MP5*SD*?" I asked. "What's that?" I knew a good bit about guns, but still half the time I didn't know what they were talking about.

"Integrally suppressed," Bob told me. "It's about as loud as a BB gun." He flashed a quick, knowing grin my way. "Works really well at taking out sentries."

"Well, nobody's skulking around downstairs," Ron announced to the room. He looked at me and tipped his beer. "So what's up?"

"The Detroit Police Department pulled one of your father's coworkers out of the Detroit River last night with a bullet in his neck." The four of them drew close, standing in front of me with a mixture of excitement and concern on their faces.

"A .380?" Jerry asked me.

"Unknown. It was still in him when I saw the body."

"Nobody's said shit to me about this," Ron began to bitch.

"They probably don't know yet," I explained. "Since it was a white guy in a suit instead of a sixteen-year-old black kid missing his Nikes, the cop thought Scott might be interested. We went to the Wayne County Morgue last night and checked him out as soon as we heard. I found a wallet on the guy with an ID badge from your dad's company."

"What was this guy's name?" Ron asked me.

"Frank Hohimer."

Ron shook his head after thinking for a second or two. "Doesn't sound familiar." He shook his head again. "But I only met a few of the people Dad worked with. Just 'cause I don't know the guy doesn't mean anything."

I dug the picture out and showed it to him. He looked curiously at Hohimer's dead face.

"Nope," he said finally. "Don't recognize him." He passed the photo around and they all looked at it.

"If the FBI isn't already pawing over the body in the morgue, they will be soon," I told them. "We really lucked out, what with Scott Copley knowing one of the guys who was on-scene when they fished this guy out of the drink. Normally, the first we'd have heard of the guy would be after the FBI got a warrant and searched his condo. Show that picture to your mom, see if she knows him. Don't let the feds see it though, or I'm screwed."

"Last I heard, State of Michigan doesn't put down on your license whether your address is a house or a condo," Bob said suspiciously, eyeing me. "You find anything interesting?"

Damn that boy was quick. "Not a thing. If the feds don't discover him by the end of today I'll give them an anonymous call. Since he worked with your dad, maybe that'll encourage them to redouble their efforts and re-interview everybody at Consolidated Systems, Inc. You think of anything new about why your dad might have been grabbed?"

Ron could only shake his head and look discouraged. I couldn't think of anything to say that'd cheer him up, either.

"Should I give you some cash or something?" Ron asked me. "Make this an official PI/client relationship? Tell me how this works."

"You try to give me any money and I'll knock your block off," I told him roughly. "That's how it works."

"So now what?" Steve asked.

"We wait."

"Wait for what?"

"Wait for the kidnappers to contact us, make demands. Wait for the feds to search Hohimer's house in case they find something I missed. Wait to hear what the feebies find out talking to your dad's coworkers. Wait for something new to pop up. However long it takes."

"That sucks."

"What do you want me to do?" I demanded of them. "I've done everything I can think of. The cops have done the crime scene and trace evidence thing, but that won't get us anywhere until we have a suspect, unless they got a print, and if they found a print I'll eat my shoes. The feds have your phone tapped and taped and if the kidnappers call, they'll be all over them. I bet they're interviewing the shit out of everybody your dad worked with. Probably for the third or fourth time."

"They've talked to me three times already," Ron admitted.

"The feds have gotta be as confused about this case as

everybody else is. I mean, why do people get kidnapped? Either so the kidnapper can make some sort of public statement, or for money. Well, your dad isn't a political figure. And even if he is working for the CIA, he's not a bigwig or he'd be in Langley, or D.C., or New York. So we're left with the money angle. How much money does your dad make a year?"

"Over a hundred grand," Ron told me.

"Not bad," I said. "Not something you'd turn your nose up at. But not enough for someone to target your dad because he's rich. There are probably a thousand Chrysler and GM execs living within five miles of here that make that much and more. Hell, if someone grabbed your dad because they hoped for a big ransom, wouldn't you think they'd have gotten around to asking for some money by now?" They all grudgingly nodded their heads.

"Motive." That summed it all up in one word. "That is the one thing we don't have. **Why** was he kidnapped? If it's something to do with those computer disks, until we know what was on 'em there's no way to know who'd be after your dad. Foreign agents, his own people, Greenpeace, the Michigan Militia for all I know. If it doesn't have to do with those disks—which, I might add, we're not even sure are missing—then we're in for a long wait."

Ron sank onto the couch next to me, his face suddenly tired. "I'm too old for this shit," he mumbled.

"You want me to talk to the feds?" I asked him, hating to see him in this state. "Maybe chew some ass, try to motivate them?"

"Hell, his mom could outbitch you in her sleep," Steve said. He kicked at the plywood floor with his shoe.

"That's what I'm trying to tell you guys. If you can think of something I should do, let me know, because I'm out of ideas. You want help searching your house again? For those disks, or whatever else we might find?"

Ron shook his head. "Naw, I've searched the damn house twice. I know all the hiding spots, and I haven't found shit. Well, a bunch of my old *Penthouses*, but those don't count. And these guys helped me take apart the study and my parents' bedroom this morning before you showed up. Just on the off chance they'd see something I'd missed. Nothing."

"What about your dad's car? Has that been searched?"

"Yeah, I think so." Ron paused for a minute and thought. "I don't know, actually. I assume the feds searched it, or the cops. I never did."

"It's in the garage, right?"

"Yeah."

Well, since I didn't have anything better to do…"Whyn't you dig up the keys for me, I'll paw through the car. I doubt I'll find anything, but at least we'll know for sure it's been searched."

Ron headed back down the stairs to locate a set of keys, looking grim. I suppose if I'd been in his shoes, I'd be having trouble staying upbeat too.

"You ready to get your ass kicked, Gimli?" Jerry cockily taunted Bob.

"Oh that's smart, piss him off," Steve scolded. "He already has trouble understanding the term 'light contact'."

Bob moved onto the open area of the floor, windmilling his arms to loosen them up. He beckoned to Jerry playfully with a crooked finger.

"You spar with Bob?" I asked Steve.

"Only when I'm really drunk. That way it doesn't hurt so much when he kicks my ass."

"Not until the next morning," Jerry added. He threw off his sweatshirt and began stretching.

"Well c'mon, let's go," Bob told him.

"You better watch it," Jerry told him, popping his neck with a savage jerk of his head. "I've been watching a lot of Jackie Chan movies."

"Yeah? I hear he does all his own stunts too." As they faced off, it looked to me like Jerry was a little more confident on his feet in front of Bob than Ron had been. Whether or not that meant anything.

"I'd be able to have a lot more fun if Ron put some mats down up here," Bob complained.

"Right. So I can end up airborne half the goddamn time," Jerry replied. "No thank you. That's the only thing that keeps you from doing the opening scene from *Above the Law* on us every time."

"Try not to kick his ass as quick as you did Ron's," Steve called out. "My beer's only half finished."

"Thanks for your support," Jerry replied, his voice dripping with sarcasm. He never took his eyes off Bob.

"Remember," Bob said, "the trick isn't necessarily being better, it's being willing to escalate the conflict beyond your opponent's ability—or willingness—to cope. They think fight, you think maim. They think maim, you think kill." Jerry nodded, still sidestepping.

Ron trudged back up the stairs as Bob and Jerry slowly circled, the soles of their shoes hissing as they slid over the plywood floor. At the exact same instant, like they'd both heard some distant starting gun, the two of them lunged, hands moving to strike.

Jerry somehow managed to deflect Bob's left hand as it tried to bruise his ribs, and retaliated with a left hook. Bob moved inside the hook and nudged Jerry off-balance with what looked like his hip. Jerry went hopping on one foot across the floor, trying not to land on his face. He recovered without taking a dive and came back for more, a look of intense concentration on his face.

Jerry was quicker than Ron, and Bob knew it. All Jerry had to do was twitch his knee and Bob reacted, turning his body to protect his groin and moving in to strike. That was just what Jerry was looking for, and did his best to crease Bob's forehead with his right elbow.

Bob dodged the elbow in an amazing display of reflexes, and, as Jerry's momentum carried him forward Bob socked him in the back of his head with an elbow just hard enough to get his attention. Almost at the same time he kicked at the back of Jerry's support leg. Jerry tried to land soft, but gravity had the upper hand, and his knee hit the floor hard.

"That sounded like it hurt," Steve commented. Jerry didn't answer, he just sat on the floor rubbing his knee with a pained expression on his face.

"You're lucky you just said something about there not being any mats," Bob said to Jerry. "When you missed with that elbow I almost clotheslined you, landed you on your head."

"Yeah, I feel real lucky."

"Don't bitch. Just think if I didn't suck at sparring."

"What do you mean by that?" I asked him.

"I mean I'm not very good at sparring," he explained. "It's a psychological thing. I know it's not for real, so I have to think about what I should and shouldn't do next, instead of just doing what feels natural and instinctive. I have to make sure nobody gets hurt, so that forces me to think instead of just react. I really have to slow down."

Jesus, that was slow? "You looked pretty damn good to me," I said.

"Actually, my sparring looks prettier than if I was fighting for real."

"How's that?"

"My natural instincts tend toward eye gouging, throat crushing, joint breaking, neck snapping kinds of moves. Breaking fingers, face biting, kicking knees so hard they bend backwards, dislocating shoulders, palm strikes to the nose. The kind of moves you can't really do in sparring, even at half speed."

"Oh. You, ah, doing a lot of that at work?"

He made a face at me. "Seriously? I'm carrying two guns and a big fucking knife. And grenades. I'm with a bunch of guys who have guns and grenades and knives. And we've got radios, for air support. The only thing I'm hitting bad guys with is bullets and bombs. Most of the time."

"Most of the time?" I repeated.

He shrugged. "Shit happens."

Ron handed me the car keys and I stuck them in my pocket. "You want me to come along?" he asked.

"You can if you want," I said. "If you're that bored. Be about as exciting as watching paint dry."

"Maybe I'll just stay up here, watch Jerry get his butt kicked by the bearded wonder."

"You want to go a couple rounds?" Jerry said defensively. "I'm sure it can be arranged."

I headed down the stairs. "Now kids, you play nice," I called out. "If I hear anybody crying I'm going to send you all to your rooms."

They were blowing off the stress and fear they were all feeling and trying to hide. In all honesty I wondered just how rough it might get before it was all over. And whether they'd be able to handle it if George Kelly turned up dead.

12:11 p.m.

I entered the house's garage through a pedestrian door next to the large overhead door. The garage was about two-and-a-half cars wide, and the pedestrian door opened onto a ribbon of concrete next to the two parking spots. Both of the spots were filled, one with Carla's big Ford pickup, and the other with George's Lincoln.

Enough light was coming in through the windows in the garage door that I didn't bump into anything as I made my way across to the Town Car. It was new, and big, and grey, and I couldn't imagine the cops and feds not having searched it half a dozen times already.

I unlocked the driver's door, hit the button to unlock the other doors, then used the key to open the trunk. My plan was to work from the rear of the car forward. If I didn't find anything on the inside then I'd check in the wheel wells and behind the bumpers and anywhere else that would be a quick convenient hiding place for…whatever.

The trunk appeared never to have been used. Maybe I was the first person to even open it—it smelled just like "new" car. I checked all the nooks and crannies anyway, and pulled the carpet up as best I could. Nothing.

The back seat was next, and took a little longer to check out. Most of my time was spent checking under the seat cushion, trying to lift it up for a complete visual inspection. It was having none of that, so I did the best I could wedging my hand down between the seat back and cushion and feeling for anything unusual.

I checked under the rear of the front seats while I was back there, but all I discovered was the first sign of litter in the otherwise spotless car. A candy wrapper, a used Kleenex, and the cap to a ball-point pen. Nothing else, and nothing under the floormats.

The front seat held a lot more opportunity for success. Most large or old cars had so much room behind the dash and glove box a family of Filipinos could hide there from the INS without much chance of being discovered. The first car I ever owned was a '72 Caprice Classic, and I could've hidden half a dozen bowling balls inside its dashboard if I'd been so inclined.

I first checked the driver's seat. Did the fabric have any rips or loose seams where something may have been inserted? Nope. Was there anything wedged up into the bottom of the seat? Nope. I checked the passenger side seat the same way, with identical results.

Laying half on the seat and half on the floor, I looked and felt underneath the dash on the driver's side. A flashlight would have helped, but I took my time and made sure I checked every nook and cranny with my fingertips. Then I checked the dashboard itself, glove box, and the heater vents. A lot of the people who smuggle drugs in cars like to stuff the contraband down the heater vents. Even in small cars the vents can hold a surprising amount of cocaine. I stuck the key in the ignition and turned it so the accessories would come on. I flipped the fan on high and stuck my hand in front of each of the vents in turn, to make sure air was blowing out. No blocked vents, and no rattling sounds.

I halfheartedly checked the doors for hidey holes, but nothing seemed to be loose. The dome light checked out fine, and so did the fabric covering the ceiling. I sank back dejectedly in the driver's seat and looked around the inside of the car. I couldn't think of anywhere else to look.

The sun visor above my head caught my eye, and I flipped it down. Air bag disclaimer. I hitched my butt across the front seat and flipped down the visor above the passenger seat. Nothing there either, except the closed flip-top of a vanity mirror.

I flipped open the lid of the vanity mirror and jerked as the makeup light blinded me. The mirror didn't hold any surprises—I was still a lot less handsome than I felt. I closed the lid, cutting off the light, then paused. That lid seemed awfully hard to pivot.

I opened and closed the cover on the mirror again. Something seemed to be binding on the hinge, and it took three times more effort to move the lid than I thought it should. I flipped on the dome light and knelt on the front seat to get a better view.

The vanity mirror had a flat plastic frame that was set into the visor. The top of the frame, closest to the ceiling, seemed to stick out further from the visor than the rest of the mirror. It was too close to the roof for me to get a good look at it, and my fingers were too big to explore the crack I found between the mirror's case and the visor.

Hoping George, wherever he was, would forgive me, I opened the mirror, took hold of its lid, and yanked ferociously. Instead of the whole mirror coming off the visor, like I had hoped, the lid just ripped off the mirror. But the mirror did separate a little from the visor, and I was able to get my fingers around its corner. Another fierce jerk and I managed to pull the mirror off. It hung forlornly, swinging back and forth on the electrical cable that supplied power to the vanity mirror's light.

I reached down to the floormat and picked up the object that had been wedged between the mirror and the sun visor. It was a computer disk. Unmarked, and externally undamaged from the fall. I turned it over and over in my hands, wondering what answers were contained within.

Realizing none of my questions were going to get

answered kneeling on the front seat, I stuck the disk in my jacket pocket. The vanity mirror would have to be replaced with a new factory part -- it was unrepairable. I grabbed hold of the mirror and placed it against the visor, which I then flipped up against the ceiling. The result would pass a cursory glance. Then I switched the dome light off, locked the doors, and closed the car up.

"What the hell are you doing in here?"

I jumped and spun halfway around, my heart slamming into my ribs. One of the FBI agents that I had seen sitting at the table in the breakfast nook stared at me curiously. He was stopped halfway through the doorway that led into the house, a black plastic garbage bag dangling from his fist.

"Jesus, you scared the shit out of me," I told him. "I never even heard you open the door." He stepped the rest of the way into the garage and pulled the door shut behind him.

"So what are you doing?" he said again.

I held up the keys to the Lincoln. "Just checking George's car."

His eyes darted back and forth from the truck to the Lincoln, finally settling on the Lincoln.

"Checking it for what?" he said suspiciously.

I waved vaguely in the direction of the barn. "Oh, you know. Ron's all nervous and upset, he just can't stand the thought of sitting around. He had his friends help him search the house this morning for the fiftieth time, see if there were any clues laying around that he missed." I rolled my eyes when I said 'clues'. "When I got here today he asked me if I'd search his dad's car. I told him it'd be a waste of time, that you guys had probably searched it ten times already, but he insisted. Gave me the keys. So I did it, just to humor him. D'you guys find anything when you searched it?"

The agent seemed at a loss for words. His eyes were locked on the Lincoln, and he looked like he was dying to step over and peer inside it.

"Uh, no," he finally got out. "That is, I really couldn't say." He strode purposefully over to the garbage cans in the corner and stuffed the bag into one. I shrugged and headed toward the door I'd come through. Out of the corner of my eye I saw the agent staring at the Lincoln, deep in thought.

"Hey," he called out to me. I stopped, my hand on the door leading outside. "Did you find anything?"

"If I find anything, you guys'll be the first to know," I told him. He was still staring at the car when I went out the door.

I figured it was a waste of time, but had to ask anyway. Ron had no idea why his father would hide a computer disk in his car, but the discovery got him excited. It got them all excited, and I had to spend ten minutes reminding them to keep a low profile. Then I drove straight back to my office. I wanted to see what, if anything, was on the disk. The boys offered to accompany me, but them breathing down my neck and pacing my small office, wired with pent-up energy, would be highly annoying—at best.

I dropped into my desk chair, rolled it over in front of the computer, and began switching everything on. I was eager to see just what was on the disk that made it so important George felt he had to hide it.

Half an hour later I was still at it. I'd managed to get the disk to display its directory for me, such as it was. There was only one small file listed, something labeled Travel. But every time I tried to get into Travel, my screen filled up with a meaningless jumble of letters and numbers. The first time I figured it was my fault, and had screwed something up—when it came to computers I knew just enough to get myself into trouble, but usually not enough to get myself out. After the third time I began to detect a pattern. I'd never seen encrypted data, but I suspected that was what I was looking at. I was pretty sure I was looking at the contents of Travel, but those contents were hieroglyphics. I tried every command and help code I could think of, with zero success. And all I knew about encrypted files was what I'd read in spy novels.

Finally, I gave up. My meager skills were no match for the task before me. No wonder I hated computers. I probably could've had the disk spilling its guts to me with one simple command, but I just didn't know enough to figure it out.

I sat and stared at my blinking cursor. Barring the sudden appearance of that code word, locating a computer expert seemed the smartest move. The only problem was that I didn't know any, and was hesitant to have a stranger looking over a disk that might contain CIA secrets. Steve and Ron fiddled around with computers, but when it came to encryption I really didn't think they knew any more than I did. Kelly used a computer at work, but her expertise was limited to proprietary software programs nobody else used.

Suddenly I remembered Kelly's brother-in-law. He was a computer programmer, and designed high-tech computer adventure games on the side. He lived and breathed computers. If anyone outside of CIA cryptography could help me, he'd be the one. The only problem was that he was in Los Angeles.

I dug his number out of my desk. It was nearly noon in

California, so I got the answering machine. I left Jeff a message to call me and hung up. My hope was that he could walk me through decoding the disk over the phone.

Next I called Scott, who was actually in his office. I asked him if he'd heard anything new about George.

"Nope," he told me. "Nothing. Far as I know the feds are still nosing around, trying to dig something up. Our guys don't have anything, that's for sure. Other than headaches, from fielding all the stupid questions the reporters keep asking."

"Better you than me. What are the feds doing, other than sitting in the house waiting for the phone to ring?"

"I hear they're spending a lot of time talking to George's coworkers, but I don't think they suspect anyone specific yet. Of course, you realize, I'm getting this all third-hand. There could be stuff they're learning that they're not telling anybody, not even our dicks that are supposed to be working with them. You know how the FBI works, you were a fed."

"DEA makes the cases, FBI makes the headlines." *That* should have been engraved on the Hoover Building. Local and state cops around the country were convinced FBI stood for Famous But Incompetent, but I wasn't willing to go that far. I knew a lot of really good FBI Special Agents.

"Yeah. Anyway," he told me, "I'm gonna make an anonymous call in about an hour, let them know about the guy in the morgue. As far as I know they haven't picked up on him yet."

"Doesn't fill you with a lot of confidence, does it?"

I hung around the office for another hour, then packed it in and headed for home.

When I got home I found my wife and the dog in the family room. Oscar ran up and greeted me in her usual manner, and my wife looked up from the book she was reading. She gave me one hell of a look.

"What?" I said. "What'd I do now?"

"You'll never guess who I got a call from today," she said. She set the book down and struggled into a sitting position.

"From the look on your face I don't want to know."

"Bonnie Jenkins," she told me, slowly enunciating every syllable. "From Channel Seven Action News." The name wasn't familiar at all, but then again I tried not to watch the news. Too violent. I found a chair and looked at Kelly questioningly.

"She wanted a comment from you on the story they're going to run on tonight's newscast. Apparently she or someone she was with recognized you at Ron's yesterday. They found out who you were, but instead of calling your office and asking why you were at the Kelly's, I guess she checked with some of her hush-hush sources."

"A television personality that has sources? She must be young and hungry."

"That's the impression I got. Between your presence at Ron's and the information her sources gave her, she decided she knew what was going on."

"About what?"

"About how George's kidnapping is probably the Detroit mob's revenge for you and Ron killing some of their guys two years ago. Or is in some other way related to your underworld ties. You like that? She actually said 'underworld ties'."

I sat there, stunned. The local news media had done

some unbelievably stupid things over the years, but this was...

"Wha— you've got to— you're serious, aren't you? Oh my God, I don't believe this! She's going to do a story on that?"

Kelly nodded at me. "And she had all sorts of questions about why the shootings then had been covered up, and if you had ties to organized crime before the shootings, stuff like that. I guess she and a camera crew stopped by your office earlier today, but you weren't there. She said they came by here, too, but that must have been while I was out walking the pooch." My wife seemed more amused than anything else. I should have been grateful for that.

I was still shaking my head in denial, and rambling. "What, is she an idiot? And how did she find out about the shootings, anyway? The Justice Department handled the whole thing, they wouldn't release any of their reports to her. And I know if she went to them for a quote all she would have gotten is a 'No Comment'. If the press ever got hold of the facts they'd destroy the feds and the credibility of the whole Witness Protection Program. And mob ties! MOB TIES? Me and the boys put bullets in ten of 'em, that's how I'm connected to the fucking underworld! Ron was in a wheelchair for a month and a half! Hell, the Sopranos in this town love me. Ron and Bob and Steve and I fucking destroyed the only challenger that Bufonte has ever had to his empire, trying to get Jerry back. I go to Bufonte's restaurant downtown, I can't even pay for the meal, he won't let me. I cleaned his house for him. There's no way he's involved in George's kidnapping. This Bonnie Jerkoff should go downtown and ask *him* those fucking questions, see what response *he* gives her." I paused, but only long enough to get more air in my lungs.

"Besides, if the mob was pissed off at me for something, why the hell would they kidnap George? They'd just go after Ron. It makes no sense! If they wanted me, they'd bomb my car, or come to my office and cap me there, and it wouldn't have taken them two years to get around to it! You know what this is going to do to my business? Jesus. I'm going to be fielding calls from jittery adjusters for days." I know I shouldn't have been so angry; idiots in the media is old news. I reminded myself the media had no obligation to get anything right, they just couldn't deliberately get it wrong. That was called "absence of malice", and it was fucking up my life.

My wife just sat there smiling at me as I ranted. After another five minutes of angry venting, enough to make the dog leave the room worriedly, I calmed down enough to converse rationally.

"So," I asked Kelly, "what did you tell this beacon of truth when she called?"

"I told her you had no comment."

"That's it? That's all you said to her? No comment?"

"Well that, and I made several comments about her having relations with animals, called her a body part, questioned her intelligence, character, and motives, and then suggested she perform a physically impossible act."

"That's more like it. But were you polite?" My wife had the enviable ability to insult and embarrass people while still seeming excruciatingly polite.

Kelly held out her hand daintily and I helped her off the couch.

"Every second. You ready for dinner?"

"I don't know if I can eat, now, I'm so upset. But I'll do my best," I added quickly, after she shot me a withering glare. "Maybe I'll jog after dinner, work off some of my frustration."

"You know, we still have to name her," Kelly said to me. We were cuddled up on the couch, in front of a roaring fire that I'd built a half-hour earlier. The logs crackled and sparked as they settled in the fireplace, giving off a comfortable sound.

"What do you mean, *her*?" I said. Through all the tests Kelly had undergone in the past months we'd had many opportunities to learn the sex of our child. We'd requested the doctors not tell us, though. We'd find out soon enough, and were content enough knowing that whatever sex our child was, it was healthy.

"Her?" I repeated. "Remember, it's the male that determines what the kid's going to be. You know, those guys with the wiggly tails? You don't have anything to do with it. And I told them that it'd better be a boy, or they'd have to jump ship."

"They all did anyway," she replied, and poked me in the ribs with her elbow. The movement almost caused us to slide off the couch, but we managed to straighten everything out in time. Our couch was not built to hold two people side by side, especially when one of those people was the size of Kelly.

After we settled back into place, I rested my head on the pillow and stared at the fire for a while. I was comfortable, warm, and full of a delicious dinner. It rarely gets any better than that.

I looked at my watch. Six fifty-five. Outside the windows the sky was long dark. We'd missed the local news, on purpose. If the story they broadcast was half as bad as I figured it would be, I would've ended up doing an Elvis and shooting my TV.

"Well?" Kelly said. "Are you going to answer my question?" It took me a moment to remember what question she was talking about.

"Oh," I said. "Well, if it's a boy, Jose Enrique de la Peña, and if it's a girl, Soliloquy Abstruse." She elbowed me again and we both half-fell/half-slid onto the floor. Both of us were giggling and snorting like a couple of high school kids, our faces inches apart.

"Going my way, sailor?" she asked me wiggling her eyebrows. I felt her hand work its way around and start doing something to me that would not be acceptable for a PG-rated movie.

"I think you should go see Dr. Prescott," I told her.

"Why?" Her hand kept doing what it was doing.

"There's something wrong with your hormones," I explained. "You're supposed to be a rabid sexual animal in order to *get* pregnant, not after the fact."

She moved her head back an inch so she could focus on me. "You want to come over here and say that, mister?" It was the worst John Wayne accent I'd ever heard.

"If I get any closer I'll be inside you."

Her hand stopped moving and grabbed me firmly. "That's the idea," she growled.

FIVE

Tuesday

8:01 a.m.

I was drying off from my shower when Kelly opened the bathroom door and told me I had a phone call. When she told me who it was I tied the towel around my waist and hurried to the phone.

"Hello?"

"Mr. Phault? This is Special Agent Reilly, I talked to you yesterday at the Kelly's." My heart was beating fast, hope rising in me that he was calling with good news.

"Yeah, hi, how are you doing? What's up?"

"I was wondering if you'd be available to answer some questions sometime today. There are several things that have come to our attention and we need to talk to you."

I agreed immediately, thinking that they'd finally dug up something unusual talking to George's coworkers. "I was planning on heading over to the house this morning," I told him. "If that's where you're calling from I can just meet you over there."

"Actually, we'd prefer to talk to you in private," he said.

"Was that about George?" my wife asked me when I was off the phone.

"I don't know. He said they needed to ask me some questions, but about what he didn't say. I hope they're finally making some progress."

Kelly scratched at her belly and looked at me with a wry smile on her face.

"They probably just saw that 'exposé' Bonnie Jenkins broadcast last night," she told me.

"You're always so negative," I told her with a grin, but a cold knot of worry began forming in my stomach.

The coffee machine was just about done brewing a full pot when there came a knock on my office door. I let Reilly and another man he introduced as Special Agent Griffin into my office. They were both in suits. Griffin held an expensive looking briefcase in his left hand. They both shook my hand, but not with a whole lot of enthusiasm.

I offered them coffee but they declined. Trying not to look like my feelings were hurt I prepared myself a cup, then took a seat behind my desk. They sat in the chairs in front of my desk. They'd originally wanted the meeting at their office downtown in the McNamara Building, but all of us driving all the way down there was stupid when my office was a lot closer. I'd told them so, and apparently Reilly couldn't think of a reason to say no.

"So, what can I do for you gentlemen?" I took a sip of my coffee and waited.

"We need to ask you several questions," Griffin told me, pulling a legal pad out of his briefcase. Reilly just looked at me, and I realized in an instant that this wasn't going to be a friendly visit.

"Exactly how long have you known George Kelly?" Griffin began.

"I first met him in August, two years ago."

"What were the circumstances of that meeting?"

They were obviously on a fishing expedition. They probably already knew the answers to most of the questions they'd be asking me, and wanted to see if I'd tell the truth. And what else I might say.

"I was hired to look for Jerry Phillips by his parents. He was missing. Ron is one of Jerry's close friends, so I drove over to the house to talk to Ron. While I was there I met George Kelly. We became friends."

"Uh huh." Griffin scribbled on the pad. Reilly just sat there and stared at me, his arms crossed over his chest. Then Griffin reached into his briefcase and pulled out a thick sheaf of papers. He thumbed through them for several minutes without speaking.

"You said Jerry Phillips was missing," he finally said. "Exactly what do you mean by that?"

"I mean he was missing. Nobody had seen him for two days and his parents were worried. They knew Lieutenant Copley, and the Lieutenant recommended me to them."

"And you located Jerry Phillips?" The question came from Reilly.

"More like Jerry located me," I explained. "It had been more or less a voluntary disappearance, and when he found out his parents had hired me to look for him he tracked me down." Which was all true, as far as it went.

Griffin gave me a look I couldn't decipher and began flipping pages. He stopped and read something, then looked at me.

"Jerry Phillips was kidnapped, Mr. Phault." He stared at me accusingly.

"Well, yeah, later." It sounded lame even to me.

"Is there some reason you felt you had to lie to us about this easily verifiable information?"

"Whoawhoawhoa, I didn't lie," I said defensively. "And I wasn't aware that it was easily verifiable. That whole incident was shoved under the rug by your Department of Justice buddies, and the paperwork was supposedly buried because of how embarrassed they were."

Griffin held up the papers in his hand. "I guess not," was what he said. Reilly shifted in his seat and clasped his hands loosely in his lap. "Why don't you tell us who kidnapped Jerry, and why."

If they knew about Jerry being kidnapped, they'd know about everything, so I gave them the short version.

"Jerry had the bad luck to witness a murder. A mob hit, if you want to get colorful about it. He went underground because he figured it was the only way to stay alive. I guess the bad guys were following me, because when he surfaced to meet with me he was grabbed."

"Grabbed? Not killed?"

"They didn't try to kill him because they thought he had something of theirs. At first I thought Bufonte was behind the whole thing, but it turned out to be his number two guy, Reginald Kellogg, making a play for the throne."

"So Jerry Phillips, two years ago, was kidnapped by members of Detroit's organized crime community," Griffin stated.

"Yes."

"And you didn't think that this was important enough to even mention it to us?" Reilly's voice rose sharply.

"I didn't see how it was pertinent." I shifted restlessly in my seat.

"You didn't think it was pertinent?" scoffed Griffin. "Two people you know in two years come up missing, the first one grabbed by individuals known to have connections to organized crime, and you don't even mention it to us? What's wrong with this picture? Am I missing something?"

I felt my ears go hot. I've never taken criticism well. "Listen, tell me if I'm wrong here, but last I heard you guys don't even know for sure that George has been kidnapped. Am I wrong? 'Cause if I'm not, you'd better not be jumping in my shit."

"Mr. Phault, exactly what is your relationship with what, for convenience's sake, I'll call the Mafia in Detroit?"

"Excuse me?" I said, eyes wide. That one had taken me off guard. "My God, my wife was right. You guys saw that thing on TV and are taking it at face value. You've got to know better than that. You know how fucked up the media is."

"Mr. Phault," Griffin continued as if I'd never opened my mouth, "how many times have you personally met with Pietro Bufonte?"

"Oh Jesus." I threw up my hands in disgust.

"Are you going to answer the question, Mr. Phault?" Reilly asked me.

"Once," I spat. Griffin thumbed through the papers in front of him.

"Only once?" he said.

"Okay, twice, but the second time was only because I was eating at his restaurant with a client who'd wanted me to meet him there. I didn't want to say no. Bufonte saw me, and came over."

"And your first meeting?" Griffin said. "What prompted that?"

"He wanted to meet me. This was while I was looking for Jerry Phillips. By that time I'd figured out that it was Kellogg who was after both Jerry *and* Bufonte. Bufonte wanted to find out if I knew where Kellogg was, so he could take care of him. I didn't. I agreed to the meeting in hopes of getting some helpful information out of him, get some ideas about where to look for Jerry. Both of us came away from the meeting empty-handed."

"Uh huh." Griffin scribbled some more, then set down his legal pad and dug around in his briefcase.

"I stayed up late tracking this down and copying it," he said. He set a small tape recorder on the edge of my desk and pressed a button on it.

A faint hum, and light static. "*Well?*" I heard myself say. "*You called me.*"

"*Watch it*," someone with a deep voice told me.

I leaned back in my chair, overcome with deja vu. A whole flood of memories washed back over me, sights, smells, the everpresent sense of fear because I knew someone was out to kill me. I could see myself sitting in that dark booth across from Bufonte in his restaurant in Detroit's Greektown, sunk deep into the burgundy leather. Bob had been there, too.

"*Now August*," a third voice said, "*is that any way to speak to our guests?*" Bufonte, his rich voice unmistakable, chastising his huge bodyguard in front of us. That's when I knew Bufonte was really in trouble. He'd never have said a word to one of his people in front of me under ordinary circumstances. But he thought I might know where Kellogg was, so the standard etiquette was suspended. "*He's young and foolish yet*," Bufonte told me, "*but he's loyal.*"

"Really? I had a dog like that once," I said.

"Does he do any tricks?" Bob asked.

"I'll show you a trick, you little fuck," August said. I saw them in my mind's eye, squaring off, August nearly a foot taller than Bob and just as muscular. Bob had been grinning like an idiot.

"Butch, Spike," I said. *"Heel."*

I snorted at the tape player, shaking my head. Reilly and Griffin just sat there and stared at me.

"I have business to discuss with these gentlemen, August," Bufonte said.

"What business?"

"I was hoping you might have some information that I need," Bufonte said warmly.

"Let me guess, you want to know where your protégé is. Please, tell me if I'm wrong."

Griffin leaned forward and shut off the tape, then sat back. The two of them stared at me as if they'd just shown me video of a second gunman in the Kennedy assassination.

"Wow, that was a trip down memory lane," I said.

"Robert Grinnand was there for that meeting also?" Reilly said. He was very disapproving.

"You heard him, didn't you? Pardon me a second, but what was that tape supposed to prove? I told you I was there, and what happened. Play the rest of the tape if you want. There's nothing incriminating on it." If they'd been hoping to rattle me with a tape of a conversation that had been a waste of time to begin with they were going to be very disappointed.

"Why was Grinnand there?" Griffin asked me.

"It's called backup. I wasn't sure what the hell I was walking into. Could've been a trap set by Kellogg for all I knew." Griffin scribbled furiously, and I just knew they'd be questioning Bob about his involvement.

"You took a 20-year-old kid with you as backup for a meet with *Pietro Bufonte*? At *his* restaurant?" Reilly was staring at me.

"You mean the kid who's currently a Green Beret? Who I bet has killed more people by now than you've arrested? What was the question again?" I couldn't decipher his look. I was having a hard time keeping my temper under control.

"And you'd never met Pietro Bufonte before that day?" Griffin continued the questions.

"No."

"He seemed awfully friendly."

"Of course he was friendly! He was trying to pump me for information about the guy planning to kill him and take over his whole organization. Listen," I spoke up. "I can see you guys are getting all interested in this, and I'm telling you it's a waste of time. Bufonte didn't have anything to do with it."

"You know him that well, do you?" Griffin said snidely. He put down his pen and glared at me. "Mr. Phault, if you were in my place, wouldn't you find it highly coincidental that you are so closely involved with two possible kidnappings? And you with admitted ties to prominent local organized crime figures. The problem I have with all this is that I don't believe in coincidence." He paused. "It seems that anybody who associates with you better watch out."

"George isn't an associate. He's a friend." I was about at the end of my patience. "And use your brains, guys. It makes no sense for Bufonte to grab George. He's nobody to them. You're grasping at straws because you've got nothing to go on. But I'm telling you, this isn't the way to go."

"Then why are you getting so defensive?"

"Wouldn't you be defensive if the local TV news ran a story on you full of innuendo and half-truths and then a couple of FBI agents come to your office and start interrogating you?"

"This isn't an interrogation," Reilly said.

"Could've fucking fooled me," I snapped back. "And give me some credit. I was a federal agent, remember? If I had anything incriminating to hide, do you think I'd be sitting here talking to you without my lawyer present? I wouldn't be talking to you at all, period."

"You know what I think?" Griffin said casually. "I think you're dirty. Big time dirty. I think you're in bed with Bufonte, and I think you're involved in this somehow. I don't know how, or why, but you're in it up to your eyeballs, buddy." He jabbed a finger in my direction. Reilly looked at him but didn't say anything.

I took a deep breath and did my best to appear undisturbed. My pulse boomed in my ears. "Oh really?"

"Yeah, and we're going to find out everything. Sooner or later, it's all going to come out, you know it will. If you've got anything to tell us, now is the time. Before this has gone too far."

"You've got nothing. That's it, right? You've got nothing on the kidnapping, no leads, no ransom demands, no evidence, so now you're on a fishing expedition."

"Yeah, and we're going to find something, too. You're dirty. You know it, I know it, and your wife probably knows it too."

Okay, I admit it. That's when I lost it.

"You want to know what's going on between me and Bufonte?" I said loudly. "I'll tell you. He loves me, he fucking *loves* me! He wouldn't even let me pay for my dinner at his restaurant. You know why? Because I killed the only guy that was ever a serious threat to him. Kellogg." I took a deep breath and charged ahead.

"And not just Kellogg. I put a bunch of his fucking people in the ground. I shot them, I kicked them to death, you name it! August, that guy on the tape? Dead, fucking *dead*. And if Bufonte ever decides he doesn't like me alive and comes after me, I'll put *him* in the fucking ground too. I don't have any loyalty to him, and never have." I was halfway out of my chair, stabbing a finger at them.

"What I can't figure out is how the lot of you never spent a full day in jail," Griffin said, appearing only slightly disturbed by my yelling. "You and those kids. You shot half a dozen people in the middle of a parking lot, for Chrissakes."

"We killed a hell of a lot more people than that," I said quietly, my eyes fixed on his. He broke off from my gaze, blinking.

"Why don't you just tell us what you're trying to hide," Reilly said softly. "It's not too late."

"Get the fuck out of my office."

I stood there and glared at them until they stood up and walked out.

I don't know how long I sat in my chair, hands clenched, but eventually I calmed down enough to use the phone. Ron was home, and I told him I'd be over in fifteen minutes.

10:52 a.m.

I parked next to Steve's car and climbed out. There were three plain Chevy sedans parked nearby, but I didn't know if one of them belonged to Reilly and Griffin.

The boys were in the barn again, I could see movement

through a second-floor window. I went straight up and avoided the house altogether.

"What's up?" Ron asked me. He and Steve were hunched in front of a computer that they must have dragged over from the house. It was on a table they'd probably brought over at the same time, since I didn't recognize it from the day before.

Ron and Steve were taking turns playing a video game, and I could hear what sounded like gunshots and animal howls coming from the computer's speakers. Bob was in the far corner of the room in a T-shirt and shorts, working out on Ron's weight set.

I walked over and watched them play for a minute. The object of the game seemed to be to kill as many monsters with a shotgun as possible. The shotgun was visible at the bottom of the screen, and every time Ron fired it, I could see the hands of the main character as he racked a new shell into the pump gun. Ron was doing pretty good mowing down the bad guys, blood flying wherever the scattergun's pellets hit, when he was blindsided and killed by an ape-looking thing throwing orange fireballs.

"What the hell are you playing?" I asked, aghast.

"**DOOM**," Steve told me. "Cool, isn't it."

"It's something." Steve switched places with Ron and began playing, firing at another ape-man with a chain-gun and sending him flying down a flight of stairs, spraying blood.

"I think the last video game I played was Pac-Man, twelve, fifteen years ago, when I was in the Army and drunk at a shithole bar."

"Boy, you are old," Ron said. He gestured at the screen. "*This* is ancient."

"Hey Bob, where's your Blazer?" I called out to him as he finished a set of curls.

"Oh, don't get him started," Ron warned me.

"I'm gonna have to stop coming home to Michigan when I get leave," Bob began bitching. He began sliding weights off the barbell and putting them on a larger bar set up for bench pressing. "You guys are bad luck." It looked like he was putting every weight Ron had onto the bar, which began to bend slightly.

"What happened now?"

"How long have these newspaper guys been on strike?" he asked me.

"Why?"

"Hold on." He laid down on the bench, lifted the bar off its rest, and began moving it up and down smoothly.

The weight set was made out of cheap concrete-filled plastic forms, the type sold at K-Mart or Sears. Bob had every weight I could see stuck on the bar, and near as I could figure it totaled about 175 pounds. He did thirty or so repetitions, then set the bar back in its rest, breathing hard.

"Should you be doing that with your finger?" I asked him as he panted.

"Benching's no problem, but curls hurt like a bitch."

"So are you sidelined until you're all healed?"

He snorted and gestured at his finger. "Because of this? This is nothing."

"What about your back? That burn's not healed all the way."

"Shit's about to pop off," he told me. "I'm actually surprised they even gave me a few days leave. I'm not missing all the fun just because of a few scratches." He paused, said, "We're all playing hurt," then changed the subject. "So, you want the long or the short version?" he asked me.

"I don't know if my heart can handle any more stress today," I told him. "Better give me the short version."

"Yesterday, I'm driving down the road minding my own business when I get a blowout. Surprised the hell out of me, what with the tires I've got on the truck. I pull over and get out, and discover that I drove over a caltrop. You know, a star-nail? I haven't seen one of those since I was doing jungle training in Honduras." A caltrop was several nails welded together and bent so that no matter how it was thrown on the ground, a point would always be sticking up. Their sole purpose, currently, was puncturing tires. They'd been invented to deal with the opposing army's cavalry.

"Oh, you weren't driving by the plant, were you? Everyone avoids that area just for that reason."

"Thanks for the warning," he said disgustedly.

"Picketing strikers."

"I figured that out. I went over there and saw a bunch more caltrops on the driveway leading into the plant."

"The management hired scab workers," I explained. "The union guys are really pissed. They've been destroying paper boxes, or setting them on fire, harassing the delivery people on their routes. One of the things must've got kicked into the street."

"I might've been a little more understanding of the working man's plight if they hadn't been standing there laughing at my flat tire. You know how much it costs to get a tow?"

"Waitaminit! I hear about this on one of the top-of-the-hour updates on the radio yesterday? They said it was a scuffle between union guys and scab workers."

"Would have been a hell of a lot more than a scuffle if the cops hadn't shown up when they did."

"Well, you're not incarcerated, that's a good sign."

"Aw, it never came to anything." Bob smiled evilly. "Cops rolled up right then, and all they saw was one lone passerby being set upon by union thugs. They called for backup and ran to my rescue."

Ron laughed and shook his head. Bob went on. "Bunch of fat beer drinkers. By the time the cops pulled everybody off me and cuffed them two more squad cars had shown up. The cops thought *they* were the ones responsible for all the injuries to the strikers, although I bet they're still not sure how they managed to break all those fingers."

"I thought I heard there were a couple strikers in the hospital," I said.

"Well, I did get hold of one of their picket signs," Bob admitted with a smile. Then he frowned. "But I've been spending a lot of time killing actual real bad guys. These strikers were just morons. So I had a little fun with them, nothing serious."

The news report I'd heard had made it sound like a near-riot, with half a dozen guys in the hospital with broken bones and contusions. "Bob," I said, "sometimes you are one scary motherfucker."

"Everybody thinks they know how to fight, but hardly anyone does," he said, and I had to agree with him. "The cops didn't seem too upset about the broken bones," he went on. "There wasn't a lot of love lost between the cops and the strikers. While they were waiting for EMS to show up the cops were falling all over themselves to convince me to sign a complaint against the union guys for assault."

"God I wish I'd been there," Ron said, chuckling.

Bob laid back down on the bench and did another twenty or so reps.

"To make a long story short," he said when he'd finished, "that blue Lumina outside is my Mom's. The Blazer's spare was flat, if you can believe it. Apparently the bead wasn't sealed right when they put the tire on the wheel."

Ron came over to me, a can of Coke in his hand. "Any news?"

"Any of you guys happen to see the local TV news last night?"

After being treated to a universal chorus of shaking heads I informed them about the whole Bonnie Jenkins incident, then told them about the visit I'd had from Reilly and Griffin.

"And I'm really worried about it too," I told Ron. "Who knows how far they're going to get thrown off track with this stuff. I'm almost tempted to have you tell them about your dad working for the CIA or whoever, but if there ever was a chance of convincing them of your seriousness, it's gone now. They'll just try to connect you or me to Bufonte or who knows what, maybe Jamaican drug smugglers." I pointed at Bob. "And they're definitely going to want to talk to you, give you the third degree about any 'mob ties' you might have."

"It'll be my pleasure," Bob said with a big nasty grin.

"No, you don't," I scolded him. "You don't know how this goes. They talk to you twice, and you accidentally tell them blue one time and green another, they'll lock you up for lying to the FBI. It's called a process crime and they'll do it just so they can sweat you. Refuse to talk to them without a lawyer present, and don't worry about them telling you it makes you look guilty." I waved my finger around the room. "That goes for all of you. They want to ask about George

Kelly, fine, but anything about two years ago you say nothing."

"I could tell Griffin was an asshole the first time I met him," Ron said. "One of those guys you want to slap just to get that superior expression off their face." He paused. "Anybody, ah, mention anything about money?"

In the process of looking for Jerry I, or actually the boys, had come across a large sum of cash. Kellogg had paid three techs handsomely for some stolen computer equipment, and the briefcase we'd found had been what was left of that payoff. Kellogg's people had killed the techs, and we killed Kellogg shortly after finding the money. Which meant no one knew we had it.

The boys hadn't seen any need to turn the orphaned cash over to the authorities, and I can't say I had much of a problem with their decision. They split it amongst themselves, and while none of them were rich, they each could have bought a nice starter home for cash if they'd been willing to brave an IRS audit. So far they'd been smart about the money, doing nothing to attract attention, but they were also college-age males—none of them had cheap, slow cars.

I shook my head. "No." I nodded at the computer. "Can any of you guys do anything with that thing other than play games?"

"I know a little bit about programming," Steve said. "Why?"

I told them about my lack of success in getting the disk to cough up any secrets.

"That's way beyond my pitiful skills," Steve apologized. His eyebrows went up and he turned to Bob. "What about your Mom?"

"Yeah, she might be able to do something. She does a

lot of computer stuff at work," he told me, "and I know she knows about encrypting disks and passwords and stuff. Maybe she knows how to un-encrypt one."

"What do you think's on it?" Ron said.

I shook my head. "We find out the answer to that, maybe we'll be closer to figuring out what happened to your dad. But, for all I know, 'Travel' is a list of expenses from the last time your dad went to the Windsor Ballet." To native Detroiters, *Windsor Ballet* meant any one of the numerous totally nude strip clubs across the river in Canada.

"Where is it now?"

"At my office. You want to head over whenever you're done here?" I said to Bob.

"Yeah, I'm just about done lifting, then I was going to run for an hour. And I wouldn't be surprised if some of the Extra-Special Special Agents stop by to ask me some questions before I got out of here. So I'll see you when I see you."

"Don't mess around with those guys," I said warningly. I waved my hand to include the room. "Any of you." I felt it bore repeating. "These guys are all bent out of shape already. Just be nice and polite and answer all their questions about George, claim ignorance on anything mafia-related, and maybe they'll lose interest in all this mob bullshit once they see there's nothing to it. Something's gotta break soon, this is ridiculous." I paused. "You're running for an hour? How far do you go?"

"I have an alternating schedule when I'm not deployed," Bob told me. "I run for an hour one day, not trying to go fast. Usually do nine- or ten-minute miles. Next day I do six miles as fast as I can. Slow one day, fast the next, slow, fast, then I take a day off."

"How fast can you run six?"

He made a face. "I've been trying to break six-minute miles, but so far no joy. Best I've ever done is thirty-six fifty-eight, which works out to six minutes and ten seconds a mile average. I think I'm carrying too much muscle. And I've dropped fifteen pounds of muscle since high school."

"I hate you," I told him, and sighed. "I hate running fast."

"So do I," he told me. "But I've never been in a gunfight that didn't start or end in a footrace. Except with you guys."

On the drive over to my office I thought there might have been a car following me, but my route was so direct, and traffic so heavy, that I never could tell for sure. If I was being followed, it had to be the feds. They were so ballsy and cocksure they wouldn't care if I spotted the tail.

As I walked in the door my phone was ringing. I somehow managed to snag it before the machine answered.

"What is it with you?" Scott said by way of greeting. "Are you cursed or something?"

"Nice to talk to you, too."

"I mean, I'm assuming you saw the story on the news. They said they tried to talk to you, but that you had no comment."

"I don't even want to talk about it."

"I bet. What's Kelly say?"

"You know the feds are taking that load of bullshit seriously?" I told him. "Two of them came into my office this morning and gave me the third degree."

"I guess it was only a matter of time before that came back and bit us all in the ass. I'm surprised nobody's called me yet. My name's all over that paperwork, and Scarelli had more bullets in him from my gun than yours."

"Yeah, well, you never met with Bufonte while the feds

were rolling tape." I sighed. "Do you have any good news? Do the feds have any leads on a suspect? Besides me, that is?"

"They don't have dick. I hear they're interviewing George Kelly's coworkers for the third time, and our detectives have been asked to help in looking through old phone records and tax returns. I'm told a couple of the agents have been heard mumbling that they think this thing is just a big setup, that Kelly staged his own disappearance so he could run off with some slut."

"You've got to be kidding."

"Aw, it's just their frustration talking," Scott told me. "They've got nothing."

"What about the dead guy, Hohimer? Didn't you make an anonymous call?"

"Yeah, last night. So far I haven't heard anything on that. Probably because they didn't find anything more than you did. That's got to be why they're re-interviewing George's coworkers. They've got a whole new set of questions to ask, now that Hohimer's inconveniently popped up with a bullet in his throat."

"Christ. I'm down to one idea, and I'm not too hopeful about that."

"That's one more than I've got. Care to tell me about it?"

"Maybe tomorrow. I don't want you to get your hopes up."

Ninety minutes later I was four pages into a report I was typing for a client when Bob walked through my door and threw himself onto the couch I keep in the corner.

"Dealing with these FBI guys might actually be fun if I could forget why they're hanging around. They're so torqued up."

"Yeah, well, your idea of fun is a lot different than mine."

I finished typing a sentence, then got up and walked over to the couch. I'd hidden the disk inside the base of a lamp on the table next to the couch. Bob's eyes followed me, not saying a word. He knew I came by my paranoia honestly. He then asked about getting together for dinner Wednesday night. I'd completely forgotten his fiancée was flying into town that evening until he mentioned it.

"Yeah, that sounds good," I told him. "I'm dying to meet her."

"Maybe we can go out to eat someplace nice. You're an old guy, you probably know where to find a fancy restaurant around here." He looked at me out of the corner of his eye.

"Do you know how to eat steak without using your fingers?" I asked. With a smile on his face he flipped me the bird and headed out.

I went back to work on my report. I got another page done before the phone rang again. It was Jeff, my wife's brother.

"So what's up with this disk?" he said. "You working for a company having internal theft problems?"

"Could be," I said. I explained, as best I could, everything I'd discovered about the disk, and all the failures I'd had trying to get it to run. Of course, I'd just given Bob the disk, but maybe Jeff could give me instructions and I could write them down and use them later if Bob's Mom didn't have any luck.

"This guy whose disk it is," Jeff said. "Would he have had access to good encryption programs? Or just some stuff he might've pulled off the Internet?"

"Anything he had would have been the best. Like, CIA good. Does that make it a lot more difficult?"

"You could say that. If he had a top-of-the-line encryption program, it might take me years to decode the data. Even the crappy programs sometimes take a Cray hours to crack. You mentioned the CIA, and I know you were joking, but seriously, the encryption stuff that's free for the taking on the Internet now is better than anything the CIA had back in the early eighties."

"You're not filling me with a lot of optimism. I was hoping you could tell me over the phone how to break this sucker. I've got a pen ready to write down all the commands and everything." He laughed so hard I thought a lung was going to fly out of the phone.

"Oh man, that's good," he said. I could imagine him wiping the tears out of his eyes. "I've got to tell the guys that one. Hell, if computers were that easy to figure out, they wouldn't need programmers like me, and I wouldn't be making six figures a year." I'd been wondering if he would somehow find a way to work a mention of his income into this conversation. I shouldn't have worried. "I'dve had to become an accountant, wear a suit to work every day."

"Maybe you'd have been able to find a firm that would let you to wear your Metallica shirts on casual Fridays." I thanked him for nothing and hung up.

I'd finished the report and was busy printing it out when the phone rang yet again.

"Hi honey," I heard in my ear. "I can't believe you're actually answering the phone."

"Why?"

"Well, so far today both Channels Two and Four have called, asking for your comment on the so-called story Channel Seven ran last night."

"Oh Christ."

"I'm still waiting to hear from Fifty. Maybe they're actually doing an investigation to double-check their info before they broadcast a story. Most of these bozos are as bad as *The Enquirer*. Pretty soon they'll allege the KGB, UFO's, and the Girl Scouts of America are involved in George's disappearance."

"What'd you tell them?"

"No comment, what do you think? I managed not to blow up at anybody this time. But I figured at least one of the crack media investigators over there might have two brain cells working in tandem and look up your office number in the yellow pages."

"Not yet. Thankfully."

"What time are you going to be home tonight? I know you've got that house call over in Birmingham today."

"Oh shit! I completely forgot about that." A high-end clothing store had been robbed recently, and had contracted me to see what needed to be changed with their alarm system, if anything. I quickly checked my daily planner for the appointment time, then looked at my watch. I just might make it in time, if traffic cooperated.

"Igottago—couplehours—seeyoulaterloveyabye," I blurted into the phone and threw it down.

5:46 p.m.

Kelly was making another grandiose dinner in the kitchen, and the smell had begun to drift through the house. In spite of the aroma, all I could think of was Bob lifting weights with his broken finger, while I'd only run twice in the last week and a half, and the only weightlifting I'd done was a few pushups. I walked over to the kitchen and stuck my head through the doorway. After greeting me at the door, Oscar returned to her spot behind Kelly, eyeballing the stove with single-minded intensity.

"How long 'til we eat?" I said to Kelly as she stirred something in a bowl.

"I just started making dinner! You want fast food, go to McDonalds. I try to make a nice meal and—"

"Hold it, hold it," I cut in. "All I wanted to know was if I had enough time to go jogging before we eat."

"Oh. Yes, you can go, but be back and ready to eat in an hour. Are you going to take the baby with you?"

I looked at Oscar and made a face. "What, with food cooking? I'd get more exercise trying to wrestle her away from the stove than I would running." I gave Kelly a quick smooch on the cheek and then ran upstairs to change.

My winter running attire was pretty utilitarian, a thick grey Michigan State hooded sweatshirt, olive drab army fatigue pants, and well-worn running shoes. If it was bitterly cold outside I might throw on another sweatshirt, or a knit cap.

After all the things that had happened to me in my short life, I'd made a promise to myself to never step out of my house unarmed. I had no interest in dying young, and now that Kelly was pregnant there were two people depending on my continued existence. Jogging, however, presented a bit of a problem: running with a gun is a pain in the ass, sometimes literally.

The sweat alone would ruin my good leather holsters in just a few outings—I knew that from experience. Fanny pack holsters were an improvement, but I hated how they bounced even with an airweight .38 snubnose inside. I normally wore my .45 on my right hip, but I didn't like jogging like that—I was paranoid it would fall out of the holster, and I wouldn't notice for half a mile. Besides, my

.45 was way too heavy to run with, no matter where I wedged it on my body. I didn't want to carry a little mouse gun, though—a little .22 or .25 could kill someone, but in the sixty seconds or so it took for them to bleed to death they'd probably keep busy expressing their displeasure with me for shooting them. They were called 'mouse guns' for a reason.

I was cruising the aisles of a gun show, looking for something suitable, when I saw it. A titanium-framed snubnose revolver. Lighter even than the aircraft-aluminum framed "Airweight" snubbies that had been around for years, and just as rust resistant, this gun came with a nice rubber grip that no amount of my sweat would ruin and held five rounds of .38 Special. Especially coming out of such a short barrel, a .38 was no match for my .45, but it beat the heck out of a .22. The little gun was so light it bucked like a mule, and its small sights with their short radius were wishful thinking at best, but if I had to use it while jogging it would be at conversational distances anyway. Six or eight feet, max, which meant I'd be pointing, not aiming. I also picked up a cheap inside-the-waistband nylon holster. Tucked into the front of my pants it held the gun securely and wouldn't get ruined by sweat the way a leather holster would. And if it did, it was cheap and easily replaceable.

Paranoid? Obsessive, taking a gun everywhere I went, even jogging? My theory has always been that it's better to have a gun and not need it, than to need a gun and not have it. Like a seatbelt, or a fire extinguisher. I wasn't alone. Most cops I knew carried backup guns on duty even though most of them had never had to fire a single shot. It was also why they carried at least one spare handcuff key on their person, on or off duty. Bad guys using handcuffs on hostages is common. No cop would ever want that to happen to him.

Thank God most criminals were idiots, otherwise they'd all be secreting handcuff keys about their person on the off-chance they'd be nabbed. I could only remember one instance where that had happened, but one dead and one injured US Marshall was more than enough to burn the lesson into my brain. I still had a handcuff key on my keyring, and I hadn't carried a badge in years.

I loaded the snubbie and set it on the bedside table as I quickly stretched, then wedged it in its holster halfway between my belly button and my hip bone before heading out. Kelly yelled goodbye as I pulled the side door shut, then I was outside and heading down the street at a decent pace.

After about ten minutes I'd worked up a good sweat, and had hit my second wind. It felt like I was doing better than my normal eight-and-a-half-minute miles as I headed into the setting sun.

The sun dropped close to the horizon, and even though the sky was brightly lit the ground around me was getting dark and hard to see. Most of the occasional cars passing me had their parking lights on, if not their headlights, and I began to question my habit of running in the evening without the benefit of reflective clothing. If my subdivision had had sidewalks there wouldn't have been a problem, but apparently the city planners had decided sidewalks should be reserved for poorer neighborhoods. Up ahead was the intersection with Brewster Road, where I would turn right and then have a wide asphalt path to run on.

With my breath coming easily and my legs pumping evenly on the slight downhill I angled for the corner. I heard faint automobile noise behind me and turned my head. In my peripheral vision I could see a car had just turned the corner a few hundred yards behind me. The sky was so bright the driver probably didn't even know how hard he was to spot without any lights on. And was I silhouetted against the bright sky, or just a dim shape against a dark background? I picked up my pace a little. The intersection with Brewster was dark, and I wanted to make the corner ahead of the car so I didn't get accidentally run over.

Fifty yards out I turned my head again and saw the car was closer behind me than I expected. I did a few mental calculations, gauged the remaining distance to the corner, and accelerated into a sprint. What the hell, I'd race the car to the corner. Bob wouldn't let an imminent cramp slow him down, why should I? I began pumping my arms to gain speed, and could feel the .38 bouncing hard against my pubic bone. Maybe I should have put a belt on.

The last thirty feet to the corner was an incline, which meant the driver behind me would be looking right at the bright sky as he reached the corner. I could only hope he'd already seen me, since he was damn near on my ass. A car swooshed by on Brewster, its tires hissing on the pavement made wet by melting snow.

Determined to win this race of my own making, and not get killed in the process (the more important of the two objectives), I gave my all in the last five yards. I hooked the corner onto the asphalt path barely fifteen feet in front of the car. I heard the driver hit the brakes, like he'd just seen me and panicked even though I was no longer in danger. I slowed down, breathing hard, and looked behind me to see the car stopping quickly at the corner, its tires skidding slightly on a wet spot. For some weird reason, its passenger door swung open, and I thought I heard a muffled male voice, almost sounding like a curse. Maybe the door hadn't been securely closed. Of course, looking over your shoulder while you jog is a dumb move, and my toe took that particular moment to catch on an upthrust crack in the asphalt. I stumbled.

An orange light winked at me from inside the darkness of the car as I fell to my right. My knee banged off the pavement; then, hands outstretched, I slid down fifteen feet of wet grassy bank. I splashed to a stop wrist deep in icy water.

"Ow," I said reflexively, but I wasn't quite sure if I'd stupidly managed to actually injure myself or just add an extra bruise or two to the collection.

A buzzing, burning sensation set fire to my left shoulder blade, and for a second I wondered if I'd pulled it in the fall. Then the reality of what had happened reared its ugly head and slapped me in the face.

The orange light I'd seen flare at me from inside the car had been the flash from the muzzle of a discharging gun. The thomping metallic cough which accompanied the light I'd seen hadn't been the sound of nearby traffic. It was the unique signature of a sound-suppressed gun being fired. And the itchy, roaring pain now lancing through the left side of my back meant I'd been hit.

I climbed to my knees in the muddy, frigid water, darkness all around me. Shocked, panicked, mind racing but in neutral, I froze, then grabbed at the gun in my waistband. It wasn't there. Biting back a curse, I looked around frantically for the snubnose.

The ditch and embankment were black with encroaching night. I shoved my hands into the ice-cold ditchwater, searching under and around my knees. Rocks and sticks were all I found. Then I saw an off-color glint four feet up the bank and lunged for it. I fumbled with the snubbie, finally getting it into my wet, numb hands. I pointed it up the slope where the dark bank was silhouetted against the greying sky.

Crouched in the dark I waited, shaking with cold and fear and adrenaline, staring past the pitifully small gun that I had somehow believed would be adequate. Without a sound the silhouette of a man's head and shoulders appeared against the night sky at the top of the bank. I fired twice, the report loud and sharp in the ditch. A huge fireball ballooned from the revolver's short barrel, and my vision sparkled orange and green. When I could see again the man was gone. I assumed I'd missed, but at least I'd made him duck.

If I stayed where I was I was dead. Nearly half my ammo was gone, with unknown results. At least one person was in the dark above me. He was better armed, on the high ground, and knew exactly where I was. Backing away from the bank would just expose me to whoever was up top, and charging up the slippery grass in an imitation of a frontal assault, toy gun in hand, was not an option. I swung my head frantically left and right, looking for hard cover or an exit route.

The gully was so dark I missed it the first time, but then my eyes registered the darker black. It was the mouth of a culvert. The hole was maybe three feet wide, a concrete pipe running under Brewster to the opposite side, designed to drain the ditch during rainstorms. No grate blocking it, rusted away or never installed, I couldn't tell. I looked up at the top of the slope again, at the small gun in my hand, and then scrambled into the dark pipe.

In front of me was nothing but black. The only sensory input I had was the scrape of concrete on my hands and knees, the gurgle of water. At any moment I expected a hail of bullets to come tearing after me, ripping me apart from the ass up, but more speed was impossible in the cramped quarters. I tried to keep out of the small stream running through the conduit to eliminate any splashing. My ragged breathing echoed loudly in my ears.

After what seemed like ten minutes of scrambling and still nothing in front of me but more darkness I began to panic, thinking I had crawled into a dead end. Just when I was about to stop and turn around I saw the lighter patch of black in front of me. I put even more speed into my shuffling crabwalk and the patch resolved itself into a grey circle. The end of the pipe.

I pumped my arms and legs faster than I thought humanly possible, scraping all of my knuckles raw and feeling my pants rip. I wanted desperately to glance back and see if anyone was peering into the pipe, or coming after me, but that would only have slowed me down and my only interest in life was speed. That and not dying while inside a cement drainpipe.

I finally reached the end of the concrete tomb. As great as my desire to get out of there was, before emerging I raised the snubnose and stuck my head out of the pipe mouth, looking around and up at the top of the slope over the top of the gun. As soon as I saw I was alone, I got my ass out of that hole. It felt like it had taken me an hour to traverse the concrete pipe, but it had probably been less than a minute.

Breathing heavily, I crawled up the short, grassy slope on my knees, the little pistol held ready. When I got to the top I poked my head up and looked across the road to see the car still parked at the corner, its headlights now on and pointed directly at me. I ducked involuntarily, then raised my head to look again. With the headlights right in my face I couldn't tell if anyone was inside the car or not. On the opposite sidewalk at a point near where I had tripped I saw the faint outline of a crouching man. He was moving slowly along the sidewalk, head bent down and moving back and forth, something in his hands.

My little pistol with its negligible sights was useless beyond fifty feet in daylight, and he was that distance from me or more, in near darkness. Maybe I should have backed off, or gone home to better arm myself, but all I could see was red. Whoever he was, he had just tried to kill me, and I wasn't about to let him go.

As a car approached from the north, tires hissing on the wet pavement, I got into a crouch and waited. At just the right moment I darted out across the sidewalk and into the street, passing just behind the car's bumper as it sped by. The hiss of tires drowned out the wet slap of my shoes as I ran across the road, but as I reached the far curb the man crouched in front of me must have sensed something. He spun around, standing up and bringing whatever was in his hands to bear. I fired instinctively at him and dove to the ground with a grunt, slamming my chin on the asphalt, fired twice more, and rolled away from him.

The man gasped and the dark object in his hands sputtered once, then he fell over sideways. In the dim light I saw him clutching at the wet sod. He muttered something, gurgled, then rolled onto his back and lay still. I didn't move for quite a while. My ears were ringing from the gunshots and sharp blow to my chin. I bit back the pain as I lay belly down on the wet grass, feet hanging into the gutter, eyes wide and heart beating, the now empty snubnose still clutched in my hand.

When no one came out of the car after me, and the man I'd shot remained still, I low-crawled across the sidewalk. In the dark, I discovered two bodies in front of me, side by side.

The indirect glow from the headlights of occasional passing cars helped somewhat, but I still had to use my hands as much as my eyes to examine the bodies. The man I'd just shot was hot to the touch, a dark shiny spot on his throat where one bullet had entered. The puddle of blood beneath him was black as oil. The second man was curled into a fetal position. The left side of his shirt was sticky to the touch; I assumed the stickiness was blood.

The guy with the chest wound had to've been the person I'd first fired at, and I was crawling through the pipe while his partner got out of the car and tried to figure out what had happened, and where I had gone.

I felt around blindly in the wet grass until my hand found the object the second man had dropped. It was heavy and blocky, and when I held it up to silhouette it against the sky I saw it was a MAC-10 submachinegun with a sound suppressor screwed onto its barrel. It was an ugly, compact, and very size-efficient package. It was also something I'd only ever seen in movies.

I stuck the snubbie back into my waistband. Holding the MAC-10 tightly in front of me I approached the car, its passenger door still hanging open, headlights streaming across Brewster. Even with the door open, no dome light illuminated the passenger compartment. It was empty.

Unsure of what to do next, I looked back and forth from the bodies to the car. Then I heard the crackle of a radio from the car. I found the walkie-talkie on the front seat and picked it up.

The radio crackled again. "Two's in position," I heard.

"Oh fuck." I threw the radio into the car and scrambled in after it, tossing the SMG onto the dash. The car was already running and I threw it into drive and floored it. The passenger door slammed closed as I slewed onto Brewster and tried to put the pedal through the floor.

A quarter mile from my house, doing eighty on a residential street, I cut my engine and lights and coasted in Neutral. One hundred and fifty yards out I hit the parking brake, no brake lights to flash, and pulled to the curb.

As soon as the car was stopped I was out the door running, the MAC-10 in my hands. Six houses before mine I angled away from the street and hugged the front porches, slowing to a walk. I unfolded and extended the gun's wire stock and planted it firmly against my shoulder. Then I stopped, and scanned the neighborhood.

My street was typically quiet, a few porch lights on here and there. No movement on either side of the street, but it was dark enough so that twenty people could have been hiding in the nearby bushes and I never would've seen them. What I did see, however, was the dark sedan parked on the street two houses past mine. Nobody ever parked on the street there, and I didn't recognize the car. I moved closer and squinted. The car was empty.

Two yards down I paused and scanned the front of my house. Even though it was dark I knew the shapes and colors of my house well enough to tell there was no one hiding in my front yard. I moved closer again and crouched in the shadow of my next-door-neighbor's bushes. From there I could see my front yard and most of the side of my house. My kitchen light and a few others were on, but I didn't see any movement through the windows.

Cheek pressed firmly against the weapon's wire stock, looking over the crude sights of the SMG, I slowly stepped around my neighbor's front porch and moved toward the back of my house, keeping to the shadows. Frost was just starting to form on my lawn.

Just as I reached the back corner of my home I heard Oscar erupt inside, barking and snarling like I'd never heard before. My heart leapt into my throat and I charged into my backyard, vaulting the railing onto my deck. Just as I landed outside the sliding glass door, which to my horror I saw was slightly ajar, I heard a quick volley of shots from inside the house. Then a woman wailing in pain.

I shoved open the glass door and went in gun first, hooking left toward the kitchen. The lights were blazing and the whole house smelled like food, but the kitchen was empty. I followed the sound of moaning through the dining room, coming around the corner into the living room with my finger on the trigger, palms sweaty on the gun.

My wife was on the floor, on her knees beside Oscar. Both of them were covered in blood. Kelly had Oscar's head in her hands, rocking back and forth, keening and moaning. I swept the room, but the only other person there was the guy on his back in the middle of the floor.

The man's shirt was rapidly turning red, and his left forearm was a total loss, the flesh punctured and ripped. Another suppressed MAC-10 lay at his side. I lowered my SMG slightly.

"Kelly," I said. No response. "Kelly!" I said again, louder. "Is there anyone else in the house?"

She struggled to her feet, eyes wide, tears streaming down her cheeks. She wiped at her face, but only succeeded in smearing blood across herself.

"He killed her," she said disbelievingly, her voice faint. She looked down at the body on the floor.

"You killed my baby. YOU MOTHERFUCKER, YOU KILLED MY BABY!" she screamed. She raised her right hand and pointed her .357 at the dead man. I was nearly knocked off my feet by the deafening, concussive blasts of the Magnums as she fired and fired and fired, until the only sound I could hear was the hammer snapping down on spent primers and her weeping. I walked through the smoke and stood at her side.

"Are you hurt? Are you injured?" I said forcefully, trying to get her eyes to focus on me. Finally she looked up and gave a little shake of her head, eyes haunted. Her gaze started to turn inward again and I grabbed her shoulder and shook it.

She looked at me, and new tears started to flow. But her eyes stayed focused. I stepped to the small wood chest with the open drawer and grabbed something out of it.

"Speedloader," I said, holding it up. I tossed it at her, and somehow she managed to catch it. "Reload!" I told her sharply, trying to get her to snap out of it. I knelt by the dead man, popped the magazine out of his MAC, and shoved it into my pocket as a spare.

"You're bleeding," she told me. "Your whole back's covered in blood." Her voice was dull with shock, with a fine edge of hysteria.

"I'm okay," I snapped. I shouldered the MAC again and headed up the stairs. By the time I'd cleared the second floor and come back down Kelly had reloaded the Smith and stood there uncertainly with it in her hand. I pointed up the stairs.

"You've got three minutes to pack," I told her, trying to keep my emotions compartmentalized and out of the way. "Your purse, contact lens stuff, and whatever else you can't live without."

She blinked, confused, and opened her mouth. "Wha—"

"You're going on a trip," I told her. Then I checked the garage for uninvited visitors. From there I went down into the basement. My house was secure, but the rounds Kelly had fired into the man's prostrate body had gone through him, our living room floor, and ricocheted all around the basement. Blood was already seeping through and dripping onto the concrete floor.

Back on the first floor I was glad to see Kelly was gone. Even through the ringing in my ears I could hear her upstairs frantically grabbing things. I set the subgun down and called Scott on my cell phone. While I was listening to it ring my eyes were drawn to a swirled, pitted spot on the MAC's receiver. Someone had professionally removed the weapon's serial number with acid.

"Hello?"

"It's me. I need you. Walton and Old Perch, bank parking lot, fifteen minutes. Bring a change of clothes and guns." I hit **END** before he could get a word out and dialed again.

"Hello?"

"Carla, put Ron on. This is John Phault." There must have been something in my voice, because she didn't offer one word of argument. I heard the phone being set down and her say something. Twenty seconds later I heard approaching footsteps.

"Yeah."

"It's me. Are the feds still taping this or did they shut it off when I didn't turn out to be a kidnapper?"

"Off, I think, but who knows for sure with them? Your name no longer brings smiles to everyone's face around here."

"Okay. Shut up and listen. Twenty minutes, the Fish and the Farmer. Don't be late."

"What's the occasion?"

"Fire Drill." It was a prearranged signal, and I didn't have to explain. I hung up without waiting for a response, grabbed the MAC, and ran up the stairs. "Time to go."

Kelly had a small bag and was stuffing underwear and toiletries into it. She looked a little more focused but still quite rattled.

"I need another minute."

"I'll go get the car. Come outside when you see me pull up." I grabbed my Colt off the bedside table, stuffed it in my waistband, then ran back down the stairs, yanked open the front door, and jogged down the sidewalk. Hopefully none of the nearby porchlights were strong enough for my neighbors to see the SMG in my hand. They were my only real worry. If anybody had heard the shots and recognized them for what they were the cops could already be on their way. I was pretty sure my house had muffled the shots sufficiently, but even if it hadn't, no one kept their windows open in December. I hoped.

The driver's door was still hanging open and I jumped into my confiscated vehicle. It was an older Pontiac, something nobody would remember seeing. Stolen, I'm sure. I popped the parking brake, started the car, and flipped on the lights. I crawled slowly down the street, eyes darting rapidly back and forth, checking for anything unusual. Nothing caught my attention, so I eased to the curb in front of my house.

Kelly came out a second later carrying the overnight bag in one hand and her revolver in the other. Ten feet away she stopped, realizing she didn't recognize the car.

"It's me, it's me!" I said quickly, opening the door so she could see me and waving for her to lower the gun that was pointed at my face.

"Whose car is this?"

"I'll tell you about it later. Get in," I urged her. She was standing in the middle of the sidewalk, looking ten months pregnant, with a gun in her hand and blood all over her face and clothes. Any cops driving by would think we were filming a Stephen King novel.

The car was moving before she had her door closed. "Where are we going?" She pulled back a sniffle and set the revolver down in her lap.

"We're meeting Scott in about eight minutes. I think he might be in danger too."

"You said we were going on a trip."

"Yeah, you and Scott."

"You're leaving me?" she said, horrified.

"No, you're leaving me. Listen," I said slowly, trying to soften the impact, "I don't know what the hell is going on. This has to be related to George's disappearance. I can't think of anybody other than spooks that'd send three guys with suppressed submachineguns after me. It's fucking nuts, there's no reason for them to want to kill me." I thought of the disk. "Grab me maybe, see what I know, but not kill me just straight out of the blue. Which means there's shit going on I don't know about, but should, and that scares me."

"But why do I have to go without you? I'm pregnant!"

"Honey, if they're after me I'm the last person you want near you. Look what happened tonight. They don't care about you except to get to me. Besides, I won't be able to find out what's going on if I'm spending all my time worrying about you. Especially when you're pregnant."

"I don't want to leave you. I don't want you to leave me. What if something happens with the baby?"

"Kelly! If we're both dead, it won't really matter, will it?" I hated doing it so roughly, but I didn't see any other way. "I'm not a damn doctor, if anything happens I won't be any help anyway. I'm in danger, which means anybody around me is in danger too."

"That's not the only reason you're doing this," she said angrily.

"Godammit, we've had this conversation! I refuse to let my life be dictated by fear or the actions of others. I will not allow myself to be threatened or intimidated. If I leave now with you I might be safe, momentarily at least, but it won't solve the problem. I'll have disappeared and have no idea why I had to." *And I'd have a hard time living with myself, and you'd have a hard time living with me*, I declined to add, even though it would've been true.

"Look, if you're around I'll be worrying about your safety instead of trying to find the motherfuckers that did this to us. That's why we're meeting Scott. The two of you can get out of here until it's safe. He can look after you."

"*He's* the cop," she said indignantly. "*He's* the one that should be staying put, not you. And *he's* single."

"Goddammit, I'm not just responsible for your safety, I'm responsible for the guys' safety too. I did something to piss someone off, and for all I know they're going after Ron next. He's the one that called me into this. And you and I both know there is no way in hell I'll ever be able to convince Ron or the rest of them to leave. No matter what happens. If I can get you out of harm's way I'll be able to concentrate on keeping them alive and out of trouble."

"Why don't we just go to the cops? Can't they protect us?"

"Maybe," I said. "Which isn't good enough. Besides, if I'm locked up, I won't be able to find out who did this. And dropping bodies means they're going to put me behind bars until they figure out what the hell happened."

"That's their job!"

"Yeah, well, I don't care. And I don't trust them to do the job right. Look, if these guys had succeeded in killing us the cops would probably figure it was some sort of mob payback after all the bullshit that's been on TV. I might be the only chance Ron has of finding out what happened to his father. Until you're out of danger I'll be worried and distracted and that won't do me, you, or the baby any good."

"But—"

"I'm not going to talk about this any more," I said firmly.

We sat in strained silence for the next two minutes. I couldn't even look at her, I felt like such a shithead. But that was the way it had to be.

I tapped the brake and then swung the car up the driveway and into the bank's parking lot. The lot was empty and I turned the car around so it faced out.

"Tomorrow, have Scott take you to the bank where we have the safety deposit box. Take the money, but don't take the gun out of there unless you really feel you'll need it. Scott should know the right way to do this, but if you've got questions, just remember to use cash for everything, no credit cards. Go somewhere you've never been before, someplace you've never thought of going to. Someplace I'd never think to look."

6:19 p.m.

Scott pulled in with a squeal of tires and the smell of burning brakes. I got out of the car as he stopped in front of us and threw open his door.

"What the fuck is going on?" He looked from me to

Kelly in the car, then did a double-take and stared at me again.

I guess I was a sight. I sure felt like I'd been run over by a truck, but I had more important things to think about than my own injuries. There were scrapes and cuts all over my face and hands, not to mention all the blood on my back from the gunshot wound. It had to be what John Wayne used to call a simple 'flesh wound', a graze, because even though it hurt like hell I was still able to move my left arm freely. Scott stared at the MAC-10 that I'd unconsciously grabbed off the dash, and kept staring at it as I gave him a thumbnail sketch of the last half hour of my life.

"You've got to be fucking kidding me," he said, still sitting in the car and looking a little dazed. His gun was in his hand, and a shotgun was propped against the passenger seat.

"Do I look like I'm fucking kidding?" Kelly got out of the car and stood beside her open door. I jabbed a finger at her. "Does she look like she's fucking kidding?" Scott saw the blood all over Kelly and the look on her face, her gun held uncertainly down along her leg.

"Holy Christ."

I waved to Kelly and she jerkily walked over and stood beside me.

"I'm telling you," I said to Scott, "I don't know what the fuck is going on. I can't think of any reason for anybody to want to kill me. And the way these guys worked it, I can't help but think it has something to do with George."

"The way they did it doesn't make any sense. Two separate teams? And while you're jogging? Be easier to have hit you at your office, or at home when you open the door."

"It's not the way I would have done it, but who cares?"

Scott shook his head. "This has got to have something

to do with George's disappearance, but I'll be damned if I can figure out the connection. You've been out of the DEA for too many years for someone to be coming after you for that, especially using three guys with submachineguns. If this was 1985 and we were in Miami, maybe. But here, now…"

"That's what's scaring me. If they're coming after me, and Kelly, who knows what's gonna happen next? I'm thinking, everybody knows me and you are tight, and have been talking about the case since this thing started. I wouldn't be surprised if they came after you, too."

"Why?"

"How the fuck should I know? Why did they come after *me*? Maybe they think I'm getting too close to something, or saw something I shouldn't have."

"But who the fuck is *they*?"

"I don't know!" I shouted, then took a breath. "Probably the same people that snatched George, whoever that is. Listen," I told him, "I want you to take Kelly."

"What?"

"Take her, take her and disappear, before they come after you."

"You're crazy."

"Am I?"

"John, there's no way they'd come after me. I'm a fucking Lieutenant with the Oakland County Sheriff's Department. Not only wouldn't they want the heat involved with killing me, they've got no reason to do it. I'm only peripherally involved in this."

"How do you know you're only peripherally involved? I'm just a friend of the missing guy's son, and they send three guys in two cars with radios and suppressed submachineguns that've had their serial numbers removed! If they decide to come after you, God knows how many people they'll use."

"I am not running and hiding," he said firmly.

"Don't be stupid," I told him. "Now is not the time to be stubborn."

"What do you think you're doing? You're sending Kelly with me, but where are you going to be? Are you running?"

"Somebody's got to stick around and try to find out what's happening."

"Yeah, well, I don't have a pregnant wife."

What was this, a conspiracy? Didn't I just have this conversation? "They're not after Kelly," I said. "She just got in the way. I want you to get her out of the way."

"What's wrong with you?"

"I've got other commitments. Ron and Jerry and the rest of the boys, they may be in danger too. And you know them, there's no way in hell they'd ever back away from a fight, take off, or disappear. Especially Bob. No matter what I tell them, no matter what I do. And this is way over their heads."

"So?"

"So I have a responsibility to them, just like I have one to Kelly. Kelly cannot stay, they will not leave. And I can't be in two places at once. The only reason I'm alive right now is ungodly luck, and that's not gonna happen again if they come after you. So would you *please* take her."

He sat in the car, looking from me to Kelly for what seemed like five minutes.

"I'm not leaving," he said finally, shaking his head. "I don't care if they do come after me, I'm not leaving. Fuck 'em. They're gonna have to kill me before I give them the pleasure of seeing me turn tail and run."

"What is wrong with the two of you?" Kelly said plaintively. "Why do you have to be such assholes?" She started to cry again and sat on the hood of Scott's car. She hugged her bag to her chest and looked at the two of us, tears streaming down her cheeks.

"Oh Christ," Scott muttered, looking away uncomfortably.

I was as close to losing it then as I have ever been in my whole life. I looked down at the ground and concentrated on my breathing. "You killed the guy who killed Oscar," I told my wife. "I'm going to find out who sent him." That got no response from her, so I looked to Scott.

"Would you do me one favor, then?" I said pleadingly to him. "Please."

"What?"

I dug around in my wallet and found the business card I'd hoped was there. "Call this number," I told him. "You're looking for Charlie Kang. I'm not sure if this is a business number or not, so you might not get any answer 'til tomorrow morning. Tell him what's going on. I think he'll be able to do something for Kelly—transportation, maybe paperwork, I don't know." *For an exorbitant fee, to be determined later,* I thought.

"Who is this?"

"An old friend who chose a different career path," I told Scott. "Until you can get ahold of him, would you take Kelly somewhere tonight? Someplace safe, not your place, and just look after her 'til morning? Then maybe in the morning drive her to the bank so she can get some emergency cash out of our deposit box. Would you do that for me?"

"Yeah, sure. Christ, of course." He moved the shotgun and Kelly walked around the car and climbed woodenly into the passenger seat. She stayed unsettlingly quiet. "You going home and calling the cops?"

"I'm going home, but I'm sure as hell not calling any cops."

Scott blinked a couple times in surprise. "John you've got to. You've got dead guys laying in the middle of the street. A dead guy in your house. You've got to call the police. For all you know they're there already, anyway."

"If I call the cops the first thing they're going to do is put me in handcuffs and take me down to the county jail for three days until they can sort this thing out. If these guys still want me dead I'm not convinced I'll be any safer in jail. Right now the number of people I trust I can count on one hand, and the only cop on the list is you."

"John, you've got to turn yourself in. It'll already look bad enough that you grabbed that guy's gun, got your prints all over it."

"Scott, you're so busy thinking like a cop that you're forgetting to think like a person. You're thinking about the crime scene, and collecting evidence, and maybe finding some witnesses that saw the guys drive up, for some future court case. All of that is BULLSHIT! None of it is going to help me find who sent these guys or figure out what to do next, and that's the only thing I care about right now."

"We have to find out who these guys are. Get their prints."

"Right. Which is exactly why when I leave here I'm going to go back and look through their pockets. If you want to call the cops, fine, but give me half an hour head start."

"As soon as they find out about this they're going to be looking for you. Hell, as soon as they check your phone records the cops'll be knocking on my door. If I don't call it in, and damn soon, they're going to find out you called me and then I'll be under a microscope."

"Give me half an hour," I told him. "Tell them I called you and told you what happened, that you thought I was joking at first, that's why it took you a little while to call it in. Or something, I don't know. I used my cell phone anyway, they wouldn't even be able to track that number down until tomorrow. They'll want to talk to you about the call, but not right away, so you'll be able to stay with Kelly tonight."

"The police are probably already crawling all over your house."

"There's only one way to find out. I'll call you in a day or two, see if anybody's found anything out on the guys I shot."

I walked around the car to Kelly's side and leaned my head in the window.

"Use the ATM cards and the credit cards to take all the money out that you can right now, in case you can't get to the bank in the morning," I told her. "Charlie'll probably have something all set up and in place, if I know him, but if he doesn't, you know what to do. Use cash for everything, never use your real name. Go out of state if you have to. Try to get wherever you go without using a car registered or rented in your name. And don't tell me where you're going, I don't want to know. Don't tell Scott, either. Call Carla Kelly in a week to find out if it's safe to come back. If it's not, wait another week before calling. George Kelly is in the phone book."

My wife's pale face was unreadable. I couldn't tell if she was in shock or furious with me or the guy who'd killed Oscar. Maybe all of the above.

"You be careful," I told Scott. "These aren't crackheads on an armed robbery spree."

Splashback

"I've had some experience with unsavory characters before," he reminded me.

"Yeah, but I think these guys play in a different league."

I heard the growl of a powerful engine and looked up to see the Diplomat burn into the lot. Barely before it had stopped Ron was out the door, a riot shotgun in his hands, a revolver in a holster on his belt. His eyes swept the lot and surveyed the situation.

I turned back to Scott and Kelly. "Go." I kissed her on the cheek. "Everything is going to be fine," I told her gently. And got no response. Scott threw an eyeball over her shoulder that let me know he didn't think that was very fucking likely. He tossed his car into reverse, and I kept my eyes locked on Kelly until she was out of sight. Then I turned to Ron.

"The balloon just went up," I said. I suddenly noticed my whole body was clenched and shaking. I ran a hand through my hair and tried to take a deep breath to calm myself. Ron stared at me, wide eyed and wary.

"You are *fuuuuucked* up."

"You don't know the half of it." I jerked my head. "Help me search this car."

We pawed through the confiscated sedan without success.

"What were we looking for?"

"Anything. Alright, let's go, get in the car." I jogged around the Diplomat and got into the passenger seat.

"Where are we going?" he said as he climbed in, handing me the shotgun. I set it between my feet.

"Head back toward my house."

"What the hell's going on?" he asked as he threw the car into gear and rocketed out of the lot. "Whose car was that?"

"Slow down!" I said sharply. "The last thing we need is for the cops to pull us over."

"Never happen," he said, but slowed down anyway. "Where'd you get the Ingram?" I looked at the subgun in my hands.

"Two guys just tried to kill me when I was out jogging. That's their car. One of them had this." I hefted the MAC-10. "When I got back to the house there was already somebody inside. Kelly shot him."

"Oh man, oh man," Ron said, shaking his head. His fingers clenched and unclenched on the wheel.

"This has got something to do with your dad, but I'll be damned if I can figure out what."

"Why would they want to kill you? Even if they knew about that disk you found, wouldn't they want it back first?"

"Ron, I just don't know. I don't know anything anymore. Take a right here," I told him. "If nobody's stumbled across the two guys I left on the sidewalk I want you to help me search them. Wallets, checkbooks, passports, any paper you can find I want. Guns you can leave. After that's done we head to my house. If that's still clear you can search the guy in my living room while I pack a bag."

"Where are you going?"

"I don't know. I'm halfway tempted to not go anywhere, just stay at my house tonight, hope somebody else shows up I can shoot." I caught Ron looking at me out of the corner of his eye.

"You're not calling the cops?"

"Explain to me what good that would do," I snapped.

"Hey, it was just a question. Relax, man, you're so wired you're making the hair on my arms stand up."

"I just sent my pregnant wife away covered in blood. You tell me how I should feel."

I was trying not to think—about anything. If I started thinking about what had happened, I wasn't sure I'd be able to function.

"I'm not gonna call the cops, but Scott Copley is," I explained. "We've got about half an hour, then they're going to be like ants around here. I plan to be long gone by then."

We drove in silence until Ron pulled off Brewster onto the peaceful side street I'd been jogging on half an hour ago. He shut off his lights and parked at the curb, then we trotted over.

The bodies were hard to find in the dark even though I knew right where they were. I quickly frisked one while Ron took the other.

My guy was wearing jeans and a button-down shirt. All I got out of his pockets were keys and some paper that in the dark felt like cash. A minute after we'd left the Diplomat we were back in it. Ron and I tossed our handfuls of pocket clutter into the glove compartment. No time to look at it now.

"My guy had a gun on his hip," Ron told me as he started the car. "No wallet, though."

As we turned the corner onto my street Ron cut his lights and we coasted. Everything looked just like I'd left it, no cops in sight. Ron parked behind the strange sedan two doors down from my house. I pointed it out to him and we double-checked the car as we walked by. Empty. I didn't know if Kelly had locked the front door behind her, but I knew for sure the family room's sliding glass door was still open. We walked briskly around the side of my house, Ron holding the shotgun down along his leg. I went in through the open door first, SMG ready, but could tell immediately no one else had been inside.

Ron cut through the kitchen and front hall while I walked straight through into the dining room. We met beside the dead man.

"Oh fuck, John, he killed Oscar. Goddammit." Ron lowered the shotgun and squatted beside my dog. He reached out a hand and touched her fur. "Those motherfuckers, I can't believe they killed your dog."

"She probably saved Kelly's life," I said, my throat tight. "I was outside when I heard her barking. She grabbed onto his arm and that gave Kelly time enough to get to the gun." He'd shot Oscar in the throat, her fur singed around the wound. The bullet had exited halfway down her back.

"John. John! You better get upstairs and grab whatever you're gonna grab, change your clothes." I realized I'd been standing there staring at Oscar for over a minute, white-knuckling the SMG.

"Go on." He put a hand on my elbow and propelled me gently. "I'll search this guy."

I headed upstairs to the bedroom. The smell of Kelly, her perfumes and powders, hovered in our bedroom and nearly brought tears to my eyes. I tossed the MAC, the empty snubnose, and my Colt onto the bed and stripped. The drying blood on my back had glued the T-shirt to me and I nearly cried out from the pain as I pulled the shirt over my head. I felt fresh bleeding. In the bathroom I tried to get a look at the wound in the mirror, peering over my shoulder. The blood made it hard to see much of anything.

I grabbed a towel and soaked it in warm water. With a few contortions and a not insubstantial amount of pain I managed to get almost all the blood off my back. The wound was a glistening red stripe about five inches long across my left shoulder blade. It looked a lot worse than it felt, but my body was still humming along on endorphins and I was sure the pain would be four times worse in the morning. If I'd been a little slower in turning the bullet would have gone in through my shoulder blade and exited my upper arm, completely destroying my shoulder joint in the process and permanently crippling me. If I'd lived, that is. The wound was still oozing blood, but very slowly.

I tossed the crimson towel into the sink and hunted up a clean shirt. My Colt 1911 went into an inside-the-pants holster behind my right hip, and a double magazine pouch went on my belt behind my left. There was a dufflebag inside my closet and I filled it with underwear, socks, a bunch of spare shirts that I wouldn't mind leaking blood on, the reloaded snubnose, and a full box of hollowpoints. Federal Hydra-Shoks, the best on the market. I also grabbed all my spare Colt magazines.

"Not a damn thing," Ron told me as I came down the stairs, a jacket in one hand and the duffle bag in the other. His hands were bloody halfway to his elbows. "We gonna leave this Ingram here or what?"

I looked at the gun. "Leave it."

Ron examined his bloody fingers. "I sure hope this guy doesn't have AIDS." He went off to find towel and I stood there, trying not to look at anything or think about anything.

Ron walked back in, wiping the blood off on a pretty white patterned towel, part of a set Kelly's mom had given to her for her birthday.

"What now?"

I stared at the floor six feet in front of me, eyes unfocused.

"Oscar always loved running around in the fields behind your house," I said softly. "I know you buried your old dog out there somewhere. Do you mind if I put Oscar to rest down there too?"

"I'd be honored to have her," Ron said after a half-second pause.

"Whyn't you go out and see if you can find anything in that car outside," I told him. "Then just pull up out front and I'll bring her out." I handed him my bag and jacket. He went to head out the door, then paused.

"You gonna be all right?"

I just looked at him. After a couple seconds staring at my face he turned away and stepped outside, wrapping his shotgun in my jacket.

I had a difficult time keeping my footing. The ground was very uneven and the moon had disappeared behind some clouds. Oscar was in my arms, wrapped in a blanket, and I couldn't see my feet to watch my step. Ron led the way, shovel in one hand, a pick in the other. I'd waited outside by the barn while he went into the house.

"I thought you went to get a shovel," I'd said to him when he came out empty-handed.

"Shovel's in the barn. I went in to let the feds know it was us out there in case they were looking out the window when we went by. No way to do this without them seeing."

"Shit, really? Maybe this was a bad idea. What'd you tell them we'd be doing?"

"I told them your dog got hit by a car and you wanted to bury her in my backyard." He then stepped into the barn and came out with the shovel and pick.

"And they bought it?"

"The two of them looked at each other and shrugged, whatever that means. My mom sure as hell didn't."

Splashback

I fell silent and concentrated on not tripping as I followed Ron through the horse pasture and into the overgrown field behind it.

"This is it." He had stopped on a small rise. Beside his leg was a badly weathered makeshift wooden cross, sunk deep into the ground. **BEAR** was scratched into the crosspiece in childlike block letters.

I gently set my bundle down and took the shovel. The ground beneath me was a dark blur as I stepped on the blade to take the first bite out of the earth. The long dry field grass held onto the clump of dirt as I levered it free.

I tuned everything else out and concentrated on digging. The dirt was thick with roots, and I had to fight and heave and pry to get every shovelful out. A foot down the soil turned to solid clay, and I discarded the shovel for the pick.

Sweat began to trickle down my forehead as I hacked and swung. I paused only to lift the chunks of clay out with my hands. Ron never said anything, he just stood a few feet away, looking at me and out over the field toward the house. Gradually the hole grew deeper. In the dark I couldn't even see the bottom and had to work by feel. When the hole was deep and wide enough I climbed in and kept chopping.

I tossed off my jacket and attacked the ground with fury, hacking and slicing at the hole's walls and floor. My hands burned on the pick's hickory shaft and blisters started to form. In the cold air I could feel my shirt sticking to my back. I couldn't tell if it was from sweat or blood. Vaguely I heard Ron ask if I wanted him to spell me. I never paused, swinging the pick with both hands into the clay as hard as I could, prying each chunk loose with a grunt. I'd hurl it to the side, then take hold of the pick again and start anew.

I wasn't just burying my dog, I was burying any hopes, any illusions I'd had that I could lead a regular life, that things had ever gone back to normal after what had happened two years ago, not just to me but to my wife.

Finally I stopped, chest heaving, covered in sweat, and leaned against the side of the grave. I had no idea how long I'd been digging. My cheeks were wet, and I looked up in surprise to discover it was raining. I blinked the sweat out of my stinging eyes and stared at the hole I'd dug. Oval, almost five feet long and four feet deep. The freezing rain soaked through my shirt but I barely felt it as I climbed out of the grave and got my dog. As he stepped forward to help I motioned Ron away with an angry jerk of my head. I laid her body in the blanket down at the edge of the hole, then jumped in.

Gently I picked up the blanket off the edge of the grave and set her down inside it. I climbed out and stood at the edge for a while staring at that blanket. My hands were raw, throbbing and sore, but the pain seemed distant, incomplete. Irrelevant. It couldn't have been more than thirty degrees out, but I didn't feel cold in my T-shirt. Ron joined me at the foot of the open grave and looked down. A long time passed before either of us spoke.

"She was a good dog," he said finally.

I clenched and unclenched my fists. A vision of Kelly staring at me out the window of Scott's car as he drove away floated before me. Her eyes were haunting.

"Yeah."

Together the two of us filled the grave with the chunks of clay, tossing them in by hand. Only at the very end, when we got to the first dirt I'd removed, was I able to use the shovel.

"You want to put a cross or a marker here or something?"

"Later."

"Where are you going to stay tonight?"

I looked around the empty field, but I could see nothing but dark muted shapes. Finally I said, "Hell if I know."

"Why don't you stay here?"

"No thank you. One look at me and the FBI is going to lock me in a room with a whole interrogation team."

"Not at the house. You could sleep in the barn, on the couch upstairs. There's a couple blankets in the closet up there." He pointed west. "A quarter mile down the road there's an overgrown two-track. Pull your car in there, no one'll ever see it, and it's a quick walk back. The feds'll think you left, and with those creaky wooden stairs in the barn no one'll be able to surprise you."

When I hesitated, he moved a step closer to me. "You're in no shape to go anywhere," Ron said firmly. "Save it 'til morning. It'll take that long for whoever sent those guys to realize you're not dead." He took hold of my shoulders, turned me toward the barn. "You'll be safe, at least for tonight."

SIX

Wednesday

8:53 a.m.

"Bang, you're dead." Steve said it as he came up the stairs, just as his head cleared the second floor. His eyes searched the room and found me on the couch. I lowered the Colt pointing at his head and flipped on the safety.

"I thought I recognized your thundering tread coming up the stairs, but I wasn't sure," I told him. He swallowed a bit nervously and lost most of his smile. He plopped himself down in a chair across from me and looked me over.

"You look like shit," he observed.

My response was a groan. "I feel like shit. What time is it?" If I'd had any idea my body would feel like this when I woke up I never would have fallen asleep. My whole body ached. It even hurt to breathe, thanks to the new groove I had in my back.

I did my best to regain vertical status, grunting and muttering like a hobo in a boxcar. I managed to get upright and slide my feet off the lumpy couch and onto the floor. When I stretched my back six somethings popped.

"I heard that over here," Steve marveled. He pulled a second chair over and propped his feet on it. I could see the brown leather of a shoulder holster where his jacket gaped.

"What time is it?" I asked again. I hawked up a big wad of phlegm and spit it into an empty Coke can.

"Nine o'clock. Time for you to find another place to stay. You ought to hear what they're saying on the radio about all the dead guys at your place. It's all over the news. The reporters are practically coming they're so excited."

"I don't want to know."

"This one guy even said—"

"I'm serious, I really don't want to hear about it."

He heard my tone. "Okay, whatever. You know, I'm sort of pissed that Ron didn't call me until this morning, that shithead." He frowned, then changed topics. "I guess you're wanted for questioning by the cops."

"Tell me something I don't know. Where's Ron?"

"In the house having breakfast with his mom and the feds. There's more feds here today, running around like somebody stuck a stick in their ant hill. I don't know if it's 'cause of you or not. I'm up here working out," he explained to me.

"Now that's a brilliant cover story."

"You should have seen the look Ron's mom gave me. The feds didn't have a clue. I guess Ron's got them used to weirdness. And I guess they figure if you're on the run there's no way you'd be up here with them camped out at the house." He jerked his head toward it.

"If you're found up here with me, you're probably going to get in a lot of trouble."

"So what's new?"

"Just thought I'd point it out." I ran a hand through my

hair and winced as I bent my scab-covered knuckles. Somehow I managed to stand up without assistance.

"Is there any blood showing through my shirt?" I turned a little. Ron had dressed the bullet graze properly before leaving me in the barn.

"No, but that scab on your chin looks ugly as hell."

"I could sure use a shower." I examined all the blisters on my hands.

"Well, you're not going to get one here. If I can manage to sneak you out of here we can go to my house, and you can wash up there. Ron told me where your car is, I'm thinking we should just leave it there for now. I couldn't even see it when I drove past it this morning."

"My plate's got to be all over LEIN by now." LEIN was the Law Enforcement Information Network, the computer database that all the local police departments shared.

I looked at him and shook my head.

"What?" he asked me.

"Well, you were right," I told him.

He didn't know what I was talking about at first, and his eyebrows knit together. "Oh," he said suddenly, remembering his comments at my house. He'd been convinced things were as bad as they seemed, or worse. He didn't appear happy about being right, but he was right in the middle of it again, when he could have just as easily sat this one out at home.

Steve looked down and picked at the knee of his jeans. "So what are you going to do? The cops are all over your house. I drove by it on the way here to see what was up and the place is a fucking circus."

"Did you see Lieutenant Copley there?"

"No, but there had to be fifty people standing on your front lawn. It's not just the cops, the news media is going batshit over this. You can't spend the next couple months up here, which is how long this'll take to cool down."

"I know, I know. If I had any common sense I'd turn myself in. This whole thing is moving way too fast for me. I need about three days of peace and quiet to think things out, get my head to stop spinning. Are you my Ron-designated babysitter?" I pointed at his shoulder holster.

"I'm all you've got, at least for now. Ron made a bunch of calls this morning. I guess he snuck his mom's cellular into the upstairs bathroom so the feds wouldn't accidentally pick up an extension on the house phone. Bob's out and about with his fiancée, out of the loop for a while. I guess she flew into town last night. Jerry's working. Ron's practically being smothered by the feds. I guess your visit last night wasn't any big deal to them until early this morning when word came down that you'd whacked a bunch of people." He leaned forward in the chair, got a serious look on his face, and held up a hand as if to caution me.

"They're out in the back yard now digging up your dog," he said.

Blood rushed to my head and my ears started to hum. I clenched and unclenched my fists a couple times until I got control and the room swam back into focus.

"I can't believe they never sent anybody up here to check the place out this morning," Steve was saying, looking around. "I guess it'd be too stupid for you to be up here that they didn't even bother."

"Goddammit," I said weakly, drained and suddenly listless. "So you're supposed to be my bodyguard?"

"You gonna try telling me you don't need one?"

"I'll tell you this—if I run into the cops and you're anywhere near, you're gonna be in trouble. Especially carrying a gun illegally."

We sat there and stared at each other for a while.

"Well, I guess that's my choice to make," he said finally. "I hate fucking being right." He stopped and stared off into the distance. "You gonna be okay?" he asked tentatively after a few uncomfortable moments. "Ron said you were a little flipped out. Not that I wouldn't be if the same thing happened to me. Jesus, I can't believe they killed Oscar. Kelly's okay, though, right?"

When I just sat there, frowning and looking at the floor, he quickly changed the subject.

"So, do you have any idea what you're going to do next?"

"Last night when Ron was bandaging me up I remembered I used to know a guy in the Miami DEA office that had a lot of CIA connections. I'm pretty sure I've got his home number at my office."

"Will he be able to help?"

"Even if he can, I don't know if he will. I haven't talked to him in almost seven years, and we were never that close to begin with. But he's the only person I could think of who might be able to get me inside information."

"Might as well go pretty soon, before one of the FBI guys decides to come up here and work out with me. Besides, sitting around feeling sorry for yourself isn't going to do anyone any good."

"If I didn't feel so shitty I'd be tempted to slap that snotty look off your face."

"I guess if I felt the way you look I'd be cranky too. You need help getting up, old man?"

11:04 a.m.

Splashback

At my insistence Steve pulled into a gas station just before my office building's parking lot. When I told him I didn't want him tagging along he didn't take the news too well.

"Fuck that. I'm coming up with you."

"If the cops are up in my office waiting for me I don't want you anywhere around."

"How am I supposed to bodyguard you sitting on my ass down here in the car?"

"Steve, for God's sake, all I'm doing is running up there to grab a phone number. Then I'm coming straight down. I don't want to make this call from one of my phones. Ten minutes, tops. If the cops are there you'll be able to see them dragging me out from here."

"Oh, come on. What are the chances the cops are even up there?"

I climbed out of his car and stuck my head in the open door.

"Steve, you idiot, I killed two people in the street last night and left a third lying in a pool of blood in the middle of my fucking living room, and the FBI thinks I'm somehow mixed up again with Pietro Bufonte and the Detroit mob." I took a deep breath, looked around, then attempted a comforting smile. "I'll be all right. I've got a forty-five on me, two spare mags, a pocket knife, a pen, a sharp wit, and bad breath. Now sit there and be quiet and I'll be back in a minute."

At Steve's house I'd soaked under a hot shower for thirty minutes, then let him rebandage the stripe on my back. A scab was starting to form, and I could feel it pull when I moved, but the wound didn't hurt too badly at all. My hands hurt a lot more. I did what I could for the blisters and left the scabs on my knuckles alone. My whole body ached, but the short walk to my building helped work out some of the kinks in my muscles.

Nobody in uniform was lurking in the lobby for me. I'd doubted they would be, but didn't want Steve taking the chance, risking his future. I rode the elevator to the floor above my office, then took the stairs down. I didn't see anybody that looked like a cop. The hallway outside my office was clear and my door was still locked when I tried it. Inside I found I had the place to myself.

The message light on my answering machine was blinking frantically. I hit the button and listened to a seemingly endless stream of reporters, TV and print, frantically trying to reach me for comment, debasing themselves in hopes of getting a good quote. A couple even left me their home numbers. When the tape finally finished I erased it. No reason to save the messages, I sure as hell wasn't going to talk to a reporter. The person I should have been talking to was a lawyer. Or better, a bail bondsman—I didn't need to pay someone two hundred dollars an hour to tell me I was in deep shit.

I had to go through my entire Rolodex, business card file, and three desk drawers before I found the phone number I was looking for. I stuck the card in my pocket and looked around the office to see if there was anything else that needed attention. Nothing caught my eye. I decided I'd better hustle downstairs before Steve got too nervous.

The hall was clear as I shut and locked my office door and headed for the elevators. I had to wait a hell of a long time for a car to arrive, and when the doors finally opened I stepped onto the car before my brain registered what my eyes were seeing.

The man in front of me looked to be about forty, with a bunch of long, hard years behind him. As the doors opened and I stepped in his eyes locked with mine. His right hand appeared from behind his back, holding an industrial-sized can of pepper gas. As the can came up the two rough looking men on either side of him each took a step my way. The guy on my left had a scarred-up chin, the guy on the right wore an amazingly ugly checkered shirt.

Pepper gas was getting really popular with the local law enforcement agencies. OC gas, as the cops called it, oleoresin capsicum, was originally developed as a bear repellent, and worked even better on people. One good spray in the face and most males, no matter their size or constitution, were on the floor blind and hacking for at least twenty minutes. The guys in front of me were in street clothes, not uniforms, and were definitely not cops. If I'd had time to think about what I should have done I wouldn't have done what I did.

Just as the can reached eye level a liquid stream of OC leapt from its nozzle toward my face. I smacked the can away with my left hand, taking spray on my cheek, and punched the guy in the face as hard as I could. I felt something pop, but couldn't tell if it was something of mine or his. Scarface on my left took a direct hit from the deflected can—right in his eyes. He yelled and instinctively batted the can away. The can sailed into a corner of the car, still spraying.

I cranked my arm back, bent a knee, and drove my shoulder into the chest of the guy to my right as he made a grab for me. His forward momentum ceased, and I tried to spin around and dive back out the still-open elevator doors.

The can man somehow managed to get a hand on me and we wrestled as the doors began to close. I tried to knee him as my eyes started tearing up from the OC filling the car. He twisted his body, taking the knee on his thigh, and slammed me in the side of the neck with a forearm. I saw orange flares.

Scarface had his eyes squeezed shut in agony, his face already red and blotchy from the spray. Even though he was gagging uncontrollably and could barely stand up he still tried to fight, grabbing blindly at me. I used the distraction to knock the can man off balance. When his grip on my shirt loosened I chopped at his elbows and managed to knock one of his arms loose.

The air inside the car was so bad my eyes had involuntarily slammed shut. I tried to keep them open, but I could still hear the can spraying, and every exposed inch of my skin was on fire. I was trying to hold my breath so I didn't inhale a lungful of gas and start convulsing in coughs, but it wasn't working too well.

Nearly blind I tried to break free, hoping to reach the control panel and find the button that would open the doors. Hands grabbed me from behind, my third assailant getting back into the fight, and I whipped an elbow backwards. It connected with something hard, and the grip he had on me loosened.

Something hit the side of the head as my legs were kicked out from under me. I hit the floor badly, saw blurry movement to my right, and kicked at it, screaming hoarsely as I expelled the breath I'd been holding in forever.

My shin connected with a knee and someone fell on top of me with a cursing shout of pain. The curse was all I needed to locate his head and I began hammering at it with fists and elbows. He grabbed at my hair and tried to find my eyes with his fingers. As I sucked in a breath I nearly bucked off the floor coughing and hacking. The OC flowing into my lungs felt like wet razorblades.

Somehow I managed to get a foot between me and the

thrashing guy on my chest. I kicked hard and heard him sliding across the floor. The whole car echoed with coughs and gagging, and I wondered if any of them could see much better than I could.

I was just pulling a knee under myself in an attempt to stand when the grenade went off in my side. I found myself on my back, head wedged into a corner. Another kick I couldn't see coming blasted into my upper arm as I tried to shield my ribs. The force of it bounced me off the wall, and my entire arm went numb. I kicked a foot out wildly but connected only with air. Then someone did a knee-drop onto my stomach and I nearly passed out.

As I frantically tried to suck in air, the guy on top of me began using my head as a punching bag. I grabbed at him but he slapped my hands away. The third time that he hit me so hard my head bounced off the floor I blacked out.

I think I was only out for a couple seconds, then consciousness returned briefly. The man kneeling atop me was coughing and spitting and cursing up a storm. The sound faded in and out while my brain decided whether or not to shut down again. I couldn't see or feel my limbs, or even tell if when I tried to lift my hand it moved. When a loud buzzing sound started up, I had no way to tell if it was from the elevator or only in my head.

"Asshole, the OC was to use on him in his office, not a fucking elevator," the guy on top of me gasped. He was coughing so hard he was shaking my body, and I started to fade out again.

Pain.

If I didn't know anything else, I knew pain. I knew what

it looked like, and I knew what it felt like. I even knew what it tasted like—bloody Tabasco.

There was no way for me to tell what hurt, no way to isolate any specific part of my body in my mind, pinpoint any exact source of hurt. My whole universe was aching.

Sometime later the one big roaring hurt separated into a bunch of slightly smaller snarling pains. My head felt like a kettledrum being kicked by a rugby team, thumping rushes of red racing through my skull with every heartbeat. A sharp pain kept appearing and disappearing in my side for no apparent reason, until I realized it only hurt when I inhaled. Well, at least I was still breathing.

I couldn't feel my arms or legs at all, and couldn't tell if I was lying down, standing up, or hanging upside down by my ankles. I experimentally flexed my arms, trying to get some response, and stabbing pain lanced through my shoulders. As it subsided I figured out that I was sitting up, with my hands pulled behind my back. My chin rested on my chest. A little feeling returned to my arms, but my hands remained totally numb. My wrists were tightly bound by something, I had no idea what. After tensing my leg muscles a couple times I determined my feet were on the floor, but I wasn't able to move them.

After a lengthy discussion with various parts of my body we came to the possibly rash conclusion I should attempt to open my eyes. They were still burning slightly from the OC, which meant I couldn't have been unconscious more than a couple hours. The inside of my nose and the corners of my mouth still burned a little.

I cracked my eyes open and the tears welled up. After blinking several times I was finally able to get my eyes in focus. Between my thighs was the grey metal seat of a 1950's-style office chair. The chair seat had at one time been painted, but most of the paint was long gone, leaving only bare metal. Beyond my knees I could see the floor, covered in ugly mustard yellow squares of linoleum. I shifted my eyes left and right, not moving my head, but all I could see was more linoleum. Wonderful.

Pins and needles began dancing in my hands after I wiggled them around a bit. From the feel it was probably handcuffs around my wrists, and they seemed to be attached to the chair back.

I was hit by a flurry of coughs, so strong I bounced in the chair. My frantic jerking against the cuffs tore the hell out of my skin. My throat burned, and the buzz in my sinuses jumped up a notch as my body tried to expel the last of the pepper gas in my system. My shoulders started to cramp up.

I raised my head in time to see a door a dozen feet in front of me open. A man I thought I recognized stuck his head in and looked at me.

"Yeah, he's awake now," he said over his shoulder, then shut the door again. He'd been one of the guys I battled in the elevator, the one with the scar on his chin. The room started to spin and I had to clamp my eyes shut and lower my head to keep from throwing up. Apparently my head wasn't fully recovered from being used as a punching bag. It was about ten times worse than any hangover I'd ever had. I probably had a concussion.

When my stomach settled I raised my head again and looked around the room. It was about fifteen feet wide, with a small desk in the far left corner near the door. The walls were covered in very old gray-brown paneling. To my right was a tall counter about ten feet long, reminiscent of a bar. I could turn my head just far enough to see the blank grey wall six feet behind my chair.

The only light in the place came from the glass block window high up on the left wall. As I looked at the window the light would dim and then brighten. I think it was just my banged-up head doing weird things.

The door opened again and Scarface, as I now thought of him, stepped into the room. Behind him were two more men, the second one closing the door. I had a brief glimpse of the room beyond, bright with sunshine, then the door cut off the light.

I recognized another of my captors. He'd been the idiot with the can of OC. I felt a certain amount of satisfaction when I saw how swollen and purply-red his nose was. In two days he'd be a raccoon. The third guy was new to me. He had a thick shock of blonde hair that seemed out of place above his craggy, fifty-something features. In fact, he looked disturbingly like Robert Redford. They stopped a few feet in front of me. I had to grit my teeth to stop the room from spinning as I looked up.

"Well, you're a royal pain in the ass," the Redford look-alike said, frowning.

"Bite me, Sundance," I told him.

Scarface took a step forward and slapped me hard across the face. His eyes were still amazingly red from the dose of pepper spray. While he did his best to produce a Hollywood-quality villainous sneer the room started to spin on me again and I let it. I opened my mouth and he leaned forward slightly.

"Yeah?" he said cockily. I covered him in puke from the knees on down. He leapt back, cursing.

"Goddammit! First Johnson fucking sprays me in the face with that shit and now this asshole pukes all over me. I ain't getting paid enough." He stomped his feet, trying to shake some of it off. Sundance did his best, but I still saw the brief smile. Johnson didn't seem to think it was funny. With that nose his head probably hurt at least half as much as mine did, and that was a hell of a lot of hurt.

I spat out bitter dregs and licked my lips. They felt weird and misshapen, and not a little bruised.

"Want to try that again?" I asked Scarface. He didn't seem in any hurry to step back in. I'd regained feeling in my fingers and had ascertained that yes, I was indeed handcuffed. Since I was still alive, I figured that whoever these guys were they needed something from me. And I could guess what.

Shit. There was no way in hell the three of them could have carried me out of my office building, in the condition we'd all been in, without Steve noticing. Therefore, since I woke up with the bad guys, Steve was probably dead. With a gargantuan effort I filed that thought away, unobserved, in a corner of my mind. At the moment I had to devote one hundred percent of my attention to my situation. I was in bad shape, tied up, and outnumbered by a bunch of guys that all seemed to be armed.

"You feeling a bit more yourself, now?" Sundance said.

"You've got to be kidding." The skin on my face pulled in weird places when I spoke. From trails of dried blood? Thank God there were no mirrors around. I shifted in the chair, and for the first time noticed a distinct lack of gun on my hip. The three of them kept looking at me, not saying anything. Trying to gauge my state of mind? Who knew. I quickly tired of it.

"You know, I loved you in Butch Cassidy and the Sundance Kid," I told him. He seemed to be the leader. "'*Who are those guys?*' Too bad you had to die in the end."

He smiled. "Uh-oh, looks like we've got a comedian on our hands." He leaned close and stared into my eyes. "Well, your pupils seem to be acting normally. Looks like you avoided any brain damage."

"Who could tell?" I grumbled. Sundance looked at Johnson and gave a little jerk of his head. Johnson went into the front room briefly, then returned carrying something in his hand. When he handed it to Scarface I saw it was two somethings—a disposable hypodermic needle and a small rubber-topped bottle.

"You've got to be shitting me," I said.

"Nope," replied Sundance. "You ought to be thankful," he said. "If we weren't in such a hurry it'd probably be torture for you. There's a guy, out of the country right now, he's practically a magician. Everybody uses him. Running electrical current through your balls or a drill bit through your kneecap works better than any drug, but you're lucky —we don't have the equipment, and none of us has enough experience doing that to guarantee the results."

"How 'bout you tell me what it is that I'm supposed to know? Or just what the fuck is going on?" I kept an eye on Scarface, who was fiddling with the bottle.

"I'm not going to waste my time asking you anything now. When the drugs start kicking in, then we'll talk."

"If you guys really want to get some answers, stick me in a room with a ringing telephone and don't let me answer it. I hate that. Or better yet, make it country music." I watched as Scarface filled the syringe with clear fluid from the bottle. I was getting nervous and made no attempt to hide it.

"Who are you?" I asked. Both Sundance and I watched as Scarface squirted air bubbles out the end of the needle. I involuntarily sucked in air.

He looked at me. "Does it matter?"

Scarface moved around behind me and I felt the cold prick of steel on the inside of my left forearm. As the needle withdrew I scowled and shook my head, feeling a sudden rush of anger.

"This is the most fucked-up operation I've ever heard of," I spat at them. "First you try to kill me, and *then* you kidnap me and ask me questions. What the hell is that? Does that make sense to you? Because I'm fucking lost."

Sundance regarded me flatly. "If I was calling the shots we wouldn't be talking. I think we'd all be better off with you dead. Keeping this covert is no longer an option, obviously. But until I can convince them that your death would be of more value to us than whatever information you might be able to provide…" He shrugged. "Call it a conflict between different management styles."

Jesus. My wife gone, my dog dead, my house trashed. And he was talking about management styles, like we were a bunch of MBAs arguing over spreadsheets. I clenched my hands into tight fists and vowed not to die in that shitty little room. Not cuffed to an old chair, helpless. Sundance gave me a little smile and motioned at Johnson.

"You stay here and keep an eye on him. It'll take ten minutes before he's under far enough."

Scarface slapped the back of my head and then he and Sundance left the room. It took nearly a minute before the pain in my abused head subsided enough for me to open my eyes.

Johnson took the chair behind the desk and propped his feet upon its scarred surface. It might take two days, but he was definitely going to have a beautiful black eye. Probably two. Hopefully his nose was broken too, the bastard. Had to hurt. He sure wasn't looking at me with a lot of love in his eyes.

The pain in my floating ribs when I inhaled made me worry I had a cracked rib, but there was nothing I could do about it. I concentrated on moving my fingers, keeping the blood flowing so they didn't go numb again. I did a quick physical inventory: maybe a broken rib, and a concussion, but everything else was just bruises and scrapes. Nothing actually serious, or life-threatening. Yet.

"You guys do any background on me?" I asked him. They appeared to be professionals, of one sort or another. Scarface glared at me evilly and felt his nose gingerly with his fingers.

"Why?"

"Because if you did, you'd know I won the Florida State Lottery six years ago."

"So?"

"Two hundred grand, if you get me out of here now."

"Don't waste your breath. If all I wanted was money there are half a dozen Cayman bank accounts I could hack into with more money than you'd ever see in your life, lottery or no lottery." He stopped fiddling with his nose and crossed his arms. "It'd be child's play."

"Like ambushing a pregnant woman?"

"Shut up," he said tiredly.

"You're gonna look like Rocky Raccoon," I shot back. His hand went halfway to his nose, then he caught himself and crossed his arms again.

I stared at him for a few minutes, until I noticed that he was starting to get fuzzy. My body went all warm, my aches and pains drifting a comfortable distance away. They were still there, but they didn't seem part of me anymore, more like I was watching a movie of hurt. My head swirled as I looked around the room. Boy, the sunlight coming through the window was sure soupy. I could see it flowing into the room like water, weaving and burbling like a small brook in the woods.

Splashback

"Wow," I heard myself say. "This is some good shit." My voice sounded strange. Somebody had dunked me in a vat of molasses when I wasn't looking. Sink or swim, women and children first. I saw my thoughts float away before I had a good grasp on them, and I couldn't seem to paddle fast enough to catch

up.

Johnson drifted by, his face all melted like candy. Maybe Willy Wonka was nearby. I loved his movie.

The molasses current started to pick up and my head began to sway with it.

The ceiling bobbed in and out of view.

There went Sundance. Happy, happy Sundance. Happy to see me. Pull up a chair, come on in, the water's fine. Everybody join the party. I grinned stupidly, and the flurries cleared up briefly.

"He too messed up?" Johnson asked.

"He's just about right."

I was a melted marshmallow, all smushy and happy to help. I rode on clouds, answering all the polite questions I was asked. No problems, just warm and fuzzies.

My jeans floated by. What an amazing pattern. Tiny alternating lines of blue and white, line after line after line after—hey! There went some tan stitching! My eyes followed the stitching up my leg, fascinated, until I was distracted by a gleam.

The shining string of spit hung from my lower lip.

Someone kept asking me questions, distracting me from the swaying gleam, and I answered them as quick as I could in hopes whoever it was bugging me would go away. When I talked the spit globule wiggled around, swaying in figure eights. I moved my jaw left and right and the string described an infinity sign in the air above my fly.

I vaguely remember Sundance asking me questions about George Kelly. How did I know him, why was I looking for him, who was I working for, and a lot of other questions that faded into the background mist. At some point we got around to discussing the mystery disk. I don't know how the subject came up, but we sure talked a long time about that disk.

The next thing I knew I was jerking awake, still in the chair. My head was more or less clear of the drug, but I still felt slow and stupid. Once again I was alone with Johnson. He was back in his chair, feet up on the desk. At some point during the questioning I'd emptied my bladder. As if I hadn't smelled bad enough before, reeking of sweat, blood, and vomit.

I was ashamed of myself for talking. They'd used a so-called 'truth agent' on me and I'd blabbed like a third grader caught in some bully's headlock, without even a hint of resistance. I couldn't remember exactly what I'd said, but maybe that was better. If I'd been as free with information as I suspected, bad things were going to happen, and not just to me. I yanked at the cuffs again, cursing.

I had no idea what time it was, but the light outside the window was definitely weaker, and fading fast. The interrogation had lasted a good while, but I didn't think it had lasted all day. I must have slept for a while. Maybe I'd been given a second shot.

If my life was a cheap action movie I'd have lured Johnson over with a snappy insult and, still bound, rendered him unconscious. A turbo head butt maybe, and then I could say something cool. *Hasta la vista, Raccoon.* Instead, I knew I wasn't getting out of the chair until they let me out of it. When they did, I hoped I'd still be alive—my captors had never bothered to hide their faces from me, and I knew Johnson's name. Not a good sign.

The door to the front room was just a simple wooden thing with a plain doorknob, the hinges exposed and facing me. They didn't seem worried about security or witnesses, which meant we must've had the building to ourselves. I'd never been gagged, so I knew yelling would be a waste of time. With some effort I'd be able to tilt my chair over, but then I'd just be lying on my side on the hard floor, wearing a chair for jewelry, Johnson ten feet away laughing at me. They hadn't left me alone yet, but even if they had I couldn't see how I'd ever get out of the chair without help. I had no idea where I was, either. Hell, I could be in Chicago, but I didn't think it was likely—the effects of the OC would've worn off by the time we got to Indiana.

The outer door opened and Sundance reappeared, accompanied by a new face. Well, relatively new—I'd seen the guy before. In an elevator.

He looked like a weightlifter, maybe in his late thirties. He had an ugly raised bruise on his forehead, and as he came into the room I saw he was limping. It must have been his kneecap I connected with. I gave myself a mental pat on the back, rather proud of myself. Outnumbered three to one in an enclosed space, caught by surprise, and I still managed to inflict some serious damage. Of course, I would have felt even better if I'd escaped, but I took what little comfort I could in the situation. I doubted even Bob could have done much better, given the circumstances.

"So what's the scoop?" Johnson asked.

"Other team is on its way," Sundance announced. "Should be here tomorrow, probably when we don't need them, but that's as quick as I could arrange it."

"Not that. What are you doing ordering a hit? You know the man's going to want us to talk to him first, with what we know now."

"I know, which is why I'm not going to make the mistake of asking permission. The man's got some personal issues clouding his professional judgment that I don't have. I think he's been making some bad calls, which is why this thing has gone so far sideways already. We need to wipe the slate clean and get the fuck out of Dodge, and he doesn't seem to want us to do either."

"When he finds out you went off the reservation…"

"Listen, let me just say that there's a time element involved here. You don't know the big picture— "

"And I don't want to know," Johnson said. "I never do. I don't want the headache."

"So forget about it. He'll come down on me, not any of you. You're just following orders."

Johnson shook his head. "I still don't like it. I hate rush jobs. There's so many more ways to fuck up when you're in a hurry."

"This target's no amateur, we have to do it quick, before he's suspecting anything."

"I know, I know. Happen tomorrow morning, latest."

Sundance nodded. "Then it'll start to get really hot around here, but it won't matter."

"I still think we should be trying the snatch," Bruise-head complained.

"Me too," Johnson agreed, "but that's not our decision. Besides, that's what we tried to do with this asshole here, the first time," he said, pointing at me, "and look how that worked out. Three guys dead, and *he's* just a lousy peeper."

"And how are you, Becky Sunshine?" Bruise-head said to me. "Still causing trouble?"

"My throat's sort of dry, I could use a glass of water."

"I bet." He made no move to get me anything.

"Again?" Johnson asked. In response, Sundance moved to the counter and picked up the bottle and syringe.

"Oh Christ," I said.

SEVEN

Thursday

The next time I woke up it was daylight again. My arms were numb even while my shoulders were screaming in pain. And my bladder was joining in the chorus with an enthusiastic voice.

"I really have to take a piss," I announced. Johnson and Bruise-head were at the desk playing cards. Johnson was the only one who looked up.

"So go," he told me. And that appeared to be that. Inwardly grumbling and cursing at being reduced to the actions of an infant, I again suffered the indignity of pissing myself. Pissed off and pissed on, all at the same time.

"Feel free to untie me, you guys need a third," I told them. They ignored me. Neither of them looked good. Hair slightly mussed, a day's growth of beard. They'd probably slept there too, on the floor or in chairs.

My stomach started to growl. Even if it hadn't been the only sound in the room everyone would've heard it, gurgling and groaning at an impressive volume. Bruise-head even looked at me briefly, to see if I'd let a gorilla into the room.

His watch glinted in the light, and I strained my eyes in an effort to see its hands. Under normal circumstances I might've met with success, but my eyes didn't seem to be working at one hundred percent.

I vaguely remembered Sundance asking me a lot of questions about the two guys I'd killed while out jogging. He didn't seem to believe in blind luck any more than he believed in coincidence, and couldn't seem to accept the fact that a lowly Detroit PI had killed three of his men armed with submachineguns. When I told him my pregnant wife had taken out his third man, not me, he'd gone ballistic. I learned a little about him then. To Sundance, nothing was as it seemed. A private investigator, even one that was a former DEA agent, armed only with a snubnose .38, could never kill two trained men unless he was something more than he appeared. He questioned me for hours about what in my past I was hiding—because there had to be something—and I don't think he ever got an answer that satisfied him.

Somewhere a phone began ringing. Bruise-head got up with a grunt and went into the front room, leaving the door partway open. I heard several affirmative noises, then a "Yeah, okay." He came back into the room, and I suddenly noticed the gun stuck into his waistband, bandito-style, was *my* Colt. With the hammer down, so that it appeared safer to the uneducated. Idiot. He'd have to cock it before he could even fire a shot. Hammer down it was just a brick.

"That was him. Says they'll be here in about fifteen minutes. We're supposed to give Junior a sleepy-time shot and sanitize the place."

"We're supposed to clean this whole fucking place in fifteen minutes?" Johnson bitched. "Jesus, where are my gloves?"

The two of them pulled on leather gloves, hunted up some greasy rags, and began wiping the place down furiously. They hit every surface that could possibly hold a fingerprint. Even in such a small place, that was a lot to wipe. Johnson started in the front room, then was back in five minutes to work on the desk and chairs.

"What a waste of time this is," Johnson complained as he worked. "Shit, it'd be easier just to torch the place."

Ten minutes into the cleaning frenzy I began to wonder if they'd forgotten I was supposed to be drugged again. I needn't have worried. As Johnson began scrubbing the countertop he came across the vial and syringe.

"Oh shit," he said, "I was supposed to shoot him up again." He hurriedly grabbed the stuff, filled the syringe, and stuck me in the forearm.

I wondered what was going on. If they were wiping the place down it was obvious they planned to abandon the location. Reason as yet unknown. Drugging me yet again meant they had no immediate plans to kill me. Emphasis on "immediate".

Not even a minute later I heard banging beyond the door. Bruise-head went out and came back into the room with Scarface and a tall skinny guy I'd never seen before. He had black hair and was the youngest of the bunch, maybe thirty years old.

"You ready?" Scarface asked. The two makeshift maids looked around the room, then at each other.

"Yeah, I think so," Johnson said. "How you doin', Larry?"

"Fine, 'cept for having to drive all the way from Maryland for this corkscrewing goatfuck," the skinny guy said. Another man appeared in the doorway, middleaged and stocky, wearing a red baseball cap. He looked around the room and then glanced at me disinterestedly. Larry's partner? That was my guess.

"It snowballed on us," Bruise-head said a little defensively.

"Well no shit."

"You shoot him up?" Scarface said, pointing at me. I gave him my best blank stare.

"Yeah."

So, they were going to move me. Where? Unknown. Why? Unknown. What I did know, however, was that I had at least another couple of minutes before the drug started kicking my ass.

Larry approached me and wrinkled his nose. "Oh, gimmee a fucking break! What, have you guys been pissing on him? I'm s'posed to ride in the car next to this?" As he complained he knelt down in front of me, pulling a folding knife from his pocket. I felt him sawing around my ankles, and then he tossed away layered shreds of duct tape. He moved around behind me and somehow separated my cuffs from the chair with one deft motion.

I didn't have to pretend I was shaky on my feet when Larry yanked me upright by the collar. I swayed back and forth and tried not to fall down even as Bruise-head moved close in case I decided to get frisky. Shit, I'd been in that damn chair for at least twenty-four hours, I wasn't about to make a run for it. I could barely stand. Larry kept me at arm's length so he didn't get messy.

"Let's go, let's go." With Larry on one arm and Bruise-head on the other I was walked toward the door. Scarface went ahead of us, opening the door, while Johnson finished up the cleaning job by pouring bleach over my chair and splashing it around the floor.

Once through the doorway I found myself in a

windowed anteroom. Abandoned desks and chairs filled the dusty space. The sunlight streaming in hurt my eyes and I had to squint. Through a window I could see that the front door led out onto a small patch of pavement with four spaces marked off. Past that was a huge boulevard of a street, three or four lanes on either side of a grassy median. Lots of traffic flew by, but no pedestrians. If we were still in Metro Detroit, the area wasn't immediately identifiable to me.

"I'll give the place the once over and catch you on the way," Ballcap told Larry.

"Check the dumpster out back," Bruise-head told the man. "I don't think we used it, but...."

Scarface opened the front door and looked left and right.

"Clear," he called out.

I was practically lifted off my feet as we went out the door. Cold winter air blasted me and I shivered. Parked in one of the spaces was a nondescript Ford Crown Victoria. Square, brown, easy to miss. Scarface pulled open its back door and I was bent over and shoved inside. I landed on my side and bounced on the seat.

I was never going to get a better chance. I squirmed around like a clumsy, drugged idiot trying to sit up. Meanwhile I twisted my arms furiously, trying to work my hands, even as I lay on them, around to my right front pocket. My fingers scrabbled at the denim of my jeans, trying to find purchase. I grunted and looked around stupidly when someone kicked me in my calf, which was still hanging out the open door.

"Sit the fuck up."

My fingers finally found the pocket. I used a knee to lift

my body slightly and with the increased freedom of movement jammed a hand inside.

"What the hell? How much of that shit did you give him?" Hands grabbed my shoulders just as my fingers closed on the keys. I was yanked sharply vertical and tossed against the back of the seat. "If he pisses his pants again I'm going to lose it, I just got over the stomach flu."

Larry thumped onto the bench seat to my left, and Bruise-head sat on my right. I felt blood trickling down my knuckles. When they'd slammed me back into the seat—and into my cuffed hands—one of the keys stabbed deep into my palm. I ground my teeth together and tried not to change expression.

Johnson drove, with Scarface riding shotgun. I tried to look around while appearing to be incoherent. The area didn't seem too badly maintained, more middle class than anything else. The boulevard was looking more and more like Woodward Avenue, someplace in Ferndale or Royal Oak.

From the outside, the building I'd just spent the last twenty-four hours in didn't look like much at all. One story, small, with a plain brick exterior and a "FOR LEASE" sign in the window. I didn't catch any more detail, I had to keep bobbing and swaying my head to keep up the illusion I was under the influence.

When the traffic cleared Johnson pulled out. He stayed in the left lane, heading southeast, if the sun's position was any indication.

My time as a functioning adult was growing short. The drug would start kicking in in just a minute or two; if I was going to do something I had to do it quick. However, I was wedged tight between Larry and Bruise-head. Any movement I made they'd notice. I sorted through my keys by feel, an agonizing process, reminding myself to slow down every time I started to hurry.

Every time the car slowed down for a light, Larry would reach his right hand inside his jacket underneath his left arm and focus more of his attention on me. Once, as he shifted his hand, I thought I saw a gun butt. When I glanced at the front seat, luck was on my side. Scarface seemed more interested in the passing scenery than me, and Johnson kept busy driving, his eyes on the road. Both of them were wearing their seatbelts.

My heart started to beat faster and my palms started to sweat. I'd found the handcuff key with my fingers, and edged it close to the cuff around my left wrist.

"What the hell are you doing?" Larry said to me. I looked around the car, like I was trying to find the voice. As I did, I saw the world in front of me begin to blur slightly. The drug was kicking in, and while I wanted to panic, and rush, I knew I had to time it perfectly. We were slowing down for a red light, and Larry reassuringly touched the butt of his gun again.

"I don't feel so good," I mumbled. "Car too bumpy. Can you open a window?" I hiccupped.

"Open a window, open a window!" Johnson said frantically from behind the wheel. "He's puked enough already, I don't want the whole car smelling." The light in front of us turned green before we'd come to a stop and Johnson accelerated. Larry relaxed, and his right hand moved away from his gun. "Open the windows back there halfway or something."

I stared at the seat between my thighs and tried to look harmless. The seat shifted as both Larry and Bruise-head turned away from me and began powering down the back windows. For that brief moment, no one was pressed against my arms. I unlocked my left cuff, and leaned forward just enough to free my wrist. Then I brought both my hands around in front of me. Bruise-head finished rolling down the window and glanced disinterestedly at me.

Kelly, covered in blood. Oscar dead on the floor. I forced those images into my head. My whole life, I'd always kept myself under control. Even during the infamous parking lot shootout I was thinking, planning. I was the most tightly wrapped person I knew. I never let myself lose control, had never let myself lose control, ever, because I was afraid of what would happen.

Not.
Any.
More.

The world shunted and a black-red mist drifted across my eyes. A white-hot, brilliant pinpoint of hate blossomed in my head. I focused myself, and welcomed the hate. I nurtured it, I lost myself in its heat, I put aside reason and tried to forget everything but the hate. I found an infinity of hate in half a second and lost myself to it.

I focused every atom of my being into the point of my right elbow and drove it so violently into Bruise-head's throat his head bounced off the corner post.

"What!" someone yelled. Larry had his hand inside his coat, reaching for the gun. I leapt on top of him, trapped his arm under my right knee, screamed in his face and hammered him across the face with my forearm. His head bounced off the seatback and I could feel his hand fluttering under my knee. A fiery haze seemed to fill the air between us. I grabbed hold of his collar with my left hand and pounded him again across the nose. Spit and blood sprayed the seat, my elbow tingling.

The whites of his eyes showed briefly, but his hand kept tugging frantically at the gun. I drew back my arm, but before I could hit Larry again Johnson slammed on the brakes. Rubber shrieked on pavement. I held fiercely onto Larry's collar and tried not to fly into the front seat. A glimpse of Bruise-head out of the corner of my eye, face purple, running out of air, eyes bulging as he clawed at his sunken throat.

The car's momentum pulled me backward, backward, until the front seat's headrest dug into my spine. The car skipped sideways to a stop, curses flying from behind me. Blaring horns filled the air. As I came back off the front seat I hammered Larry again in the face, my whole body behind the blow. I hit him harder than I'd ever hit anyone before, hit him harder than I thought humanly possible. His body went limp and my arm went numb from the elbow on down. I slid off him and fumbled for the gun under his arm, pulling his limp hand away.

Johnson and Scarface were still caught up in their seatbelts when I spun around. They'd tried drawing their guns without unfastening their belts and had gotten tangled up.

Scarface was half-turned around, his hand under his coat and pinned in place as he leaned into the seatbelt. The double-click of the Smith and Wesson as I pulled the trigger back was the loudest sound in the universe. His skull exploded from the .357 Magnum and the windshield shattered as the bullet kept on going. Johnson screamed something unintelligible through the smoke and spraying blood. He twisted in the driver's seat, ripped an automatic out past his seatbelt and fired at me. His hand banged against the seat's headrest as the hammer fell and the shot went wild.

My cheek burned from the muzzle flash as I twisted around and shot him three times high in the chest. His gun fell out of his hand into the backseat and he slumped backward against his door. He looked confused, and grabbed weakly at the steering wheel.

The interior of the car started to get all wavy and incandescent. I held tight to the seatback as the world spun around once, tilting crazily. Sunlight glinted off the handcuffs as they dangled from my right wrist. Wisps of smoke drifted lazily in the air, curling toward the ceiling. The copper smell of blood hung in the air.

"Goddammit, goddammit," I muttered. The gunfire had left me nearly deaf. The ringing in my ears was loud as church bells.

Larry was slumped awkwardly in his seat. The left side of his face was strangely sunken, the eye bulging out and showing only white. Dropping the revolver, I climbed over him and fumbled with the door. The world was shifting around me, a big vat of Jell-O swaying back and forth. When I finally got the door unlocked I shouldered it open and saw the car was slowly drifting forward, still in gear. With a groan I flopped backward and dug inside Bruisehead's coat. He never moved as I roughly reclaimed my Colt from his belt. I climbed back over Larry, grabbing my keys off the seat, and stumbled out of the car, gun in hand. Cars flew by me, horns blowing, and it was all I could do to remain upright.

I was in the middle of the street, wind from the traffic tousling my hair. The Crown Vic rolled slowly away from me, angling gently from the center left to the center right lane. Its left rear door hung open, Larry's trailing hand just visible. Cars slewed around it as it crossed into the next lane.

I shoved the Colt into my waistband and somehow managed to stumble across three lanes of traffic without getting hit. Objects moved in and out of focus and my mind kept wanting to drift. The bright yellow of a sign caught my eye and I squinted to read it. A Shell gas station. I jogged haltingly in that direction and found what I was hoping to see. A pay phone.

From some locked vault inside my head I managed to conjure up a phone number. I dug some coins out of my pocket, but my vision was so bad, fading in and out, that I couldn't tell which were quarters. I fed the phone half a dozen at random and punched in the number before I forgot it.

"Hello?" I heard a loud, horrible screech and then a resounding crunch. A block away I could barely see the Crown Vic sideways in the middle of the street, T-boned by a big Lincoln. A motorcycle was wedged halfway under the Lincoln, and I could hear screaming.

"Jerry?" My voice was slurred and barely comprehensible.

"No, this is his mother. Which drunken idiot of a friend is this?"

"Don't hang up. John Phault. Need to talk Jerry. Portant." Speaking clearly took more energy and concentration than I thought I had left.

"John! Where the hell have you been? Jerry's been looking all over for you."

"I'm all fucked up. I need pick someone up. Me. I mean, need someone to come pick me up. I need help, can't drive. Where's Jerry?"

"Are you okay? You sound horrible."

"Shut up!" I yelled. "Can't talk long, I think I'm gonna pass out. I'm at…" I lurched away from the phone and looked for a street sign or anything else that would tell me where I was. "Telegraph, Six Mile!" I managed to slur while yelling into the phone. My hands were shaking so badly I was having trouble holding onto the receiver, and it wasn't just from standing outside in the December air wearing nothing but a T-shirt and jeans. "Gas station! Fore I freeze to death."

"Jerry's out," I heard her saying. "I'll call his cell. If he doesn't answer I'll come get you myself." I think she said something else, but I sort of drifted away from the phone. The receiver fell out of my hand and swung back and forth. They could be looking for me. Better get out of sight.

I staggered toward the gas station. There seemed to be a lot of activity further down the road, everyone was looking in that direction, away from me. Horny, horny cars. I found the gas station wall and bounced along it for a while until I hit something metal. I tried to go around the metal thing but couldn't see well enough to figure out where I was going.

The rancid smell of rotting garbage drifted up from somewhere and I threw up, this time all over myself. That exhausted my energy supplies and I fell to the ground, banging my knees. I was cold, so cold, my teeth chattering. I curled up into a ball on the hard ground, the earth swaying and tilting. Light came and went with the waves, and the rhythm finally put me to sleep.

"Oh, Jesus."

I felt hands lifting me, helping me stand. My whole body was shaking uncontrollably.

"Give him a coat. Hurry up, give him your coat. His skin's like ice." A coat was thrown around my shoulders. I let them lead me, my teeth chattering like a machine gun. I was physically lifted into the truck, set on the backseat. Jerry flipped a switch and the fan went from low to high, blasting hot air at me.

"Let's go, let's go!"

Bob jumped behind the wheel. I laid on the seat and bounced around as he pulled out of the gas station over a curb.

"Are you okay?" Jerry climbed into the backseat and started checking me over for injuries. "Jesus, he's covered in puke." I felt myself being pressed into the seat as Bob accelerated.

"Sorry," I mumbled through my chattering teeth. "Drugs. Spinning all around."

Bob turned halfway around in his seat. "What did he say?"

"Something about drugs. He's tripping on something, that's for sure. Are you okay?" he asked me. "Are you hurt? You've got some blood on you."

"Sick," I mumbled. "Maybe broken ribs. I'm okay. Grabbed."

"Are you following this?" Jerry asked Bob. "I think he's got hypothermia. God knows how long he was out there. I don't think it's his blood."

"Drugged!" I said forcefully. I couldn't believe they were so thickheaded. "Got grabbed. Fucking Robert Redford." I looked at Bob plaintively. "I'm sorry! Fucked up, I think. Couldn't help it. Don't remember. Goddamn motherfuckers. Fuckin' killed 'em."

"John, what were all the police cars doing on Telegraph right near where we found you?" Jerry said very loudly and very slowly. "The whole street's blocked off. Do you know anything about that?"

"Motherfuckers," I asserted. "Sundance wasn't there, but just about everyone else. Tried to steal my gun. Birthday present." I tried to pull my Colt from my belt then, and Jerry restrained me. He took the .45 and set it aside.

"Is anybody going to be coming after us? I mean, is there anybody in the area we should be looking out for?" Bob said.

"Think I killed them all. Nice and warm," I said. "Feel a lot better." I tried to organize my thoughts into a coherent pattern. It took a while. "Got kidnapped," I said finally, laboring over each word. "Drugged. Bunch of spooks I think. Got away in a big brown car. Blew his head all over the glass. Is Steve dead?" I said worriedly.

"No, but he feels like shit, if that helps," Jerry told me. "Never saw you leave. Man, look at all the cop cars, they're coming out of the woodwork," I heard him marvel from the front seat as yet another siren flew past us.

I faded out again. Jerry's worried face hovering over me was the last thing I saw.

A couple of sharp bumps brought me to. I had no idea how long I'd been unconscious. I cracked an eye and saw I was still laying on the backseat of the Blazer, Bob behind the wheel. Jerry had moved into the front seat and they were talking. I was only shivering half the time, and my mind seemed a lot clearer. Maybe near-hypothermia made the drug wear off faster.

"So where the hell are we going to take him?" Jerry was saying.

"Man, I'm fucked up," I mumbled. They didn't hear me. My swollen lips felt like balloons. My whole face hurt when I talked. Hell, my whole body hurt without me having to do anything. Another bout of shivers hit and I pulled the coat closer around me.

"You're asking me?" Bob said. "What have I got in this state, other than my parents' house and Ron's?"

"Both out," Jerry agreed. "His house is no good," he said, stabbing a finger at me, "and there's no way Steve's mom could handle this."

"Motel?" Bob kept his hands on the wheel, his body still as he drove. He never took his eyes off the road. I could see his hands clenching and unclenching, the skin around his knuckles whitening.

"Seriously? Look at him. How the fuck are we supposed to get him in without someone calling the cops? Manager'll think we're dragging in a corpse to have sex with."

"I'm not that bad," I said defensively. I blinked my eyes a couple times, trying to clear up the fuzzy edges. It didn't work. I managed to sit up. Sort of.

"So you're back, huh?" Jerry gave me a look. "You shouldn't say anything until you see yourself in a mirror. I won't even mention the smell."

"I think I messed up." I reached up a hand to feel my lips. They weren't nearly as big as they felt. My hand gently explored the rest of my face. No cuts, but a whole lot of swelling and sore spots. My upper right arm hurt enough to be broken, but I didn't think it was. I remembered blocking a kick with it.

"What about your house?" Bob said to Jerry.

"Ahh, I really hate to go anywhere that someone might look for us. Hell, we still don't know what happened to Mr. Potato Head here."

"I got kidnapped. I'm guessing they were spooks, but I never asked and they didn't tell." I started to feel weird and woozy again. The drug in me was hitting its second wind, or coming out of hiding now that I was warming up. I reached out a hand and grabbed the seat to steady myself. "Whoa, *jeezus*. Drugged the shit out of me." I slid down in the seat until I couldn't see the road or the other cars.

"What'd they do, give you drugs to make you talk?" Jerry said. I nodded drunkenly.

"I'm sorry, I'm sorry, I fucked up," I said. "Drugged me all day and night, don't even know what I said. You see someone that's the spitting image of Robert Redford, you run the bastard over. I'm glad Steve isn't dead, I thought I'd killed him." Jerry and Bob traded a look.

I leaned forward slightly to get a better angle on Bob. "I think I told them I gave you the disk. I don't remember. Better be careful."

Bob slowed the truck down for a traffic light and turned and looked at me with a dead face. Jerry had the weirdest expression on his face, sad and horrified at the same time.

After opening and closing his mouth twice, Jerry told me, looking like he wanted to cry, "They blew up his fiancée." His eyes darted to Bob, then back to me.

"What?" The fog in my head was drifting in and out, but I was pretty sure I'd heard him correctly.

"Cathy. They put a bomb in her car. It went off this morning. She's dead."

My mind couldn't seem to accept it. "Why would they want to kill her? That doesn't make sense."

"It was my mom's car," Bob said slowly, with absolutely no emotion in his voice, staring out the windshield. "The one I was driving yesterday because of my flat. The one I drove over to Ron's. My mom let her use it to run some errands. Cathy hated driving this thing. She said it was too big, that she was afraid she'd hit something."

I felt like a sledgehammer had hit me in the chest. "Oh God, Bob, I'm sorry. It's my fault. I must have told them about the disk." And they'd gone out and mistakenly blown up Bob's fiancée, on the information I'd given them. "I got her killed. Oh Jesus." I couldn't move.

Bob didn't say anything for a long time. He sat rigid in the seat, staring forward out the glass, both hands clenched on the wheel. Jerry never moved, maybe never even breathed.

Finally Bob spoke. "*They* killed her, not you," he said through gritted teeth. I could see his huge jaw muscles bulging. He never looked at me, just stared straight ahead. "I can't hold you responsible, they did it. I know you wouldn't have told them anything voluntarily. All the new drugs they've got, I'd probably have blabbed too."

I wished then that I'd been physically tortured. Fingernails pulled out, cigarettes put out on me, anything. Just so that I'd have something, some visible evidence of resistance, to help me retain some measure of self-respect. Giving up everything under the influence of chemicals, without even token resistance—pathetic. And Bob's fiancée was killed because of it. Because of me.

"Bob, I…" What the hell was I going to say? *Sorry?* "It's my fault," I finished lamely. "I'm the one to blame."

Bob turned around in his seat then and gave me a look I'll never forget.

"If I held you responsible for Cathy's death you'd be dead already," he said, absolutely no emotion in his words. And I had no doubt he meant it. "I don't want to talk about it anymore." He turned back around and kept driving.

After that the Blazer was quiet for a long time. Jerry, obviously uneasy, finally broke the silence.

"You think there were a lot of feds at Ron's, you should have seen Bob's house. The police called the ATF and they were rolling up with a whole shitload of explosive analyzers, fume sniffers, all sorts of equipment while we were scooting out the back."

The Blazer hit a couple of hard bumps and my stomach flip-flopped. I grabbed hold of Jerry's seat-back and swallowed. "I don't think I've got anything left in my stomach to throw up, but you better be prepared anyway." My mouth was dry and I was sweating even while I shivered.

"Listen, does that make sense to you guys?" I said. "Blowing up Bob? I mean, if they were after the disk, wouldn't you think they'd be more interested in retrieving it than killing anybody who might've found it? If they know what's on it, they've got to know it's encrypted, so it's not like we know what's on the damn thing." I vaguely remembered a conversation Johnson and Sundance had about that very subject, but the details escaped me. "Where is the disk, anyway?"

"I've got it in my bag," Bob said. "My mom couldn't do shit with it."

"Aren't you the person they just kidnapped?" Jerry said. "The same person they tried to kill first, not one day before? I'm just a fucking college kid, so maybe I'm missing something, but *none* of this makes any fucking sense to me. Speaking of that, if they were using drugs, how come your face looks like it was slammed in a car door twenty times?"

"I didn't go quietly when they grabbed me. Three on one, in an elevator."

"Ouch."

"I gave as good as I got, for a while. I must have bad karma or something."

"Join the fucking club," Bob muttered. "The cops think I blew Cathy up."

"What?"

Jerry elaborated. "The ranking guy on the scene, a

sergeant or something, it only took him ten minutes to figure out that it wasn't a *bomb* bomb, it was a grenade. A frag, wedged between the seat and the door, with the pin pulled. I guess he was EOD in the Army." He shook his head. "So half of them figure—Hey! He's in the Army. Army, grenade, two plus two equals he blew up his fiancée, arrest him. At least they weren't all thinking that. The rest of them hear he's a Green Beret, they wonder if he's been overseas pissing off any terrorists lately." Jerry frowned. "I knew something was up when I called his house and cops answered. Just like Ron's, déjà vu all over again. I had to park on the next street over, walk through his backyard. They've got him in the kitchen, asking dumb questions like have he and Cathy had any fights recently. Unfuckingbelievable. Then my mom called me, and off we went."

"The cops didn't mind you leaving?" I said to Bob.

"I didn't ask." His voice was flat. I could see him struggling to keep himself under control. One moment he stone-faced and still, the next he was vibrating with pent-up rage.

"Well, we might as well all be in trouble with the cops," I grumbled.

"Hey, I just thought of somewhere we might be able to hole up for a while. Pull over wherever you see a pay phone," Jerry said.

"Do I look as bad as I feel?" I groaned, shifting in the seat in a fruitless attempt at comfort.

"You look two hours dead," Jerry said. "How do you feel? How'd you get away, anyway?"

"They were moving me. I have a handcuff key on my keyring and managed to get to it. Incompetents." The Blazer slowed and turned, then bumps like going up a driveway.

"Why were they moving you?"

"Hell if I know."

"There's a phone," Bob announced.

"I'll be back." Jerry hopped out and disappeared. I was still nearly horizontal on the seat.

"What the hell's our next step?" Bob asked, staring out the window. "About the only organization that isn't involved in this is the Coast Guard."

"Damned if I know." I could feel myself starting to fade fast after my short burst of coherence. "I feel like shit." It was getting to be an effort to even think, much less carry on an intelligent conversation. I laid across the seat and closed my eyes. For the first time the Blazer decided not to spin around me.

"How many guys were on you in the car?" Bob asked quietly.

"Smashed one guy's throat, got the other guy's gun. The two morons in the front seat had their seatbelts on."

The next thing I knew the truck was moving again, Jerry back in his seat.

"You sure they're going to be okay?" Bob was saying. Apparently I'd missed the beginning of the conversation.

"You'll know when you see them. They're good guys. They're a little bit country, we're a little bit rock and roll, that's all. I told Dave everything that's going on, he was glad he could help. He's heard me talking about you before. Hell, he was already worried. You should hear what's on the TV. I guess CNN's all over your house, blathering about terrorists and Homeland Security alerts. This sounds big. Like *big* big. You want me to turn on the radio?"

"No," Bob and I said together.

"Where're we going?" I asked, my eyes still closed.

"Two brothers I work with live up in Lake Orion. Their house is nice and secluded, and no one would know to look for me there, much less you guys. Don't even have to worry about their parents, they're in Hawaii for a week."

"Oh Christ," I mumbled.

I came to again when Bob cut the engine. I cracked my eyelids and saw both of them turned in their seats, staring at me. "Can you walk or do we need to carry your battered ass?"

Jerry climbed out and held the seat forward so I'd have room to squeeze out. I moved like an old man, slow and hunched over, but I got out on my own, without throwing up or passing out. The cold winter air hit me again but the Blazer's heater had chased the shivers from my body.

The Blazer was in the center of a circular gravel driveway, trees all around. Twenty yards behind it I could see a patch of dirt road, nothing but woods on the other side. In front of me was a large two-story house, white with green and brown trim. The house was decorated country rustic style, with a lot of woodwork around the porch columns and window shutters.

The house's front yard sloped down sharply toward the rear of the property. The basement was probably a walk-out. Beyond the back yard were more trees. I couldn't see any other houses, but I could hear the faint sound of heavy traffic on a paved road, so we weren't as removed from civilization as things first appeared.

The front door opened. A young male a few years older than Jerry stepped out, holding the door open for us. He had a lever-action Winchester in one hand, and a revolver was stuck in his belt. He looked around before he looked at us.

"Damn," he said, looking at me. "Better get him inside

before someone drives by. There's some antiseptic in one of the bathrooms, don't know what else. Park the truck around back, we can stick it in the barn out of sight."

"There's still time to back out, Dave," Jerry told him.

"What, and miss all the fun? Hey Doug!" A younger version of Dave stepped around the back corner of the house and looked our way. He held a scoped pump shotgun in his hands. "Go open up the barn, we'll put the truck in there."

Jerry and I stepped past Dave into the house while Bob started up the Blazer. Jerry kept a cautious hand on my arm. I was swaying a little but didn't feel nauseous anymore.

"I really appreciate this," Jerry said.

"You'd do the same for me. Straight ahead, just put him on the couch." I heard him close the front door with a thunk. The door was an antique, solid wood two inches thick, with detailed nature scenes carved into it.

I half-fell onto a couch that had seen better days. I faced a huge stone fireplace, the mantel made of rough-hewn four by sixes. Dave came into the room and looked at me. I looked back. He was maybe five nine and lean, with sandy brown hair. His body was compact, his arms ropy with muscle. One of those people blessed with good genes. I went through basic training with guys like him, guys that could do pushups and pull-ups all day, backpack their bodyweight on long road marches without breaking a sweat. He looked worried and scared and excited as hell.

"I'll go see what kind of first aid I can dig up," he said. He propped the rifle against the hearth and left the room. A few seconds later Doug came into the room from a back hallway, Bob on his heels carrying two large gear bags. Doug had the same build as his brother, and they both had dark farmer tans from working outside all summer at the plant nursery. Doug was maybe half an inch taller and two or three years younger. His sandy-blond hair was cut into an absolutely perfect flattop.

Bob dug into one of his bags and pulled out his suppressed MP5. He snapped a magazine into place and chambered a round. Doug gave him a wide-eyed stare.

"What's up?" Jerry asked.

"You willing to bet your life that no bad guys are going to track us down here? This place is pretty defensible. Really only need two people to cover the whole perimeter. One guy in the front room, and the other one on the deck out back. You can cover three sides of the house from back there." The deck was reached through a sliding glass door on the far side of the room I was in. Since the lawn fell away the deck towered nearly fifteen feet off the ground. "Four-hour watches, everybody can get some rest."

"I know you guys never threw away the vests I got from the feds," I said. "I can't think of a better time to start wearing them." Bob looked at me, thought a second, then dug into the second bag and pulled out his Kevlar vest. He set the MP5SD down, pulled off his jacket and then began removing the hardware that interfered with his taking off his shirt. I saw the Browning still on his right hip, but at first I couldn't figure out what the leather harness around his shoulders was. Then I realized it was the rig for his big Randall knife, his engagement present, hanging upside down under his left arm. He had to remove that before he could pull on the vest.

"I'll give Steve a call, let him know where we are," Jerry said. "I can have him drop by my house, grab my stuff."

"These guys are probably really good at following people," I warned.

"Once he gets his Mustang up to a hundred and twenty

on Lapeer Road he'll lose them, no matter how many people are on him, unless they're using a helicopter. Or they'll start chasing him. Either way we should be okay, he won't show up unless he's sure he's clear."

Jerry turned to Bob. "The Blazer's hidden now. Anybody comes here, they're gonna have to knock on the door or look in the window to find out if we're here. The three of us should try to keep out of sight, have only Dave or Doug wandering around outside or up on the deck." Bob looked at him silently.

Dave returned, his hands full of bottles and gauze. "This is what we've got. I'm not much for first aid, though."

"Set it down," Jerry said, pointing at the end table beside the couch. "Anything else fucked up beside your face?"

"I'm getting twinges in my ribs." I pointed at the offending area.

"Take off your shirt. Hell, take off all your clothes. You smell like a barnyard. We'll get 'em washed. You got anything that'll fit him?" he asked Dave.

"I'll see what I can do." Dave disappeared while I gingerly removed my clothes. I put my belt and hardware on the floor and handed the clothes to Doug. He kept them at arm's length and headed for a washing machine. I looked down and saw angry red marks on both sides of my ribcage. I hoped my face didn't look that bad.

"I think I see a tread pattern," Jerry marveled. The bruise was definitely shoe-shaped. Doug returned with a thick blanket and I wrapped myself up in it.

"I'm going to need a couple towels soaked in hot water," Jerry said. "Old towels, not the good stuff."

Bob was only slightly bulkier under his clothes with the vest on. He grabbed the MP5 and started toward the front room, just off the front door. It had a small bay window, the sill covered with houseplants. From there he could see the entire front yard and as much of the road as was visible from the house.

"Bob?" Jerry said questioningly. Bob stopped and looked at him. "You've got more first-aid training than me, do you want to check him out?"

"You can handle it." With that he walked into the front room, a grim look on his face.

Doug returned with the towels. Jerry spent ten minutes swabbing at my head. By the time he was done both towels were pink. Dave reappeared, and Doug drifted off toward the back of the house, shotgun in hand.

"I'm, uh, gonna wander around," Dave said, obviously trying to think of something useful to do. Jerry nodded at him, and he picked up the Winchester and disappeared.

"You don't look so bad, all cleaned up," Jerry said to me. "Your face, that is. There are a couple of nice splits in the back of your head, probably should be stitched up. Your face is all swollen, but I don't think anything's broken. You'll be a nice shade of purple tomorrow."

"How 'bout my ribs?" He'd felt along them with his fingertips.

"I think they're just bruised. We'd need an X-ray to know for sure."

"Well, it only hurts when I breathe." My eyes darted in the direction of the front room and lowered my voice. "How's Bob doing?"

"How's he look like he's doing? I've barely gotten five words out of him all day."

"How bad was it?"

He leaned close and whispered. "That grenade, Christ, it blew her intestines all over the road in front of the house.

By the time I got there the whole area was covered, walled off with yellow tape, but I heard the cops talking about it. Neighbors all over the place, gawking, cop cars parked on everybody's lawns. When I walked in the back door and saw Bob talking to the detectives I about shit. I mean, he's covered in blood. Covered like Carrie at the prom. He was in the house when it blew, but I think he tried to do first aid on her, CPR or something. Maybe tried to stuff her guts back in. And the detectives are having him stand around like that, you believe it? Shouldn't they have taken his shirt as evidence or something?"

"Maybe they were waiting for the evidence techs. Pictures first, then bag the shirt. I don't know. I can't really think straight right now." Actually, I was trying not to think about Bob's dead fiancée. And how she was dead because of me. No matter what Bob said, no matter who had actually planted the grenade, they'd gone after Bob because of what I'd told them.

"I don't think they were either," Jerry told me. "Nobody was really thinking, everybody was really freaked out, learning Bob's Special Forces got them thinking this was some sort of terrorist attack. I don't even think he knew he had the blood on him. He was all wild-eyed, just sitting there, not moving, not focusing on anything. The detectives, I think they'd only been there a few minutes, I don't think they even knew who I was, maybe they thought I was his brother or something. My guess is they don't go on a lot of bombing slash terrorism slash whatever calls. Place was like a Chinese fire drill, which I guess worked out for us, I'd never have been able to slide him out of there if they'd had their shit together. He had the Blazer parked on the street around the corner, and I don't think anybody knew it was his."

We both looked toward the front door. I could hear the hardwood floor creaking as Bob paced back and forth in front of the window, got brief glimpses of him as he turned and headed back around. "I grabbed some clean clothes for him out of his room and then I got the call from mom. The detectives were on the phone with the ATF or somebody and we just scooted out the back with his gear and jumped in the Blazer. I'm glad no one thought to stop us, I don't know what Bob would have done." He sighed, and all the energy seemed briefly to drain out of him. "It seems like that's all I've done today, clean blood off people."

He threw the towels down and looked me over. "Go find a bathroom, take a shower. You don't have anything I can bandage anyway, 'cept those cuts on the back of your head. And I can't do anything with them unless I shave around the wounds first. I can do it, but you'll look like a radiation victim."

"Thanks, I'll pass. This thing'll be over, one way or the other, before the cuts have a chance to get infected."

"I hope you're right. Dry off, then come back and I'll slather you in whatever Dave managed to dig up."

It was the longest and most painful shower I'd ever taken. By the time I dried off and stepped out of the bathroom I could smell the dryer going. I wrapped myself tight in the blanket and shuffled back to the couch.

Food was cooking somewhere. My stomach growled, but I didn't trust it. Not yet. I dropped onto the couch and took a good look around the room for the first time. Comfortable, worn furniture, slightly western in style. A picture on the wall of Dave, posing with a huge, dead elk. Another of a much younger Doug, with a deer. Maybe his first? He only looked about ten in the picture. Hell, they looked so much alike, it could've been Dave, but I didn't think so. There was a slight difference around the eyes.

A wave of exhaustion hit me, the events of the past twenty-four hours taking a heavy toll. I wrapped myself tighter in the blanket and reclined on the couch. I didn't feel nearly as doped up as I had just half an hour earlier, but the drug kept hitting me in waves. I'd get woozy and light-headed and stupid, and my heart would thump oddly. I hoped whatever they'd given me hadn't done any permanent damage to my head. Jerry came into view, eating a big sandwich.

"Lay on your side, I'll dab the cuts on your head so they don't get infected. Hopefully. You hungry? Dave's got sandwiches, some chicken cooking."

His sandwich smelled good but the aroma made my stomach dance around uneasily. I turned on my side away from him and tried to find a position where my ribs didn't hurt.

"Thanks, maybe later," I told him.

I could hear him chewing as he worked on my head. Whatever he was using burned like a lit match. I closed my eyes and tried to relax.

"What are we gonna do?" Jerry said. "We can't just sit around waiting for somebody else with a gun to show up."

"What's this 'we' shit?"

"I'm your designated bodyguard now," he told me. "You're such a shit-magnet I'm sure something else will pop up before this thing's finished." I could only groan.

"Hey," I said suddenly.

"What?"

"Someone should go out and try to find that building where I was held. One of those guys might have left something laying around. At least get the address, so I can run a utilities check and see who's paying the bills."

"Well, describe it."

I did the best I could, but I'd only caught a brief glimpse of the exterior of the building. I told Jerry what side of Telegraph it had been on, how long we'd been driving before I escaped, and what plants had been growing on the boulevard across from its front door.

"Me and Bob'll check it out," he assured me. I don't know if I had the courtesy to wait until he was done treating my wounds before I fell asleep.

I awoke with a start, heart racing, sweaty. I rolled onto my back and stared at the ceiling. No way to tell how long I'd been asleep, but my neck was at least two hours worth of sore. I felt like I'd been beaten unconscious. About the only part of my body that didn't hurt was my feet. I would have taken more Tylenol, but I'd swallowed six earlier and was afraid more would just make me queasy. I'd thrown up enough for one week. I'd thrown up enough for the year.

The house was quiet. Somewhere I could hear the hum of an appliance, and outside the creak of bare branches in the wind. I struggled into a seated position and found my clothes neatly folded on the floor beside the couch. All the stains and smells seemed to have come out nicely. With a groan I got to my feet and hobbled toward the bathroom, the blanket clutched around my shoulders. On the way I ran into Dave.

"Back among the living?" he said.

"Technically. Where is everybody?"

"Doug's out back on the deck, Jerry's in the front room. You want anything to eat?"

"Where's Bob?" I couldn't read the expression on his face.

"He's out walking the perimeter." He gave me the look again.

"Walking the perimeter? I thought he agreed we should stay out of sight."

"I don't think he's doing too good." Dave was concerned, and I could see he was more than a little scared. Which was sort of ironic, seeing as he had a rifle in one hand and a pistol stuck in his belt, and was locked up safe in his own house.

"He'll be okay," I told him, trying to convince myself as much as him. I started toward the bathroom again.

"So you want something to eat?"

"I guess I'm willing to try. You got soup or a sandwich or something like that?"

"Sure."

I took care of business, then inspected my face in the mirror for the first time. I looked a lot better than I felt, which was scant comfort. A lot of the sore spots on my face weren't even bruised. At least not visibly, not yet, and the swelling wasn't so bad I looked like Frankenstein. I wrapped the blanket around myself and headed to the front room.

"Clean as a whistle," Jerry told me. He handed me a piece of paper with an address scribbled on it. "Whole place smelled like bleach. Even took all the trash out of the dumpster behind the building."

"It was a long shot," I admitted, trying not to show the disappointment I felt.

He gave me a look. "Telegraph is still roped off. Traffic was a nightmare. I didn't even know the Detroit Police Department had that many helicopters."

Bob was in the family room. His face was shiny and red.

The MP5SD hung across his chest by its complicated sling, stock extended.

"Hey Bob, what's up?" He acted as if he hadn't heard me. He had one of his black nylon gear bags and was digging furiously through it. "Bob?"

He wouldn't meet my eyes, instead pulling out several more magazines for his submachinegun. Boxes of ammunition followed, and he began filling the mags. I moved closer and saw the veins in his neck bulging, his jaw muscles clenched. Dave wandered in from the kitchen, wiping his hands on a towel.

"What are you doing?"

Bob still wouldn't look at me. The clicking continued as he kept loading magazines. Jerry walked in from the front room, a curious look on his face.

"I can't…I can't stand staying here, doing nothing," Bob said finally, not looking up. He topped off the third thirty-round magazine and put everything back in his bag. He unhooked the MP5 from its sling and stuck the sling into a pocket of his bag. When he picked the bag up, he looked around the room. His face was set into a blank, determined mask.

"So where are you going?" Jerry demanded of him.

Bob looked him right in the eye. "Looking for trouble."

I didn't even try to stop him. He went out the back door, bag in one hand and MP5 in the other. Two minutes later I heard the Blazer as it came around the front of the house and rolled out to the street. He spun a little gravel pulling out, then was gone. The rest of us looked at each other.

Doug came into the room wearing a brown Carhartt jacket, his crewcut covered by a knit cap. "Where's Bob going?" he asked us. He saw our expressions. "What?"

2:24 p.m.

Dave fixed me a delicious bowl of chicken soup and a turkey breast sandwich with mayo and lettuce. My stomach welcomed the soup but wasn't sure about the mayo on the sandwich.

I wasn't tired anymore. I was bruised, sore, cut, pissed off, and had one hell of a headache, but I wasn't tired. I put my clothes back on, then took my pistol apart. Everything appeared normal, so I put the .45 back together, loaded it, and stuck it back in its holster, hammer cocked and safety on. Somehow I managed to tie my own shoes without assistance, although it took me twice as long as it should have. For lack of anything better to do I prowled the house.

Jerry sat watch at the front window, staring out the glass from the wide oak seat of a beautiful antique rocking chair. He'd taken his 1911 out of the holster and set it on the sill so the gun butt wouldn't scrape the chairback.

I stood beside him and gazed outside for maybe ten minutes. Neither of us said anything. The sun was out, highlighting several stray leaves blowing around the yard. A few squirrels ran about, gathering last minute additions for their winter larder. Steve was on his way over.

Nothing was happening in the front yard and I finally wandered off. Doug was in the kitchen, noisily fixing himself something to eat. I nodded at him, then walked through the rest of the ground floor. The house was pretty big, maybe three thousand square feet, with a magnificent stone fireplace. If I'd been house hunting it would've definitely caught my eye.

Dave was out on the back deck, wearing a thick jacket and wool pants. His bare hands were stuck in his front pockets as he slowly wandered back and forth across the planks. I saw his rifle leaning inconspicuously in a corner, against the deck railing.

A small bookshelf held an eclectic assortment of titles. I grabbed a thriller and spent forty-five minutes trying to read it. Finally I gave up. I stuck the book back in its slot, and in a last-ditch effort to forget my worries I did a desperate thing—I turned on the TV.

All I could find was garbage. Channel after channel of talkshows, featuring an endless parade of defective humans talking to earnest, clueless hosts. I channel surfed for fifteen minutes, until finally one of the shows ended and a *Simon & Simon* rerun came on. I sighed with relief, sat back, and tried to relax. It worked, at least for a while.

I was jolted out of my semi-trance by an urgent, obnoxious musical burst. I focused my blurry eyes on the TV and saw a blank screen with the station logo. The slightly familiar face of a second-string anchor appeared, a busy newsroom behind him. In fact, the room was literally boiling with activity. People were running left and right and talking on phones, not making any attempt to keep the noise down. The words **Breaking Story** appeared at the bottom of the screen.

The anchor's eyes were wide as he looked into the camera. He could barely sit still, he was so excited.

"This is Bobby Collins, Channel Seven Action News. We're interrupting this program to bring you a breaking story." He was talking too fast, spilling the words out on top of each other.

"We go now, live, to Bill Mitchell on Detroit's northwest side. Bill?"

The view changed and I was looking at another reporter I vaguely recognized, standing in somebody's front yard, his back to the street. He wore a suit underneath an expensive topcoat, his tie an expensive silk job that probably cost eighty bucks. Mitchell, however, even in the fancy getup, looked bad. His face was pale and he kept blinking weirdly, like he'd just been hit in the head.

"This is Bill Mitchell, reporting live from northwest Detroit." He sounded a lot more together than he looked. "Not twenty minutes ago," he went on, "standing practically where I am now, I personally witnessed a horrific gun battle on the street you see behind me." He gestured without turning, while the cameraman pulled back and did a wide angle of the street.

The unmistakable awkward shapes of dead bodies littered the street. I saw at least four corpses, scattered around a grey Ford that had been broadsided by something big. Half a dozen cop cars were visible, lights flashing, with more screeching up every second. Between the sirens and the loud chop of a helicopter overhead, Mitchell practically had to shout to be heard. Whatever had happened was barely over.

"I was on this quiet Detroit street talking to the residents, asking them about the proposed racetrack project that would, if approved, require them to move and their houses to be demolished. Then the violence erupted." He paused dramatically. "We have video of the entire incident."

"Please be advised," Mitchell went on, "that the footage you are about to see is very graphic. I personally urge anyone with children present to have them leave the room. Again, what our reporter witnessed today was very violent, and we want anyone who might be disturbed by it to have ample warning."

Mitchell stopped speaking and stood there expectantly. The picture changed and suddenly I was looking at a huge black man in a stained T-shirt, standing on a porch. He was holding his screen door open while he talked.

"—what do you think? Naw, man, I don't want to move. And I sure as hell don't want my taxes raised to pay for no damn racetrack that we ain't even—" I became aware of the roar of engines, getting louder. The interviewee stopped in midsentence and looked past the camera just as the sound of squealing rubber filled the air.

"What's—" I heard someone, probably Mitchell, say.

The camera spun around to show the street. A grey Ford was sideways in the road, facing us. It still rocked from the skidding stop as four men piled out. They all had guns. The cameraman pulled back and I could see a black Caprice angled across the road on the left, forty feet from the Ford. It was pointed away from the camera. Two guys had already jumped out of it, one with a shotgun. The one with the shotgun ran around the rear of the car to the driver's side and ducked down. From fifty feet away the camera's microphone had no trouble picking up the hollow *ka-chunk* as he chambered a shell. Nothing else in the world sounds like a pump shotgun being racked.

Between the two cars was a black Blazer, one lone occupant behind the wheel. The Blazer wore handsome oversize tires as well as a gleaming back steel push bumper/brush guard. Its exhaust was a quiet, throaty rumble.

"'Nother Goddamn drug bust," I heard the black man say disgustedly, off camera.

"Oh, fuck. Hey. *Heyyy!*" I shouted. I bolted upright on the couch, grabbing at the cushions. The floor shook as Jerry and Dave came running in, alarmed.

"What? What!"

I never took my eyes off the TV, only pointed.

Two guys had dived out the Ford's driver side doors

and were now crouching behind the car, pointing pistols at the Blazer. The two men that had exited the Ford's passenger side stood there, next to the car, facing the Blazer in the open. One of them had an Uzi in his hands—its ugly lines were unmistakable. His partner wore a hideous orange shirt and was brandishing a revolver.

"Out of the car!" Orange-shirt was yelling at the Blazer. "Out of the fucking car!"

You idiots, I thought distantly. *Your two teams are looking right at each other. If there's any shooting you're going to kill yourselves.* But then it became clear, from their body language, that they didn't think there was going to be any shooting. They were in charge, in control, and had their man surrounded. Outnumbered.

The Blazer was broadside to the camera, its passenger side toward us as it faced the Ford. The dark form of the driver was visible inside the cab as he sat, unmoving.

"Shit," Jerry said weakly. "That's Bob." It sure was. His massive jaw was clearly identifiable even in silhouette.

"Is this live?" Dave asked.

Bob slowly leaned forward over the steering wheel and looked at the four guys in front of him. Orange-shirt was yelling again for him to get out of the car, while the guy with the Uzi had unfolded its stock and set it against his shoulder. He aimed it at Bob over the Blazer's grill.

"No," I told Dave.

Most of the yards on both sides of the street had chain link fences running almost all the way down to the curb. No room to drive around the Ford, no way. At the corner of the TV screen, past the guys crouching behind the Ford, I saw the silver back end of a Chevy Suburban. Channel Seven's blue logo was on both its rear doors.

Didn't Bob see the news truck? Somebody had to've seen the news truck, they couldn't all be that blind. Could they?

"It looks like the police are stopping someone, possibly a suspected drug dealer," Mitchell lamely attempted to narrate from offscreen. "You *are* getting this," he quietly asked the cameraman. "I believe the police call this a felony stop," Mitchell said, back in narrator mode.

Bob leaned back, left hand still on the wheel, and turned in his seat to look out the Blazer's back window. I could see the seatbelt over his shoulder stretch. The two guys were still there on the far side of the Caprice, pointing guns at the back of the Blazer.

And then History was burned permanently into my brain.

The cars had been stopped maybe ten seconds, and Orange-shirt began for the third time ordering Bob out of the truck. Bob was still turned in his seat, looking out the rear window.

Then the Blazer's back end dipped, and the murmur of its exhaust kicked into a high-volume roar. The truck jumped the ten feet to the Uzi-wielder in the blink of an eye. The steel bumper knocked him up and back, and the submachinegun sailed away into someone's yard. The Blazer, still gaining speed, thundered into the Ford, crushing the descending gunman's body between the two vehicles. Orange-shirt dived out of the way, dropping his gun.

The Ford bounced and skidded sideways from the impact, throwing the two men crouched behind it to the ground. The one farthest away started yelling. It looked like he was pinned beneath the car. Someone off-camera gasped.

Bob rebounded against his seatbelt, then was out the door. The driver of the Caprice, as soon as the Blazer began moving, ran around the front of his car. He was at the Blazer's rear bumper, charging forward, when Bob bailed out the door.

All I could see was feet underneath the Blazer as they met near the rear axle. Then Bob's feet were alone, and the man came crashing down headfirst onto the concrete, his pistol clattering. The man began kicking spasmodically, clutching at his throat.

Bob dropped to the ground and rolled under the Blazer toward me in one smooth motion as a shotgun boomed. He popped up and charged at Orange-shirt, who'd regained his feet near the front of the Ford. The man with the shotgun sidestepped right, pumped a fresh shell into the chamber, and took a bead on Bob's back.

Orange-shirt saw Bob coming and yelled, firing two panicked rounds at him. The guy with the shotgun, directly in the line of fire, dropped like a stone as only someone shot in the head can. Then Bob was on Orange-shirt.

He was amazingly, inhumanly quick, yet moved with such economy of motion the video looked like a slow-motion instant replay. Bob insolently slapped the man's revolver away, then grabbed the guy's chin with one hand and his hair with the other. He twisted violently, and Orange-shirt's feet came off the ground. The microphone picked up the pop of snapping neck bones quite nicely.

Bob never stopped moving, leaping on and over the Ford's hood before Orange-shirt even hit the pavement. The blonde near the driver's door had been kneeling with his gun out when Bob had rammed the sedan with the Blazer. The Ford's front fender had caught him square in the face, and hard. Blood covered his chin and streaked the front of his shirt as he sat dazed on the pavement. When he saw Bob, airborne over the car's hood coming at him like the

Angel of Death, he fired two wild shots, neither of which came close. As Bob came down he kicked the pistol out of the man's hand so viciously it flew out of sight down the street, then hammered the man in his bloody nose. The blonde hit the concrete hard and rolled onto his side.

The fourth man out of the Ford was still pinned under the car, its rear tire on top of his leg. He'd been kicking furiously at the Ford, trying to free his leg, denting the quarter panel and rocking the vehicle on its shocks, when Bob flew over the hood. He swore and pounded the body panel with his foot hard enough to sway the car, and suddenly his leg was free. The man lunged away from the car, his freed leg bent oddly, and got to his feet. He realized he was unarmed just as Bob laid out the blonde a few feet away, and looked around frantically for his pistol. He spotted it on the ground fifteen feet from the car. He paused half a second as he saw Bob turning, obviously wondering if he could reach the gun in time, then realized he was out of options. The man dived for his gun but he was too slow.

Bob caught him in midair and jerked him upright, taking a punch meant for his head on one muscled shoulder. The defiant man yelled in pain and rage and pounded his fists at Bob, who used his big arms to block. Bob then shot out a fist, catching the man under his left arm. Bob was so fast I didn't see his hand move until he was pulling it back. Bob's hand flicked out again, fast as a snake striking, tagging the man under his right arm as he swung at Bob's head. The man began to fold into himself and started to collapse and it was only then that I noticed the glinting spike protruding from Bob's fist. The instant I realized the thing in Bob's hand was the Randall his fiancée had given him, Bob kicked out at the man's injured leg. The man cried out as his knee buckled.

Splashback

Bob's left hand shot out, grabbing the man's hair as he started to go down. Bob held him up off the ground with one hand like he was made of straw. The knife darted in with a kind of swooping, corkscrewing hack, and suddenly the camera zoomed in and to one side and all I could see of the action was Bob's big shoulder and the back of his head. I sat up straighter, wondering if perhaps the cameraman had hit the wrong button, then I realized what was going on. Some editor, sitting back at Channel 7, had cropped the video, which could only mean that something *worse* than what we'd already seen was taking place.

"Look at me. ***Look at me!***" Bob had turned and was yelling at the blonde still lying ten feet away. Bob was directly facing the camera, his face huge in the frame. I could see dark splotches on his face, and he was holding his left arm straight out in front of him. Whatever was in his hand was out of the shot, but Bob held it out at arm's length for the one man still left alive to see. The view widened slightly, Bob still off-center, and the body of the man he'd just downed could be seen on the pavement behind him, flopping and twitching.

"Holy Mother of God," someone said.

"You tell them!" Bob roared at the blonde, shaking the object in his hand. Dark drops splattered his arm and face, and dripped down Bob's shirtfront. His face was red with blood and purple with rage, ropy veins climbing his thick neck, eyes bulging. Knife in one hand, covered in blood, he was Rage incarnate, the stuff of nightmares and legends. "You tell them they sent five people and it wasn't enough!" His deep voice echoed thunderously off the houses. A dark pool was forming at his feet as the body behind him grew still. "You tell them. You send more people, I don't care. I'm not done yet. Next time send twenty, I'll put their fucking heads on pikes! **YOU TELL THEM! Send me more! I'm gonna fucking kill you *ALL!*"** Channel Seven cut out the profanity, but a six-year-old could have read Bob's lips.

Bob threw the object he'd been holding at arm's length at the blonde, who made no attempt to dodge. I caught a brief glimpse of it as it hit him in the chest and thudded wetly to the ground. The blonde lay, unmoving, as Bob stared at him, panting. After a few seconds that seemed an eternity, Bob bent down and wiped his knife clean on the dead man's pants, then stuck it back under his arm.

Bob looked around, searching for threats. He looked surprised to still find himself on planet Earth. Then he walked quickly to the Blazer and climbed in. As he backed up the mangled body hung briefly on the Blazer's brush guard before it slid off and hit the pavement with a wet thud.

The Blazer's impact had pushed the Ford sideways a good six feet. Bob eased forward, angling two wheels up onto the curb, and managed to squeeze past the vehicle's back bumper. The camera followed Bob as he accelerated down the street, around a corner, and out of sight. I noticed, with some relief, that his license plate had never been in focus. Not that anyone who'd ever met Bob wouldn't be calling up the station right now with his name, address, and date of birth. Maybe they wouldn't recognize him because of the beard. A man could hope.

The whole incident had taken less than a minute.

"I sure hope those guys weren't FBI," Jerry said, stunned.

"C'mon, let's go!" Mitchell said. He came into view, jogging toward the street, microphone in hand. The picture bounced as the cameraman gave chase.

"Y'all are nuts," I heard the black guy yell, then the slam of a door.

The blonde struggled to his feet, eyes glued to the object Bob had thrown at him. He turned around just in time to get a microphone stuck in his face.

"Bill Mitchell, Channel Seven News," he said breathlessly. "Do you need us to call nine-one-one? What can we do? Which department do you and your men work for? Who was the individual you were trying to arrest? Should we call for an ambulance?"

Even with a misshapen nose and the bottom half of his face smeared with blood I recognized him. Sundance's eyes went wide as saucers. "Oh shit," was what he said. He looked frantically around, then began hobbling furiously toward the Caprice. Several fingers on his right hand were bent at odd angles and I suspected they were broken from when Bob had kicked his gun away. Mitchell stayed with Sundance the whole way, yelling stupid questions at his back.

"Is that—?" Jerry said.

"Yep," I said, looking grim.

The cameraman had to dart out of the way as Sundance wrestled the Caprice around and sped off, running over one of his dead accomplices in the process. When the car was out of sight Mitchell had the cameraman pan the carnage. Neighborhood residents began appearing hesitantly at their doors as the camera swept the scene.

The view changed and we were looking at Mitchell, **LIVE!**. Behind him were too many cop cars to count, lights flashing like fireworks. At least two sirens were still going. The DPD helicopter whup-whup-whupped out of sight overhead. Uniformed officers were busy stringing yellow crime scene tape around the street, looping it around fenceposts and telephone poles. At least thirty neighborhood residents were milling around, pointing and talking. One of the teens was pantomiming cutting someone's throat. A few stood behind Mitchell, waving at the camera or making faces.

"Police still are not commenting on the incident you've just witnessed," Mitchell told us. "We've provided them with an unedited copy of our tape but it will be some time before they have a chance to analyze it. No one here seems to know which police department or federal agency the murdered men were with, or who the suspect was they were trying to apprehend."

I found the remote and shut the TV off. Then I set the remote down and stared at the TV screen.

"I want a copy of *that* fucking tape," Jerry said. His eyes were blinking erratically.

"He cut his head off," Dave said in disbelief, looking as stunned as I felt. "He cut his head off. Right there in the street. And *threw* it. They can't...they're going to lose their license, showing that thing."

"No they won't," I said. "I doubt they'll even get fined, although I'm sure the FCC would love to do it. Hell, what they were showing was news, wasn't it? Ever heard of the First Amendment? *They* sure have. And they did edit it. They cropped the picture. It'll probably win an Emmy. Make that a Pulitzer."

"This is going to go national, isn't it?" Dave said. "Peter Jennings, Tom Brokaw, all those guys. There's no way they could pass up that video. And then they're going to start asking a shitload of questions."

"This changes things, doesn't it?" Jerry said to me.

It took me a few seconds before I realized what he was asking. "It shouldn't, not with all the shit that's happened already," I said. "But yeah, I think you're right. It changes things."

"So where is he?"

"He'll be here," I said.

None of us said anything for a while.

"Six," Jerry said finally.

"What?"

"Bob said they sent five people and it wasn't enough. He got it wrong. It was six. They sent six people."

"Nobody's perfect," I said.

The Blazer pulled into the driveway forty-seven minutes later. It didn't take that long to drive from northwest Detroit. From the dazed look on his face he'd probably been cruising aimlessly. How he'd avoided being spotted was yet one more unanswerable question I had no one to ask.

I met Bob at the front door, pulling it open as he came up the steps. Jerry, Dave, and Doug stood silently behind me, watching. Steve was back there too. He'd shown up fifteen minutes earlier, loaded down with what at the time had seemed an absurd amount of gear.

Bob's hair was clotted with blood, his clothes stiff with it. There were tear tracks through the blood spackling his face; dry now, but he still had a haunted look in his eyes.

"I think I fucked up," he said, his face contorted in an ugly rictus of pain. He kept looking at me strangely, and I finally decided he was waiting for me to start yelling.

"It won't be the last time," I told him. He stared at me, blinking slowly, for some time, finally realizing that was all I had to say. I stepped aside and he moved past me, zombielike. He smelled like a butcher's shop.

EIGHT

Friday

8:48 a.m.

"I don't like it," Jerry said.

"Okay, you got a better idea?" I asked him. We were sitting at the kitchen table, eating breakfast. Mine consisted of a bagel, a Pop-Tart, and orange juice. My head was tender and felt like it was swollen. Hell, it probably was. My right arm, where I'd been kicked, was sore as hell, but I didn't think it or any of my ribs were broken. I was popping Tylenol like popcorn but if they were working I couldn't tell.

"Well...no, but--"

"Listen, no offense, but this doesn't even concern you."

"Not yet."

I shook my head. "This can't go on. I'm not getting pulled over on a felony stop, everyone pointing guns at me. That's a Lose-Lose situation."

"There aren't any charges against you," Jerry said. "They still just want you for questioning."

"How the hell would you know? Besides, I'm sure

there's a warrant out on me for questioning, as a Person of Interest, at the very least." God was I depressed. And a long night of fitful sleep hadn't helped. I looked around the room, first at them, then at Jerry's and Steve's rifles locked and loaded and leaning within easy reach.

I shook my head and looked at Bob. He hadn't said a word since I'd gotten up, and Steve wasn't real talkative either. Steve was a little freaked out—well, we were all more than a little freaked out, but Steve was showing it the most. He kept pacing back and forth, occasionally shaking his head. He kept staring at all the firepower too.

"And you're next," I told Bob. He just stared at me, face completely devoid of expression. "After that little stunt, in front of a fucking camera crew for Chrissakes, there're are gonna be more people after you than looked for Lee Harvey Oswald."

"I told you, I didn't see the guy with the camera."

"Yeah, but you saw the goddamn truck! You didn't think there might be a reporter nearby, somebody might have a fucking mini-cam? Don't you get it? You're famous now. CNN's showing that clip every ten minutes. Osama bin Laden's squatting in a cave right now somewhere in lower Asscrackistan and *he's* fucking seen it. You know they've got your name, address, date of birth, bloodtype—you name it—by now. The only reason I can imagine they haven't released it publicly yet is because of the possibility of terrorist involvement. They know you're a Green Beret, what they don't know—and this is a guess—is who the fuck those guys you killed were, and how does it relate, if at all, to the death of your fiancé. Which are the same questions I have." When he just stared at me I gave up and dropped it.

"Now's the best time to do it," I told Jerry. "That shit with Bob is the corker. Maybe that's better, nobody can lie about what happened, it's on video. If we turn ourselves in now, they already know something is going on larger than us. There's going to be two dozen detectives working on this in a couple different jurisdictions, plus the FBI. Hell, the FBI's probably going to take the whole thing over, just because they can. If anybody can find out what's going on, they will. Throw all those man hours at it, something's going to give. And they just won't be able to bury it, this thing's way too high profile." *I hope*, I added silently. Truth was, none of us had any idea what the hell we'd gotten ourselves involved in.

"Yeah, we'll get locked up," I kept at them, "but if we ask for protection, we'll get it. Big time. Anybody looks at that video, they'll know people are really serious about stopping our clocks."

"Let's hope to God none of those guys really were feds," Steve said.

"Even if they were, that operation was off the books, I'll tell you that." It was a guess, but the only legitimate interest Bob had to law enforcement agency before that incident was as a murder suspect, and that was with the Sheriff's Department. Those guys in the video were not with any Sheriff's Department.

"I don't want to get locked up," Bob said. "How'm I supposed to get these guys?" I turned to him and did my best to get through.

"Bob," I said, "you are amazing. That video is the most unbelievable thing I've ever seen in my life. I can see, you still don't get it when I say you're going to be famous. Garbagemen in Berlin'll recognize you if you walk down the street. I mean, that was like Sergeant York Medal of Honor stuff. But he didn't do it on video, and your guys weren't enemy combatants."

"The fuck they weren't," Bob spat. I went on like I hadn't heard him.

"Even you know that if they try to hit you again like that, you're going down. You've used up enough luck for three lifetimes. You might get one or two of them, but if it happens again they're not going to make the same mistakes. It won't be a kidnap attempt, it'll be a hit. If any of these guys knows how to work a rifle you'll probably never see it coming. If they'd been trying to whack you last time, chances are you wouldn't be with us any more. And I'm not even going to try to figure out what's going on. First they try to blow you up, and I heard them say they didn't want to try an abduction, then the next thing I know they try to abduct you. If something's changed since then, I don't know what it is. It's the same bassackward thing they tried with me.

"I can't go on like this," I told the three of them. Doug was in the front room, watching out the window and eavesdropping on our conversation. Dave was wandering the backyard, freezing his ass off voluntarily. He didn't think Bob was wrapped too tight, and figured it was only a matter of time before he snapped again. He didn't want to be around when it happened. "I don't know who's after us, I don't know why, and I've exhausted all my options. Yeah, it's probably some spooks, probably because of that disk, but so what? We can't decipher it or the situation. We hand the damn disk over and if that's why they're after us, after me, maybe they won't be interested in killing or kidnapping us anymore."

"That's a hell of a lot of ifs" Jerry said.

"I don't like it any better than you do. But if these people are still after me, I don't know who they are, where they are, or why they want me, so I have no way to fight back. Same goes for Bob. I might get lucky again too, but they're going to get me sooner or later. I'm choosing the less shitty of two shitty choices. Jail is better than dead."

"You really think you'll do jail time?" Steve said to me.

I didn't really want to think about that. "Who the fuck knows? My specialty's federal drug laws. I'll find out as soon as they figure out who those guys were that I killed. I bet you I'll get to spend more than a few nights in the county jail, though. I killed people. And left the scene. I might not even be offered bail. Charged? Convicted? Don't have a clue."

"What about me?" Bob said dully.

"Depends on who those guys were. In court we could say you recognized Sundance from my description, so your…negative reaction upon meeting him is explainable. Justifiable even, to the right jury. That is, up until the decapitation."

Even though I hadn't actually seen it, because of the careful framing, there was no doubt in my mind about what had happened in the middle of that blood-soaked street. Anyone who saw that video, even the edited version we'd been treated to, knew exactly what Bob had done.

"Too bad you didn't grab Sundance so we could ask him a few questions," Jerry said, giving Bob a dirty look. "The one guy there you should have killed or grabbed and you didn't do either." I was still tiptoeing around Bob, trying not to set him off, but Jerry was having none of that. Jerry'd had to knife two guys to death on this run from the Detroit mob, so I guess he figured he had a right to call Bob on his blunder.

"I told you, I didn't recognize him because of the blood on his face."

"What'd Ron have to say?" I asked Jerry. He'd gone out early to a pay phone to make the call.

"Not much. The idea was to *not* say anything, remember? The line practically vibrated with all the people listening, waiting to hear you or Bob call in. Ron had seen the Hurricane Bob video, that was obvious."

"But you did give him the word that we might be dropping by."

"Yeah. I had to dance around; it took a while before he figured out just what the hell I was trying to tell him. He didn't shoot down the idea of a visit, if that's what you're worried about. He was wired as hell, though. I bet the feds are just batshit over there."

If and when I turned myself in I wanted it to be a surprise. Show up at Ron's unannounced, turn myself over to the deputies and feds and let them fight over me. With all the people that probably had government connections after me, I didn't want anyone, not even the good guys, to know my schedule.

"I'm not ready to stop the fight now," Bob said.

"Bob, you're smart," I pleaded. "Ignore the rage for a second and think. Who are you going to fight? You going to drive around, drive by Ron's house again like a fucking idiot, get another couple cars full of guys to follow you? This time, the guys behind you will be feds. Or deputies. Or both. With helicopter support, probably. You know someplace we can go to get some bad guys, or Ron's dad, you tell me."

He didn't say anything, and wouldn't meet my eyes.

"I know you're hurting," I told him. "I am too. God only knows where Kelly is, if she's all right. I have to force myself not to think about her, because I get so angry at what those bastards have done to us I can't think. I can't imagine what she must be thinking after seeing the news last night, and that's nothing compared to what you've gone through. All I've really lost is a dog." I took a deep breath.

"I'm not asking you to stop the fight. *But we need to know who we're fighting.* We need to know what's going on. And why. I can't find out on my own. We need help."

I was trying to convince them as much as myself. Bob didn't like it, not at all, but I think even he realized we were out of options. He would've been happy to keep on killing people if he just knew where to find them. Sounded reasonable to me—I was getting a little short on feelings myself. He'd keep going until he caught a bullet or ran out of people to shoot at. Grief and rage and vengeance and no small amount of survivor's guilt was driving him. We couldn't stop him, and knew it; I was trying to get Bob to stop himself.

I wasn't sure anymore if Bob cared whether he lived or died, but I knew he didn't want to die needlessly. He wanted a few more bodies behind him, or more than a few, and was willing to do whatever it took. I hoped that included waiting, and letting the good guys do their job.

10:12 a.m.

"I'll go in first," Bob said without much feeling. "I'm the man of the hour. By the time they get done yelling and screaming and running around," he told me, "you ought to be able to walk in without a fuss. You think they'll have two sets of cuffs?"

"I wouldn't worry about it."

He scowled at nothing in particular.

"I'll give you a minute or so, then wander in," I agreed. "Maybe Ron can soothe some of them with sweet talk. And then I'll stroll in, give them another huge headache to start their day. Hell, if there are any deputies there, they're gonna love to see me. I've single-handedly doubled the county's homicide rate this year." Bob, on the other hand, had done his nasty business in Detroit, where five corpses were an average week. Statistically he was just a blip.

I was with Bob in the Blazer, on the way to Ron's. Jerry and Steve followed us in Steve's Mustang. They'd refused to stay behind, absolutely refused, even though I told them the FBI would most likely arrest them just on principle. They didn't care, and I knew better than to try and press the point. All of us had used up our logic without success; we were running on pure emotion now.

Two cars, because I figured the cops wouldn't be satisfied with just Bob; they'd want to impound his car, too. Dave had hosed all the blood off its front end, but it was still evidence. Plus, it was all over that video; driving it around was like playing Russian roulette, sooner or later a cop would flip his cruiser in a smoking U-turn and the Blazer would end up surrounded by a dozen squad cars. We'd stopped en route and unloaded Bob's gear at a mini-storage facility where Steve rented space, and honestly I was shocked we hadn't been spotted on the way to Ron's house.

Bob still wore the Randall and the Browning. No way was he going anywhere unarmed, even for a second. He ignored me when I told him it would probably mean a CCW charge added to his arrest report. I didn't even want to know if anybody else was carrying. The only silver lining in that cloud was that the law was on our side—they'd be arrested on Ron's property, so as long as they could prove they had the permission of the homeowner to carry guns there was nothing to charge them with, but I knew that wouldn't stop the FBI.

What a clusterfuck. I'd killed people on two separate

occasions and still had no idea what the hell was going on. And if I had to bet, I'd be spending the next six months or so in jail, waiting for my trial, as bail would be denied.

Bob sat silently, staring straight ahead, both hands on the wheel. Never a big talker, he'd become so uncommunicative, going hours without saying a word, that it was starting to give me the jitters.

Much too soon for my taste we arrived. Bob pulled into the gravel driveway and parked on the side of the house between the garage and the barn. Steve slid his Mustang to a stop next to us and we all got out. Two bland sedans of the species the feds favored were parked near the front door.

"This is shit," Bob muttered so quietly I almost missed it.

"You got a better idea, big boy, you should've said something earlier," I snapped at him. He looked at me, a tiny sliver of regret peeking through his stony facade.

"Somebody had to see us pull in, you better go before they pile out the door waving their guns around," Steve said. Actually, I was surprised there were only two cop cars in the drive. I'm not sure what I expected, maybe I just hoped George was still a huge priority for everyone. Truth was, there were probably more people out looking for Bob and me than for George. A lot more.

Bob lowered his head and started around the corner of the house toward the front door.

"Keep your hands in sight," I called after him.

"You got a lawyer?" Jerry asked me.

"Yeah, I've got a guy I used before. Remember when I got sued by the family of that guy Scott and I shot two years ago?" He nodded and we stood silent, waiting. I'd give Bob another minute or two, then head in myself.

The muffled, stuttering boom of gunshots echoed inside

the house, then the chiming crash of breaking glass. I found myself running toward the front door, gun in hand, without any recollection of having willed my body to move. I rounded the corner of the garage and tore across the front lawn. The front door was hanging partway open, only darkness beyond. I jumped onto the porch and hugged the bricks. There was a ragged exit hole from a bullet near the top of the door.

"Ahhh! Fuck! Fuck! Shit! Oh my *Fucking* God!" Ron was the one doing the cursing, I would've recognized his speech patterns anywhere. He was in pain. A lot of pain.

"DownDown***Down,*** motherfucker!" Bob shouted. "Let me see your hands! Let me see your hands! You too, fuckface!"

"Coming in!" I yelled, waiting half a second. Then I shouldered open the front door and sidestepped to the left. Jerry and Steve barreled in right after me, one low and one high, all our guns out and sweeping the room.

Ron was bent halfway to the ground, the whole side of his head covered in blood. He had a revolver in his right hand while his left was pressed against his head. He kept trying to keep his gun pointed at Special Agent Reilly, but the pain had him weaving. Reilly, neatly dressed in a navy blue suit, was kneeling on the hallway carpet, holding shaking hands above his blood-spattered face.

On his back at Ron's feet was a stranger in a suit. He had a surprised expression on his upturned face. The bullet hole in his forehead, rimmed in black with half-burned gunpowder from a nearly contact gunshot wound, probably explained his expression. The back of his head was mostly gone, his limbs at awkward angles on the floor. A Glock was on the floor near his leg.

Bob held another neatly dressed white male at gunpoint

in the front room. The man was on his knees, fingers laced behind his head. Shiny spent cartridge cases littered the floor near his feet.

"Turn around motherfucker! Turn around!" Bob kept yelling. The guy shuffled around on his knees and put his back to us.

"Check the house!" I yelled at Steve and Jerry. They headed out.

"Oh Jesus, Oh Fuck!" Ron's head was bleeding profusely, thick streams of it covering his hand and running down his arm. I could smell the warm blood in the air. I wanted to go help him, but not before I knew my surroundings were safe.

"What the hell is going on in here?" I demanded of the room. I didn't know where to point my gun.

"It was a fucking setup!" Ron gasped. "Bob walks in the door and the next thing I know people are shooting at me!"

"What happened?" I yelled again. Bob had his back to the rest of the house as he covered his man. I kept spinning left and right, gun up and tracking with my eyes. Until Jerry and Steve got back the house was a free fire zone. Ron's head would have to wait.

"As soon as I walk in the front door," Bob spat, "this guy pulls his gun out and starts unloading at me. No 'Freeze', no 'Police', no 'FBI motherfucker, let me see your hands', he just draws and fires when I'm standing there, hands wide and empty. That other cunt tried to cap Ron in the head. If Ron hadn't been so quick on the draw we'd both be dead."

"Yeah!" Ron screamed at the dead man on the floor, rage and pain speaking. "Didn't know I was carrying, did you? Fucking ruined your whole day, didn't I?" He kicked the body hard enough to rock it. Jerry and Steve came running back into view.

"It's clear," Jerry said. "There's nobody here. Nobody at *all*."

"Where's your Mom?" I said to Ron.

"Got a call, she needed to go look at a body that might be Dad. Couple of feds and the County dick that was here went with." A wave of pain made his features collapse and he bent over, almost dropping his gun.

"Get him out of here, see what you can do for him," I told Jerry. Ron stumbled off, barely able to see through the pain. Jerry helped him along with a hand on his arm.

"Watch your guy, Bob," I said. Bob nodded, his back still toward me. He hadn't taken his eyes off his man yet.

"You got a gun on you?" I said to Reilly.

"R-right hip," he stammered. The spreading pool of blood from the dead man's head was slowly soaking the hall carpet, and Reilly watched it inch closer to his knees with some trepidation.

I nodded at Steve and he carefully disarmed Reilly while I covered him. Then I kicked Reilly in the chest and he went over, arms flailing. Before he could get righted I knelt on his chest and pressed the muzzle of my Colt against his upper lip. That calmed him down right quick.

"I just don't give a fuck anymore," I told him. "I'm going to cover this nice floor with your brains if you don't tell me what I need to know. You believe that?" He looked into my eyes and nodded.

"Good. What the hell is going on? What happened here?"

"I don't know," he said earnestly, hoping I'd see how honest he was being. "The doorbell rings and suddenly everyone's shooting."

"Who fired first? Did you see?" He shook his head fractionally, the Colt still glued to his upper lip.

"Bob, you sure of what you saw?" I asked without turning around. I figured the normal reaction of any cop who recognized Bob from his TV debut would be to pull his gun out and start yelling. "They fired first?"

"Ain't no doubt afuckingbout it. And it wasn't just jitters, or accidental."

I looked back at Reilly. "Who is this guy?" I pointed back and down at the dead man.

"Rivers, Special Agent Rivers, with the Bureau. Out of the Cleveland office." His eyes kept crossing as he stared at my pistol.

"What about the other guy?" I said, heart sinking.

"Rivers' partner. Green, I think his name is."

"They're feds, then? Both FBI?"

"Sure. Yeah." I saw some infinitesimal shadow of doubt cross his face.

"What?"

"I saw their ID's," he said. "The Cleveland office faxed us here and told us they'd be coming. It was their phone number on the fax, I saw it. They told us we'd be getting an additional two agents for the detail, okayed by the Division chief."

"The return phone number on a fax can be changed to read whatever you want it to," I said. "When did you get the fax?"

"This morning, about nine o'clock. They showed up around nine-thirty." If I remembered correctly, Jerry had called Ron just after seven.

"You know these guys? You ever seen them before?"

"No, not personally. One of my guys had heard their names before, though."

"Find me a cordless." Steve was back in seconds with a

phone. I handed it to Reilly, pulling the Colt back a few inches.

"Call Cleveland," I told him.

He punched in the number from memory. "There's no way," he told me, comprehending. "I know what you're thinking. No way in hell. Not so quickly."

"When'd you get the call about the body?"

"Half an hour ago. They've been gone about twenty minutes." Half an hour back we'd been on the road, on the way to Ron's. But five minutes before that we'd been at Steve's mini-storage place, unloading everybody's gear.

"Let me guess. These two guys volunteered to stay here."

"Yeah, this is S.A. Reilly, out of Detroit," he said into the phone, not having a chance to answer my last question. "Let me talk to the SAC." He waited while he was put through to the Special Agent-in-Charge of the Cleveland office.

"You guys are fucking crazy," he told us around the cordless. "Like you weren't in enough trouble already. You just killed a federal officer, you know that?" He looked at me, feeling more confident every second.

"I hope you're wrong," was my sincere reply.

"Yes sir!" Reilly puffed up visibly. An impressive feat for someone in his position. "This is Special Agent Reilly, Detroit office. I'm Agent-in-charge of the Kelly disappearance, up in Rochester Hills. Yes sir, that's the one. Yes. It should, we met at a wedding this summer. In Pontiac. Yeah. Right. The reason I'm calling, did your office fax us this morning, let us know you were sending two agents over to help with this Kelly thing? Temporary reassignment, two guys? No, no ransom demand yet. Yeah, we still think it's a kidnapping. Yes sir, I know what the protocol is, but there was a slight mix-up on this end."

"No?" Reilly looked at me, uncertainty in his eyes. "By any chance do you have two agents in your office named Rivers and Green?" I could hear the SAC's affirmative reply.

"Get a description," I told him.

"Could you describe them for me sir." A pause. "If you could just humor me, I assure you that as soon as I figure out what's going on here, if your people are involved you'll be the first to know about it. Please."

The SAC didn't sound too friendly anymore. Reilly's eyes never left mine as he was given the descriptions. "You have no other agents in your office with the same last names?" he asked for verification. When the SAC was done Reilly thanked him politely.

"When I get this thing all sorted out I'll call you back," Reilly said. He pulled the phone away from his ear and hit the off button, cutting the SAC off in mid-question. The most telling point was that Reilly didn't even try to tell the Cleveland SAC that he was a hostage. And I knew why, I'd seen the surprise and hurt in his eyes when he'd discovered my suspicions were correct. Reilly gave me the phone, looking tired, and I handed it back to Steve.

"They're not ours," he told me. "Green is African-American, or at least the real Green is. And this guy is four inches too short to be Rivers." I climbed off Reilly and gave him a hand up.

"Steve, you accompany Special Agent Reilly into the family room and keep him company."

"Now wait a minute——" Reilly began. I held up a hand.

"We're on the same side," I told him, "but people keep trying to kill us and I'm done playing by the rules. I want you somewhere where you can't be a witness. I'm going to ask Mr. Green some questions."

"What are you going to do?"

"Where'd they go to look at this body?" I asked him, ignoring his question.

"Wayne County. If there ever was a damn body."

"Now you're getting the picture," I told him. If Reilly's coworkers were heading to the Wayne County Morgue, they'd be gone another half hour at least. Even if they turned around as soon as they got there.

Gun in one hand, Steve took hold of Reilly's arm and led him away. Steve and I traded looks, and then he ushered Reilly out of sight.

"He been disarmed?" I asked Bob, looking at the kneeling man's back. Bob jerked his head toward the front window. A SIG Sauer semi-auto was lodged in the glass, muzzle stuck halfway through the double-paned window. Bob must have smacked it out of the guy's hands.

"Artistic. You pat him down?" Bob nodded again, standing six feet behind Green with the Browning pointed unwaveringly at the back of his head.

"Turn around and stand up," I told the man. Green, or whatever his name was, did so, slowly. He looked tense, but not scared.

"Mr. Green—you don't mind if I call you that, do you? Even though we both know it's not your real name—I'm having a hell of a week. *Believe* me when I tell you that I am through fucking around. You would do well to believe everything I tell you as though it was the word of God. Now, we're going to play a little game called Clue. If I don't like what you have to say, the answer's gonna be Mr. Grinnand in the front room with the Browning. You get what I'm saying? I'm not going too fast for you? Do I need to paint you a picture?" I pointed at bullet hole in the forehead of the dead man on the floor.

Green shook his head and lowered his hands. If he recognized Bob from television he gave no sign.

"Talk to me."

"Anything you guys want to know, you ask. This is just a fucking job to me, I've got no loyalties here. I've obviously stepped into something big."

"Tell me how you got here."

"You're going to be disappointed," he told us. "What I can tell you ain't much. I got a call yesterday afternoon when I was in Chicago. I don't know by who," he told us, "and I didn't recognize the number or the voice."

"Freelance?" Bob said.

"Yeah. My number's available to most everyone in the business. This guy knew the right names, so I knew he was serious. He tells me to get a clean car, check into a certain hotel in Detroit, and wait for a call. He said the thing might not go down, but I'd be paid for my time either way."

"How'd you end up in this house?"

Green nodded at the dead guy on the floor. "He showed up at my hotel room about seven thirty this morning. Took my picture, left for an hour, and when he came back he handed me my own FBI badge wallet. My picture in it and everything."

"You know him?"

"As far as I know he's Special Agent Dwayne Rivers, FBI. That's what he told me to call him. I'd never seen him before this morning."

"He show you our pictures or something?"

Green nodded. "He told me how it was supposed to go down on the way over here. I about shit. I mean, the work I normally do, it's the shitbags that get hurt. Here he's telling me I'd probably have to whack at least one FBI agent. Prick."

"You could have said no," I told him.

Green rolled his eyes. "Gimmee a break. He'd have capped me right then and there. I did good in getting him to double my fee."

"You got paid already?"

"Partial. After the deed was done I was told to disappear, show up tomorrow night at the Columbia Inn in Columbia, Maryland. Supposed to be a reservation there for me, Mr. Green."

"Maryland?"

"Don't ask me. I figured they wanted to make sure I really got out of town. Or maybe there was another job out there tied in with this that they were keeping close to the vest. After I checked in someone was supposed to call and arrange payment."

"Was the idea to make it look like we died in a shootout with the FBI? Plant your guns on us?"

"That was one contingency."

"Christ."

Bob safed his weapon and handed it to me butt first. I took it reflexively, then wondered what the hell he was doing as he took off his jacket.

"Bob?"

He tossed his jacket behind him. The harness holding the Randall followed.

"Bob? What are you doing?"

"Me and you," he said to Green.

"Helllooo, Bob?"

"You get by me and you walk," Bob told him. Green tilted his head at him, confused. I stood behind Bob, a pistol in each hand and a dumb expression on my face. I had to be hearing things.

"The FBI really needs to talk to this guy," I said.

"He's not going to tell the FBI shit. Why should he? He never fired a shot, so all they've got on him is impersonating a federal officer. What's that, a year or two in some federal country club? When he gets out, well read, in better shape from pumping iron, he just goes right back to work for the same people.

"Maybe they might try to nail him on attempted murder, if Reilly can remember just what the hell happened and the jury believes me and Ron. If he talks he just digs himself a deeper hole, and the only way he'd talk is to give them a bigger fish. The only guy he knows to give them is lying on the floor there with half his head gone."

"This isn't the way," I said. From the expression on Green's face I could see that everything Bob had said was true. This guy had no one to give up but himself, so why should he talk?

"It's my way." Bob shrugged his muscled shoulders and stared Green in the face.

"You've got to be shitting me," Green said. He stared at the overmuscled kid in front of him, trying to decide if it was some sort of joke. That cinched it—he definitely hadn't seen the Hurricane Bob video. Bob just stared at him.

I stuck the Browning in my belt and looked around for some support. None was to be found.

"I'm not going to fight you," Green said indignantly, with just a hint of disbelief in his voice.

"Then this won't take very long." Bob inched closer. Green looked to me for some help.

"He's serious," I assured him. "Believe that."

I watched the expression change on Green's face from

disbelief to anger as he finally realized that Bob was, indeed, serious. Then his eyes narrowed, and he glanced at the SIG still lodged in the window.

"I kick his ass and you're going to let me walk?" He still wasn't one hundred percent convinced.

"You know what?" I said, disgusted. "I wash my hands of this whole fucking thing. Bob, you're an asshole." I holstered my Colt, stuck Bob's Browning in my belt, crossed my arms, and leaned against the wall.

They stood about eight feet apart. There was a small table under the front window to Bob's right. To his left was a low rectangular coffee table, and the couch on which I'd sat while Ron told me his Dad worked for the CIA. It seemed like a year ago.

Not enough room to really circle, no place to hide. Green's face darkened and his eyes locked onto Bob's. He bent his knees and inched his left leg forward so that he stood in a fighting stance, hands in loose fists at chest level. He looked like he knew what he was doing.

Bob held his arms loosely at his sides, fingers flexing. He didn't get into any stance, he didn't clench his fingers into fists, he didn't look like he realized he'd just challenged someone to mortal combat.

Bob slid another step toward Green and raised his hands to waist level. Green moved sideways six inches and backed up half a step. Then he was effectively out of room. I saw his eyes dart right and left, measuring distances. Bob took another half step, and I could see Green studying him, trying to evaluate Bob's skill.

Green slid back to his right and readied himself. This was going to be quick and brutal. I stopped leaning on the wall and waited. Time slowed, and the air became thick.

Bob's left hand drifted up and Green decided that

second to move. He feinted left and charged to his right. Bob floated toward him, hands moving up.

Green surprised both of us, angling away from Bob. He went airborne, planting a foot on the edge of the coffee table for leverage and driving a fist at Bob's neck from the side. Still moving forward, Bob twisted to avoid the brunt of the blow, took hold of Green's arm and collar, and executed a hasty judo throw. Then, way off balance, Bob deliberately fell sideways and rolled away from Green.

Green's heel splintered the table under the window on the way down. He hit the carpeted floor hard but was up by the time Bob reached him.

"Aaaaaah!" Green's fists and elbows were blurs as he hammered at Bob, high/low, left/right. Bob blocked most of it, but there was a meaty *Thwock!*, and Bob's head snapped back. He took half a step back, looking stunned, and Green moved in for the kill. Eyes clearing, Bob smacked the grasping hands away from his eyes and throat. His foot flicked out. There was a crunch, and Green's knee folded. Spitting out a gasping grunt, Green landed hard on an elbow and tried to roll away.

Bob knee-dropped onto Green's back, locked both hands under his chin, and heaved upward mightily. The sound of his snapping vertebrae was like soggy branches underfoot.

And that was it.

Panting, Bob let Green's head go. It hit the floor with a thud. Then he stood up, and faced me for the first time since I'd entered Ron's house. Time began moving normally again, and I finally remembered to breathe.

"Bob," I said, "when did you get shot?"

He looked down at the bullet holes in his shirt.

"I forgot about that. No wonder it hurt so much when

he hit me." Two round holes punctuated the weave of his shirt. One was down low, near the floating ribs, the other centered over his left breast. "I told you, I walked in, and they started shooting."

With obvious discomfort, he pulled the shirt over his head and looked at the shiny slugs still embedded in his Kevlar vest. As he moved to touch one it fell out and bounced on the carpet.

"I think my rib's fucked up." He winced and held his side, stretching away from the hurt. It didn't seem to help. "I think I made it worse with that roll." He held his side gingerly, still breathing hard from the fight.

Since I'd never before heard Bob complain about pain, he had to be suffering some serious hurt. I could only imagine what his ribs would feel like when the adrenaline wore off. Kevlar saves lives, but instead of holes in flesh the result is bruises four inches across and fractured bones. If he were a normal person he'd be heading to the hospital for at least two days. Of course, if he were a normal person, he'd be dead.

With a look of disgust he tugged at the other slug until it came free. He looked at it briefly, then tossed it away.

"Let's go see how Ron's doing," he said.

We found Ron and Jerry in an upstairs bathroom. Bloody towels covered the entire floor.

"Oh shit."

It looked like Jerry had finally gotten the bleeding stopped. Drying blood covered Ron's left arm to the elbow, and his neck and bare chest were streaked crimson. The bullet had passed through the cartilage in Ron's ear and cut a short furrow in his skull before moving on. Ron's ear was split in half from the impact, but I couldn't tell how much flesh was actually missing. Ron's shirt was a total write-off, soaked in blood and tossed into a corner.

"Ahhh, fuck! Fuck!" Ron was still cursing, his head hanging sideways over the bathtub while Jerry poked around in his ear. It looked like Jerry was trying to figure out what to do next.

"Well, this was a fucking great idea," Jerry spat at me, nearly yelling. "Let's turn ourselves in. Yeah, sounds like a fucking piece of cake." The bathroom was filled with the coppery smell of blood, and the walls seemed to shrink around us as tempers flared.

"Ow, shit! Watch it! Goddammit," Ron cursed, "why am I the one that always gets shot? Fuck! So what the hell are you going to do now?"

"I'm pretty sure I've got a suture pack inside the first aid kit in my truck," Bob said.

"The FBI's going to fry our asses now." Jerry was boiling mad, his ears red. He waved around a bloody washcloth. "I can't fucking believe this. You think of anybody else we should shoot today, you let us know. Judges, maybe a cop or two?"

"Shut the fuck up!" Ron bellowed, veins bulging as he fought the pain.

"Damned if I'm turning myself in now," I told them. "I'm not suicidal. Four hours warning and they manage to get two guys with the right names and authentic-looking FBI creds on the inside? With a fax as a backup? Fuck that. I can't compete with that. They can do that, they can do anything, far as I'm concerned. I can't even figure out how they knew we were coming. Can you? From now on, I'm gonna stay on the offensive until I'm arrested, dead, they run out of bodies to throw at us, or the President calls me up personally and says all is forgiven."

Splashback

"You thinking Maryland?" Bob said.

"It's all we've got. One of the guys that was interrogating me mentioned he'd come from Maryland. I've got the feeling Green wasn't lying about that reservation, but I'm sure as hell not going to make any calls from here to confirm it. And we need to go *now*. Say goodbye to Mr. Reilly, call an ambulance for Ron, and take off before anybody else shows up. Next people through the door are either going to be the real FBI or a platoon of bad guys with belt-fed machine guns. They've tried everything else."

"Fuck you!" Ron exploded. "Get that stitch kit. I'll do my ear my damn self if I have to. You guys forget why the fuck you're here? It was *my* dad they kidnapped." His hands clenched and unclenched. "What the fuck am I going to do here by myself?"

"We still don't know if he was kidnapped!" I shot back.

Jerry jabbed a finger at the bullet wound in Ron's head. "Something's fucking going on. Something big."

Shit. I knew he was right. We all did. "You up to that?" I said to Bob, nodding at Ron's chewed up ear. He nodded.

"It won't be pretty, but it'll travel. If we were in the jungle it'd be another story. I'll need twenty minutes and some disinfectant."

"Go get the suture kit," I told him. "Twenty minutes is all you've got." He disappeared.

"How bad is it?" Ron said through gritted teeth.

I leaned close and studied it. "It's torn up like hell, but it's not life threatening. Head wounds always bleed like a bitch. Whenever we get out of prison you can look up a good plastic surgeon. Or maybe not, chicks dig scars. Find some antibiotics," I told Jerry. He started looking through the bathroom's cabinets. "Some painkillers couldn't hurt either."

"Somebody needs to get my gear out of my room," Ron said between pants. "I've got a go bag and my shotgun behind the false wall in my closet."

I shook my head. "Am I the only person here who wasn't expecting the shit to hit the fan?"

10:39 a.m.

"We're leaving," I told Reilly twenty minutes later.

"What'd that guy tell you?" he said to me.

"I told you, he slipped and fell and broke his neck before I could ask him anything." I tossed Green's FBI badge wallet onto the table in front of Reilly. I'd seen a lot of real FBI creds—which do not resemble, in any way, the FBI IDs flashed on TV shows—and Green's looked authentic.

Reilly gave me a dirty look. "What'd he tell you?" he repeated. I pretended like I hadn't heard him and changed the subject.

"George Kelly's a spook," I told Reilly. That brought him up short. He sat there and looked at me, for once with nothing to say.

"CIA? This is fucking Detroit. They're not allowed to work inside the U.S."

"I don't know if he was CIA, NSA, or what," I explained. "Neither does Ron. George was out of the country a lot, but I don't think the NSA has operatives, per se. I thought all they did was signal intercepts, but who knows what kind of equipment they've got at his workplace. That Consolidated Systems, the whole place is a front. I don't know if even Carla knows anything more than that, but now's the time to start asking."

"How long have you known about this?"

"What, are you going to yell at me for withholding information? Hell, you don't know whether or not to believe me now. I can see it in your eyes. And that's with two dead guys in the other room with perfect fake Bureau ID's. If I would've said anything to you after I found out last week, you would've thought I was a loony. Tell me I'm wrong."

Reilly looked down at the kitchen table and shook his head.

"Is that who those guys were?" he said to me. "CIA?"

"Those guys? Fuck if I know. My guess would be hired guns contracted for this one specific job, who didn't know jack about anything else, but that would be just a guess since Mr. Green slipped and fell before I even had a chance to talk to him. Now it's your turn with these bastards. Did the prints on the guys I left in the ditch and at my house lead anywhere?"

He hesitated, as if debating whether he should tell me, then shook his head. "Not yet. All former military, no criminal records."

"What about the guys Bob killed in Detroit?"

Reilly looked like he'd eaten something sour. He debated with himself, then admitted, "We don't know. Nobody knows who they are. They all had FBI creds, but they're not FBI." He peered up at me. "Their badge wallets looked real. Hell, I think they were real. Real IDs…in the names of actual agents. Except these weren't the guys. Everything was correct but the pictures."

Holy shit. It was even worse than I thought. I threw my hands up. "You're proving my point."

"Why do they want you?"

"I think they think I've got something of theirs."

"What?" he asked.

I just smiled.

"Do you even have it, whatever it is?"

"Now what fun would that be, giving away all my secrets?"

He stared at me awhile. "You're trying to draw them out. That's it, isn't it? You want them to keep coming after you."

"Not really, but how else am I supposed to find out where George is, why he was grabbed?"

"You don't even know for sure he *was* grabbed! You're fucking suicidal."

"Suicidal is sitting around here or locked up somewhere, trusting my safety to you or the locals. These guys can be anyone they want, go anywhere they want to be. The list of people I trust with my life is about six names long, and yours isn't anywhere on it."

"Whatever this thing is that you have, you ought to give it to me. Your having it doesn't seem to be stopping them from trying to kill you."

"I'm almost tempted, but I don't want your death on my conscience," I told him pointedly, and stuck a thumb at the front room. "Right fax number, real creds, and the names of actual agents. All accomplished in hours. I give you any kind of evidence, I've killed you for sure." That sobered him up. "Maybe after I find out what happened to George."

"That may be never."

I couldn't let myself think that, give up hope. "Time for me to go."

"Where?"

I just shook my head at him.

"You don't want to do this," he told me. "If everything you say is true, we can protect you." His statement sounded so lame, even to him, that he looked embarrassed he'd said it. He looked down, shook his head, then looked back up at me. "This is going to end badly for you." He wasn't trying to scare me, he was trying to warn me.

I just gave him a look. "No shit."

"Goddammit." He tugged viciously at the handcuff binding his left wrist to the heavy dining room table leg. That had been Steve's idea. Reilly couldn't reach any of the phones in the house while he was attached to it, and the table was too damned big and heavy to break.

I hefted Reilly's SIG nine-millimeter in my hand, then set it down on the table in front of him. It was still loaded.

"In case your guys aren't the first people that show up," I said. "Remember, they were going to kill you too, FBI or not." He looked from the pistol to me, and I finally glimpsed a tiny bit of fear in his eyes.

Jerry was standing outside the Blazer as I jogged up, Ron's shotgun held down along his leg. Everyone else was inside the vehicle, nearly frantic with the desire to get the hell away from there.

"You said there was a back way out of here?" I said as I climbed in.

"This whole area used to be farms," Ron said through clenched teeth. The big white bandage covering his ear had a few dark spots where the stitches were bleeding. "There's two-tracks all over." We all jerked at the sound of gunshots from inside the house.

"What the fuck was that?"

I looked at Jerry, and he had Ron's shotgun up and trained on the house. I cocked my head and listened. There was another gunshot, a pause of a few seconds, then another. Jerry started to twitch.

"Reilly's trying to shoot through the table leg," I told them. "Let's go."

For almost a mile we traveled cross-country, through

fallow fields and the overgrown windbreaks between them. Ron cursed at every bump and jolt. Apparently the Tylenol-3 with codeine Jerry'd found for him hadn't worked its magic yet. Bob wasn't too fond of the rough ride either. I could see him in the front seat, one arm looped around his ribs. I was feeling better, or maybe I was just getting used to the pain. I felt like I'd fallen down a flight of stairs, which was an improvement from the night before.

"We need to get rid of this thing," I said.

"What, the Blazer?" Jerry asked.

"Even if every cop in three states wasn't looking for it, it sticks out like a sore thumb," I told them. Bob glanced at me, a sour look on his face, but he knew I was right.

"You going to rent something?" Jerry asked.

"You need a credit card for that," Steve said.

"No, I've got another idea," I said. "Give me your cell phone," I said to Jerry.

With no warning we popped through a line of trees and found ourselves on a wide, well-traveled dirt road running east-west.

"Pick up our gear first?" Bob asked me.

"We sure need it. But I've got a feeling that's where the bad guys picked us up. That storage area's under your name, right?" I said to Steve, as I dialed Jerry's cell phone.

"Yeah. I arranged to have my monthly storage fees automatically billed to my credit card."

"Maybe that's it, then," I said. The scary thing about that scenario was the manpower and resources required to pull it off. "I hate going back, but I want some heavier weapons around, and I can't see them still having somebody stationed there."

"A pistol's what you use to fight your way back to the rifle you never should have put down in the first place,"

Jerry said, sounding like he was quoting someone, or something, but I was damned I could figure out what. I listened to the phone ring in my ear, hoping the number I had was still good.

"Who are you calling?" Bob asked me, hunched over behind the wheel.

"You remember how I found out who was actually after Jerry last year?" I asked them.

"That guy you were in the Army with, the smuggler."

"He'd be offended at your characterization," I said.

"You sure he'll help?" Bob asked. "We're sort of high profile."

I smiled. "Let's just say Charlie and I bonded through adversity, same as with you."

Jerry turned and looked at Bob with an expression of disbelief. "*Sort of* high profile?"

Steve unlocked the roll-up door and we hurriedly grabbed the gear bags we'd dropped off less than two hours before. Jerry unzipped his bag, pulled out his M4 carbine with its Aimpoint red dot sight, slapped a loaded magazine into place, and chambered a round. He looked much happier with the rifle in his hands, and covertly covered us, from the shadows, as we loaded the Blazer. I checked under the hood and all through the undercarriage, just in case, but didn't find anything that looked like a tracking unit attached to the Blazer.

"Well," I began, hands on my hips. "I don't think—" I froze, staring at Jerry. He'd grabbed his cell phone back and was talking to his girlfriend Jodi.

"Gonna be gone for a while. Can't say where, can't say how long," he told her, his voice low and serious. I grabbed the phone out of his hand. There at the top of the screen was the GPS locater icon.

"Goddamn it!" I swore. "I'm an idiot. Cell phones, now, everybody give 'em here. He'll call you when he can," I said to the open phone in my hand, then snapped it in two before Jodi could answer. I tossed the pieces to the ground with the other phones and smashed them with the butt of Ron's shotgun.

"You think that was it?" Bob asked me.

"If it wasn't, it would have been before the day's out," I told him.

"You thinking they're just tracking us, or actually listening in?" Jerry asked me.

"We'll know when we drop off the Blazer," I told him. "This could get interesting."

Charlie Kang hadn't relocated his warehouse, it was still in the same bad area of Detroit, in the shadow of the I-96/Southfield Freeway interchange. From the outside it looked abandoned; what few windows it had that weren't boarded or painted over were coated with grime. There were a handful of clunkers scattered around the parking lot, but no sign of life as Bob wheeled the Blazer around the back of the building as we'd been instructed. As we approached the grey, rust-speckled overhead door it rolled up quickly and a man in greasy coveralls stepped out and waved for us to enter. All we could see past him was black.

Bob gunned the engine and we rolled under the door, which barely waited for us to pass before running back down its track to smack hard against the concrete. The inside of the warehouse wasn't dark, just poorly lit compared to the parking lot. Huge metal containers of some sort blocked our view of most of the building. Before the Blazer had even stopped moving Jerry was out the passenger door, the butt of his M4 tucked into his shoulder as he scanned the building from behind the vehicle's engine compartment.

The guy who'd opened the door for us never looked back once the overhead door was down, trudging toward the back of the warehouse, wiping his hands on the seat of his coveralls.

"You're right, I *do* recognize the truck," I heard from somewhere, as I climbed out behind Jerry. I spotted Charlie off to the left, emerging from the door of what looked like an office. I walked around the front of the Blazer toward him, and his eyes went past me. "Among other things." I glanced over my shoulder and saw Bob getting out of the truck, MP5 in hand.

"Like I said, you wouldn't believe the week I've had," I said tiredly. I shook his hand, and he smacked me on the shoulder and gave me a big smile. As usual, Charlie looked like a million bucks, dressed in a black suit, navy blue shirt, and a silk tie that probably cost as much as my gun. "Whatever you paid for that suit, it was worth it," I told him.

"You don't know how much I paid. You look like shit," he said cheerfully. He squinted at my face. "Ouch." He'd noticed how slowly I'd gotten out of the Blazer. "You okay?"

"Nothing a week in the hospital wouldn't fix."

His eyes looked past me again and the geniality left his features. "Are you expecting trouble?" The question, I'm sure, was more of a reflex than anything else. Charlie was a lot of things, but stupid wasn't one of them.

Steve had exited the Blazer with Ron's shotgun in his hands, and Jerry had stepped out from behind the far side of the vehicle, the M4 still tucked into his shoulder. Their heads were on swivels, moving back and forth constantly.

"You're goddamn right we are!" Ron said, climbing out of the back seat. The codeine in the Tylenol was helping the pain in his head a little bit, which was why Steve had his shotgun—painkillers and firearms were a bad mix unless there was no alternative. Ron stumbled a little getting down off the running board, and put a hand on the door for support.

Charlie looked at the fresh bandage covering the left side of Ron's head and winced. He loved to play the inscrutable Chinaman, but even he was having trouble keeping his face blank at the sight of us—my banged-up face, Ron's bandage, the bullet holes in Bob's shirt—hell, Bob alone would probably have been enough to crack Charlie's façade, he obviously recognized him.

"I don't know if they're tracking us somehow or we're just really unlucky," I told my old friend, pointing at the Blazer, "but driving around in that thing'll get us nowhere fast."

Charlie nodded, then turned his head to look at Bob, who was a few feet away examining the bullet holes in his shirt and shaking his head.

"I wasn't sure what you meant when you said 'celebrity'," Charlie told me, inclining his head toward Bob.

"You see why I said tinted windows?" I said.

He then did a very odd thing, at least for Charlie. He walked up to Bob and stuck his hand out.

"Charlie Kang," he said.

Bob looked a little surprised, and glanced at me, but took the offered hand. "Bob, Bob Grinnand." At that, Charlie nodded and turned back to me.

I looked down at my feet, then back up at him. I so

wanted to ask him about my wife, but I dreaded hearing anything, good or bad. "Kelly?" I said finally.

"I have no idea where she is," he told me. "Which is exactly how she said you wanted it."

I took a deep breath and nodded.

"What are we waiting for?" Ron said a little too loudly. Apparently the painkillers had damaged his volume control. There was a loud BEEP BEEP! just outside the overhead door and the boys spun that way, guns going up. After seeing Bob probably every time he turned on a TV, the boys on edge and geared up like a SWAT team about to hit a drug house apparently didn't seem odd to Charlie.

"You said big enough for five guys plus gear, right?" Charlie said, walking over to the door. He peered out a crack, then threw the sliding deadbolt and heaved upward on the door. A black Chevy Suburban with tinted windows that looked about five years old sat idling in the lot nearby, another man in grimy coveralls climbing down from behind the wheel.

I'd decided something the size of the Blazer was our best bet, but our transportation choices were limited. None of us knew how to hotwire a car, and Steve was right, we couldn't rent one—that required a credit card. Two vehicles would have been more comfortable, but might attract attention. Jerry knelt next to the Blazer, nervously scanning the empty lot over the top of his rifle.

"That thing clean?" I asked Charlie.

"As the wind-driven snow," he told me.

"Is it a problem, leaving the Blazer here?" I asked Charlie. He shook his head.

"The guys I know, they'd chop up the Popemobile if they thought they could make a buck off it," Charlie told me. Bob looked pained, but he was a professional, and knew about operational security.

"What do I owe you?" I said.

He shrugged. "What do you have?" he said with a smile, thinking our wallets were probably pretty thin. He wouldn't turn down money, but if I hadn't brought it up we could have walked out of there without paying him a dime. I didn't want to do that—he was my friend, but he was taking an awful risk with the Blazer, and Suburbans, even used ones, weren't cheap.

Ron's go-bag was on the concrete next to the Blazer and he hefted it onto a small metal table and zipped it open. "Take what you need," he told Charlie.

Charlie wandered over to the bag and did a doubletake, then looked over at me. I didn't know how much of his cut of the orphaned mob cash Ron had in the bag, but apparently it was more than enough. Charlie looked at me for a few seconds, then nodded. He reached in, took one packet of bills, and slid it into his pocket. I stared out the open door at the Suburban, wondering just where it might take us.

"Registration should be in the glove," Charlie told me. "If you'd given me enough time I could've gotten you a driver's license to match. Or some more hardware. How long can you stick around?"

"You know that scene in *Raiders of the Lost Ark*?" I asked him. "Where Indy's running down that hallway with that huge boulder right on his heels? That's where we are. We stop moving and we'll get crushed."

"Except our boulder's fucking invisible," Ron said, his voice far too loud.

NINE

Saturday

7:18 a.m.

"Oh my God."

I grunted in pain and fought to get vertical. My fingers clawed at the seat upholstery, finding no purchase. Jerry groaned from the front seat and coughed.

"I can't believe I did this voluntarily."

"What are you complaining about?" Jerry said. "Look how big that seat is."

I finally struggled upright and looked blearily around. We were in the Suburban, faint morning light starting to burn through the fogged-up windows. I shivered and pulled the jacket I'd been using as a blanket closer around me.

Jerry stretched in the front passenger seat and raised the seatback. He rubbed a circle in the condensation on the window and I saw it was frost.

"Start this thing up, get some heat going." He turned the key while I peered out the window.

We'd stopped at a rest area somewhere along Route 2 in

Ohio. The plan had been to get a little farther away from Michigan before stopping, but none of us had remembered the bottleneck construction on I-75 in Toledo.

If anybody had been following us in a car, none of us had been able to spot them after an hour of improvisational driving. Switchbacks, U-turns, going the wrong way down one-way streets, driving half or double the speed limit. The only option left to the people after us was airborne, and Bob had a pair of binoculars. After half an hour of scanning the skies we'd eliminated that possibility. After that, I was as confident as I'd ever get that we weren't being followed. Still, any time anybody in a passing car even looked our way I worried they'd recognize Bob and call the State Police on their cell phone, but Bob had claimed the driver's seat and glared down anyone who tried to spell him. Thank God for the tinted windows.

After an hour of stop and go traffic outside Toledo, however, tensions were running a little high. Jerry'd climbed into the back and stared out the rear window with his rifle across his lap, which hadn't helped my stress level. To distract them I asked their opinions about just what the hell could be going on. Who did they think kidnapped George, and why? And if they didn't think he'd been kidnapped, then what? In half an hour they tossed around enough conspiracy theories to fill a whole season of *The X-Files*. Nobody came up with anything new, but the distraction kept them calm and thinking. I had several interesting minutes of conversation with Bob.

"What's your take on the CIA?" he asked me.

"You mean in general? Well, I worked for the federal government, so I have no romantic ideas about the people that do those kinds of jobs. Regardless of what Tom Clancy says, or maybe even believes, the sad fact is that the CIA is just another bloated inefficient bureaucracy, run by a political appointee who may or may not know his ass from a hole in the ground, staffed by people for the most part who have no real-world experience and are pretty much guaranteed to keep their jobs no matter how badly they fuck up. While there are hard-chargers and true believers in the ranks, I'm guessing close to half the people in Langley are only interested in doing the minimum required to keep from being fired…and that's it. Add to that the castration it suffered under the previous administration and the never-ending budget cuts since the Cold War ended, is it any wonder we never saw 9-11 coming?"

"When I was in the DEA," I'd told him, "every once in a while we'd liaison with the CIA. Usually to trade information, although they always got a lot more than they gave. But I always dealt with intel guys, not operators, and I know they have some sort of special operations people. The guys we're running into aren't the clueless MBA's I'm talking about, that's for sure, these guys know how to get their hands dirty. You ever meet any?"

"There are a few guys that move on from SF to the spooks," Bob said, "and they've got home-grown trigger pullers, but this isn't the Cold War anymore—the number of operators they've got is pretty damn small, even after Nine-Eleven. Hell, they never really had that many, but after the Soviet breakup the Operations end really downsized. I think they're trying to build it back up now, after the cow's out of the barn, but that'll take 'em a while. I don't think any of the other intel agencies have operators, but I don't know."

He got a thoughtful look on his face. "Say this whole

thing with George has been an authorized op," Bob said, thinking out loud. "Probably only a few guys at the top of the food chain know what it's all about, the rest are just following orders, completing a mission. Then consider how many people have been involved in this. It's incredible, even assuming a lot of them are freelance, contractors, ex-SF or whatever, not officially on the payroll. Hell, the DDO can't have much more than fifty or a hundred guys immediately available – in country – for this kind of work, total. How many do you think have been on our case? Between the people we've seen, heard about, or killed, we're talking close to twenty-five bodies. Even assuming contractors, that's a lot of people. And a budget expenditure that's not insubstantial."

"So what are you saying?"

"I don't think this is an authorized op. How many people have died? Damn near a dozen, right? You're talking way too high profile for the CIA which always run in the opposite direction from publicity. And authorized doesn't necessarily mean legal anyway. Not on U.S. soil. If this were an authorized op it would've been called off long ago because of the publicity. Too much chance of exposure. They lose one guy and they call operations off. And remember, too, somebody has to justify their expenses to someone else. People that do this kind of work don't come cheap. An operation this size, authorized or not, sure as hell should have attracted the attention of the big dogs in the intelligence community."

"Some sort of rogue agency then, or rogue operation?"

He shrugged. "You tell me."

"I'll tell you one thing. If you're not talking national security, people only usually take these kinds of risks for one reason."

"Money."

"You got it. And a lot of it, I'm betting, from the sheer size of this beast. Whoever's at the top of this thing calling the shots is wearing one hell of an expensive suit, I'll tell you that."

That conversation had taken place yesterday afternoon. Now I was peering out the frosted window, trying to see how the day was shaping up outside. The Suburban rocked slightly and I heard Ron yawn from the back.

"Get up, sleepyhead," Jerry told him.

"I'm freezing," I heard Ron mumble.

"I'm not the guy who said he didn't want to be sucking carbon monoxide fumes all night," Jerry bitched back.

Steve had grabbed a small tent and two sleeping bags from his storage garage when he heard we had no set ideas on where we'd be sleeping. He and Bob had disappeared out into the woods on the far side of the parking lot.

"I wonder if they froze to death."

"No such luck. That mummy bag Steve's got is good to ten below." Jerry headed out, first for a bathroom stop and then to wake up our two campers if they were still asleep. Half an hour later the tent and sleeping bags were stowed in the back of the Suburban and we'd all visited the restrooms.

"You look like hell," I told Bob as he returned from the restrooms with Steve. He was pale and looked sick. All I got was a glare as he climbed into the driver's seat and started looking over the maps. Steve made eyes at me and jerked his head.

"I'm gonna go stretch my legs," I said. "Be back in a minute."

"I'll come with you," Steve said.

"So what's up?" I asked him a minute later when we were out of earshot.

"I'm worried about Bob," he told me.

"Aren't we all."

"No, I mean I think his ribs are really messed up bad. I don't think he slept at all last night. He kept tossing and turning, finally he sat up and dozed that way. In the bathroom just now I could hear him spitting into the toilet, and when he came out his lip was bloody."

"You mean like he's coughing up blood?"

"I don't know, but have you seen how he's been driving? All hunched over? Watch him, every time we hit a bump it hurts. And he's not exactly a pussy about pain."

I sighed, and zipped my coat up a little higher against the cold morning air. The rest area was starting to get a few more visitors, mostly truckers up late or starting early. The sound of traffic whooshing by on the freeway echoed off the leafless trees.

"What do you want me to do about it?"

"I don't know. Nothing, I guess. I just thought you ought to know."

When we got back to the Suburban I hopped up on the running board beside Bob's open door. "Want me to drive?" I asked him. "You've been doing all of it so far."

"I'll drive," he told me.

"You sure?" He ignored the repeat question.

"There was a big trucker's gas station a few miles back with showers," I told them. "You guys want to stop there or just wait 'til we hit the hotel?"

"How much farther do we have?"

I looked at Bob.

"Staying off the interstates, mostly? About eight hours, no more than ten, long as there's no snow," he said.

"Let's just get there," Ron said, expressing the mood of the group.

Somewhere in Pennsylvania Jerry found a radio station playing Rush Limbaugh. I've always enjoyed Rush, but Iraq didn't interest me anymore and somehow his jokes about the latest outrages coming out of Washington didn't seem funny to me. My sense of humor seemed to have been seriously impaired by the events of the last few days. Everyone else in the truck seemed amused, though. Except for Bob. Steve had been right—Bob barely took his arm from around his ribs, and even though he hid it well I could see the pain in his eyes every time the Suburban hit a bump. He wasn't just steering, he seemed to be using the wheel to hold himself up.

4:52 p.m.

"You drink any more of that stuff, they're not going to have to use embalming fluid on you when you die," I told Jerry. He was drinking what had to be his fourth bottle of Diet Coke since we'd gotten underway.

Bob was filling the Suburban up while the rest of them used the Amoco's bathrooms. I'd grabbed a Diet Coke myself and was back in my unofficial spot in the back seat.

"You be nice, or I'll have Ron put that **Tool** back in the CD player," Jerry said.

"You want to hear something scary?" I said. "I actually kind of liked it." I watched Bob as he headed off to use the bathroom. He moved slow and careful, one arm unconsciously protecting his ribs.

"Now I know we're in trouble."

We were using cash to pay for everything—the boys knew enough about paper trails to not leave any. Between my two ATM cards and a credit card I'd gotten my hands on a thousand dollars before we'd left Michigan, and I had a hunch Ron wasn't the only one of them to bring along a chunk of mad money.

"I can always tell when I'm out-of-state," Ron said, climbing in after paying for the gas. "*Hustler* for sale at the gas stations and condoms in the bathrooms, but we're not allowed to pray in school. America. What a country. No wonder Al-Qaida wants us dead."

Steve appeared with a bag full of fluorescent orange Cheetos in one hand, a huge Coke in the other.

"I hope we get there soon," he said. "I've had just about enough of riding in the car."

"Bob looked on the map and said it should only be about another hour," I told him. "That is, if he doesn't pass out from the pain and drive off the road first."

"You noticed that too, huh?"

The four of us watched Bob as he pushed the gas station's glass door open and walked toward the Suburban. A nice egg-sized shiner was growing on his cheek, courtesy of the late Mr. Green. Bob had listened to my concerns and put on a baseball cap and sunglasses before getting out of the Suburban, but still I was eager to get moving. I nearly laughed at the absurdity of our situation. We were so damn banged up only Jerry and Steve could show their faces in public without eyebrows being raised.

Bob was concentrating so hard on not limping or showing any pain he didn't even see us staring at him.

"You gonna say anything?" someone asked me.

"And just what would you have me say?" was my reply. Nobody responded.

Bob carefully climbed up into the driver's seat, still refusing to be relieved.

"He needs to shave that damn beard," I said. "It's like Rudolph's nose-so-bright. They got razors in there?"

"No. I thought of that, and checked," Jerry told me. He huffed. "So what's the plan going to be when we get there?"

"Plan? What, are you kidding? I stopped thinking about thirty hours ago." I wasn't joking, either. If I stopped long enough to seriously consider my actions I'd spin around and head back to Michigan to turn myself in.

"So, what? We just check in and then see what happens?"

"Well, we know the reservation's good." I'd confirmed it around lunchtime from somewhere in Pennsylvania. "Unless they plan on stiffing Mr. Green on his money, somebody'll get in touch. I'll talk to them and insist on a person-to-person for the cash if they want to do a dead drop. I'm hoping that whoever shows up with the payoff doesn't know what Green looks or sounds like. It's a good bet, since he had no idea who hired him—I'm betting that goes both ways. Even if that's not the case, we still grab whoever shows up and find out what or who he knows and go from there. Work our way up the chain of command."

"That's a plan? Calling that a plan is an insult to real plans everywhere."

"You asked." I looked at them, at their young faces, and contemplated the enormity of what we were doing. The oldest of them was twenty-two years old, and here we were heading cross-country, riding on a pile of guns, some of them taken off dead men, on what at best could be considered a fool's errand. And I knew that if I told them—again—they didn't have to come, that they could turn back, they'd be insulted.

"What do you think the chances are that it's just one big setup?" Steve asked.

"Oh, I don't know," I said, looking to Bob for input. "About forty percent?"

"At least," Bob growled.

"Good thing you got laid this summer, huh?" Jerry said to Steve. "Be shitty to die as a virgin."

For nearly a minute, Steve was speechless. He sat there blinking, his mouth working soundlessly. "Fuuuuuuuck *you*," Steve finally shot back, his face beet red.

I just prayed to God we didn't get stopped by any cops. I knew them better than anyone else did, and even I wasn't sure what they'd do.

It was amazing to me just how much traffic there was in Maryland and along the whole eastern seaboard. Detroit, the Motor city, on its worst day, could barely compete with D.C.'s standard Monday morning rush hour.

Maryland roads were weird in other ways, too. The first time I'd ever driven around the Columbia and Ellicott City area in the late eighties, two things had caught my attention. First, how new everything looked. New malls, new office buildings, new residential subdivisions, new roads. I got the impression that ten or fifteen years earlier the entire area had been farmland and forest. But as new as it all was, the whole place was wall-to-wall people. Where the hell did all the people come from? Did the contractors ship them in after they finished the roads and malls?

As we rolled into Columbia, Maryland, I saw that nothing had really changed. It was an upscale area, and I'd heard somewhere that it was a planned community, whatever that meant. Tasteful, pretty, with winding wooded boulevards nearly bumper to bumper with traffic.

"It's supposed to be up here on the left," I told Bob. The

Columbia Mall appeared on our right as the road took a gentle turn to the left. We rolled past an office building, then saw the green sign of a Bennigan's.

"Take the loop-around, go down that street there," I told Bob, pointing at the Bennigan's. As soon as he did the Columbia Inn was right in front of us, a couple hundred yards down a side street. It curved past the front of the hotel and disappeared into a two-story parking structure beside the restaurant.

"Might as well park in the ramp," I said, "get this thing out of sight."

"We're getting a second room, right?" Ron said.

"That's the idea. Hopefully they'll have connecting doors. We shouldn't all go traipsing past the front desk," I told them as they started climbing out. However, I sure as hell wasn't going in alone. I ended up with Jerry and Ron.

The lobby of the place was quite attractive, done in peach and other soothing pastels. Poofy couches and glass-topped tables filled the center of the circular lobby, arrayed around a bigscreen TV. Across the way I could see French doors leading to the hotel's restaurant.

"Hey, look! Wow." I followed Jerry's gaze upward and saw the whole center of the hotel was hollow. We could see fifteen stories straight up. Colorful streamers hung from the glass ceiling all the way down to the second and third floors.

"C'mon," I said, jerking my head. We headed for the front desk. "Keep your eyes open."

The clerk was blonde, and gorgeous, wearing a maroon blazer with the hotel logo on the pocket. She couldn't have been much older than my companions.

"Welcome to the Columbia Inn," she said brightly. A nametag said GWEN.

"Hi," I said. "Reservation for Green." She began typing

on her computer. Jerry was doing what he was supposed to, looking around the lobby for anyone brandishing an Uzi, but Ron couldn't keep his eyes off the girl.

"Yes sir. One room, non-smoking, with a king-size bed."

"Would it be possible for me to get a second room? Preferably adjacent to the first?"

"Let me check." Thirty seconds of typing followed. "I'm sorry sir, we're pretty well booked up. The closest I can get you is one floor up. Non-smoker, two double beds. We're almost sold out," she said apologetically. "There's a convention in the hotel. Accountants."

She looked at Ron's bandaged head, my lumpy face and scabbed knuckles, then back at Ron's head. "What happened to your ear?"

He leaned forward and lowered his voice. "Gunfight," he said confidentially. She blinked once, then looked at me and rolled her eyes.

"Car accident," I told her, and pointed. "*He* was driving."

She giggled. A sure sign as to how my life had changed—and not for the better—was how weird it seemed to be having a normal conversation with a pretty girl. "And how would you like to pay for this?"

"Cash," I said, digging in my pocket.

"We'll need a credit card number on file for security purposes," she informed me sweetly. I froze.

"Use this," Ron said, handing over a credit card. I shot him a worried look but he gave a little shake of his head.

"Put the second room in my name," Ron told her.

Gwen looked at the card. "Of course, Mr. Reilly." Jerry practically blew snot out his nose and had to start coughing to cover up his laughter. I rubbed the bridge of my nose and wondered how long it'd be before the headache set in. I glanced over my shoulder, then did a doubletake. I kicked Ron in the shin and nodded my head. He turned and looked around the lobby. The bigscreen TV was tuned to Fox News, and they were showing the Hurricane Bob video.

Even though I'd seen it half a dozen times already I couldn't take my eyes off the TV. They stopped the tape before the beheading this time, and I noticed that Bob's face was pixeled out. So were the faces of the faux Feds. That was no accident, but what did that mean?

When the clip ended they cut to a split screen shot featuring a hot anchorette and a guy who could only be retired military.

"Stay here," I told Ron and Jerry, and walked across the lobby.

"—which only raises more questions, of course," I heard the female anchor say. "A lot more questions. Here, Colonel Patrick, let me read the statement to you again, and I want you to tell me what you think of it. Remember, this is coming from the FBI late yesterday, this is their official statement, so far the only statement they've made concerning the incident we've just witnessed. 'To our knowledge, and contrary to initial reports, the men shown on this video were not members of or acting on behalf of any local, state, or federal law enforcement agency, and anyone who has any information concerning them or this incident should immediately contact their local FBI office.' That's the official statement. That's one heck of an admission if you ask me. They were quick to assure the public that the incident had nothing to do with terrorism, but that begs the question— How do they know? If they don't even know who the dead men are, saying it's got nothing to do with terrorists or terrorism seems rather fatuous. We've got another quote, an unofficial one, from an FBI agent, who told us, 'They're not ours, they're not locals, we don't know who they are, and we don't know if this incident is related to the other homicides in the Detroit area. But you can bet we'll find out.' Colonel, your comments?"

The short-haired man looked a little ill at ease. "Well," he began, "my background's military, of course, Special Forces, not law enforcement, but the fact that they're willing to come out and say they don't know who these individuals are, that they've got nothing, and basically beg for any help they can get, tells me something. Frankly, it tells me a lot."

"That's what I was thinking," the anchor said. "What about the man shown on the tape? The FBI has stated this wasn't a terrorist act, but when half a dozen heavily armed men apparently unaffiliated with any law enforcement agency get killed during what looks to me like an attempt to abduct someone it leaves you wondering who they were, who he was, and exactly what was happening there, especially when the FBI has asked that we please stop showing the tape until they sort things out. We've agreed to obscure the faces of the men in the video, but again, this leaves me with more questions."

"All I can say," the colonel said, "after watching that video more times than I care to remember, is that none of those men fit the standard terrorist profile, and they've all had training of some sort." He blinked once, and with an expression on his face I couldn't read said, "Some, apparently, more than others."

"What about that?" the anchor asked him. "You know about these things. Have you ever seen, or I guess been taught, that technique? The decapitation? We can't actually show it, it's far too grisly, but the public has seen edited versions of the incident, and it's pretty obvious what took place. You've seen the raw footage, Colonel, as have I.

Admittedly, it's horrific, but what struck me was how fast he did it. I didn't think you could remove a person's head that quickly with just a knife. I would think it would be... tougher." She made a face. "Forgive me for being so graphic."

The colonel's mouth drew into a thin line. "I've never been taught any techniques to remove someone's head, and I don't think that's something that really gets taught. Not since we moved away from fighting with swords. You don't need to take someone's head all the way off to kill them. Beheading is and always has been done to send a message. As for tough, well, when the adrenaline gets going you'd be surprised at what you can do. Or how fast you can do it. Depending on how motivated you are." He paused and stared hard into the camera. "That gentleman appeared very motivated."

I had to wonder what kind of urgent phone calls were going back and forth between USSOCOM—Special Operations Command, the entity ultimately in charge of the Army's Green Berets—at MacDill AFB in Tampa and the FBI. And the Department of Justice. And probably the Pentagon. Bob wasn't just a soldier, he was a decorated Special Forces soldier, on active duty, and America was a country at war with unconventional foes. The men involved had been in possession of fake FBI credentials, although apparently that detail hadn't been released to the press yet. Just who those guys were who had tried to abduct him, and why, was a question I was guessing was bouncing around corridors at the Pentagon, if not the White House. I also had a strong suspicion that there were large numbers of people all around the country who knew a lot more about what was going on than us, even though we were in the middle of it.

I tore my eyes away from the TV set and looked around the lobby. Everything looked just the way it was supposed to, no matter how surreal my life felt at the moment. I walked back over to the check-in counter where Ron was still flirting with the clerk.

"You guys have any aspirin?" I asked her.

"There are vending machines on every floor," she informed me with a perky smile. "Aspirin, Alka-Seltzer, Tylenol, all that."

"What about razors?"

"Those too," she said helpfully.

"Any messages?" I asked tiredly. Her fingers flipped quickly through the message box.

"Not yet."

"Jesus." I looked at Jerry, who'd spoken, and saw that he was looking across at the TV, where they were showing the video of Bob again, this time in slow motion. Even in slow motion he was fast. And every time I watched it Bob looked angrier.

The clerk saw what he was looking at. "It's horrible, isn't it," she said sympathetically.

Jerry looked at her. "Horrible's not the word."

6:34 p.m.

I felt two hundred percent better after showering. I came out of the bathroom and sat on the bed with my hair still wet so Ron could get under the water. We were sharing the room with the king size bed. Jerry, Steve, and Bob were one floor up and almost halfway around the hotel. None of them were thrilled about splitting up but nobody wanted to line up for a single shower when two were available. They'd be down as soon as they cleaned up. The schedule for the evening consisted entirely of sitting around and staring at the phone in my room, waiting for it to ring. I hoped somebody had brought a deck of cards.

11:07 p.m.

Ron was laying on the bed, feet flat on the floor, hands clasped behind his head. He was staring at the hotel room's textured stucco ceiling, had been for quite a while. God only knew what he was thinking.

I could only hope George was still alive. We'd been doing our own version of Sherman's march to the sea, pretty much destroying everything in our wake, and that was without knowing what had happened to Ron's father. If it turned out George was dead I shuddered to think how my companions would react. I wondered if, at the end, we'd find out that we would've been better off just turning ourselves in.

I rubbed my face vigorously between my palms, then pushed myself off the hotel chair by its arms. "I'm beat," I told him. And broke, I added silently. Three of them had spent the last four hours pummeling me in poker. Bob spent the whole evening hunched over in a chair, not talking, his face chalk white. He'd made regular trips into the bathroom, where behind the closed door we could all hear him spitting into the toilet. The look on his face did not invite comment, not that anyone was in a talkative mood. They tried to put on a brave front, but I knew them too well. I don't know if *scared* would have been the right word to describe them, but we were all suffering from a sort of battle fatigue. The not knowing was the worst part. Doctors like to call it Post-Traumatic Stress Disorder. I was pretty sure this counted as Mid-Traumatic, but whatever. All I knew was in the middle of a bet Steve's hands started to shake so bad he dropped his cards. He went into the bathroom, and when he came out ten minutes later he appeared back to normal. We all pretended not to notice, and went back to playing.

For most of the evening we'd had the TV tuned to CNN, but after an hour and a half with no new news about our situation Bob had snapped, "Would you please shut that fucking thing off!" They were about to show the video yet again, and Bob seemed near the breaking point.

"Is this as big as I think it is?" Jerry asked me as he shut off the TV.

"The attempt on Bob is the lead story on every news network. The media hasn't tied it yet to the dead bodies at my house, or George Kelly's kidnapping, but they will. And soon. Especially after word gets out that we dropped two more bodies at Ron's house. In front of the real FBI, no less. Who we told about George Kelly being some sort of asset with the intelligence community. And, to top it off, the real FBI and military knows that a bunch of guys with not-real/real FBI creds tried to abduct an active duty Green Beret. In the middle of a street. In the middle of the day. After trying to blow him up. While we're at war with terrorists and about to head into Iraq. So yeah, however big you think this is, it's bigger."

"And we still don't know shit," Jerry felt obliged to add.

I looked around the room. Bob had always been light-skinned, it went with his pale hair, but now he was nearly as pale as milk except for the dark circles under his hollow eyes. His skin was so pale it made his beard look brown. The bandage over Ron's ear covered half the side of his head. I felt like I'd been attacked by a troupe of midgets wielding hardwood fish bats.

I'd been trying for two days, but I tried again. I spoke to Jerry and Steve.

"Look, Bob, Ron and I are in this. We've killed people. But you guys haven't. Not yet. You get out now, it won't be nearly as bad for you. Us, if we live through this, no matter what happens we're going to spend serious time in prison. I don't want to see that happen to you."

"You shut the fuck up with that shit," Jerry growled at me, eloquent as always.

Steve looked at me tiredly. "I'm not just here for you. I'm here for him," he said, nodding at Ron. "And him." He nodded at Bob. "We're in this together." He paused. "Whatever the fuck 'this' is."

"Morons," I told them. "Idiots." Name-calling didn't have any more effect on them than logic and reason had.

After the last big pot everybody decided to call it a night. The consensus was that it was too late—the bad guys would've already called if today was the day. Steve, Bob, and Jerry headed back upstairs, but would be back bright and early in the morning. "And shave that goddamn beard," I told Bob as they headed out. Now all I had to do was convince Ron he wanted to sleep on the floor.

"I don't know if I can sleep with this fucking ear," Ron said. "That Tylenol's doing dick. Besides, it's barely even eleven o'clock," he protested, propping himself up on his elbows. He pointed at the TV. "We get free Skinemax. It'll be tits and ass until dawn. *The Golden Child* with Eddie Murphy starts in half an hour, it's got the most gratuitous wet t-shirt shot in Hollywood history. Which is saying something." I only groaned in response, and hobbled my various aching parts into the bathroom to relieve myself. Two days in a truck hadn't done my abused body one bit of good. I peered into the mirror—my face was lumpy, but the bruises were deep enough that they didn't show through too well. The shoeprint on my chest was getting darker, and now I could see a tread pattern.

"How's your ear?" I called out. "Hurt much?"

"Only when my heart beats. You thirsty?" Ron asked as I was washing my hands. "I want to get a Coke."

"Sure, what the hell," I told him. "A little caffeine couldn't hurt. As beat to shit as I feel I don't think I can sleep yet." I sat back down in the chair and slowly put on my shoes, then shrugged on my jacket to cover the Colt and the two spare magazines that adorned my belt. Ron made sure his sweatshirt was pulled down over the revolver on his hip and then we were ready to go public in search of the nearest pop machine. People from other states would have referred to it as soda instead of pop. They'd be wrong.

Not wanting to die from laziness, I peered through the peephole in the door before opening it. Ron pointed a finger down the hall to our right, his eyebrows arched questioningly. I shook my head and stuck a thumb to our left.

The hotel was surprisingly quiet. Maybe all the conventioneers were at the bar or something. Then again, I doubted accountants kept late hours. I peered over the waist-high railing down to the lobby as we walked. There were two couples sitting on the sofas, but I didn't see anybody coming or going from the restaurant.

The Coke machine was beside the elevators at the long end of the oval open-air courtyard, atrium, or whatever the architect called the fifteen stories of nothing he'd designed into the center of the hotel. Our room was nearly halfway between the elevators, in the middle of one of the long sides of the oval, guaranteeing we'd have a long walk no matter where we wanted to go. Curiously, though, the stairs weren't next to the elevators. Our room was only one door away from a stairwell, with another stairwell on the far side of the oval. Wings led off the long ends of the oval, and that was where the majority of the hotel's rooms were positioned. The hotel was attractively designed, but not very space efficient. I guess with the prices they charged it didn't have to be.

Two steps behind Ron, I passed the elevator doors and stopped in front of the Coke machine. On the right was a candy-filled vending machine, and next to that was an ice machine. Ron put his hands on his hips and stared at the Coke machine with its six-foot-tall backlit red and white logo, then turned and looked at me, not saying anything. Then he spun back to the machine, spine stiff. The orange light was lit beside every single button, indicating the machine was totally out of cans. I tried not to laugh, God knows I did, but a few snorts still escaped. Ron turned around and looked at me, torn between anger and disbelief.

"I can't believe those fucking bean-counters drank all the pop," he said. He took two steps sideways and punched the elevator call button angrily, crossing his arms across his chest. I looked across the open air and saw another pop machine on our floor, next to the opposite elevator.

"C'mon," I told Ron, and headed down the curving hallway back the way we'd come. Even with no one in the hotel, we'd be standing there ten minutes waiting for an elevator just to take us down one floor. We'd learned that immediately after checking in. Choice profanity erupted to my rear but Ron fell into step. I elected to head for the pop machine I could see ahead instead of taking the stairs to another floor where there might not even be a machine.

I glanced to my left at the decorative streamers hung from the atrium's ceiling seven floors above us. The streamers ended around the third floor. They were made of some shimmery translucent material that changed color depending on how the light hit them. Then I heard a mechanical rumble and turned my head to see the elevator doors some forty feet ahead of us open and two men step out. They paused just outside the elevator and looked at the sign mounted in front of them, on one of the rectangular support columns, explaining to guests which rooms were in what direction. A one second pause and then they turned our way.

I took another step in their direction and then

THUMP!

my heart slammed in my chest and the whole world went into slow motion. The man on the left turned toward me. He was wearing a black jacket and khakis. The man to his left, my right, was in a brown leather bomber jacket and jeans. As my right foot touched the ground, my stride unbroken,

THUMP!

they began to walk, and the man in the black jacket started to turn his head my way. Ron was to my right, a step and a half back, saying something about the hotel. The tiniest details, like the pattern on the maroon hallway carpet and the pebbled surface of the walls, jumped out at me, as if I'd inherited the Six Million Dollar Man's bionic eyes. I brought my right hand back and swept the jacket away from my right side. My left foot swung forward to touch the

THUMP!

carpeted floor, and my right hand closed on the Colt's grip, drew it from its holster in one smooth motion. As soon as the pistol's muzzle cleared leather I began to bring the gun forward, clicking off the thumb safety just before my left hand closed over my right. The man in the black jacket had light brown hair and I saw him lock his eyes onto me, thirty feet away, as I brought the automatic up. He had brown eyes. The pistol's front sight was in sharp focus as it settled into the rear notch, centered on the man's chest as

THUMP!

I pressed the trigger. The gun bucked in my hand, soundless, the muzzle rising to obscure the target as I swung right to acquire the second man. As the front sight came down to where I knew the second man would be I fired, glimpsing only a flash of brown as he dived to the side.

THUMP!

Rooted in place in a textbook shooting stance, I pivoted slightly right and saw where the second man had thrown himself. The Coke machine stuck out of its alcove no more than eight inches and he'd pressed himself against the wall behind it. I fired ***ONE-TWO-THREE-FOUR-FIVE*** times at the leading edge of the illuminated Coke dispenser, trying to punch one or more .45's through it into him, then pivoted left

THUMP!

and reacquired the man in black. He was flat on his back in the hallway, not moving.

From behind me I heard Ron yell "What the fuck are you—" as I swung back towards the Coke machine and a glimpse of movement. The front end of a gun poked around the corner of the vending machine and I threw myself backwards behind one of the rectangular support columns lining the inside of the open hallway, almost flipping myself out into space as the top of the low wall caught my butt. The roar of a full-auto weapon filled the hotel, and pieces of plaster erupted from the front of the column. I backed off a step to give myself some room to maneuver as another long, wild burst chewed up walls and the carpet to my right. It sounded like a roaring metal dragon had been let loose in the hotel.

"Jesus Christ!" I heard Ron shriek as I brought my gun up and quickly fired a double-tap around the corner, then ducked back as the man filled the space I'd just occupied with hot metal. Whatever he was using, it had an extremely high rate of fire. The long bursts, combined with the weapon's recoil-induced muzzle rise, caused most of his rounds to sail high and wide. A small, unharried part of my mind considered this while the rest of my body was struggling at bladder control.

The column I was hiding behind stuck out into the hallway less than a foot. The solid waist-high stuccoed wall that ran along the fifteen-story cave of an atrium merged into a column like the one I was behind every fifteen feet around the entire circumference of the floor. The design prevented little kids from falling to their deaths but left me little room to maneuver as I endeavored to slam a loaded magazine into my empty gun without toppling over the railing or exposing vital body parts to a bullet.

I hit the slide release and chambered a round from the fresh magazine, then leaned out from the column and fired four at the corner of the Coke machine. In a phenomenon the doctors call auditory exclusion, I could clearly hear the heavy .45 rounds thumping into the machine's metal body, and yet the gunshots were mere muffled thuds, sounding far away. More pieces of red and white plastic fell from the no-longer illuminated front of the pop dispenser, and I could hear a hissing gurgle as some perforated cans discharged their contents onto the floor. None of my shots, however, had any sort of visible effect on the guy squeezed behind the rectangular chunk of metal and plastic. Machines designed to thwart thieves with crowbars and drills also apparently did a good job of stopping low-velocity pistol bullets. The guy behind the machine didn't have a lot of room to move either, but he wasn't about to give up such superior cover. As I ducked back behind the column—which was doing a pretty good job itself of stopping bullets—the guy fired another short burst at me. I could feel the bullets slamming into the opposite side of the column. The machine pistol he was using had been small enough to hide under his jacket, but that meant it was a bitch to control on full-auto.

The gunfight was maybe ten seconds old and just then I heard two quick pairs of amazingly loud gunshots from behind me. I turned my head and saw Ron crouched down behind the curving parapet wall some ten feet to my rear, out of the line of sight of the guy I had pinned down behind the Coke machine. Ron had his Smith & Wesson .357 out and pointing across the open-air courtyard to the other side of the hotel.

I spun my head left to see what he was shooting at just as he fired another two quick shots. There, across the way, on our floor, were two more men crouching down behind columns, bringing pistols to bear. They split, one heading left and one right, dashing from column to column as they worked their way around the oval toward us. I twisted my upper body to the left as far as it would go without moving my feet and was able to get the men in my sights, some fifty feet away. I fired a wild double-tap at each of them, to no effect, and then reloaded quickly with my last mag.

"I'm out!" Ron yelled at me, patting his pockets just to make sure.

"Goddammit!" I screamed back at him, firing again at the two guys across the way, trying to keep their heads down as much as hit them. It worked, briefly. They both fired in my general direction, trying to buy themselves some time so they could get closer. Unbelievably, I saw one of the room doors across the hotel open up and a guest stuck his head out, trying to see what was going on.

"I didn't think I'd need extra ammo to get a fucking pop!" Ron yelled back. "I'm gonna try to make it to the room!"

"Go!"

I was between a rock and a hard place. Standing as I was, I had cover from anything the guy behind the Coke machine might want to throw at me, but I was completely visible from the waist up to the two assholes across the hotel. If I ducked behind the wall away from the two guys I'd stick out from the column and be exposed to the guy at the Coke machine, who took this moment to fire another burst my way. He must have reloaded. This close, the sound of his full-auto weapon was deafening. More plaster dust filled the air. I edged out from behind the column and fired twice at the corner of the machine where he was hiding, then leaned back, twisted my body, and fired a round at each of the guys edging toward me. They scrambled for new cover and fired blindly in my direction. Now, a mere thirty seconds into what I figured would be the last gunfight I'd ever see, I'd lost count of how many rounds I had left in my gun.

I'd just decided to try and make it back to our room, hoping to manage a retreat without being riddled by the guy with the submachinegun, when somebody began cracking a hundred-foot long bullwhip in the hotel. After half a dozen of these rapid roaring echoing cracks I looked over at the two guys trying to flank me and saw they had gone to ground somewhere behind the curving waist-high stucco wall. One raised his handgun into view and fired at something above and behind me. He was greeted with a quick volley of return rifle fire, the wall disintegrating around him, and I saw shiny spent cases tumbling past me towards the lobby eight stories below. I leaned out over the wall and craned my neck upward. Thirty feet behind and one floor above me I saw the barrel and distinctive front sight of an M4 poking out over the railing. The rifleman poured rounds into the wall, the brass falling toward the lobby like a golden waterfall.

One of the men across the way fired twice at the rifleman's position, then made a quick dash for the next column. The rifle spoke twice, loudly, and the man stumbled and fell behind the wall. The rifleman then put another six or so rounds into the wall where the guy had disappeared from view. Suddenly realizing that the guy I'd pinned down behind the Coke machine could have skipped up to me and sent me to hell while I wasn't paying attention, I edged out gun-first from the column, prepared to fire more rounds into the indestructible pop machine. Instead, I saw that I wasn't the only person caught up watching the action on the other side of the hotel. As my sights cleared the side of the column I was rewarded with a glimpse of a partial silhouette. I'd caught the guy looking someplace other than where I was, and I fired once.

He went down, skidding across the wall to the floor in front of the elevator. His left hand clawed out for something to hold on to and bright red arterial blood sprayed out of his neck in a fantail. He tried to sit up, right hand dropping the gun and grabbing at his neck in a panic. I shot him again, this time in the head. He dropped to the ground and flopped and twisted for several seconds, then was still. Rifle fire still echoed loudly through the hotel, as well as return fire from what sounded like a pistol. I stepped out from behind the stucco column, putting it between me and anybody on the far side of the floor. My .45 was trained on the bodies of the two men I had killed, laying in the unnatural positions of death beside each other on the hallway carpet.

I spun and aimed at a thumping sound and saw Ron running up the hallway toward me, the MAC-10 subgun in his hands. I lowered my pistol and we both noticed that its slide was locked back, the gun totally empty. For a fraction of a second I thought I was going to lose it, and my hands started to shake, then I dropped the Colt's slide and fumbled it back into its holster as Ron tossed me his revolver.

"You got six!" he yelled. The .357 in a firm, two-handed grip, I spun toward the far side of the hotel and searched for a target. I saw one of the gunmen as he headed for the stairwell in a faltering run. I spun to Ron and pointed at the two bodies on the floor.

"Check 'em out," I ordered him, then jumped over the two forms and ran full out down the curving hallway at the guy who was limping toward the stairwell. His left hand was pressed against his side, red with blood, and he was using his right to propel himself along the wall. I didn't see a gun anywhere.

The man pushed open the stairwell door just as I reached his companion. The gunman's partner was crumpled, unmoving, in a large puddle of blood on the carpet beneath the low wall which had been shredded by rifle bullets. I dashed after the fugitive, reaching the stairwell door before it had closed all the way. I kicked the door back open and pointed my revolver at the figures on the stairwell landing.

"Shit!" exclaimed Steve, lowering the pistol he was pointing at my head. The gun visibly shook. I depressed the muzzle of my own gun and stepped onto the landing next to Bob, who had the injured man pinned against the wall. Bob's left hand was around the guy's throat, holding him still. In his right hand Bob held the MP5, the smooth black cylinder of its suppressor resting lightly against the man's cheek.

The guy was panting and his eyes were wild, his right hand pressed back against the wall and his left against his side where his shirt was soaked in blood. He tried to look tough, but he couldn't help but stare at the bore of the weapon that was an inch from his left eye. His eye kept darting from the muzzle to Bob's impassive face back to the MP5's muzzle. It looked like he recognized Bob; I would have been surprised if he didn't. I gave him a reassuring smile and moved a step closer. My smile might have had more effect on the guy if Bob hadn't been looking at him like he was ants on a sidewalk. Steve moved to the door and held it open with his body, covering the stairwell both up and down, with occasional glances out the door at the hallway corridor.

"Questions," I said. The guy grunted and struggled in Bob's grasp. In response Bob let the subgun drop to his side on its sling and gave a vicious openhand slap to the guy's left hand where it pressed on his fresh bullet wound. The guy let out a gurgling scream and scrabbled at Bob's forearm with his right hand, his knees buckling. I saw the muscles in Bob's arm tense as he squeezed the guy's neck and held him upright against the wall. The gunman's face turned a shade darker and he gave a little chirp like a demented bird. Bob was slightly hunched over, his face pale.

My head filled with red. I cocked Ron's Smith & Wesson and pressed its barrel against the injured man's forehead. "We're pressed for time and we're only going to do this once," I told him, steel in my voice. "Do you want to talk or would you rather we just kill you right now and leave your body in this hotel stairwell?"

"I'll talk, I'll talk," he gasped. "But I don't know shit." I removed the .357 from his head and lowered the hammer.

"I'm looking for George Kelly," I told him. "All I want is to know where he is."

"Who the fuck's that?" he said hoarsely. He was looking at me but every couple of seconds his eyes flicked over at Bob. Yep, he recognized him.

"The guy you people fucking kidnapped in Michigan last week!" I said angrily, showing heroic restraint by not shooting him right then. "Mid-fifties, halfway bald, built like a fifty-gallon drum on two stumps. George Fucking Kelly!"

Out in the hotel I could faintly hear Ron yelling. "Police! Stay in your rooms! Don't come out until we tell you it's safe!"

"I don't know, I swear to God I don't know!" Bob's captive pleaded frantically, looking for any sign of compassion in my or Bob's face. Still holding him by the throat against the wall, Bob punched the guy just above where he'd been shot. The failed gunman screamed pitifully, sounding like a woman, and weakly kicked at Bob. Bob took the kick on a knee without a sound or change of expression.

I heard a sound and a middle-aged couple appeared on the landing above us. Dressed in their pajamas, hair mussed, looking scared. They stopped when they saw us.

Steve refrained from pointing his gun at them, and held up a hand. "Police," he said in a deep voice. "Back up the stairs. Stay in your room."

"Help me," our captive squeaked as them, Bob's hand still around his neck.

Dredging an admirable knot of courage up from somewhere, the grey-haired man protested. "What are you doing to him?" he asked indignantly. I got the impression he was used to wearing a suit and barking out orders that were followed without question.

Bob turned his head and, without releasing his grip on the gunman, just stared at the couple. It took a second, but then they both gasped and took a step backward. He still hadn't shaved that damn beard. The woman's finger came up and pointed at him reflexively as her mouth opened.

"Go away," Bob said dully.

The wife grabbed at her husband's arm, eyes wide. They turned and scrambled back up the stairs without a word. Sometimes fame works in your favor.

"We need to get the fuck out of here," Steve said, nearly vibrating with adrenaline.

"You're about two seconds from past tense unless you can tell me something useful," I informed the guy stonily.

"I don't know about any George Kelly," the guy pleaded with us. "I've only been on this thing two hours. I got paged, and got rolling. That's it. I just do contract work!" He looked from my face to Bob's.

"Were you here for us? Or Green?"

"I don't know who Green is," the man told us, wheezing around the hand clamped over his throat.

Shit. "So us? How'd you know we were here?"

"Reilly, some guy named Reilly. They're into his phones, and I guess were watching his credit cards. You used one to check in, right?"

Steve glanced at me, his face dark. I frowned. We were paying cash, the credit card was only in case—"Shit," I muttered. The front desk clerk would have run the card just to make sure it was valid. And that, apparently, was all it took with these guys.

"Who are you working for?" Bob growled.

"Man, I don't ask names. I only know work aliases, nobody uses their real ones on these jobs."

"Not people, organization. What organization?"

"I don't know. No, really!" he squeaked, as Bob lifted a fist. "I'm on a list. Independent contractor. A very private list. I don't know who contracted me this time, but my name's not on a board at McDonalds."

"CIA?" I said.

"I don't know, maybe," he said.

"This is getting us nowhere," Bob said, grabbing the pistol grip of his MP5. He began to raise it.

"No, wait!" the wounded man said suddenly. "CIA. One of the other guys said something on the way over about a guy they were keeping locked up at the estate. He didn't say anything about any kidnapping, though. Or mention any names."

"What about the CIA?" Bob asked him.

"The guy said they were keeping this big guy locked up in one of the basement rooms of the estate, and that he was a real pain in the ass. Something about homeland security or something, I don't know." Questioning yells bounced around the eighth floor's hallway and echoed up from floors below. Screams, slamming doors, running feet. And very, very faint, sirens.

"What estate are you talking about?" I asked the guy.

"The estate, the *Estate*, it's about ten, fifteen minutes from here. It's, shit, what the hell's it called? Granger, no, Wesley-Grange, the Wesley-Grange Estate. It's a mansion on a bunch of land, used to be a historical site in all the books, open for tours 'til they ran out of money and the Company bought it. CIA. Now it's an off-the-books vacation spot for the brass and other guys need a little vacation. I've only been inside it once, couple years ago."

I turned and looked at Bob. "You believe him?"

"I'm telling you the truth, I swear to Christ!" the guy blubbered. "I don't even know who the fuck you guys are." He moved his head as well as he could, with Bob's hand firmly locked onto his throat, and looked down. He was soaked in blood all the way to his knee. The sight of the wound seemed to weaken him. "I got to get to a hospital," he moaned, dropping both hands to his injured side.

"Let's go," I said. Bob's feet remained planted. He let go of the MP5's pistol grip and drew the Randall from underneath his left arm. The guy's eyes widened as Bob held the knife up to his nose.

"You see this?" Bob asked him calmly.

"Bob!" I yelled at him, as the hired gun, recognizing the knife as well, found a reserve of strength and punched Bob in the side of the head with all he had. Bob's head rocked back. Steve turned around to see what the hell was going on, just as Bob plunged the knife deep into the man's armpit. As the blade sunk home the guy's mouth opened wide in shock, then Bob twisted the knife and yanked it sideways out of the man's chest, spraying me with blood. Aorta severed, the man went down clawing at his shirt as the fierce beat of his heart covered the wall and floor in splashing blood. Steve and I just stood there, stunned.

As the gunman, twitching and shuddering and making horrible sounds like an injured kitten slowly started to side down the stairs, Bob carefully bent over and wiped the Randall's blade clean on the guy's pantleg. Then he put a hand against the wall for support and straightened up like an old man with arthritis.

"What a pussy," Bob spat down at the body, his teeth gritted against the pain. "These guys are pathetic." The man's punch had split open his left eyebrow. Blood ran freely down the side of his head from the inch-long gash.

"If we don't leave now, we might as well drop our guns and put our hands behind our heads 'til the cops come," Steve told us, his face white from shock. Once he'd said it, I couldn't believe we weren't already surrounded by cops. I'd fired the first shot nearly five minutes before. I pointed at the two of them.

"Upstairs. Grab your shit out of your room and get Jerry, wherever the fuck he is, and meet me and Ron at the far stairwell, this floor, in one minute. Go!" I spun before they could move and began running. There was shouting and the faint static of prep radios echoing up from the lobby but I had neither the time nor the inclination to stick my head over the railing and count the cops coming my way. Ron met me outside of our room, MAC-10 held down alongside his leg, looking scared and relieved to see me. He'd probably been wondering whether to stay or run over to where he could Steve standing in the open stairwell door.

"Time to go," I told him, rushing past him into the room. "Grab your shit and let's skedaddle." I tossed my bag's shoulder strap around my neck so that it rested against my left hip and waited a second while he did the same.

"Where's—" he began to ask.

"On the way," I told him. I pointed at the MAC-10. "Stick that thing in your bag. The only way we're getting out of here is if we look like regular joes." I headed out the door of our room and took a sharp right. Several doors up and down the hallway were open, people sticking their necks out to see what, if anything, was still going on. Twenty feet down the hallway and I was at the stairwell door. I turned the knob and pushed it open, waving Ron through. Two seconds later Bob, Steve, and Jerry pounded down the steps to our floor.

"Put the hardware away," I told them, holding the stairwell door open with my foot. "There's cops all over down there. We gotta walk out like we don't know from shit."

"How the fuck they gonna let us do that?" In response I took half a step to my left and yanked down the red handle of the fire alarm on the wall. A klaxon began blaring, and I immediately saw a dozen terrified people reflexively bolt from their rooms, just on our floor alone.

"Fire!" I yelled as loud as I could, trying to sound terrified, hands cupped around my mouth. "Oh, God, it's a **FIRE!**"

"Terrorists!" Jerry shouted, trying to one-up me.

The response was immediate. The thunder of feet, and there were even a few screams. Steve took the cue. "Anthrax!" he screamed shrilly. Bob frowned at him.

"Beautiful," I murmured, then pointed down the stairs and kicked Ron in the ass to get them moving. We'd only descended a floor and a half, feet pounding on the steps as we circled down, before the stairwell began filling above and below us with frightened people.

We spun around and around and down, our feet beating a rapid tempo on the steps, our haste as we pushed by people helping to heighten their sense of fear and increase their speed. My ribs hurt with every bounce, but I ignored the pain. We were down to the third floor before the stairwell became so thick with frightened hotel guests that we had to slow our pace. Some of them had even grabbed small pieces of luggage, so with our large bags slung we didn't look so out of place.

As I rounded the corner of the stairwell just above the second floor landing I spotted a cop. He'd obviously realized there was no way to contain or control the hundreds of people stampeding down the stairs, so he was standing in a corner of the landing, next to the door, just watching everybody who was coming down the stairs, not saying or doing anything. He'd taken his prep radio out of his belt and was holding it in his left hand, eyeing the face of each person who passed him, ignoring questions. I tried to blend into the mass of people, putting a dull worried expression onto my face and looking at the center of Steve's back as he jogged down the stairs in front of me. Thinking back on it, I guess my time would've been better spent if I'd used it to wipe all the blood off my shirt, sprayed there when Bob'd ripped his Randall from the gunman's chest. That cop took one look at my blood-speckled face, did a double-take, and then his right hand went to his weapon as he yelled "Hey!" Everyone was flying down the stairs so fast that by the time he got the word out Bob was already two steps past the officer. Three steps up from him, I heard the cop pop the thumb break on his holster as he raised the radio to his lips.

Terrified down to my very marrow with the thought of what Bob, in his messed-up state of mind, might do to this officer only trying to do his job, I froze. At which point Steve took it upon himself to pull the inhaler-sized spray can of pepper gas out of his bag and empty it into the cop's open eyes and mouth. For a fraction of a second we were all frozen in time, not moving, then the officer's eyelids snapped shut of their own volition and he let out a howl, dropping his radio and scrabbling at his face as he tried to draw his weapon. Bob was on him immediately, wresting the pistol from his grasp just as it cleared the holster. Steve grabbed the radio off the cement floor as my eyes began to water from the OC spray now filling the entire stairwell. Not this again.

Splashback

The cop blindly tried grappling with Bob, fear on his face as he figured he'd be shot with his own gun if he lost control of it, but Bob just swept the officer's legs out from under him while keeping an iron grip on his gun.

The whole thing had happened so quickly that the three or so people near us in the stairwell who had been in a position to see what happened weren't sure exactly what *had* happened. When they began to blink and cough from the OC gas, however, a lot of them realized that the only thing they really cared about was getting out of the hotel.

"Anthrax!" Steve screamed again, his acting aided by real coughing.

As the five of us ran down the last flight of stairs I saw Bob eject the magazine from the cop's automatic, rack the round out of the chamber, and then drop the gun just before we hit the outside door. My eyes burned as we hit the cold nighttime air and I looked around to see where we were. Off to our left a half dozen or so cop cars were parked haphazardly in front of the hotel's entrance, blue and red lights spinning erratically. At the moment, though, no uniforms were visible.

I grabbed Ron's shoulder and pushed him toward the parking structure. "C'mon," I managed to choke out between coughs. More people ran out of the stairwell door behind us, a few of them sneezing and coughing. They couldn't decide where to go, and while a few of them ran toward the cop cars and the main entrance, and a few moved toward the two-story parking structure, most of them just stood in small groups in the middle of the street, staring up at the hotel. Looking for smoke, I guess. As we jogged past concrete pillars, trying to spot our vehicle in the dimly lit cave-like parking ramp, I could hear more sirens in the distance, getting closer. A lot of sirens.

Steve gave a long, hacking, ragged cough and spit on the floor as we reached the Suburban. "Fuck, that shit's nasty," he said to no one in particular. "I can barely keep my eyes open." Bob got the doors unlocked and we threw ourselves inside, sitting on top of our bags.

"Go Go GO!" Jerry kept saying. His hands were shaking as he pulled the two receiver halves of the M4 from his bag and tried to reassemble it. Ron slid over the top of the back seat into the rear of the Suburban where he hunkered down on top of the rifle cases. Steve held the cop's prep radio in his hand, trying to decipher the excited babbling filling the air. It seemed like five minutes before Bob got the Suburban started, out of the parking spot, and rolling, but that was just because my heart was leaping in my throat and I expected to be surrounded at any second.

Bob whipped the big SUV around a corner and accelerated down a line of parked cars, slowing as we approached the exit. As the hood of our car nosed out of the structure we looked left and right. Another cop car or two had arrived in front of the hotel, and I could see a few people in uniform standing out front, radios in hand, but there was nobody near us or looking our way. Bob activated the turn signal and pulled out into the street, slowly and calmly accelerating away from the chaos. We passed the Bennigan's a second later. Twenty people lined the curb, trying to figure out what was going on down at the hotel.

At the light Bob hooked a right and we were finally on a main road, out of sight of the hotel. Bob punched it. We caught up to a crowd of cars and settled in with them just as two cop cars and a fire truck, all with their lights going, flew by in the opposite direction. Ron, sitting on the floor behind the rear seat, watched through the back window as they grew smaller. The MAC's wire stock was pressed firmly into the pocket of his shoulder.

"Everybody okay?" Jerry inquired loudly from the front seat. His ears were probably ringing horribly from firing the M4, which he'd finally gotten back together. He held it out of sight between his legs. A chorus of "Yeahs" was his reply.

"Anybody starts following us in anything but a fully marked cop car, you let me know," I told Ron pointedly. "Anybody on the radio saying they've spotted us?"

"I don't think so," Steve said, bent over, his ear close to the radio. "Lots of calls for ambulances, though. What the fuck happened?" he asked, sounding hoarse and a bit bewildered. He slid open one of the rear windows and spit, then tried to blow his nose out the window with only minor success.

"How the hell did you know?" Ron asked me as Steve wiped his nose on his sleeve. I looked over and in the glow of passing streetlights saw his eyes locked onto mine.

"One of those guys showed up to sanitize the place where I was interrogated. He was with Larry, the guy who said he'd come all the way from Maryland. I almost didn't recognize him without his baseball cap. There's no way he wouldn't have recognized me."

"Thank God you remembered his face. When you pulled your gun out and just drilled him without even a 'Fuck you' I thought you'd lost it."

Thinking about what had just happened, now that I wasn't one hundred percent occupied with staying alive, I began to get the shakes all over again. I knew it was mostly my body trying to get rid of the gallons of adrenaline it'd dumped into my bloodstream, but there was more to it than just that. The moment kept replaying itself in my head: the two guys, calmly stepping off the elevator. They exchanged one or two words, then turned my way. What if I hadn't recognized him? What if I'd messed up my draw, dropped my gun, missed with my first shot? What if one of the guys across the atrium had taken the time to aim before firing at me, stuck in plain sight behind the column? I wasn't so much shaking as shuddering, shuddering at the combination of luck and timing that let me sit here, alive, while so many others were dead.

I sat in the corner against the armrest and hugged myself fiercely, arms wrapped around my stomach trying to control the quaking that shook my whole body. If passing streetlights weren't the only illumination inside the car they would've been able to see just how damn scared I was. They usually looked to me for direction, and I wasn't sure this time I'd be able to give it to them. One too many close calls had worn down the belief that I'd get through this in one piece.

"...and then Bob practically gutted him," Steve finished angrily. While I'd been absorbed in self-pity and doubt, Steve had been explaining to Jerry and Ron what we'd learned in the stairwell, and how we'd learned it.

"Cool," Ron said from the floor behind my seat. He was still looking out the back window, the MAC-10 in his lap.

"Cool?" I echoed, getting angry. My face was covered in the man's dried blood and I could feel it pull every time I spoke. "*Cool?*" I practically shouted.

"Hey, fuck those guys!" he roared back at me. "They're playing in the majors here, they know there ain't no second-place winner! These motherfuckers grabbed my dad, and until I get him back I'm gonna rape, rob, torture, or kill anybody that gets in my fucking way. You got a problem with that, I don't fuckin' want to hear it." He reached up and pressed a palm to his injured ear, wincing.

"Relax! Just relax," Jerry said warningly, looking from Ron to me to Steve. "Nobody here is the bad guy."

"How we going to find this estate?" Bob asked from behind the wheel. He was hunched over so far he was practically chewing on the steering wheel. It sounded like he was talking through clenched teeth.

"How you holding up?" I asked him. He looked back over his shoulder at me for a second, and I saw his eyes scrunched halfway shut from the pain. "How's your eye?" It looked like the bleeding had almost stopped.

"I really fucked myself up going up and down those stairs," he said, molars grinding. "It feels like I ripped something."

"Bob, you're fucking insane," I told him. "I know you've been coughing up blood, it means you've got a punctured lung, for Chrissakes!" He wouldn't look at me, he just kept staring out at the road over the wheel. "Bob," I tried again, "one of your ribs is cutting a hole in you every time you breathe! I don't know shit about this kind of stuff, but I know that's serious. Extended hospital stay serious. I'm afraid that if you don't see a doc soon you're gonna die from blood loss or who knows what." He still wouldn't look at me, the obstinate bastard. Nobody else would say anything, either. If Bob wanted to drive himself into the grave with this, they wouldn't stop him. I looked around, but none of them would raise their eyes.

"Everybody dies from something," he told me after a while.

"Yeah, well, you're gonna die of stupidity," I told him, disgusted.

"You think this estate might be in the phone book?" Steve asked.

"I don't know. The guy said they used to give tours

there, but I don't know how long ago that was. Once the Company bought it and stopped the tours they probably took it out of the book. But it's still worth checking out."

"So all we need to do is find a pay phone," Steve said hopefully.

"When was the last time you saw a public phone that had a phone book? Stop at the next fast-food place or gas station, they'll have a phone book. You can ask if they've heard of the place."

We rode in uneasy silence for several minutes, the only sound in the car the squawking from the cop's radio, which seemed to be increasing.

"Well, somebody recognized you," Steve said, straightening up from the radio and looking at Bob. "But nobody's mentioned the Suburban yet."

"We need to get some Maryland plates on this thing," Ron said from the back. "I don't care who it's registered to, out-of-state plates stick out. Helicopter!" he called out suddenly. Then a second later, "Never mind, it's heading the other way, toward the hotel."

"McDonald's," Bob said a few minutes later, and pulled into the lot.

"I'll go," Jerry said. He waited until Bob pulled into a space off to the side, where we couldn't be seen by the employees, handed me the M4, then jumped out and headed in. Three minutes later he was back, shaking his head. "No luck," he told us. "Nothing in the phone book, and they'd never heard of it." We pulled back out into traffic, but we'd gone less than half a mile before I told Bob to pull over.

"Where?"

"Here," I said, pointing at the Holiday Inn. "Hotel employees are bound to know something about a place that used to have tours." Bob stopped a good distance away from the front doors and Jerry jogged up to the entrance.

"If this doesn't work we might have to wait until morning to call around," I said. Ron tossed me a gun cleaning rag and nodded at my face. I wet it with a half-empty bottle of water and started wiping at the sticky blood.

"Hey," Ron said, setting down the MAC-10 and rummaging around in his shoulder bag, "look at this." He pulled out something and held it up for us to see. It took me a few seconds in the dim light to figure out what it was.

"So that's what I heard," Steve said, taking the object from Ron. It was an Uzi pistol, with a wire stock folded sideways along its receiver. The whole thing couldn't have been more than eight inches long.

"This is what that fool was spraying at you," Ron told me, gesturing at the machine pistol. He was talking fast, nearly bouncing up and down. We were all still jazzed on adrenaline. "He fired almost two full magazines and never unfolded the stock. No wonder he couldn't hit a fucking thing." Ron held up two long black sticks, magazines for the Uzi that looked like they held at least twenty rounds each. I was pretty unfamiliar with the gun, and had only fired an Uzi, the full-size model so popular with Hollywood action heroes, once. I'd seen Uzi pistols before, but they were not common. The full-auto versions were especially scarce. Like I needed more convincing the people after us had a lot of resources.

"He got panicked," I said. I was talking fast too, and couldn't sit still. It was the adrenaline burning itself out. "He wasn't expecting anything walking down the hallway. Besides, he had his fancy-schmancy burp gun and figured he was invincible." Of course, if they'd knocked on our hotel room's door, that Uzi with its high RPM would have worked quite well in close quarters.

"The other guy had a pistol," Ron said.

"If they knew it was us at the hotel instead of Green, don't you think they would have sent more than four people?" Steve said to me.

"If they knew it was us at the hotel, they would have known it was all five of us," Bob said. "No way in hell would I have only sent four people to do that job. Not with our track record against these guys."

"If they'd found us all in our rooms, two guys in each doorway with subguns would have done the job right quick. I don't suppose you grabbed a wallet off of either of them?" I asked Ron.

He shook his head. "I didn't think to check."

"That's okay, probably doesn't matter. I shouldn't expect miracles, it's only freak chance that all of us aren't dead. And I'm getting really tired of questions and more questions without any answers."

"I'm getting tired of people trying to kill us," Steve said. "This thing doesn't have any serial numbers," he declared. He handed it to me when I beckoned and I examined the pistol's receiver. On its side where I assumed the serial number had been was only a grooved swirling pattern in the steel.

"Removed by acid," I announced. "Just like on that MAC-10. No numbers, no way to trace 'em, plausible deniability." Shaking my head in disgust I handed the gun back over to Steve.

Steve worked the machine pistol's bolt a few times, then unfolded the stock and pressed it into his shoulder to get a feel for the weapon. "Nice," he commented. "Compact."

He looked closer. "Muzzle's threaded. You find a suppressor anywhere?" he asked Ron.

"I was in a bit of a rush. He probably had one, too, for indoor work. Shit."

"That thing sounds like a chainsaw it's so fast," I said.

"Here comes Jerry," Steve said, nodding his head toward the hotel. Jerry had a piece of paper fluttering in his hand as he jogged back toward the Suburban.

"Well?" I asked as he climbed back inside.

"It's not Wesley-Grange, it's *Wellesley*-Grange, the Wellesley-Grange Estate," he told us with a grin.

"Yeah? So what's that?" I asked him, pointing at the piece of paper in his hand. He held up the scrap of paper with a smile.

"Directions," he said.

TEN

Sunday

12:01 a.m.

We coasted down the gleaming blacktop at a stately thirty-five. Bare-branched trees lined the road, hanging over the wide paved shoulders. The interior of the truck was quiet as we peered out into the cold night. There were fresh Maryland plates on the truck, courtesy of another Suburban we'd spotted outside a bar.

The grey line of trees to our right ended abruptly. A brick wall appeared, running along the far side of the drainage ditch about ten feet from the asphalt shoulder. The wall was over eight feet tall; too tall for even us, in the high-riding Suburban, to see over. It was constructed of oversize rusty red bricks topped with a flat runner of stone, slate or granite. Streetlights designed to look like old gas streetlamps illuminated the wall, spaced every hundred feet.

The road continued to curve gently to the left and we rolled by the front entrance. I saw a short drive, a guardhouse, and an ornate black iron gate, then we were past.

The brick wall continued for another couple hundred yards then disappeared into the trees.

The two-laner curved more sharply and we started down a slope. Once out of sight of the estate, Bob pulled onto the shoulder and cut his lights.

"Eight-by-ten guard shack," Jerry said. "Brick walls, made to look old but I don't think it is. I saw one guy inside, light blue uniform shirt, patches on the shoulders."

"Two guys," Steve added. "And the front gate's on rollers."

"Anybody see a goddamn house?" I said.

"It was way back there, couple hundred yards back behind some trees," Bob said. "I saw a couple lights."

"Is that wall just a front or did it turn at the corners and head in?" Nobody had an answer for me.

We waited another ten minutes and did another drive-by in the opposite direction. I caught a glimpse of what had to be the main house. It was a big square of black with one lone window glowing yellow and a feeble exterior light. Before we'd even pulled out of sight Jerry had the map out.

"I think there's a road just over the top of the hill," he told us.

"What hill?" We'd all been looking out one side of the Suburban while he'd been looking out the other. He explained that directly across the road from the estate the ground sloped sharply upward.

"I couldn't see how high it went, though," he went on, "and this thing ain't topographical." He waved the map. "We need some sort of observation post, we just can't keep driving back and forth in front of the place every ten minutes."

Bob pulled over again and flicked on the interior light. "Let's see." I leaned forward too. Jerry pointed out the gentle curve of the road we were on. A half mile to the north another road nearly paralleled it.

"Park on this road, maybe it looks down on the place," Jerry said hopefully, tapping his finger on the map.

"Sounds like a plan," Bob said, putting the Chevy into gear. "Now get me there."

We ended up passing the spot and had to circle back. The second time we went more slowly, craning our necks and pressing our noses against the cold windows. We turned around again, then Bob parked on the shoulder. The second road was busier, with a car whooshing by every thirty seconds or so.

"We should be directly opposite it," Jerry said. He'd been watching the odometer and quickly double-checked it against the map's scale. We all looked out the windows to our right. Nothing to see but the dark shadows of more trees.

"Guess we're gonna have to do it the old-fashioned way."

We spread out and started into the woods in a ragged line. Hopefully no good Samaritan would call about an abandoned truck on the side of the road. Our progress was slow—none of us wanted to lose an eye on a branch or twist an ankle over a stray limb. The ground was level for what I guessed was the first hundred yards, then started to slope down. My footsteps seemed amazingly loud swishing through fallen leaves I could barely see. The moon was full but the cloud cover was almost complete. Only city lights, bouncing off the clouds, helped us out.

I relaxed my pace even more as the ground sloped down at over a twenty-degree angle. I chose each step carefully, not caring to trip and carom down the hill, bouncing off tree trunks.

As soon as I hit the slope the tree cover in front of me began to thin. I scanned the blackness below as I picked my way around deadfalls and sinkholes, dead ferns and prickly bushes. I was hoping for an opening in the trees that would afford me an unrestricted view of the land below. I wasn't having much luck. The dark estate had been hard enough to see when we knew where to look.

Fingers snapped off to my right. The sound carried amazingly well in the night air and I again reminded myself to tread as quietly as possible. I began working my way toward whoever had signaled, glancing to the left occasionally in case I chanced upon a choice viewing spot.

In a minute we were all clustered around Ron. He'd found a twenty foot nearly-level clearing that gave a glorious view of the estate. We were sixty feet west of the driveway and about a hundred feet up. With the angle of the slope I figured that would mean roughly four hundred feet walking distance to the guardhouse.

The night air was crisp and cold and I had no problems seeing the well-lit interior of the guardhouse. Half of one man's torso was visible, and occasionally a second man's arm would swing into view. I think they were playing chess. I doubted we'd be able to find a better spot even in daylight. We stood there together, in silence, for several minutes.

"Anybody bring any binoculars?" I whispered. Somehow it seemed appropriate.

"Just what I was thinking," Bob murmured.

"We're gonna watch 'em?" Steve said.

Ron growled, then said, "Unless you want to walk up there right now, knock on the guard booth, ask them politely to turn over my dad. Or maybe you've got access to a transporter."

"For how long?"

"Long as it takes. Why, you got someplace you're supposed to be?"

"Relax," I hissed.

"Do it in shifts?" Jerry said.

"Unless everybody wants to do an all-nighter."

Bob tapped Jerry and they headed back up the hill. The rest of us stayed put so the clearing didn't get misplaced.

From high upon the hill, the main estate building was almost entirely visible. In the dark, details were hard to make out, although the longer I stared the more I could see. It appeared to be a three-story brick or stone edifice with a gently sloping roof. A great black cube, nearly featureless, squatting in the night. Since it was an estate, I assumed the building was a residence of some sort, although it looked more like a turn-of-the-century office building.

The slope we stood on faced almost directly south. The whole north side of the mansion stood exposed to us, and we had a pretty good angle on the building's west side as well.

The driveway leading onto the grounds appeared to be asphalt, wide enough for two cars to pass. Past the gate it wove through sparse trees to the house. It stood out nicely from the brown grass of the huge lawn. A weak light mounted near the roof on the mansion's east side lit up the driveway as it ended in a circle. Since I didn't see any doors other than one small one on the north side I guessed the main entrance was on the east by the circle drive. Something that could have been a fountain stood in the center of the traffic circle. On the far side of the circle from the house was a long low building I took to be a multi-car garage.

The red brick wall ran along the road for almost a quarter mile. The gate and guardhouse were near the center of that span. I still couldn't see whether the wall enclosed the whole estate or just ran along the road for looks and as a noise and vision barrier. Occasional trees dotted the huge expanse inside the wall but they were nothing compared to the thick woods surrounding the estate.

Only one light shone from inside the house. It was on the third floor, north side, near the northwest corner.

The three of us turned as one as we heard the swish-swish of feet through leaves. Ron snapped his fingers a couple times while I took out my newly reloaded Colt, just in case. Images from the gunfight kept popping into my head, flashes of guns or blood, accompanied by spurts of adrenaline that left me shaking.

Bob and Jerry appeared out of the blackness, carrying a lot more than just a pair of binoculars. Jerry had those, as well as the two sleeping bags. Good idea, I hadn't thought about what it'd be like sitting for hours on the cold ground.

Bob, meanwhile, shouldered his big sniper rifle and scrutinized the guard shack through the Leupold scope. He swung the bolt-action to look at the house, then after a few seconds lowered the weapon.

"How's that scope do at night?" I said. I knew certain scopes, and binoculars, had some limited light gathering ability, designed to help hunters at dawn or dusk. Bob's binoculars, for instance, brought out detail on the dark mansion when I held them up.

"No improvement." I didn't say anything, but maybe he heard me frown.

"It works well enough for me to see if George is in any car leaving there and then dump whoever's with him."

"That mom and pop motel we passed on the way here," Jerry said. "You want to get a couple rooms there?"

"Providing they're not booked up."

"Four-hour watches?" Ron said. "Two guys out at a time?" Two people had a better chance of staying alert and awake than one, especially late at night.

I thought for a second. "Yeah. You guys are really thinking. But better make this first one eight long so nobody has to blunder through the woods in the dark again. Not until we know the area better."

"I'll wait until I can actually see something," Ron said.

"Me and you?" Jerry said questioningly to Bob, who nodded.

"Find a comfortable spot, try to keep warm, and write down anything that goes on down there. Lights turned on or off, cars coming or going, guards talking on the radio."

"I have done this kind of thing before," Bob growled, his face in shadow.

"Once or twice, maybe," I told him. "I've been doing it for fifteen years. You have something to take notes with?"

"I keep a log book with the rifle."

"Then I guess we'll see you at—" I checked my watch. "Say eight a.m." Bob nodded.

I waited and let them stare at me for thirty seconds. "Car keys would help."

Bob dug them out and handed them over. "How long can we afford to wait?" he asked me.

If George was indeed inside, he could be moved offsite in a windowless vehicle, or killed, and we'd never be the wiser. And we'd have no way to predict it since we still didn't have a clue as to why he was grabbed in the first place. Then again, it could all be an elaborate ruse designed to draw us into a trap. No way to know, although the guy we'd gotten the information from had seemed sincere enough at the time.

"Not long."

Ron, Steve and I trudged back upslope and through the trees. We located the Suburban and waited until there was no traffic in sight before stepping out onto the shoulder and climbing in.

Nobody spoke as I steered the big vehicle back the way we'd come. I took one wrong turn but finally located the little motel. It was a small, L-shaped single-story place about ten minutes from the estate. I had to knock on the office door for five minutes before I finally roused the wizened manager. He was nearly five foot two and it looked like his ancestors had successfully interbred with squirrels. He had two interconnected rooms available, much to my surprise. I paid in cash and left a false name. He never asked for a credit card and mine was the only face he saw.

Each room contained a single queen-size bed. Ron and Steve started arguing over who would sleep where but I was too tired to care. The rooms smelled a little musty but were otherwise clean. The sink and tub were stained but functional. I opened the connecting door and then went about figuring how to set the alarm clock.

"I don't care if you're seven months older than me," Ron was saying. "And what the hell does that have to do with anything?"

"It means I've got seniority. Besides, you know I can't sleep if there's someone else in the bed with me."

"That's another reason you need to get a steady girlfriend."

While they kept at it I washed my face and used the facilities. I set the Colt on the bedside table next to the alarm, then stripped down to my jockeys. I'd already slept in my clothes once this trip, I'd be damned if I was going to do it again.

Ron and Steve kept the argument going even as they propped chairs under both doorknobs.

"I do not owe you twenty bucks," Ron protested. "You always think everybody owes you money." It was the last thing I heard.

7:10 a.m.

The bird was a thing out of Stephen King's mind, huge and ferocious, with a sharpened beak two feet long and fiery red eyes. It dived and swirled past me, flapping its wings and chirping as it did its best to disembowel me with beak and claw. For something so big I couldn't understand how it could have such an annoying mousy chirp. Then the ground started to roll as the earthquake began.

"Jesus Christ, are you dead?" Steve grumbled, climbing over me to angrily slap off the beeping alarm clock. As I cracked my eyelids he fell back onto his side of the bed and groaned.

I was still on top of the covers and from the stiffness in my back hadn't moved all night. I struggled to my feet and headed into the bathroom.

I had my choice of any two of the four handkerchief-sized towels hanging on the rack to dry off with after my shower. Typical. I stood in the tub and used one on my hair and one on my body, then let air and gravity do the rest. Some of the bruises on my ribcage had decided green was the color of the day. As long as I didn't take really deep breaths my chest didn't even hurt.

"Me and you?" I said to Ron when they were both cleaned up. I'd thought about it and decided that if we were going to have a rifle on site, one of the two people present ought to be competent in its use. Steve and I didn't qualify.

He admitted only a fair competency with rifles, and while I'd been through basic training, my experience with bolt-action scope-sighted rifles was exactly zero. I wasn't about to take a distance shot at a moving human target, not when George might be nearby.

Ron nodded. He'd brought in his shotgun the night before and leaned it beside the bed. It was too big for his shoulder bag, and it wasn't dark outside anymore, so he took the coverlet off the bed and wrapped it in that prior to our departure. People might be curious, but no one would scream "Gun!" None of us wanted to leave anything we might need in the room.

"I'll make you a list of things to do while we're out there," I told Steve. "Maybe you can get Bob to sleep a little, even if he says he's not tired."

"Yeah, right. You want me to tie him to the bed?"

Steve made the turn and watched the odometer. After one point seven miles he pulled onto the shoulder. Cars and the occasional truck whooshed by, rocking the Suburban. I felt uneasy and exposed. It wasn't the same as at night. The woods, which had seemed so thick only eight hours before, suddenly seemed sparse and barren, devoid of cover. The shoulder of the road where we sat was in plain view of traffic for over a quarter mile in either direction.

Ron and I waited until as few cars as possible were in sight and then jumped out of the truck and sauntered into the woods. Ron's brown Carhartt jacket blended in nicely with the tree trunks and fallen leaves but my coat was navy blue and didn't do a thing for me. The sun wasn't quite above the horizon yet but it was still damn bright out.

With only memory as our guide we headed toward the

area where we'd left Bob and Jerry. Our pace was a lot quicker since we could see where we were going. In short order the ground began angling down and we picked our way across fifty feet of brush-encrusted slope before stopping. They should have been in sight. Ron and I turned to each other, then looked around again. Neither of us wanted to be the idiot whispering their names louder and louder like we were lost.

"Over here," I heard Jerry say in a low voice. We headed toward the sound, slightly downhill and west of us. After fifty feet I finally saw the blind they'd built out of fallen branches and dead leaves. It looked like a snarled clump of bushes.

Ron and I stopped short of the A-frame blind. We couldn't see the estate yet, but that also meant we couldn't be seen by anyone down there, and I didn't know if there was room for all four of us in the blind. I leaned against a tree, putting its bulk between me and the estate. Ron did the same. We watched Bob and Jerry crawl out of the blind and head our way. Bob could barely stand upright, his face screwed up into a grimace. A night laying on the cold ground hadn't done him any good.

"Notes are inside," Bob told me. "Pretty self-explanatory." I nodded. He turned to Ron.

"Rifle's zeroed at the gate. Remember that the slant of a windshield will make the bullet deflect down if at all, not up like you'd think, so don't hold low. You shouldn't have to try for anybody at the house, but if you do, you're gonna have a drop at that distance. Don't try to dial it in, use holdover, aim right at the top of their head. Wind's been zilch so far, but there's a drift table taped to the stock if you need it." Ron nodded and headed for the blind. The odds of George being driven off while we were standing around talking were greater than zero, which was enough for Ron.

"I made a shopping list," I told Jerry and Bob. I pulled out a wad of cash and handed it to Jerry. "Feel free to add anything you think we might need. Steve's got it, he's doing the shopping. You," I pointed to Jerry. "Find the closest library, go to more than one if you have to. This estate is supposed to be some sort of local historical site. Somebody has to have written something about it. Find it. Dig up anything you can. Local papers, who knows. Copy everything. I don't know if they'll have internet. You know how to look up stuff in the card catalog, use microfiche?"

"I'm in college."

"Yeah, and I've seen your grades." I paused. "How many rounds did you fire at the hotel?"

"From my rifle? A whole mag, twenty-eight rounds."

"How much do you have left?"

He snorted. "Ten mags. Think that'll be enough?"

"Dear God I hope so."

"What do you have for me?" Bob was damn near wheezing. It scared the hell out of me.

"You're getting some rest," I scolded him. "You want to run yourself into the grave, fine, but do it on your own time." He didn't have the strength to argue. "See you later."

Before they stepped off Jerry slapped the wad of cash I'd given him back into my hand. "We can pay our own way," he said with a wink and a grin.

The blind was a six by eight rectangle of fallen limbs, their intertwined branches covered and stuffed with handfuls of dead leaves. I crawled in through the back door, a small archway. The roof was four feet above me, more branches and leaves. Inside the blind the two sleeping bags were side by side, three inches off the ground on an insulating bed of field grass and crackling leaves.

On my elbows I crawled up next to Ron, already settled into place behind the rifle. Through deliberate gaps in the front of the blind we had a panoramic view of the entire estate, guardhouse included. The sun was just breaking through the treetops around us but the estate was still in shadow.

A foot of the rifle's heavy barrel protruded from the blind but Bob had tied grass and rubbed dirt all along its length. It didn't look like a branch, but it didn't look like a rifle barrel, either. Ron had the stock tucked snugly into his shoulder pocket, his left hand under it for support. The weapon's safety was off, his thick finger alongside the trigger guard. He'd found a proper cheek weld and surveyed the guardhouse through the ten power scope.

"You shot that thing before?" I murmured, finding the binoculars. He grunted assent. I knew he was a damn good rifle shot, but every long gun had its own peculiarities. I hoped to God we didn't have to use it.

I propped my elbows on the ground and tried to hold the binoculars steady. One of the things on my shopping list was a spotting scope of at least twenty power, with a tripod, because the binoculars just wouldn't do. They were only seven power, and the main house had to be over a quarter mile away.

As I studied the estate for the first time in daylight I saw that the long, low building to the east of the main house was indeed a garage. We were on the wrong side to see how many bays there were for cars, but it appeared there was room for at least six. Behind it was a tiny brick hut that I hadn't even noticed in the dark. Not just that, there was a big garden on the west side of the house bordered by a five foot high hedge that was practically invisible at night. Every plant inside the hedgerow was either brown or had been dug up. Probably quite a pretty sight in the summer, with a brick walkway curling through the planting beds. A large bay-windowed room stuck five feet out into the garden from the house. White wood trellises surrounded the bay window and covered the brick between the panes. There was a railing along the top edge. Perhaps its roof served as a balcony for one of the second-floor rooms. The overall look of the place was very English; I expected to see Winston Churchill come strolling around the corner of the house, puffing on a cigar.

"You take the guardhouse and driveway," I said quietly. "I'll take the house and garage. We'll switch every fifteen minutes. I'll do all the writing so you stay on the gun." He grunted again, never taking his eye from the scope.

I squinted through the binoculars and swore. The brick wall wasn't just for show. It bordered the entire estate, a giant rectangle.

The hills surrounding the estate were heavily wooded, and while the estate held a few trees it was mostly just lawn. I looked down at the small spiral notebook. Bob and Jerry had filled several pages with notes, and there were drawings and diagrams of the grounds as well. The first page was a simple diagram of all the buildings and I started with that.

480 yards to main house was scribbled on the page under the picture of the mansion. Under the guardhouse was **160 yards to guardhouse.** The scope apparently had a range-estimating feature.

I didn't know what was included in current sniper training but Bob had devised a simple three-digit reference system for quickly identifying any window in the main house. N32 was the north side, third floor, second window counting left to right.

There was a door offcenter on the north side, which Bob had labeled Door 1. The pedestrian door on the side of the garage was Door 2, and the one in the side of the tiny brick hut was Door 3. I explained the whole system to Ron and he briefly checked out the house to see what I was talking about.

The next several pages in the notebook were chronological entries of everything that had taken place in the first eight hours of surveillance. I flipped to the last page and looked at the final scribbled line.

0802: 2 W/M's appear east side main house dressed in guard uniforms. Walk down driveway to gate. Gate opens before they get there. Knock guardhouse door, granted access. Almost immed. the other two guards leave hut & walk up to east side of house by driveway circle & out of sight. Go in front door??

"Looks like there was a shift change in the guards just before we got here," I informed Ron. "And they're staying on site." I flipped back through the pages and saw that the guards hadn't done much of anything all night. Every hour on the hour, though, one of them had picked up a phone visible on the wall and talked, never for more than a minute. Checking in, most likely. Except at the five o'clock hour. Why not? There didn't seem to be any explanation. Maybe

Bob and Jerry had just missed it. They'd had to build the blind sometime during the night.

I shifted on the bag, trying to find a comfortable spot, and watched.

0812: streetlights shut off.

0818: full daylight.

0832: W/M walks from east side of house to garage. Dark hair, thin, thirties, casual clothes.

0834: above W/M walks from garage into house (east-'front'-door).

0859: guard in guardhouse talks on phone briefly.

0912: above listed W/M walks from house to garage.

0913: grey Ford Crown Vic pulls from garage, down driveway to gate. Gate rolls open (left to right)—guards in guardhouse did <u>not</u> open it. Driver identified as above listed W/M, alone in car. Car heads west. Maryland plate BCD 344.

1003: guard talks on phone.

1017: two W/M's walk into view, SW corner of main house. Both dressed in blue overalls, carrying rakes. They begin raking leaves out of the hedges, W side of main house.

1039: one gardener walks to Door 3, gets two big plastic garbage cans from the hut. Walks back to the hedges, they fill the cans with leaves. Work continues.

1100: guard talks on phone briefly.

1123: the two gardeners store the garbage cans

in the brick hut, walk to garage (south side, out of sight).

1128: gardeners walk into view and enter main house through Door 1. Poss. keypad on wall beside door used to gain entry.

Not a hell of a lot of activity for four hours. After eleven thirty, not a damn thing happened worth writing about until we heard someone crunching through the woods behind us at one minute before noon.

I twisted around and looked out the back door. Jerry and Steve were side by side fifty feet northeast of the blind, looking around. I climbed out slowly and walked toward them until I was out of sight of the estate. As I came close Steve held up a spotting scope on a short tripod.

"Twenty to thirty power adjustable. Leupold. Cost an arm and a leg but I figured money didn't matter."

"Good. You can use it to check out the north door, see if that's a keypad on the wall beside it. I hope you're dressed warm, I froze my ass off just lying there for four hours."

"Ron coming out?"

"Not until somebody goes in there to relieve him on the rifle. We already had one car drive off today. You have any luck at the library?"

"Yeah. All the stuff's back at the room, Bob's going over it now."

"We need to get a little closer look. I think that glass on the guard shack is armored. It has just a little too much green tint for my liking. Ron's going to head into the woods, get a look at the back side of the place, see if we're missing anything important."

"You look at our notes?" Jerry said eagerly.

"Skimmed 'em, mostly."

"I think we might have found something," he told me. My eyebrows went up. "I'll rip out the pages, give them to Ron. See if you see what we think we did. When are you going to take that walk?"

"Soon as possible. I'd send someone else, but I think there's another keypad on that damn guardhouse and I'm supposed to be the alarm expert. There's something about that wall, too. You're going to be on the rifle, right? I doubt there'll be any problem, but…"

"Anybody tries to grab you they'll get a hundred and ninety grain telegram from God."

12:09 p.m.

I had Ron drop me off a quarter mile before the estate. A slight breeze arrived and was swirling leaves along the shoulder of the road as I stepped down from the Chevy's running board. It was cold, barely twenty-five, and that wasn't counting the wind-chill. I slammed the door, flipped up my coat collar, and started walking. At least the shoulder was paved. If I remembered correctly I'd pass the corner of the estate's brick wall and have fifty feet or so before I was in sight of the guardhouse.

A few birds cheeped and twittered, and the brown clumps of oak leaves still hanging on the branches rattled in the wind, but otherwise it was quiet. The sun kept trying to peek out from behind the clouds but wasn't having much success. I walked briskly, breath trailing from my mouth in grey clouds. The road began to curve and I moved as far to the right as possible without stepping off the shoulder.

The brick wall was a dark line in the woods that I first spotted a hundred feet out. I continued around the curve and there it was, eight red feet topped with stone. I kept my face pointed forward and slightly down. The curve of the road helped, it meant I could look straight ahead and the wall would still be in front of me.

From the style and condition of the bricks I figured the wall was at least fifty years old. The grey slab of stone topping the wall was four inches thick and overhung the bricks an inch or two. Support columns also made of brick punctuated the wall every twenty feet or so. They were maybe a foot square and stuck out slightly from the rest of the wall. The top of the wall was about a foot higher than my head, so there was no way to see into the estate grounds. I tried anyway, without being too obvious.

I was nearly across from the front gate when I saw something that caught my attention. At the top of one of the support columns I saw a metal post rising above the stone. The top of the post was only just visible to me, so it couldn't have been more than five or six inches long. My eyes darted ahead to the next support column and searched for another metal post. After a few seconds of frantic looking I found it. Then I was across from the front gate and nearing the guardhouse. I kept my nose down but nearly sprained my eyes darting them this way and that.

The gate was two feet taller than the walls, made of black wrought iron. It was on six-inch wheels and wasn't nearly as old as it first appeared. It'd be a bitch to climb—one-inch thick vertical bars four inches apart, with arrowhead tips. Curlicued wrought iron connected the pointed spikes, but only at the very top and bottom of the ten foot gate. Anyone trying to climb the thing would have nowhere to place their feet, and would then have to deal with the spikes at the top.

As I passed the gate and guardhouse I looked curiously at both, as any normal person would. The guards were both visible inside, but only one looked up as I passed. My presence didn't seem to concern him, and he went back to whatever he was doing a second later. I started breathing again.

The guardhouse was twelve by twelve, red brick with a greenish-grey slate roof. The only door faced the driveway. A nine-digit keypad was mounted on the wall right next to it. Three sides of the guardhouse had windows. It was tough to tell in the few seconds I had, but it looked like my suspicions were correct. The windowpane appeared several inches thick. It might not have really been glass, it could've been the bullet-resistant Plexiglass most banks used, but I wasn't about to tap on it to find out, and for our purposes the difference didn't really matter.

Past the guardhouse I took the opportunity to study the wall again. The posts stuck up from the center of every column. I was nearly to the end of the wall when the sun came out. Bright, beautiful sunlight lit up the fine wire stretched between the metal posts. It was like a golden laser beam running along the wall from post to post, from one end of the estate to the other. Then the sunlight cut off like someone had thrown a switch and the fine wire disappeared from view once again.

The Suburban was a half mile up the road, idling on the shoulder. I opened the passenger door and was hit by a pleasant wave of hot air.

"See anything useful?" Ron asked. He put the truck into gear and we pulled onto the road.

"There's a wire running along the top of the wall,

strung between metal posts. About four inches above the stone."

"Electrified?"

"I doubt it. Too fine a gauge, plus I didn't see any insulators on the posts."

He thought for a second. "Anybody going over the wall would touch the wire and set off an alarm somewhere?"

"That's my guess. Wouldn't even have to break it, there could just be a pressure switch, set to go off from anything heavier than a squirrel. A keypad next to the guardhouse door, but windows all around, so there's no way to get anywhere near it. And the keypad's to get in the guardhouse, there's no way for visitors to actually open the gate themselves. Which means it has to be done from inside the guardhouse. Which means it has to be occupied twenty-four-seven."

"Any cameras? Nobody saw any yesterday."

"I didn't see any today either."

"Is that weird?" he asked me. "It seems weird, that amount of security, and no cameras."

"I don't know. Maybe. If they had cameras, and a keypad to open the gate, or intercom to the main house, they wouldn't need a guardhouse at all."

"I'd rather have cameras," Ron said. "There's always a blind spot. Or we could sneak in the gate behind a car going in, if there wasn't a guardhouse full of eyeballs right there."

I shrugged. "Maybe that's why they've got this setup. Seems like they wanted the human touch." It vaguely reminded me of how the Secret Service worked the White House. Even though there were cameras everywhere, they had men stationed everywhere as well, and they rotated their posts every hour to keep them from getting complacent. Luckily we weren't dealing with the Secret Service.

Ron'd been studying the map while waiting for me. Fifteen minutes later he pulled over after having circled around to the south of the estate. We were halfway between two sprawling industrial parks, nearly three-quarters of a mile from the estate. The area was mostly young winterbare oaks and maples, with the occasional patchy field. It was the closest we could get on the south side.

"You gonna have any problems finding it?"

"I've got a compass, but I won't need it." He looked at his watch. "Pick me up here in three hours."

"I'll be here. You be careful."

Ron smiled and patted his jacket covering the gun on his hip. He pulled a black wool cap from his pocket and tugged it over his head, zipped up his jacket, and started into the underbrush.

12:30 p.m.

Bob was hunched over the room's small table. He'd pulled it out from the wall and into the center of the room, then covered the top with papers. One of the beds was covered with the gear Steve and Jerry had purchased. I'd look at it all after I'd had a peek at the paperwork. The police officer's prep radio was on the bedside table, occasionally sputtering.

"That the stuff Jerry found at the library?" He grunted in reply. "Whattaya got?"

"Floorplans, at least of the first two floors. And a few photos."

"You're shitting me." My heartbeat sped up considerably. He spread out the pages so I could see.

The floor plans were simple diagrams from the pages of the October, 1979 issue of **Architectural Digest.** Jerry'd made copies of the floorplans, but there were color pictures too of the mansion's interior and apparently he'd just decided to cut the entire article out of the magazine and steal the pages.

"Wellesley-Grange: A Study in Contrasts" was the title of the article. It was about five hundred words long, spread out over five pages amid numerous photos of the antique interior. The author spared no adjective in describing how the whole house was unique, a blend of the old and new in both architecture and interior design. Apparently the mansion was still open to the public when the article was published. I peered intently at the first and second floor layouts.

"Nothing on the third floor?" I asked.

"Nope."

"How 'bout the basement?"

"Not even a mention. The article talks about it having three floors, but never mentions a crawlspace or cellar or dungeon or anything."

"Well, hopefully that's just because there was nothing of interest down there."

"Or there is no basement," he said. "Just like the Alamo."

I shot him a surprised look. "Did our resident Green Beret badass just make a fucking *Pee-wee's Big Adventure* reference?"

"Maybe."

I snorted, then squinted. "You do that yourself?" The cut above his eye had been stitched shut. The knots weren't pretty, or even, but the wound was closed.

"Yeah," he said ruefully. "Knots look like shit, but I've never done 'em in a mirror before."

"A local anesthetic might have helped, too. What's this?"

I'd found a few pages of small type that had been copied out of a book.

"Bios of Wellesley and Grange. Business partners that made their fortune in textiles and built the place around the turn of the century. They lived there together. **Architectural Digest** made a veiled reference to the fact that they were butt-buddies."

"They use that term?"

"Not exactly."

I sat down and read everything Jerry'd found three times, trying to glean all the information I could out of the pictures and print.

The Wellesley-Grange mansion was fifty-one thousand square feet. Over three dozen guest bedrooms, two big staircases and one small circular one of steel and handcarved walnut, and a ballroom on the first floor with marble floor and tapestried walls that looked like something out of a French castle. The article made brief mention of plumbing upgrades and the installation of new furnaces and central air in the sixties. The third floor contained sixteen bedrooms and five bathrooms, but no pictures were included. Only two of the three staircases reached the third floor.

At some point I'd need to memorize the floorplans but at the moment I wanted to look over Bob and Jerry's notes from the first shift. I pulled the pages out of my pocket and sat down on the bed to read.

Two minutes later I stopped, pulled out a pen, and went back to the beginning entry. I made tick marks next to the entries I thought were significant:

0044: movement left-to-right (shadow) at window N36

0045: motion on West Balcony(WB) above garden room. Poss. person.

0049: movement(in oth direction--RTL) at N36. WB now apprntly unoccupied

0132: movement N36 -- LTR

0132: motion on WB. See tiny winking orange light, continues on & off several mins.

0137: movement N36 -- RTL

0214: movement N36 -- LTR

0215: motion detected WB

0257: movement N36 -- LTR

0257: motion on WB

0259: guard uses phone in shack. Orange glow seen on WB

0306: movement N36 -- RTL

0337: movement WB

0423: movement N36 -- LTR

0425: motion on WB

0454: orange light on WB, movement

0457: movement N36 -- RTL

0603: movement N36 -- LTR
   0606: motion detected WB

0642: movement N36 -- LTR
   0642: motion on WB, winking orange light for approx. 2 mins.

I sat back, thinking, then reread all the log entries including the ones I'd made hashmarks by.

"What do you think?" Bob asked me.

"I think somebody's got a very bad habit," I said slowly. Bob nodded his head.

"You tell me your conclusions," I said to him.

"Every thirty to sixty minutes somebody leaves that lit room on the third floor," Bob said. "A light throws his shadow across the window from left to right as he heads out. I think he goes down to the second floor, opens the French doors or whatever they are, and steps out onto the balcony."

"Where he spends five or six minutes sucking down nicotine."

Bob nodded. "Then he returns to N-three-six, passing across the light from right to left."

"What does that tell you?"

"It tells me that at least once every hour there's an open door," he said after a few seconds. "Who do you think he is?"

"Those guys at the guardshack are checking in with somebody every hour." I thumbed through my notes. "And at the three o'clock hour they checked in when this guy was on the balcony, which leads me to believe there's at least one other guy in N-three-six to answer the phone, since the guard didn't panic or call back."

"So we wait until three or four o'clock one night when this guy's working, hop the wall in the woods somewhere, climb the trellis to the balcony, and wait for this guy to come out again."

"Simple," I said.

"Relatively, yeah."

"There's an alarm trip wire running all along the top of the wall," I told him. "Cheap, simple to maintain, and probably pretty damn effective. No way to go over without setting off all sorts of lights and buzzers, probably in the guardhouse as well as N-three-six. If this was a normal mansion, the alarm'd be hooked up to a central dispatcher, or even the local P.D., but I don't think that's the case here."

"Well shit," he said. "How about the gate?"

"Alarmed?" I shook my head. "I don't think so. It rolls, almost impossible to set up any kind of sensor alarm on that. Besides, no need to do it. It's five feet away from the guard shack, no way to approach it undetected. You know, I just thought of this, I'd betcha every time the gate opens a buzzer or a light goes off both in the house and at the guard shack. And a guy left today when I was watching and neither of the guards opened the gate, someone inside the house must've."

"Take the guards out first?"

"Guardhouse is armored," I said. "Keypad on the door, bullet resistant glass. Your .300 WinMag rifle might penetrate, but there are two guards -- whichever one you didn't drop with the first shot would dive under cover and slap the hot button and we'd be shit out of luck."

"There's a way in," he said. "There always is. We just have to find it."

I sat there for a few minutes, thinking about courses of action. The only one that made sense was also the craziest. I plunged ahead anyway. "Ron's in the woods right now checking out the back side of the place. Let's say he doesn't find anything we can use. I've done a lot of raids, but nothing on this scale. You probably haven't either, but you're a lot more current than I am on assault techniques."

Bob leaned back in his chair and tilted to one side, holding his ribs. His eyes darted over the papers laying on the table.

"Can you do anything with the wire on the wall?" he asked.

"Even if I knew for sure what it was, any attempt at re-routing by me would probably set it off. My alarm experience is almost one hundred percent residential or small commercial. I don't know shit from trip wires. I might be able to disable it successfully, cut a patch or something, but there'd be no way for us to tell if I did it right until we got to the house."

"If the wall's out, that leaves the gate. And the guardhouse."

"Two guys in their thirties, armed and in apparently good shape, locked in a secured building."

"Undoubtedly within arm's reach of a panic button. Shit. There's got to be some way of suckering them out of there."

"If there isn't, I don't know how the we're gonna get in," I said. I leaned over the paperwork and looked around. "Let me see those floor plans again. At least we've got that."

"Providing the spooks didn't change it all around when they took over."

"You're just a ray of sunshine, aren't you?"

"You see much movement today?" he asked me. He was

still sitting sideways, practically arched over the arm of the chair. "Place seemed deserted to me, but maybe that's just because it was night."

"Guy drove off in a car, and two gardeners spent an hour or two raking out the bushes in the garden," I told him. "Remember, it's winter. I've done a lot of surveillance, and most people just don't come out of their houses when it's cold unless they're going somewhere. There could be fifty people in there, and unless someone wants to eat out or catch a flick, we might not see them for days."

"That guy said they used it as some sort of resort, didn't he? That would mean a regular staff."

"Probably live on the third floor or the basement, somewhere out of sight," I said. "A place that size'd need at least two full-time kitchen people, not to mention a minimum of three maids. Housekeepers. And those gardeners I saw are probably the maintenance guys. From the size of those beds in the garden, I bet they hire other people to do the plantings in the spring."

"Warm weather landscapers and lawnmowers."

"Yeah. But not for the winter months. So that makes what, seven?"

"Yeah. Minimum. Plus two gate guards, and two guys answering the phone inside. Oh," he said, sitting up straighter. "D'you see the log? Guards did a shift change at eight, and the new guys walked down from the house. I doubt they work for any company, those uniforms are probably fake. Same guys take a turn in the gatehouse as work the phone in N-three-six. With twenty-four-hour-a-day coverage, you're talking a bare bones minimum of twelve guys with sidearms on premises. Probably more like eighteen, once you figure in days off and stuff like that. That's if they're all on-site, say five days a week."

Bob took a deep breath, then said to me, "Armed, private security. Ballistic glass. Alarm wires. At a big house in the middle of nowhere Maryland."

I nodded. "Yeah." I knew what he was getting at. Nothing we'd seen made me think this was just a random location given up by the contractor in the stairwell. There was something inside there. Something that needed protecting.

"They'd need a trained wait-staff to properly serve a visiting group," I mused. "We're talking well over twenty people, just for a skeleton crew. Maybe if there's nobody staying there the help lives offsite, but we have to assume otherwise."

"Plus any guests that might be staying there. Christ." Bob started shaking his head and kept at it for so long I was worried he was having a seizure.

"What?" I asked him.

"We've got no sure way onto the grounds. I saw squirrels, and a rabbit, so I'm pretty sure once we make it onto the grass we'll be set until we reach the house. We never saw any dogs. Say we get into the house, now we're outnumbered by at least four to one. All we've got is shitty floorplans, and not even for the floor George is supposed to be on." He swung forward and with a grunt stood up. He paced slowly around the room as he spoke, moving with a shuffling half-step.

"What you're talking is a sneak-and-peek," he said. "Go in soft and quiet, because for all we know, if they think someone's busting in to get George they'll kill him rather than give him up."

"Right."

"Fuck," he said, and started shaking his head again.

"What?"

"The place is fucking *huge*," he said. "Three floors and a basement, well over fifty rooms, guys inside and out with guns. I wouldn't try this with less than two eight-man teams with state-of-the-art shit. Night vision, suppressed weapons, hard body armor, flash-bangs and frags, not including the two guys I'd leave up on the hill with sniper rifles. Make that one sniper/observer team, and one team with a heavy caliber MG in case the shit hits the fan. No, you know what, fuck that, we don't know enough about what's inside, who's inside, make it an entire platoon of Rangers, overwhelm them with numbers, with an AC-130 for close air support."

"We've got five people, Bob," I said. "Three of us injured to varying degrees, with a motley collection of weapons."

"I know," he said. "And we're going to do it anyway. And I'm in. I'm just…" He waved his arm vaguely. "I had to say something to someone," he finished, "get it off my chest."

"Did you get any sleep this morning?" I asked him, concerned. He'd been unnaturally white for a day, but now he was starting to look green.

"I'll get plenty of sleep when I'm dead," he shot back, still doing laps around the room in his shuffling gait. "Right now I've got more important things to do."

"I think you're worrying too much," I said in an attempt to get him to relax.

"When was the last time you did a raid?" he asked me. "Christ, an entry team, to get any good, needs to practice together for weeks before they've got their shit down. It takes at least a full forty-hour week of room clearing drills before you learn how the other guys move and you stop accidentally sweeping your partner's head with your muzzle when going through a doorway. And that's if you know what you're doing to begin with."

"We don't have a week," I reminded him. "Hell, none of us can bear to wait for more than another day or two at the outside. That's if nothing happens that forces our hand. For all I know Jerry's lighting up a car with your rifle right now."

Bob sat back down in the chair and hunched over. "There's got to be a light that goes on in N-three-six every time that gate opens," he said quietly. "If that gate ends up being our point of entry, we're going over it."

"It'll be a real pain in the ass," I admitted.

He was quiet for twenty seconds. "Hate and caffeine will only get me so far, there's no way I'm getting over that thing," he told me grudgingly. "Hell, I don't even know if I could climb that trellis without passing out, and that's practically a ladder."

I sat quietly for a minute, thinking.

"If that's the way it is, that's the way it is," I told him. "Don't worry about it now. If we end up going over that gate, the first problem we have to solve is how to get those guards out of the gatehouse and punch their tickets quickly and quietly when there's no cover within fifty feet." Taking them hostage never even occurred to me—so many more things could go wrong if we tried to grab them that I refused to even consider it.

"Try seventy," he said. "The bushes on the far side of the road, at the base of the hill. Right above the ditch. That's the closest you can get. A person could get there by stalking down the side of the hill through the underbrush."

"Yeah, but then what?"

"Exactly."

"Say we get into the house, unnoticed, and there aren't

any more people in there than we think," I theorized. "What do you think our chances are?"

He shrugged. "If he's there, uninjured, and can move? All of us out alive? Ten percent. Some of us out alive? Maybe thirty percent."

Jesus. "And if it's a trap?"

"We're all dead, and just don't know it yet. Unless they want to take us prisoner, ask us questions, but I don't see that happening, none of us know shit."

3:17 p.m.

Ron stepped out of the trees as I drove up. He hopped into the Suburban and I accelerated smoothly away from the curb.

"Talk to me," I said. I was more than a little relieved to see him still in one piece.

"I'll do it east to west," he said, pulling out a small spiral notebook. I glanced over briefly and saw drawings as well as writing. "Garage first. Three double-wide doors. Only one was open, and a full-size Ford van was inside. White, I think, but it was hard to tell." He paused and squinched his eyes halfway shut, then pressed a palm against the bandage covering his ruined ear.

"The cold made it ache like a motherfucker, and now that it's warming up it's hurting all over again. And the other one's still ringing from the hotel." He shook his head and looked at me, a smile tugging at one corner of his mouth.

"We're certainly in sorry fucking shape," he said with a chuckle. "Okay, I got a good look at the front door on the east side of the mansion. It's made of wood, with an arched top, about six feet wide. The front of it is covered with carved squares, and there's a six-inch square stained-glass window set in its center. My mom would kill for a door like that for our house. Beautiful. Probably weighs as much as a Caddy, too. Just to support its own weight it'd need to be four inches thick. Even if it's not reinforced with steel we'd need to set charges and blow it to get through. I can make us some plastique if it comes to that, but that's gonna take me at least another day. And we'll need a kitchen."

"How 'bout the wall?"

"Goes all the way around. Alarm wire all along the top, far as I could tell. No trees close enough to climb up and jump over it, if that's what you were hoping for, they've all been trimmed or cut down." He flipped backward a page. "Uh, that small building near the garage looks to be a tool shed or something. Maybe it used to be something else, but that's what they use it for now.

"East side of the house itself, south side, nothing much to tell. No good news. Shitload of windows, none of them open. No doors on the south side. There's a tiny balcony, about three by four feet, outside the center window on the third floor of the east side, right above the front door, but that's it."

"How'd you manage to see the front door through that eight foot tall wall?" I asked, curious.

"Climbed a tree."

"You look at the west balcony?" Ron nodded. "Can we get up to it?"

"No problem. There's trellises all over that garden room, wrapped in vines or something. I could climb it blindfolded, using one hand. There's a wrought iron railing around the edge of the balcony. It's about three feet tall and looks more decorative than anything else. The garden room, and the balcony, are in the shape of a half-circle. The balcony's reached through a pair of glass doors. Most of that stuff I could see better through the scope than I could when I was out there just now, I couldn't get too close. I sketched everything, if you want to look at them," he told me. He waved the notebook.

"You see any possible way into the house?"

"Those balcony doors look pretty flimsy," he said. "But they've got to be wired. Hell, the whole house is probably wired. Every door and window. So, other than busting a window or blowing a door? No. Unless you want to walk up to the front door and knock, see what happens."

"Don't laugh," I said. "Simple plans are usually the most successful." I told him about the cigarette smoker and his hourly visits to the balcony. He pulled at his lip while he thought.

"There weren't any exterior lights on that side of the house at all," he said, remembering how the mansion had looked when we'd first set eyes on it the night before. "Be easy to go unnoticed standing in the shadows. Say two guys, one on each side of those French doors. Take the guy down when he comes out and go in that way. Yeah, that'd work."

"Think about it," I told him. "Look over your drawings, remember how it looked in your head. Anything you can think of that might fuck up that part of the entry, you let me know."

We rode in silence for a couple minutes. Finally I had to say it. "We don't know if your Dad's in there."

Ron glanced at me. "Yeah?"

"Hell, we still don't know what happened to your dad, if he was kidnapped. If he was, why. If he's the guy inside the estate." I paused. "If he's even alive." I sighed. "We still don't know a fucking thing, other than people keep trying to kill us."

Ron took a deep, loud breath. "And?"

"And we're planning to murder people just to get in there and find out for sure. Bob's on a rampage, sick at heart, he doesn't give a shit. Jerry and Steve are here because they're backing the rest of us up. But, ultimately, this is your decision. Not anybody else. There's a chance we've totally misread the situation here. That your father is not inside. That these people have nothing to do with his disappearance. But there's no way for us to find that out before we get in, and we probably can't do that without killing people. Who may have nothing to do with any of this. We're flying blind." I stared at him. "Morally what we're planning is completely indefensible. And if we're wrong, we'll be killing innocent people."

"We're not wrong. This isn't wrong," he told me. He jerked a thumb over his shoulder at the estate far behind us. "It was good info we got, and it led us here."

"And if it is wasn't good info?"

He huffed a big breath out his nostrils and stared at the passing scenery. "I'm okay with that. What's the phrase, better to regret the things you've done than the ones you didn't do? You having second thoughts? You don't think this is a good bet?"

"It's the only bet we've got. I just want to make sure you've thought about how we could be completely, totally wrong in all this."

Ron grunted. "If there's any chance at all my Dad could be in there, I'm going in," he told me. "And I'm not going to start 'What if'-ing it." He flipped back through his notes. Having said my piece, I pondered about how best to get through the front gate guards. Because if he was going in, so was I. His Dad had been grabbed by someone, and was still missing. My wife was in hiding, and the last time I'd seen her she'd been covered in blood.

"Nobody went outside while I was sneaking around," Ron said, "but when I was sitting in the tree I saw a bunch of people moving around inside."

"A bunch? What's a bunch?"

"It was hard to tell. They were mostly just shadows and silhouettes, but I bet I saw at least six people moving around. All on the ground floor."

"See what they were doing?"

"No. But they were in some sort of big room. At the southwest corner of the place."

"The ballroom," I said. Ron looked at me. "Jerry found floor plans at the library," I told him.

"Beautiful."

"No mention at all of a basement," I felt obliged to add. Apparently Bob's bleak outlook had begun to rub off on me.

"Still better than what we had before," Ron said brightly.

This time I managed to spot the blind without any hisses to guide me. Ron and I trudged over to within fifty feet and watched Steve as he backed out of the intertwined branches, careful not to bump anything and dislodge any of the leaves wedged in place. He looked at the MAC-10 in Ron's hand but didn't say anything. Ron had figured that if the blind was spotted and the bad guys came a'callin, whoever was inside would want something more powerful than just a pistol, and the rifle was too awkward for close range confrontations. He also planned to pop a few rounds at a tree trunk to see if the MAC's sights were on, since he'd be carrying it inside, even though if he had to use it he'd probably just point-shoot the thing. I was interested to hear just how well its suppressor worked.

"Anything happen?" I asked. I handed Steve one of the Whoppers we'd picked up on the way in.

Steve shook his head, then sniffed the burger. "God this smells good. I'm starving. No, we didn't see a thing. Spotted some movement in several of the second and third floor windows, maybe a maid doing her rounds. That's it, other than that goofy-lookin' fucker that walked by on the road earlier."

It only took me a few seconds to figure out he was talking about me.

"Jerry told me about the guy on the balcony," Steve went on. "We gonna go in that way?" He peeled the wrapper down and started eating the Whopper. I'd just wolfed down one of my own and found I was still hungry. Ron had an extra one in his hand but it was for Jerry.

"That's what it looks like," I answered. I stuck my thumb at Ron. "He checked around the back of the place and didn't find anything useful."

"When are we going to do this?" Steve said anxiously. He looked from me to Ron, obviously wanting to do something other than wait and watch. I knew how he felt.

I turned halfway to Ron. "In the end it's your call," I told him. "We can wait as long as you want, but every day we put this off…The good guys'll just get closer to tracking us down, and the bad guys can move George out of there in a windowless van any time they want."

"Assuming he's even in there, which we still don't know for sure," Steve mumbled.

Ron looked down at the ground and kicked a few fallen leaves around. "I don't want to wait," he said, shaking his head. "What'd we decide, that the only way in was over the gate?"

"Pretty much," I said.

"So to go in that way, we're gonna need to figure a way to get those guards out of their bunker. Shit."

"You hopping on the rifle next?" Steve asked him.

"Uh, yeah, I guess so."

"Why don't you sit down with Jerry and Bob," Steve instructed me. "The three of you together ought to be able to figure something out. I'll head back into the hide." The Whopper was gone and he rolled the wrapper into a ball and stuck it into his pocket.

"We also need to check out some of that stuff you bought," I reminded myself aloud. I looked around. "What time does it get dark?"

"About quarter to, six o'clock."

"Go replace Jerry," I told Ron. "We'll go brainstorm, see if we can think of something. After dark we might show up here, see what's happening. There's a lot of movement in there, maybe they're expecting guests. After dark we'll be able to see inside a lot better." Ron handed me his little notebook and I stuck it in a pocket to be studied later.

"With our luck they're getting ready for us to show up," Steve said wryly.

The two of them headed over to the blind and Ron ducked inside. Jerry slid out, said a few words to Steve, then walked over to me, tearing at the Whopper's wrapper. I turned without speaking and we started back toward the Suburban.

"You looked at the log, right?" he said, his mouth full of food.

"The balcony looks like the way in," I admitted. "Once

we figure a way to take out the gate guards we should be all set."

I suddenly realized that the thought of coldly killing two men, from ambush, didn't bother me in the slightest. At one point in my life it would have, but now I had no doubts, no second thoughts. The past week had changed me into an altogether different man, one I hoped I'd be able to live with once this was all over. And one I hoped my wife would still be able to care for.

Jerry grinned heartily, nearly hopping with excitement as the Suburban came into view ahead through the trees.

Have to find a different place to park it during shift change or the cops'll start getting curious, I thought. Just one more worry on a long list.

Jerry looked at me with his big guileless smile, his face full of the confidence of youth. "This is working out great," he said to me. "Things are coming together nicely, don't you think?" He took another huge bite.

"If things go the way we plan, we'll be in and out in fifteen minutes and only have to kill four people for sure: the two guards, the smoker, and his partner in the radio room." I counted them off on my fingers.

"Sweet, huh?"

"Jerry," I said confidently, "things never go the way they're planned. Even if George is there and it isn't a trap, I'm fully expecting a clusterfuck of epic proportions. Prison time would be the best-case scenario."

"Fuck it," he said. "We've had one hell of a run, no matter what happens. When it comes time to rush that place, I wouldn't be anywhere else for all the money in the world."

4:06 p.m.

"Hey buddy, what's up?"

"Who is—oh, uhhhh, hey," Scott said lamely. "Ummm, how you doing?" My surfer dude accent had apparently thrown him.

"Good, good," I said, pouring on the cheer. "Been keeping busy?"

I could hear him breathing as he tried to figure out what to say. "Yeah," he finally came out with. "Things have been pretty hectic around here lately, lot of high-profile crimes."

"I heard something about that on the news, didn't I?"

"Yeah, it's all over the news," he told me. He didn't sound happy about it either.

"That must be cool, working on important cases like that." I did my best to sound awestruck. "You close to catching the bad guys or what?"

"The feds have pretty much taken over everything," he told me. "I'm going to be stuck behind my desk for a while. I'm out of the loop, I'm getting my news off the TV."

Well, at least they haven't suspended him, I thought. "Bummer, dude." I glanced at Jerry sitting in the Chevy's passenger seat and shook my head. He didn't look surprised.

"How about you?" he asked. "You, uh, keeping healthy?"

"Trying to," I told him. "I've been working my ass off lately, trying to land a big client."

There was a brief pause on his end. "You think you're going to get him?"

"Unless I get blindsided by the competition, I think I've got a chance here in the next few days. If it doesn't work out I don't know what I'm going to do to keep busy." I paused a few seconds. "How's that girlfriend of yours, you seen her lately?"

Scott considered how he should answer. "No, we agreed we should go our separate ways," he told me, "and I haven't heard from her since."

"Okay," I said. "Well, I better get going."

"You take care," Scott said, with sudden feeling.

Jerry'd paid cash for the cell phone and a thirty-minute calling card at a nearby gas station. I dropped them both into a dumpster behind a shoe store before heading back to the motel.

4:12 p.m.

Bob was coming out of the tiny bathroom when we let ourselves in. His face was flushed and wet, like he'd just stepped out of a hot shower and neglected to dry off.

"You running a fever now?" I asked him.

"No, I was using the sauna," he cracked in reply. He put a hand on his ribs and stretched experimentally. A gamut of expressions ran across his features, none of them reassuring. Jerry held up Bob's Whopper, figuring Bob would be ravenous for food, as it'd been nearly twenty-four hours since he'd eaten. Instead, Bob looked at the burger with unease. I wondered if the pain had him throwing up more than just blood.

"You got any blood left in you to cough up, you high-drag, low-speed, inbred, thick-skulled, chunky, ear wax eating motherfucker?" Jerry challenged him. He was as worried as I was about Bob. I kept imagining opening the motel room door to find Bob dead on the floor from blood loss.

"I thought I was supposed to be the cranky one," Bob

grumbled. He sat down at the table and looked at the log pages and pictures and floorplans laid out before him.

"You sound like you've got syrup in your lungs, and it ain't fucking syrup," Jerry told him, and he was right. Bob's voice had been getting weaker and wetter for at least a day. "D'you get any sleep, you goddamn rockhead?" Jerry asked him.

"About an hour and a half," Bob admitted. "I just woke up and was splashing my face with cold water when you showed up." He looked at the paperwork spread out in front of him, then back at us. "We gonna do this or what?" he asked.

The three of us sat down at the motel's small table and went over everything we had. I reread Jerry and Bob's nightshift log, trying to see if any other explanation for what they'd seen—other than a smoker with a heavy habit—presented itself. Nothing came to mind. I stared at the floorplans until I had them memorized, and read everything Ron had written in his little notebook three times.

Finally, the three of us developed a high-tech raid plan to follow once we'd entered the mansion through the balcony's French doors. It concluded with, "...and then we'll see if we can find the basement and locate George." Bob started shaking his head again, and I fully understood why.

"This whole thing's contingent on us getting those assholes out of the guardhouse," Jerry said. None of us was happy about it, either.

"As soon as it's dark I want to head out there," I told them. "Maybe we'll be able to come up with something when we're looking at the thing." There was something about the guardhouse that was gnawing at the edge of my consciousness, some obvious fact I was overlooking, but when I tried to focus on it it just drifted away. Maybe whatever it was would pop to the surface when the actual building was in front of me.

"You shut this off?" Jerry asked Bob, pointing at the cop's prep radio.

"Battery died," Bob told us. "I'm surprised it lasted as long as it did."

"Swell."

Jerry got up and moved to the gear piled on the bed. "While we're here, we might as well check these out," he said. He motioned to the five hands-free, voice activated radios Steve'd purchased at Radio Shack earlier in the day.

Each unit consisted of a headset with a microphone, connected via a thin cord to the battery pack that had a belt clip. They normally only came in pairs but Steve'd had the Radio Shack employee switch over some of the units so that all five were now on the same frequency. The box said the radio's range was in excess of a mile, but I was assuming that was outdoors and in a straight line.

Jerry and I turned on all the units and made sure they worked inside the room. With the headset in place and the flexible mike in front of my lips I felt like a telemarketer.

Jerry headed out with one of the headsets to test just how far they would broadcast and receive. While he was gone I shrugged on Bob's Kevlar vest. It was the one he'd had on when he was shot, and the plan was for me to wear it during the raid. Bob had a heavy-duty raid vest with plates and built-in magazine pouches that he'd be wearing when we hit the house. I wondered briefly what he hadn't brought with him from Bragg. I had a vest of my own, but it was on the floor of my closet in my house.

I had a bigger frame and was a few inches taller than Bob, but his chest was proportionally larger, so the vest fit me better than I'd expected. Still, it wasn't a perfect fit. They never were, even when new, unless you were willing to pay the extra bucks for a Second Chance. They'd measure you and then make a vest to the exact dimensions required.

"Testing, testing, come in rubber ducky, don't let your meat loaf, over," I heard in my ear. Bob, still poring over the floorplans, heard the transmission coming out of the three spare units on the bed and shook his head.

"I copy you, bonehead," I replied. "How am I?"

"Okay. A little scratchy. I'm at least a quarter mile away, so we know they'll work this far, and through one wall."

"Ten four. Come on back before you get lost."

"Horky dorky on that one, big mama."

I took off my radio and shut all of them off. Bob was looking at me from his seat at the table.

"You guys are all nuts," I told him.

"But in the right way," he replied. "Remind me, when Chucklehead comes back, I'll go over hand signals, make sure we're all clear on what means what. Once you're in the house you shouldn't have to use the radios anyway, unless something goes wrong, like you get separated."

"If that's all that goes wrong..." I began.

"Don't worry," he cut me off. "It won't be."

6:23 p.m.

With sunset the temperature had dropped again, but I'd remembered to throw on an extra sweatshirt. The walk helped keep me warm, too. Since we might be leaving the Suburban parked for a while we'd decided that same spot on the shoulder might not be a good place. I'd found a church parking lot three-quarters of a mile down the road and was now walking back to where I'd dropped Jerry and

Bob off. Occasional cars hummed by on the ebony asphalt, barely making any sound at all until they were on top of me. Hopefully a cop wouldn't stop and ask if I needed any help.

The moon was on the wane, barely half full, but clouds were scarce. I'd made the trip enough times that even in the moonlight I had no trouble spotting the dark tangled mass of underbrush that was the sniper hide.

A dark figure crawled out the rear and waited beside the blind as we approached. The three of us walked into the clearing and I looked down the hill to the guardhouse. In the crisp evening air I could clearly see one of the guards in the little house, but the only way he'd be able to spot me was if he stepped outside and scanned the slope with binoculars. Even then, as long as I didn't move, the chances of being observed were near zero.

"I'm glad you came," Steve said. Something in his voice caught my attention.

"Why?" I said. "What happened?" My breath turned to white fog and drifted slowly upward in the still air. For the first time I looked toward the main house and saw it was lit up like a Christmas tree.

"Wowzer." Over half of the windows were lit up on each of the three floors.

"We didn't start surveillance until after midnight yesterday," Jerry said. He jerked his head at the house. "That might be normal." He didn't quite sound like he believed what he was saying.

"About five-thirty, quarter to six, right around sundown, we got some visitors," Steve said. "Three white vans pulled up and went inside. The first two showed up together, and the third one drove up about ten minutes later."

"What kind of vans?" I said.

"Regular full-size vans. Fords, I think."

"Who was in 'em?" Jerry asked.

"Couldn't see. Two of them had tinted windows, and the third didn't have any side windows at all. Other than on the front doors, that is."

"Where'd they go?"

"That's what I wanted to get to. First the first two vans showed up--"

"Five forty-two," I heard Ron say from inside the blind.

"Right. The first one pulls up in front of the gate, you know, on that thirty-foot strip of driveway between the gate and the road, and the two guards come out and talk to the driver."

"Driver was a white male," Ron's muffled voice added.

"Waitaminit," I said, images flying around my head. "Hold on. Did anybody ever see an intercom on the outside of that fucking guardhouse? There's that keypad, to get in, but did anybody ever see an intercom to talk to the guards inside?"

I got mumbled "No's" and shaking heads in response.

"What happened when the guards came out?" I demanded of Steve.

"Only one guy came out at first," Ron responded from the blind. His prone position behind the rifle with his cheek pressed against the stock probably muffled his voice more than the thin walls of the blind did. "Had a clipboard in his hand. Acted casual, talked to the driver of the one van while the other one waited on the shoulder. Drivers were both white guys. Second guard came out a few seconds later and ended up leaning against the doorjamb of the gatehouse."

"I could see both the guards were talking," Steve said. Both he and Ron sounded a little pumped up. They'd probably been frantically scanning the two vans, Ron with his finger on the trigger, wondering what the vans were doing there. Were they coming to pick up George, or drop off a dozen armed guys in anticipation of our raid? "They looked relaxed, but I couldn't tell what they were saying. Then the guy leaning against the door stepped inside and the gate slid open. The two vans headed up to the house and parked right by the front door. 'Cause of the angle, all we could see was the back end of the rear van."

"They were full of people, I'm telling you," Ron said.

"I didn't see that, all I saw was two people," Steve replied peevishly. "Two guys wandered out from between the back van and the house. They looked around, then headed back out of sight. Probably into the house. Late twenties, early thirties, casual clothes. The vans pulled over by the garage about ten minutes later, and the drivers walked back over to the house."

"They park in the garage?" Bob asked.

Steve pointed in the darkness. "If you look real close, you can see the back end of one sticking out past the edge of the garage. It's parked outside, I don't know about the other one."

"That's when the lights started popping on all over the house," Ron said.

"It was getting dark out," Steve added.

"You said there was a third van?" I prompted.

"Yeah. Same thing," Steve said. "White guy driving, pulled up next to the guard shack. Only one guard came out this time. Gate slides open, van heads up to the house and parks next to the front door for about five or six minutes. Then it pulls around out of sight behind the garage. I think I saw the driver head into the house but it was sorta dark by then."

"How soon after the vans were through the gate did the guards close it?" Bob asked.

"Uh, pretty near immediately."

"Nothing else going on down there to distract them from closing it," Jerry commented.

"Okay, so we have three vans arriving within ten minutes of each other," I thought aloud. "They all pull up to the house, but you guys couldn't tell if there was anybody in 'em or not."

"Right. But if they weren't unloading people at the front door, they were unloading *something*."

"Wasn't there a white van in the garage when you reconned the property?" Bob called softly to Ron.

"Yeah."

"So we've figured out there's no speaker on that thing, that they've got to come outside or open the door to talk to somebody," Steve said.

"Build what amounts to a bunker and forget to put in a goddamn intercom," Jerry said.

"They really seem to prioritize direct human interaction before you can get in," I mused. "No cameras, no intercom, live guards."

"A chain's only as strong as its weakest link," Bob said. "I think I've thought of a way to get those guards out of the booth, at least for a few seconds.'

"How?" I demanded.

Bob explained his idea, fleshing it out as we stood there looking down at the target. It only took him a minute, then we stood in silence for five more, thinking.

"It's simple enough," I said finally. "We'll be running our asses off at the beginning, but other than that…" I scratched my head. "It still might not work," I said finally.

"Everything could go just right and they still might not come outside."

Bob shrugged. "Worst comes to worst we can wait until shift change at midnight or eight a.m. and take out all four guards."

"I think it'll work," Jerry said. "It's so simple and stupid and obvious they'll never see it coming."

"Anybody think of an alternative?" None of them had any suggestions. "Ron, this what you want to go with?" It was simple and stupid and obvious...and involved cold-blooded murder.

"Any raid plan that involves beer has got to be a winner," he said.

"Jesus," Jerry said, shaking his head.

"So, we've got our plan to get in," Steve said. "When do we go?"

Silence descended as they soberly thought of executing a raid with what little information and resources we had.

"It has to be a night when Smoker's working," Jerry thought aloud.

"Best to go in around three or four in the morning," Bob said. "Everybody but the guards should be asleep, and the guards'll be bored or dozing by then."

We stood in the clearing next to the blind and stared down at the estate for several minutes. An occasional car slid by on the road below, and now and then a faint breeze would brush against my cheeks. Far off to the southeast the blinking lights of a jet appeared as it climbed for altitude.

"Tonight."

The four of us turned and gazed at the interwoven pile of brush from where the terse word had sprung. We looked at each other, but the darkness made reading their expressions impossible. I took a deep breath and closed my eyes.

When I opened them again I still couldn't see their faces, but I could sense their resolve.

"Do we really have any reason to wait?" Jerry asked quietly.

I thought long and hard, then shook my head. "Waiting only lowers our odds. We just can't go until we know for sure Smoker's working."

"Once we spot him coming out, we just have to estimate his next appearance time and from that decide whether we go right after the three o'clock check-in or the four," Bob said.

"And then it's hey diddle-diddle, straight up the middle," Steve murmured, staring down through the darkening gloom at the estate. "Guess I picked the wrong week to stop sniffing glue."

"Roger, Roger," I said, which got a little smile out of him.

7:06 p.m.
Back in the motel room Jerry and Bob had pulled everybody's gear from inside the Suburban and laid it out.

Bob's plan required that he use a suppressed weapon, hence he'd be toting his MP5SD. Jerry'd claimed Bob's customized Remington 11-87 shotgun for his raid weapon and was busy throwing it up to his shoulder to practice acquiring a sight picture. Jerry owned a Remington pump, which was so nearly identical in operation and handling to Bob's semi-auto that I didn't worry about him using what would otherwise be a strange weapon in a life or death situation.

Steve had an expensive HK93 with a collapsible stock. It and the M4 shared ammo, but it looked more like an oversize version of Bob's MP5. Seeing as they were both made by Heckler and Koch, that only made sense. Jerry'd passed his M4 to me. It'd been a few years since I'd fired one, but as soon as I touched the weapon I knew I'd be okay. The Colt 9mm subguns we'd been issued in the DEA were virtually identical to Jerry's M4, and before that I'd been trained on the M-16 while in the army. I knew where all the controls were and practiced shouldering it while flipping the safety off. Frankly I was amazed at how quickly the muscle memory came back.

The Aimpoint "red dot" sight was new to me, but once it was switched on it stayed on and was built to handle combat. I figured it ought to last me through the night. "This brings back memories," I said, looking down at the black metal-and-plastic rifle in my hands. It seemed light now, barely six pounds I knew, but I remembered that at the end of a 20-mile forced march my rifle had seemed twenty times heavier. I looked at the weapon's selector, then at Jerry. "This thing rock and roll?"

He laughed. "No, no happy parts in that. It's just a plain, simple, legal semi-auto. And you'll get a lot faster target acquisition with that dot. You saw people using 'em at the IPSC match on their pistols. Just put the dot on the target and pull the trigger. It's a lot faster than lining up the front sight with the rear sight with the target, but I left the iron sights on it just in case."

"Did you ever use one in anger?" Bob asked me.

I looked at the rifle in my hands. "Only ever used a pistol," I replied.

"Dry fire that a few times," Jerry told me. "I've got a JP match trigger in there and it's kinda light. I don't want you accidentally touching one off."

I gave him a dirty look. I'd been shooting since he was

in diapers, but I swallowed my pride and took the advice. The trigger pull was shockingly light.

"What's this?" I asked him, looking at the rounds filling the magazine I'd just pulled out of the M4. "You got tracers in here?"

"No. The green tips are military issue armor piercing, red ones are Hornady TAPs. On impact those red polymer tips push back into a hollowpoint and cause rapid expansion. They practically explode, but that means they don't penetrate barriers for shit, which is why I've got those two kinds of ammo alternating in all my mags. Don't worry about it." Jerry looked at Bob. "What's your favorite?" he asked Bob, indicating weapons.

Bob's eyes drifted slowly up toward the ceiling as he spoke. "A Longbow Apache. AH64-D. Ducked down behind a fallen tree, all of us damn near out of ammo, seeing it pop up over the ridgeline, unload two pods of seventy-mike-mike rockets, then watching as it did strafing runs with its chaingun until the place looked like a freshly plowed field. Most beautiful thing I've ever seen."

"That's a bit out of my price range," Jerry said.

"They remember to buy flashlights?" I asked, looking around. It'd been one of the many things on the shopping list we'd made up. "What about the boltcutters?"

"Relax," Jerry said. "He got everything that was on the list and more. If it's not here it's in the other room. Hey," he said to Bob, "how much ammo should I carry?" He was looking down into the shotgun's case at the numerous five-round boxes of double-ought buckshot.

Bob sat back in the chair and whipped his head to the side violently. His neck popped so loudly I heard the echo off the wall. "Hope for the best, prepare for the worst. Try to imagine what the worst-case scenario would be," he told

Jerry. "Absolute worst case, figuring in the number of known bad guys, having to use suppressive fire to hold a position, everything. Then figure how many rounds you'd want to have with you for that. You've got seven in the gun, and between the receiver shell caddy and the buttstock shell carrier you've got another ten on the gun. Plus your pistol of course, and however many spare mags you've got. With me so far?"

"Yeah." Jerry had his eyes closed, thinking.

"Okay. You've got a number? Now double that amount, and you should be fine." Jerry's eyes popped open wide.

"You sure that's not overdoing it?" I said. Jerry had handed me ten loaded thirty-round magazines for his rifle, which at the time had seemed like serious overkill. Jerry started pawing through the pockets of the soft-sided shotgun case.

"I'm never going to die for lack of shooting back," Bob told us. "Almost happened once, and once is enough. If I've got to make a choice between food or ammo going into my pack, I'll go hungry. Tonight that won't be a problem, ammo's practically all we're going to have to carry. We'll hydrate before we go in, so water won't be an issue either."

"If I use your guidelines I'm gonna have to head out for some more rounds," Jerry told him.

"I've got more than what's in that case," Bob told him. "Between that case and my two gear bags I've got thirty slugs and over fifty rounds of Federal Tactical Twelve, the low-recoil buckshot. And Ron practically brought along a whole two-hundred-and-fifty-round case for his fucking shotgun." He was right about that—I'd worked up a major sweat carrying Ron's gear bags down from his bedroom and into the Suburban.

"Here." Jerry handed me a heavy black nylon bag and I

looked inside to see it was filled with loaded magazines for the M4 and boxes of ammo. "Better to have it and not need it."

"I've been thinking," Bob said. "I think you guys should work in teams of two. Partner up. It'll make moving around inside easier. Instead of thinking of yourself as a group of four, and worrying where everybody is, just worry about your partner, where he is. Then all you'll have to do is be aware of where the other team is and let them worry about each other. Treat each team as an individual, if you know what I'm getting at."

"Yeah, I gotcha," I said. "I think that's a good idea."

"You know, before we head out to take the next watch, we ought to go over those hand signals," Jerry reminded Bob. "And after that, maybe you can give me some helpful hints on going through doorways with a long gun. I'm used to room-clearing with a handgun."

"You should probably practice transition drills too, in case your SGO goes Tango Uniform," Bob told him.

Jerry was nodding. "Yeah."

I looked at Jerry. "Did you understand what he just said?" I asked, pointing at Bob.

"Yeah, why?"

I just shook my head.

8:05 p.m.

Jerry and I took the eight-to-midnight shift. While he settled behind the rifle I wrapped myself up in the sleeping bag in what I knew would be a vain attempt to stay warm. I made sure the bolt on the MAC—our site security weapon—was closed on an empty chamber, flicked its safety off, and laid it alongside my leg. Then I picked up the binoculars and began studying the estate. After a few moments I set them down and went to the spotting scope. I'd avoided using it first because I knew its high-magnification lens didn't work well in poor light, much less in total darkness, but at least a dozen of the mansion's windows were lit up.

"Guards're playing Gin," Jerry murmured against the rifle. "You got anything?"

"Lot of lights on, but so far no movement."

He grunted in reply. We lay side by side in the blind, eyes scanning the estate for signs of anything unusual.

It was barely five minutes later when Jerry snorted. "Jesus," he said. "I'm already freezing my ass off."

"I thought it was just me," I said. "Now I feel a little better. Don't worry, if worst comes to worst we can always strip naked and snuggle up in a bag together."

"This thing goes down as fucked up as you think it will, we're all going to be sleeping with guys in prison. Just remember," he told me, "you're only gay if you're on the bottom."

11:56 p.m.

I heard them tromping through the woods a full minute before they found us. Bob and Ron set the bags down with identical grunts and looked around. I finished climbing out of the blind and joined them. They'd already changed into their raid attire.

Bob was head to toe in black. Black leather boots covered his feet, while baggy combat fatigues, or Battle Dress Utilities—BDUs—as they're called in the military, covered him from wrist to ankle. Over his chest was the black armored vest I'd seen earlier, with thick plates. He'd said it would stop grenade shrapnel and rifle rounds, and maybe a bit more. I hoped we wouldn't find out if he was right.

Ron was in camouflage BDU's, which worked as well at night as solid black. Both of them had their winter coats on as an outer layer, but the coats were unzipped. They'd worked up a sweat carrying all the hardware through the woods.

Other than Bob, who carried his Army boots and seemingly everything else with him everywhere he went, the rest of us were going to be wearing our regular footwear. Nobody wanted unfamiliar footgear that wasn't even broken in on a high-risk raid. Luckily, because it was winter, we were all wearing boots of one sort or another.

"Change of watch," Bob said softly, staring down the hill. I looked to see two guards in uniform strolling down the driveway toward the gate.

The gatehouse door opened and a head peeked out, then ducked back inside a second later. The gate began rolling open.

"Whyn't you put on your cammies now," Ron suggested to me. "You can put your jacket back on over them if you're still cold."

"It's that obvious, huh?" I said, my teeth on the verge of chattering. "It's that lying still that does it."

"This'll help get you warm," Ron said. He produced small flat boxes from one of the bags and started handing them out. They smelled suspiciously like pizza. My mouth began watering.

"I'd marry you if you were any good in bed," I told him.

"Maybe it's not me, maybe your standards are just too high," he replied.

"Yeah, regular bathing is overrated," Bob quipped.

After flipping Bob the bird, Ron crawled into the blind

with pizza for Jerry and took my place behind the spotting scope.

While I changed into Bob's plain Kevlar vest and the newly bought black BDU's I watched the new guards enter the gatehouse. A minute later the off-duty pair headed out and started up the driveway. The gate slowly rolled closed behind them.

The bullet stripe on my left shoulder blade burned briefly as I pulled on the BDU top. With everything that'd happened, I'd forgotten all about that wound. I wiggled my arm, but wasn't treated to any more flare ups. Thank God for small favors. Now if only my face would stop hurting every time I opened my mouth.

Just the act of changing clothes warmed me up some. I pulled my coat on over the fatigues, then looked back at the estate. There were still a hell of a lot of windows lit up. Half a dozen bedroom windows on the second and third floors, plus the whole first floor glowed to one degree or another.

We heard rustling leaves and Bob pulled his MP5 from his bag. It was only Steve, returning from the church lot where he'd stowed the Suburban.

Steve stood next to me silently, hands in his coat pockets, staring down the hill like the rest of us. He checked his watch, then looked at me. I caught his glance out of the corner of my eye.

"All we can do now is wait," I said.

"And go over the plan step by step a hundred and thirty-seven more times until we've all got everything memorized," Bob said.

The fervent discussion helped to distract us from the wait, and the cold. I spoke and thought about the raid plan with the rest of them, but some small part of my brain still stayed focused on the mansion's balcony. Was Smoker working tonight? If he was, would he keep to the previous evening's routine and come outside to light up? Would he be alone, or would a second guard join him this time for a nicotine fix?

As the minutes ticked by and still no one appeared on the balcony, no shadows flitted across the curtain of N36, our talk gradually slowed and then ground to a complete halt.

I pulled my sleeve back and angled my watch face to catch the feeble moonlight. Ten minutes until one.

"You sure he hasn't been out yet?" I hissed at the blind.

"We see him, you'll fucking know about it," Ron snapped back.

I clenched my jaws together and shuffled from foot to foot impatiently. Christ, I hated this shit. Waiting was always the worst part of anything.

ELEVEN

Monday

12:57 a.m.

"I've got movement!" Ron called out a bit too loudly.

"Where?" Bob hissed.

"N-three-six," was the excited answer.

We held our collective breath and stared down past the treetops. I could see the window in question, but to my unaided eyes it was just a large yellow dot. My heart hammered loudly in my ears as I squinted, trying to see something, anything, where I knew the west balcony stuck out from the mansion. Years passed.

"I've got him," I heard Jerry say. His voice was thick with tension, and relief.

"Is it our guy?" Steve asked. "Not somebody else?"

"Uh…" Jerry said. There was a ten second delay. I stared down at the huge building, seeing nothing.

"There, I've got a cigarette glow," Ron said. I let out the breath I'd been holding.

"Christ, thank God," I said. "I don't know if I would've been able to stand another day of this waiting."

Bob dug around blindly in one of the bags and pulled out a stick of camouflage paint.

"C'mere, beautiful," he said to me.

Bob took his time painting every square inch of exposed flesh on my body with black. He didn't just dab a spot here and there, as Hollywood does to its leading men so moviegoers can still see their faces; Bob *coated* me with the stuff. Forehead, nose, cheeks, chin, then the important and sometimes forgotten areas: my eyelids, neck, and inside and behind my ears. I had a dark blue wool cap covering my hair to complete the look.

Bob inked the backs of my hands and wrists, then handed me the stick. I returned the paint job. He was wearing fingerless gloves, so once I finished streaking his fingers I was done. Seeing that mop of blond hair over two hovering white eyes was slightly unnerving.

Bob took the stick back and started on Ron, who'd climbed out of the blind. Steve slid inside and took his place.

"How's your ear feel?" Bob asked, staring at the mangled thing on the side of Ron's head. Ron tossed the spotted gauze bandage to the ground.

"Nice and warm," Ron replied. "I think its infected." He gritted his teeth and nodded to Bob, who commenced rubbing the camo paint into the stitched-up folds. When he pulled back I saw tears running down Ron's cheeks. Bob squeezed his arm in sympathy.

2:02 a.m.

"Smoker," I heard Ron say softly. He was back behind the rifle, Steve on the spotting scope.

We stared down at the dark grounds of the estate. My body thrummed with tension. The adrenaline coursing through my bloodstream could've powered Detroit for weeks. I found myself unthinkingly clenching and unclenching my black fists, bouncing on the balls of my feet.

I looked right and saw Bob nodding his head as if in time to a rock 'n roll beat. He sensed my gaze and grinned.

"You think you're wired now, just wait," he told me.

He was grunting as much as talking. I couldn't understand how he was still upright, much less functioning. His lung had been punctured for over thirty-six hours.

"All right, I think he's back inside," Ron said two minutes later. I checked my watch.

"Radio time," I told them. "Everybody over here."

Bob and I handed out the radio headsets. Battery packs were clipped to belts, headsets settled into place. We all spread out and turned the things on.

"Bob checking in," I heard in my ear.

"Bob, you're good. John checking in," I murmured.

"John, you're fine," Ron said. In a minute we'd verified that all the units were working properly.

"How long are the batteries supposed to last on these things?" Steve asked. We all gathered near the blind.

"A lot longer than we'll need," I said. *I hope*, I added silently.

"Everybody gather 'round," Bob said gently. Something in his voice made me step close and pay attention.

He nudged us into a tight circle, shoulder to shoulder, facing each other. Then, slowly, he stretched his arms out and put them around the shoulders of the men to either side—Steve on the left, Ron on the right. I looked close at Bob's face, but the black facepaint made him impossible to read. I reached my own arms out, hugging the bodies to either side of me.

Uncertainly at first, the rest of them tentatively began embracing. Soon we were as one, facing toward a common center. Their bodies were warm where they pressed against my sides. Our smoky breath formed a whirling, rising cloud in the dark night air.

They looked to Bob, and saw his head was bowed.

I closed my eyes and bowed my own head. I didn't have it in my heart to pray, somehow I didn't think our quest would rate, but I wished with all my soul for the continued safety of my companions, and of my wife, Kelly, whom I loved more than life itself. I could feel the men to either side of me, breathing, their ribcages moving against mine. They were alive, blood coursing through their veins, vibrant, young, full of hope. I wished them well.

"Wherever this road takes us," I said after a long while, "I'm glad it was you guys by my side." I opened my eyes and raised my head. They were looking at me, blinking slowly, silent.

"This is also complete insanity," I told them.

Ron snorted. Steve shook his head.

"It's only borderline insanity," Bob said softly.

A small smile slowly curved the corners of Jerry's mouth. "Let's get to work," he announced.

Our circle floated apart. Ron and Steve slid back into the blind while Jerry sat beside it, staring down at the estate.

Bob pulled out the MP5SD and hooked it onto his body via that same convoluted sling system I'd seen earlier. The Browning rode high on his right thigh in a tactical holster, and loaded magazines for both weapons filled pouches all over his vest as well as the left thigh pocket of his BDU's.

Jerry'd thought to bring four magazine pouches that

each held two 30-round magazines for his M4. After taking off my coat I strapped the mag pouches to my belt along my left side and behind my back. My .45 rode in its customary position on my right hip, and I had four spare magazines for it in pouches or pockets across my body.

I inserted the last thirty-round magazine into the M4's mag well. It clicked into place and I gave it a sharp rap with the heel of my palm to ensure it was properly seated. I chambered a round then flicked the safety on. I then popped open the hinged lens covers on the Aimpoint. I found the knob in the dark and twisted it, then peered through the short tube. There was the glowing red dot I'd been expecting.

Bob had already locked and loaded his MP5SD and was watching me.

"Jump up and down," he instructed me.

Uncomprehending, I did as ordered. He gave me a dirty look as I dug the loose change I'd automatically transferred from my jeans to the BDU's and tossed it to the ground.

I jumped up and down again. No jingling this time. So that was why Jerry had taped up the metal sling swivels on the M4. I peeled back the sleeve of my shirt to reveal my watch face.

2:15 a.m.

"Time to go," I told Bob.

He nodded, producing a black balaclava from a pocket. He pulled it over his head, then extended the MP5SD's stock with a click. The balaclava covered his entire head and neck except for an oval around his eyes. They stared at me unblinkingly. He'd blackened the skin around his eyes, and his eyelids.

Steve crawled out of the blind and stood beside Jerry. Jerry extended a hand in a silent wave, then we were off.

I mirrored the snail's pace Bob set for the first fifty yards, angling down the hill. Then he came to a near stop, taking one slow step at a time, not placing weight on his foot until he was sure there were no branches underneath waiting to crack. I was five yards to his rear, trying to move as silently as he did. It wasn't easy.

My thighs began to burn from the achingly slow pace, and the M4 started to drag at my arms. We moved downslope at an angle, in a more or less direct line for the gatehouse. Bob had made it clear he wanted to approach in total silence, so that if one of the guards happened to wander across the road to relieve himself, he wouldn't know we were there even if he was pissing on our shoes.

I tried to distract my mind from my quivering thighs. I knew Steve'd be walking back through the woods to pick up the Suburban. He'd keep it idling on the shoulder while Ron and Jerry waited for the Smoker to indulge his bad habit one final time.

Suddenly I realized Bob had stopped and was crouched in the thin underbrush. He motioned me forward and I slowly made my way to his side.

Six feet in front of us the brush ended abruptly at the edge of the drainage ditch running alongside the road. Bob's nighttime navigation skills had proved excellent—we were directly across from the gate. I rested on one knee and slowly scanned the area. Bob did the same. When we were both finally convinced we were the only people within earshot he gave me the nod.

"We're in place," I said very quietly into my microphone.

"Roger that," was Ron's subdued reply. "Steve, you got that?"

I waited for Steve's response. When five seconds had passed without me hearing his voice, my heart began to race.

"Okay then," Ron said. "Everybody hold tight for the word."

My roaring heart began to slow down. "Be advised," I murmured, sounding calmer than I was, "we can't hear Steve."

"Ten-four. He says you're weak, but readable."

I took a deep breath and tried to relax. Yeah, right. I might as well have tried to saw off my arm without bleeding.

The ditch stretched eight feet from the asphalt edge of the shoulder to the brush line. In the summer it would be green and grassy, but right then it was more mud than anything else. It was shallow, barely a foot and a half deep at its lowest point. Not much of a hiding spot, which was why we were staying in the woods until the last possible moment. Across the road, about seventy feet away, I could see the top of one of the guard's heads through the gatehouse's front window.

Something moved to my left and I instinctively shouldered my rifle, unconsciously flicking the safety off. My finger was on the trigger, applying pressure, before I'd even realized what had caught my attention.

Shaking my head, I swore silently at myself as the headlights flickered through the trees. The car continued around the curve in the road, speeding by the two of us a few seconds later. I safed my weapon, lowered it, and turned to look at Bob. He slowly pumped his hand at me, palm down. Relax, relax. I nodded and filled my lungs with the cold night air. Christ, I'd just about opened up on a passing car. I shook my head at myself again, then gave Bob a thumbs-up. He turned back to the road and continued staring at the guards in the gatehouse.

"This is fucking insane," I mumbled.

2:54 a.m.

"Smoker! I repeat, Smoker's out!" Ron's excited voice caused me to jerk involuntarily. I traded looks with Bob, then checked my watch.

"We copy," Bob said.

"We're outta here, boys and girls," Jerry said breathlessly into my ear. "Radios are coming off for the run."

I pictured them in my mind, scrambling out of the blind. Rifle, spotting scope, sleeping bags—we didn't need any of it for the raid, so they'd be leaving it all behind on their run for the Suburban. Afterwards, if everything went according to plan, we'd be able to retrieve our equipment unmolested. If not, well, what hiker wouldn't appreciate a thirty-five-hundred-dollar sniper rifle?

3:02 a.m.

I heard the Godawful music before anything else. Heavy metal, I assumed, or maybe just a recording of a train derailment. As I turned my head right the headlights swung into view. They swelled in size as the music grew even louder and more unpleasant, hard as that was to believe.

The vehicle was only a hundred feet away by the time I was able to tell from its huge, boxy shape that it was the Suburban. From the sheer volume of noise all of its windows had to be down. The truck cruised toward the gatehouse at or just under the speed limit.

As the Chevy passed by in front of us I saw Steve and Jerry silhouetted in the front seat. They were hootin' and hollerin' like frat boys at a strip club, having a good ol' time. Just as the Suburban passed the brightly lit gatehouse Jerry let loose. His aim was true, and I saw the not-quite-empty beer can arc through the air and smack into the gatehouse's front window. Foam sprayed the glass, and both guards popped into view as they stood.

One of the two guards was a blondheaded guy about my age. He said something to his partner, and they both stared after the Suburban as it zigzagged down the road. The partner, fortyish with prematurely graying hair, shook his head in reply.

The blond stepped outside and circled around the front of the gatehouse. He bent down and then held up the beer can so his partner could read the label. They both shook their heads in disgust, but I noticed the blond took the can back inside the gatehouse to be disposed of properly.

As soon as the gatehouse door shut behind the blond Bob tapped me on the shoulder and we slithered into the ditch. I laid flat in the cold mud, keeping my head down. My fingers clenched the M4's pistol grip as if they were afraid it would fly away. I sensed Bob hunkered down to my right, waiting as I was for the other shoe to drop.

It seemed like an hour later but was probably barely more than five minutes when I saw the bushes I'd just crawled out of light up. The headlights of the Suburban swung back into view far down the curve to our left. The music was still cranked up, but maybe not quite as loudly as before.

The truck grew closer at a steady rate, weaving slightly. I

tensed as it came near and held my breath. As it rolled past us, brake lights on, Bob and I both crawled up the short embankment and got into prone positions facing the guardhouse.

I watched Steve as he performed a horrible U-turn thirty yards down the road, nearly driving into the ditch under the wall. He backed up unsteadily, then pulled the Suburban crookedly up the shoulder until it was at the edge of the estate's driveway. This time I recognized the music playing. Beastie Boys, *Sabotage*. Apropos, I suppose.

Both guards had seen the Suburban as it passed by and slowed down. When Steve U-turned, the truck's headlights swept the gatehouse windows. By the time he'd shifted the truck into Park the blond guard had the gatehouse door open and was staring suspiciously at the vehicle. The M4's stock was planted firmly into my shoulder pocket, safety off. The Aimpoint's slightly fuzzy red dot was resting on the blonde's chest, but my finger was still outside of the trigger guard.

Steve opened his door and stumbled out. When two empty beer cans fell out of the open door and began rolling around in the street the blond stopped looking suspicious and started looking disgusted once again.

"Hey buddy!" Steve called out to the guard, walking unsteadily toward him. Steve'd left his door hanging open into the traffic lane. The night air was cold as hell, barely twenty degrees, but all Steve wore was a T-shirt and jeans. He looked like he didn't even notice the cold. With all the adrenaline he probably didn't.

"What?" the blond said.

"D'you know where the goddamn interstate is?" Steve demanded of him, stopping at the far edge of the driveway from the guard. "I been driving around for a fuckin' half hour trying to find it," he went on, waving his arm around wildly. It was obvious he was trying hard not to slur his words. Steve stopped, and squinted at the man's uniform.

"Hey," Steve said worriedly, "are you a cop?"

The guard, mouth open to respond, instead stared at the Suburban. I glanced over at the truck and saw a pair of feet exit the passenger side door. It was Jerry, and I watched him from the knees down as he half stepped/half slid into the muddy ditch on the far side of the road. I heard a loud belch and saw a beer can hit the ground by his feet.

The blond moved into the middle of the driveway, hand on his sidearm. His older partner appeared in the doorway of the gatehouse, wondering just what the hell these drunken fools were up to. I looked back at Jerry's legs, which had stopped.

C'mon, COME ON! I silently urged him, my whole body vibrating with tension.

Steve kept still pestering the guards with stupid questions. They were looking back and forth between him and Jerry. The blond couldn't decide whether to be amused or angry at the drunken idiots bothering him. I looked back at Jerry's legs.

"Hey, what're you—" I heard the blond guard begin. The stream of urine appeared between Jerry's legs and began splashing into the muddy ditch. I heard him heave a great sigh. I felt my own sense of relief.

"Jesus! Get the f-...get off our property," the blond said indignantly. He moved to within four feet of Steve. His grey-haired partner finally decided to leave the gatehouse doorway and stepped out into view.

I quickly looked left and right. No headlights in sight. "It's clear," I said quietly.

"You're nowhere near the fucking interstate, you

drunken imbeciles," the blond began berating them. "I ought to call the police, God knows how many accidents you're going to—" I nearly missed the cough of Bob's MP5 beside me, much quieter than that of the MAC-10.

The grey-haired guard dropped like a puppet whose strings had been cut. He landed in an ungainly pile on the driveway without even a twitch to signal the end of his existence.

I'll never know whether it was the sound of the body dropping or some strange twitch on Steve's face, but something caused the blond guard to turn his head. Bob's second bullet caught him just under the ear and he fell to the ground, bucking and flopping.

3:11 a.m.

"Go!" I yelled too loudly, pushing up and dashing across the road. Ron rolled out over the tailgate as I sprinted toward the fallen guards. He had Jerry's and Steve's gear bags in his hands and went straight for the gatehouse.

The blond was still fighting for life, thrashing on the asphalt even as Steve, for lack of a better plan, began stomping on his head. I reached the other fallen guard, grabbed him by the collar, and started dragging the body toward the gatehouse. Jerry had a little trouble shutting off the tap but reached my side a second later and together we made better speed with the body. Ron passed us in the gatehouse doorway, heading out. By the time we'd dumped the body inside and exited the brick hut Ron'd cut the blond guard's throat with a big knife. He began dragging the second guard toward the gatehouse while blood still poured from his ruptured head. Bob finally made it across the road and shuffled to Ron's assistance.

Steve was still standing in the middle of the driveway as they dragged the body away. He was staring at the blonde's open eyes as the body was pulled across the asphalt. I pushed him toward the gatehouse and looked around. Jerry was just closing the Suburban's door. Engine roaring, he took off eastward down the road.

I did a quick visual to ensure nothing had been left on the ground or driveway. I didn't see anything but blood, which looked black and would probably be mistaken for oil. Then I stepped into the gatehouse. With the two bodies on the floor there was hardly any room to stand.

Ron was already helping Steve into his BDU shirt and gear. There was no time for him to change his pants, so we'd darkened Steve and Jerry's faded jeans with black camo paint earlier. The guards had never noticed.

Steve finished buttoning the black top and shrugged on his military surplus raid gear. It consisted of olive green Load Bearing Equipment suspenders attached to a pistol belt. Magazines for his rifle and pistol filled the pouches that festooned the harness. Bob handed me the paint stick and I began darkening Steve's face.

"I'm gonna step outside," Bob said, pointing to the shadowed area between the gatehouse and the estate wall. His eyes were unreadable behind the camo paint and balaclava. "Any cars show up I'll bang against the wall, you can duck down below the windows when they drive by." Then he was out the door.

Ron pulled Jerry's gear from a bag and laid it out on the counter for easy access. I finished painting Steve just as Jerry sprinted up.

"Fuck," he panted, as we helped him put on a BDU shirt and his own LBE harness. While Ron painted Jer's face I took a moment to look around the small gatehouse. There was a small magnetized chessboard in one corner, along with a frayed deck of cards. On a tiny desk was a stack of log sheets and a couple new mystery novels. There was a phone on the wall. Above the desk they'd thumbtacked Miss July into a place of honor. She deserved it.

Metal clanked as Steve and Jerry located their weapons and made sure they were locked and loaded. Headsets were snugged into place and turned on. They looked at each other, then at me. I checked my watch.

3:21 a.m.

Bob was moving before I had the door halfway open. I headed for the far end of the gate. Once there I backed up to its iron bars and laced my fingers together. Steve planted his foot and I heaved him up. His weight left my arms as he pulled himself up and over the gate. The gate was tallest at its center, and as I helped Steve up I looked to the end nearest the gatehouse. Bob was stationed there and had already hoisted Jerry over. I helped Ron up and over next. Inside the gate, I knew Jerry and Steve would have their weapons out and trained on the mansion.

Throwing the M4 over my shoulder on its sling, I jogged over to Bob. He stuck out his hands and when I was ready heaved me up to the top of the gate with a cursing grunt. The thick Kevlar of my vest took the pointed tops of the spikes as I swung my feet over and lowered myself to the length of my arms, then dropped. I landed with a curse and staggered to my feet. My headset had bounced askew and I fixed it quickly.

Bob stared at me through the steel bars, listing to one side from his exertions and wheezing wetly. His eyes were the only part of his features not covered by the balaclava, and they burned furiously into me. Sadness, rage—I couldn't tell what he was feeling.

"Bob…" I began.

"See you when I see you," he said, then lurched back to the gatehouse and ducked inside.

3:23 a.m.

We jogged westward in the shadow of the wall. I was the last in our staggered line, darting from tree to tree. The mansion loomed off to our left, already huge, and we were still five hundred feet away.

Inside the grounds the air was still, and my breath loud in my ears. The trees dotting the lawn were scattered, but the youngest of them had been planted long before I was born. I paused at each gnarled trunk, watching, listening, then darted to the next tree. My heart was pounding fiercely, harder than it needed to for the moderate physical effort I was expending.

The three of them were flitting shadows ahead of me. Occasionally one of them would pant hard enough for their mike to pick it up and broadcast it to the rest of us, but otherwise the night was silent.

We cruised across the front of the estate, then started angling in toward the house as we moved west. The trees thinned out as we moved away from the wall, then stopped entirely a hundred feet from the thick hedge encircling the mansion's west garden. The elevated position on the hill had warped my perspective of the estate. On the ground, I saw the hedge was nearly six feet tall, and I wracked my brain trying to remember where the gaps in it were.

I paused at the last tree before the bare lawn and looked

to my right. Steve saw my look, then turned and signaled to Ron and Jerry.

Christ, here we go, I thought. There was a pause that lasted an eternity, then two dark forms broke from the trees and tore across the open grass. A low hum filled my ears as I watched them sprint toward the west garden, my rifle up and aimed at the house. My racing heart, heaving lungs, and endorphin-flooded blood filled my head with electrically charged static. The night air seemed thick as molasses, every detail clearer than if I'd had the world under a microscope.

Ron and Jerry moved in slow motion, taking two lifetimes to cross the hundred feet of moonlit lawn. Finally they reached the hedge and tore around the corner out of sight.

Around the glowing red dot of the Aimpoint I saw the light was still on in N36. Two other bedroom lights were lit on the north side. A faint glow peeked around the curtains of several first-floor windows. *Waaaay* too many lights on inside, as far as I was concerned. Outside the building, however, the only illumination anywhere near us was a feeble light above the small door on the north side of the manse. I searched the whole north face for any new lights coming on, any movement. No windows opened, no alarms went off.

Finally I heard two clicks in my ear. Behind his own tree, Steve gave me the nod. I took a deep breath and broke from cover, feeling naked as I tore across the grass for the welcoming shadow beneath the hedge.

I felt a dozen eyes upon me, imagined a hundred bullets striking my body, the searchlights flashing into my eyes as I flopped on the brown grass, dying. I pounded across the grounds, hoping Steve was close on my heels. I ran faster than I'd ever run before, my heart in my throat, but it still took forever to get to the corner of the hedge.

Finally I flew past the corner and ran along the west side of the hedge, hidden in shadow. The balcony railing above the garden room was just visible over the top of the immaculately trimmed boxwood hedge.

At the far corner I skidded to a stop and peered around the hedge. Jerry was kneeling ten feet away, shotgun pointed at my head. Ron was another ten feet down the hedge, weapon trained on the mansion. Jerry lowered the shotgun, waved me forward, then turned and moved behind Ron.

I crouched where Jerry had been, letting Steve cover the rear, panting hard. Jerry saw we were in place, then tapped Ron on the back. Together they stood and, weapons at the ready, scooted out of sight around the gap in the hedge where the garden's brick walkway started. I jerked to my feet and covered the balcony over the top of the hedge.

Because of the up angle, I could only see the top half of the French doors. They were closed, and I was pretty sure the balcony was unoccupied. Ron and Jerry came into view as they paused at the garden room. Ron had the MAC trained above him at the balcony edge while Jerry swept the garden. When he saw it was clear he looked back toward me. I wasn't sure if he could see me, painted up as I was against a black background, so instead of a hand signal I flicked my thumbnail against my mike twice.

At my "All Clear" signal, Ron slung his subgun and started up the trellis. I heard the faint creak of wood once, but Ron didn't seem worried. At the top he vaulted over the rail and hugged the wall, unslinging the MAC-10. He quick-peeked around the corner through the French doors, then darted to the far side of the doorway.

After Ron's double-click, Jerry ran up the trellis like a

monkey. When I saw they were set, backed up against the wall on either side of the French doors, I ducked down below the hedge and knelt on the cold grass.

The estate's south lawn rolled gently away from me on three sides. It was hard to tell in the dark, but the brick wall on the south side seemed closer to the mansion than on the road side. There were certainly a lot fewer trees inside the perimeter, even though beyond the wall was solid woods.

I backed up to Steve, tapped him, and together we moved along the hedge to just before the opening for the brick walkway. Hunkered down near the base of the hedge I couldn't see the balcony at all, but that couldn't be helped. Both Ron and Jerry were already up there, and I couldn't afford to be seen peeking over the hedge by Smoker when he stepped out. I checked my watch in the moonlight.

3:29 a.m.

Christ! Over half an hour since Smoker had last appeared. I hoped he hadn't already shown up again and left while we were en route, because then we wouldn't get a chance at another open door until after the guards' 4 o'clock check-in. If he still hadn't shown by 4:00, I was going to have to decide if Bob should pick up the phone and try to bluff his way through a check-in. Being an eternal optimist, I gave that plan a ten percent chance of success.

We'd busted our asses getting to the balcony and still it'd taken thirty-five minutes. Well, nothing to do about that. If we'd missed Smoker, we'd just have to improvise. However, I doubted that had happened. He'd never gone less than forty minutes between smoke breaks before. Then again, we'd only had one and a half night's worth of surveillance on him from which to try and detect a pattern.

3:43 a.m.

I'd just frantically checked my watch again when I got a double click in my ear. Even as I moved through the gap in the hedge toward the garden room's trellis I wondered what the hell was going on. If Smoker had shown up, I'd heard nothing from the balcony—a mere thirty feet away—to signal his arrival or demise. No creak of the French doors, no click of a lighter, no thumps, *nothing*.

I slung the M4 and started up the trellis. It took me only half a second to learn, as I'm sure Ron and Jerry already had, that the vines encircling the trellis were climbing roses. I grit my teeth as the thorns dug into my palms and tried not to cry.

I flipped breathlessly onto the balcony, taking a brief personal moment to ball my fists up against the pain of puncture wounds. Then I unslung my rifle as Steve clambered over the edge. Ron and Jerry stayed close to the brick walls, eyes peering through the open French doors to the dark room beyond. Looking around uncertainly, I suddenly realized the odd shadow behind Ron's feet was actually a crumpled body.

I quick-peeked past Jerry's head, but couldn't see anybody inside the dark room. Hell, if there'd been anybody there they'd have made their presence known already. Stepping quickly past the glass, I stopped at the north side of the balcony. The corner of the mansion still prevented me from seeing the gatehouse, but I was as close as I was going to get to it.

"Bob," I said in a low voice. "We're going in. You copy?"

"I copy," was the faint, scratchy reply. I spun around and signaled them to go.

Ron, MAC at the ready, slid through the open door. He went left, Jerry went right—we'd worked that out ahead of time. Steve gave them half a beat, then went in. I stepped in behind him and shut the door.

Even though I'd been in the dark for hours, the room was so black I had to wait for my eyes to adjust. A yellow glow on the far side of the room dissolved into the edge of a partially open door. Shadows appeared on either side of it as Ron and Jerry moved close.

Twenty seconds more and the hulking shapes of furniture began to appear in the edges of my vision. I began drifting toward the cracked door, feeling my way across the room.

Ron put his eye to the crack. MAC at the ready, he slowly pulled the door open. The room filled with light, and I unconsciously stepped to the side, toward the shadows. I saw we were in some kind of sitting room, filled with ornate loveseats and small tables.

The white door swung open without a sound. It was two inches thick, topped with elaborate carvings, and I absently wondered why anyone would've wanted to paint over what had to be beautiful hardwood. Ron peered past the doorframe on one side, while Jerry crouched opposite him. From ten feet into the room, I watched Ron study whatever was beyond the doorway for a good long time. Then, finally, he shouldered the MAC and carefully stepped through, Jerry on his heels.

I moved to the left side of the door, rifle up and covering what I saw was a wide, hugely long corridor. Concealed bulbs in sconces near the ceiling gently lit the hallway. A dark, intricately patterned carpet runner covered most of the ten-foot-wide hall, on top of what looked like newly refinished hardwood. Here and there a tiny, narrow table was pushed against the peach colored walls. A foot-wide border of dark green wallpaper ran down both sides of the hall just below the ceiling. Everything about the place looked new or recently refinished. The place was gorgeous, but the whole house was so quiet I started to get the jitters.

Ron and Jerry moved down the right side, hugging the wall. They were panting so heavily the radio was picking the sound up and sending it to my ear. I wanted to tell them to relax, take a few deep breaths, but doors lined both sides of the hallway, and not all of them were closed. Hell, my heart was beating so hard there could've been a disco with a hundred people in it dancing their asses off at the far end of the hall and I wouldn't have heard it. I kept my rifle trained on the nearest open door, forty feet down on the left.

Ron and Jerry reached the big staircase, twenty feet down the hall from where I crouched. Ron covered the stairs, while Jerry nervously eyed the open door he was far too close to.

I waved Steve through the doorway, then hurried after him. We moved as quickly down the carpeted hall as we could without running. Steve touched Jerry's shoulder when he was in place. Ron and Jerry started slowly up the stairs, around the curve to the left, and out of sight. The blood roaring in my ears sounded like a tornado.

I gave them five seconds, then tapped Steve and headed up. Steve backed up behind me, covering the open doorway until he'd climbed out of sight.

Ron and Jerry were laying on the steps, eyes just above floor level, peeking left and right down the third-floor hallway. I stopped four steps back and tapped Jerry on the leg. He reached over and touched Ron on the shoulder. Even under all the equipment and clothing I could see Ron's chest heave as he took a deep breath. Then he was off down the hall, Jerry in his wake. I stepped up to the top of the stairs, and saw the pair gliding tensely toward a half-open door, light spilling from it into the hallway. N36.

I covered the hallway beyond them and heard Steve move up to cover the other direction. We were thinking and moving as a team better than I could've hoped, although Steve did keep stepping on my heels—literally. We still hadn't seen or heard another person, and I was beginning to get a little spooked. Sweat was dripping from my nose just standing still.

Ron edged up to the right side of the open door and paused, practically eating the wall as he tried to look inside the room. He carried the most gear of any of us. Not only did he have the MAC-10, but his big Mossberg shotgun was tightly strapped across his back, over the top of a small backpack that contained boltcutters and a few other tools. Every pocket he had was jammed full of shotgun rounds—when he moved fast, he rattled. Jerry crouched right behind him, waiting. The doorknob was opposite Ron, the plain white door hanging open into the room six inches or more, and he inched up to the doorframe, nose against the wall, trying to see inside.

I couldn't hear anything or see any movement inside the radio room, but Ron seemed to be waiting for something. Maybe he was just gathering his courage. After a minute—that seemed like an hour—Ron finally slid forward. The MAC's wire stock went up to his shoulder, while his left hand floated toward the door. Jerry crept up behind him, probably wishing he had Bob's MP5SD. Shit. If I was going to start counting, that was our first mistake. Bob should have the M4, and I should've brought the MP5SD inside. One suppressed weapon for a four-man team on a mission that demanded silence for its success just didn't cut it, and if anybody tried to make a run for it that MP5SD would be near useless against car doors and auto glass.

With no warning, Ron suddenly pushed open the door and charged in. Jerry rushed in after him as I heard multiple metallic coughs. I winced—they seemed loud, but in all probability weren't. Harsh, adrenaline-charged breathing filled my earpiece.

I waited, hands clenched on the rifle, staring at the gaping doorway. All I could see was one of Jerry's legs. I couldn't tell what was going on, or why it was taking them so long.

C'mon. Come ON! What are you doing? I'm dying here! I wanted to scream. Finally Jerry stepped into view and I breathed easier. He raised his index and middle fingers, *two men*, then chopped his hand across his throat. I got the message. He moved toward us, Ron coming out behind him. Ron paused at the door, locking it before tugging it shut. Apparently everything had gone okay, but they were so wired, features distorted by stress and black paint, that I made no attempt to read their expressions.

Steve and I stayed in place, covering the rest of the third-floor doors. Ron and Jerry moved to us, and Ron leaned his head in close, his lips against my ear. He murmured, his words barely audible. "Security cameras all around the outside of this house that apparently we never fucking saw, and that work in low light. There were a bank of monitors in there showing the entire grounds. We were on camera for our whole approach. Neither of the guards in there was watching the feeds, one was reading, the other was sleeping. Smoker must have had his head up his ass too." He traded an incredulous look with me.

"Cameras inside?" I asked, just as quietly.

"There were a few, but I didn't see anybody. A lot of the screens were dark. There was a big control panel but I didn't want to start hitting buttons to find other camera angles and accidentally hit an alarm or something." I nodded and jerked my head, then Ron was past us and down the stairs, smelling of gunsmoke and copper. I did a quick double-check of the hallway and then we turned and headed down after Ron and Jerry.

The stairway curved clockwise and I headed down at a steady rate, keeping Jerry just in view. We passed the second floor which was still dead silent and continued downward. Jerry slowed as Ron came into view, on his hands and knees, peering down around the curve of the stairs at the first-floor hallway.

I realized that I could actually hear something in the building other than my own breathing. The faint sounds drifted up to me, and I strained to figure out what they were. My own heartbeat seemed louder than the muted sounds, and I soon gave up.

Ron kept staring at whatever he was staring at, motionless as stone. I was nearly beside myself with anxiety. *What the hell was he doing? Didn't he know that every minute we spent in this place increased our chances of being discovered a thousand percent?*

After another agonizing minute he eased forward, slowly moving down the steps, MAC pointed somewhere down the first-floor hall. We strung out behind him, arm's length apart. Third in line, I sidestepped down the stairs, eyes darting to the left and right of the first-floor hallway as it rose into view.

The first thing I saw was the floor. Four by eight white

marble slabs, charcoal veins running all through the glossy stone. Two more steps and the rest of the hallway came into view.

It was a study in white; white walls, white ceiling, with white crown molding bordering the two. Small crystal chandeliers hung from the ten-foot ceiling, glowing at what I guessed was half power. I saw one tiny rosewood table against the far wall, sporting a tiny vase of fresh flowers, with two small paintings in gilt frames above it.

When I reached ground level I peeked around the corner to my left. Big double doors stared back at me. Through beveled glass panes I could see the darkened garden room beyond. To the right the hallway stretched out forever. That's where all the noise was coming from. Twenty feet down light spilled out of open doors, and I could plainly hear voices and people moving around. After the deafening silence of the second and third floors, actually hearing people made the hairs on the back of my neck stand up.

I backed away from the hallway and continued down the stairs. The suspected basement turned into a substantiated reality as our stairway continued down past the marble and chandeliers.

Once I rounded the curve the stairway didn't get any darker, but the nature of the light changed. Near the bottom I saw the modern, suspended ceiling. It appeared as out of place in the mansion as the four of us did.

Ron and Jerry spread out as I reached the end of the stairway. The ceiling was off-white two-by-four foot acoustic panels with matching metal slats for support. I'd installed something virtually identical when I'd finished my basement. The featureless hallway had matching walls and grey utilitarian carpet, all illuminated by fluorescent lights hidden in the ceiling. The walls seemed made of something more substantial than the drywall I'd used in my own house, but other than that small detail my surroundings were eerily mundane. I couldn't reconcile what I was seeing with the ornate and ridiculously expensive furnishings of the three floors we'd just passed through. It was like we'd somehow wandered into a time machine that'd flung us from the 18th Century into a 20th Century office building.

The basement had a layout obviously borrowed from the three floors above. A main hallway ran down the middle, with doors—not nearly as many—to either side. The hallway dead-ended at our end at a brown door with a simple doorknob. It stretched away fifty or sixty feet across the basement before ending in another door.

Ron moved left to the plain door, Jerry quickly sliding in behind him. I covered the long glaring hallway and Steve stayed on the staircase, on guard for any unexpected visitors. I would've sworn my heart rate doubled as I heard the rustle of fabric when someone reached for the knob.

I heard the door behind me swing open, and hunched my shoulders in anticipation. I waited five seconds, then broke training and looked over my shoulder. I saw the door hanging open, past it only a blank wall visible. Ron and Jerry were nowhere to be seen.

I forced my head back around to my area of responsibility. No gunmen racing down the hallway toward me, no heads peeking out of doorways, no eyes wide with alarm at the apocalyptic figures crouched in the hall.

"Storeroom," I heard in my ear. Two seconds later the door clicked shut, and Ron and Jerry moved past me down the hall. I lowered my rifle so it wasn't pointed at Jerry's back, tapped Steve, and moved into their wake.

We hugged the right wall, moving at a steady but not

rapid pace. Two more doors quickly popped up on the right side, both of them unlocked. Jerry and Ron checked them both without any excitement. One of them was some sort of conference room with rows of tables and chairs. I never found out what was in the second room, but Ron and Jerry were in and out of it in seconds without incident.

Thirty feet down on the left was another closed door. Our line angled to the left wall, then paused as Ron tried the knob. He shook his head, then looked at me. He jerked his head at the locked knob to make sure I'd understood him. I shook my head in response, and described a long U-turn with my finger. I was trying to communicate to him we should do all the open doors first as a matter of expediency. Then, if we still hadn't found George, and hadn't yet been discovered, we could circle back and force our way into the locked rooms. Kicking doors open would make quite a ruckus, and until we were spotted, noise was to be avoided at all costs.

Ron either understood my gesture or pretended to. He and Jerry moved forward again. I slid back to the right side of the hallway, tugging Steve along. Since he was acting as tailgunner, I kept my left hand on the back of his LBE harness. I gently pulled him along backward, the rifle in my right hand pointing down the hallway. We shuffled nervously along on the short, thick carpet, keeping an even distance from Ron and Jerry. The tension was unbearable. Sweat dripped from my nose, ran down my spine.

Forty feet past the locked door I saw a corridor branching to the right. Just beyond this new corridor the main hallway dead-ended at a closed door.

As they neared the corner Ron and Jerry split up. Jerry jumped over to the right side of the hallway and eased up to the intersection, while Ron put his back to the left wall and began sidestepping slowly toward the corner. When they'd both reached the point of no return, Ron gave a nod and they slid out together, Ron high, Jerry in a crouch.

No screams rang out, and nobody dropped from a bullet, so I felt it was safe to assume the coast was clear. The two of them disappeared around the corner and I hurriedly pulled Steve along in order to catch up.

I looked down to the right of the 'T' intersection at the new hallway. It was narrower than the first, and ran less than thirty feet before ending in a blank wall. The only items of interest in the hallway were the two closed doors.

I knelt and covered the main hallway door, ten feet in front of me. I also kept an eye on the door on the left five feet down the new hall, although if anybody stepped out of it I'd be hard pressed to shoot them without tagging Ron or Jerry. They stood outside the other door, ten feet further down the hall on the right. As Jerry reached out for the knob I jerked up a hand for him to stop. He froze.

I couldn't decide if I was hearing it or feeling it, but something weird was going on. A rhythmic vibration was giving me the tingles. I could feel it in my bones, a buzzing coming up through my knee. Or maybe it was a noise, a real low bass that hummed in my ears at such a low tone my senses didn't know what to make of it. I knelt there for thirty seconds, trying to make sense of what I was experiencing. The vibration, or noise, or whatever, continued, never getting louder or fading away. Finally, when nothing untoward happened, I shrugged it off to some sort of machinery, maybe a running furnace, and waved Jerry on.

He tried the knob, nodded to Ron, and they charged in together. As the door swung open a low hum filled the hallway. The room they'd darted into was illuminated by a weak light, but again I couldn't see a damn thing past the doorframe.

"Furnace," I heard Ron say.

"Water heater," Jerry added. "Huge."

I remembered the article stating that the mansion had something like five or six furnaces. Even with that many, at fifty-six thousand square feet, each one would have to be gigantic.

The closed door in front of me, at the end of the main hallway, piqued my curiosity. My perspective might've been screwed up, but it seemed like the basement – if it ran underneath the entire first floor – should've been a lot more extensive than what we'd seen.

Ron and Jerry popped back out of the furnace room and closed the door. The hum filling the corridor ceased, but I could still feel the rhythmic thumping. Funny how it sounded different than it felt.

Our two point-men moved up to the last door in the secondary corridor, the one just a few feet from me. I backed up a step so I could get a better angle on the door.

Ron knelt on the left side of the door, while Jerry stood to the right of the doorframe, where the knob was. As Jerry reached for the knob I gravitated toward the two of them, sensing that was the place to be. I pulled Steve back into the side corridor. It meant he had to cover both ends of the main corridor, but if anybody showed up all he had to do was duck back and we'd all be out of sight. When Steve was settled into his new position I placed my hand on the middle of Ron's back to let him know I was there.

Jerry's hand gripped the knob and twisted slowly. The knob turned, and he nodded at us. I felt Ron inhale and tense up as Jerry raised the shotgun, tucking the butt into his shoulder. Since I'd be the third guy through the door I kept the M4 pointed down along my leg. If I shot one of them in the back it'd ruin my whole day.

The blond hairs on the back of Jerry's hand stood out against the black paste coating his skin. For some reason I could see every muscle, every tendon as he gripped the knob fiercely. Heightened visual acuity, all the stress experts called it. Just one of the many adrenaline-induced altered states I'd been experiencing since I'd charged across the road toward the fallen guards. Except for tunnel vision, I'd had 'em all—auditory exclusion, attention to irrelevant details, and my favorite, tachypsychia, or what the FBI calls "visual slow-down", where the world turns into a slow-motion NFL instant replay.

My heart was the loudest sound in the world as I watched Jerry turn the doorknob the rest of the way, pause, then push the door open. As soon as it cleared the jamb I knew we'd made a horrible mistake. Amazingly loud rock and roll assaulted my ears, something by The Stones, and I realized the door had to've been soundproofed. The rhythmic vibration hadn't been the damn furnace, it'd been Keith Richards.

The door swung open smoothly. Any noise it made was swallowed in the music, as well as, I suddenly realized, a storm of loud voices. My brain kicked into hyperdrive and the whole world slowed to a crawl. Hello, tachypsychia; hello tunnel vision.

The first thing I saw was a belt. Below it, a blue-jean covered butt, its owner bent over a table to the right of the door. As the door continued to swing wide, Jerry making a belated, terrified grab for the knob, I saw the table was a pool table, and the owner of the blue jeans had a billiard cue in his hands. His opponent came into view on the far side of the table, drinking out of a plastic cup.

Even as the door swung left I stepped right, unconsciously wanting to see. To the left of the pool table was a man in a blue uniform, eight feet away from us and facing the far side of the room. He was standing between two pool tables, both of them in use. The air in the room was smoky, and the smell of beer hit my nose even before the door stopped moving. Past the first two pool tables were another two, and a foosball game, two couches, a large screen TV, stereo equipment, and a bar. Three of the four pool tables and the foosball game were in use. One couch was occupied by people both talking and dozing, and there were people standing both in front of and behind the small bar. The room was thirty by sixty and packed with people, dense with the sound of voices raised to be heard over the music.

Blue-jean's partner's eyes were attracted to the moving door. He squinted in confusion at the black shapes in the doorway, and leaned past the guy in the blue uniform to see us better. The uniform saw his companion's stare, and turned his head to look over his shoulder. When the off-duty gatehouse guard saw the three armed men with painted faces in the doorway he gawked for half a second, then made a hasty grab for his sidearm.

"No!" I screamed, instinctively straightening up.

Ron was up and moving forward before the word had even left my lips. I saw the burst of forty-five caliber slugs chew up the front of the guard's uniform shirt as the cases flying out of the MAC hit me in the face, and then Ron moved left to clear the doorway.

BOOM! I saw another uniformed guard standing between the far two pool tables go down under a load of buckshot from Jerry's shotgun. On one knee the guard struggled to draw his pistol, staring at us in disbelief. Then his face turned jelly red under thunder. I saw the red plastic hulls of the spent shells flipping through the air as Jerry charged into the room, firing.

There was half a second of stillness, then the room erupted in chaos. Screams, yells, bodies lunging this way and that. A big guy standing next to the foosball tables dropped his can of Coke and in one smooth motion swept his button-down outer shirt off his hip to reveal a holstered pistol. I didn't know if he was an off-duty gate guard or another of the same breed that had been trying to kill us all week, but my rifle butt was against my shoulder and I was squeezing off a shot before I'd even thought about moving. The M4 gently nudged me and a tiny spot appeared on the man's T-shirt, just below the neckline. He looked at me stupidly and I shot him twice more, then launched myself through the door.

The back half of the room was a seething mass of people. Casually-dressed men and women, terrified looks on their faces, some of them screaming, were trampling each other in their haste to get away, to escape us through the open doorway in the far left corner of the room. Couches were overturned, bottles on the bar rolled off and shattered on the floor. I looked for threats between the panicked people just trying to escape.

A man next to one of the couches dropped to one knee and fired at me. I dived behind the pool tables as more gunfire erupted from the half-dozen or so armed men who'd elected to remain behind and fight it out with us. Ron and Jerry were already crouched down behind another of the slate-topped pool tables. They'd kicked the hornet's nest over and now looked like they weren't quite sure what to do.

Holes appeared in the wall behind us, and I could feel bullets thudding into the table I was using as cover, a loud crack as the slate top fractured. The air was nothing but roaring gunfire. The men opposite us were burning through their ammo, yelling to each other as they advanced, trying to keep us pinned down. We couldn't let that happen. Ron stuck the MAC over the top of the pool table and emptied the rest of its magazine blindly. The volume of incoming fire dropped slightly. I looked over at Jerry and Ron and stabbed my finger past them, urging them to move.

Steve suddenly opened up with his rifle from the doorway, shooting over our heads. He pulled the trigger as fast as he could, swinging his muzzle back and forth. I rolled to the side and stood up between the wall and the pool table as pistol bullets cracked by me. I caught a glimpse of someone crawling toward our position and fired three times at him, just as a guy popped out firing from behind the rolling bar. Dust flew from the wall next to my shoulder and I felt something hit my chest. The crawler slumped to the ground as I spun toward the bar, only to see the man duck out of sight once again. I placed the Aimpoint's dot on the bar's stained oak veneer and kept pulling the trigger until the man fell out from behind it, dead and bristling with splinters. Steve moved up behind me, firing wildly at anything that even looked like it might be a threat. Hot pieces of brass bounced off the side of my head. The noise was deafening.

Ron and Jerry were up and charging along the far wall, firing at what defenders were still left. Gleaming brass fountained out of the reloaded MAC. Someone else jumped up near the TV, firing a SIG at us, and the four of us riddled him and the TV with bullets. One of us was screaming, and I'm not sure it wasn't me.

A man struggled to his knees behind one of the overturned couches. We fired at him until he went down, then I headshot a guy crawling out from behind the bar. The wall behind him splattered dark red. I swept left, then right, then left.

Torn bodies littered the big gameroom's floor, some of them twitching, but nobody was trying to get up. I sensed movement out of the corner of my eye and spun right, only to see Steve, a faint wisp of smoke rising from the muzzle of his HK-93. The ringing in my ears was as loud as a siren, and swelled in time to my heartbeat.

"Oh shit. Oh fuck. Oh shit," Jerry kept saying over and over, the shotgun drooping in his hands. Then habits formed from a thousand hours of practice kicked in and he began shoving fresh shells into the gun. "Reloading!" he belatedly yelled.

The room was dim with gunsmoke. Curly trails of grey swam around the odd fluorescents that hadn't been nailed by ricochets. I stared at the spectacle before me, my feet glued in place. I was mesmerized by the sights, the smells. Limbs bent at unnatural angles, blood splatters on the walls, the bullet holes in everything. *Jumping Jack Flash* just winding down on the stereo. The house of cards still somehow standing on the coffee table in front of the TV. I found myself staring at the bodies, looking for answers. Had they been part of the same group we'd been fighting since this thing had started? If not, who were they? They couldn't all be off-duty gate guards. Why hadn't they run, couldn't they see they were outgunned? I looked around, unseeing, the questions running through my head, paralyzing me, until I heard a groan from one of the people on the floor.

"Shit. We've got to move, people!" I yelled at them. They were doing what I'd just been doing, standing around staring slackjawed at the carnage all around us. "This room may be soundproofed, but we forgot to shut the fucking door. Let's find your dad before anyone else shows up."

"Let's go!" Ron shouted, galvanized into action. He looked at the nearly empty MAC in his hands, hesitated a second, then tossed it into a corner. With a wicked glint in his eye he unslung his Mossberg twelve-gauge pump gun. "Let's do it!"

Werewolves Of London started up on the stereo. Aaaaoooohh.

"Bob, if you're still paying attention, the shit has hit the fan," I said warningly into my mike. No response. Hopefully that was just because the radio wouldn't reach him through the concrete.

"Try that," I instructed Ron, pointing at the door everyone had been scrambling for. I had to force myself not to stare at the bodies. I stepped over and around them to reach the door in the far corner of the room, past the overturned couch and the fractured TV. There were moans, but I didn't stop to search out their owner. We didn't have the time.

Ron rolled a body out of the way and yanked open the door. We all piled through, guns at the ready. Another long hallway. I looked left, and saw a lot of corridor before the closed door fifty feet down. I realized immediately we were back in the main hallway. That door fifty feet down had to open on the T-intersection and the door to the game room we'd just blown through.

Immediately to our right the corridor ended, and I saw the first step of a stairway headed up, with a bloody handprint on the wall. Between the stairway to our right and the closed doorway down to our left, the only thing to look at in the blank corridor was the door almost directly across the hall from us. It was wider than normal, and metal, and secured with a couple of thrown, padlocked bolts. Hinges on the outside, facing the hallway, as opposed to every other door we'd seen that night.

I saw the padlocks and a chill went through my body. Ron felt it too. He practically flew to the closed door and jerked down on the locks. They were secure, and I caught his shotgun one-handed as he blindly tossed it in my direction. While Ron dug around in his backpack for the bolt cutters Jerry moved to the right and covered the unfamiliar stairway. We had to be just under the main foyer, and the front door. I could hear movement upstairs, pounding feet, slamming doors, and shouts, lots of shouting, but the gunfire had so badly screwed up my hearing that I couldn't make out what anyone was saying.

With forceful grunts Ron frantically severed the steel shanks, then ripped the lock bodies from the bolts and tossed them down the hall. His hands nervously scrabbled at the bolts, finally getting them to slide out of the reinforced doorframe. I threw him his shotgun, just as I heard shouts echoing down the stairwell Jer was covering.

Ron and I traded glances, then he readied himself and pulled open the door.

3:55 a.m.

George Kelly was inside, sitting at a small desk. Dressed in a navy blue polo shirt and jeans, he was reading a paperback, half-glasses propped on the end of his nose. He looked up at us as the thick, soundproofed door flew open. Nobody said anything for a second.

"Dad!" Ron yelled at last.

The book fell out of George's hands and landed on the desktop with a clunk. It was a very worn copy of *Little Women*, the pages dog-eared.

"You've got to be fucking kidding me," George said, mouth hanging open.

I stepped in, rifle up, and checked the room. He was alone. Besides the small desk, there was a tiny bed with flowered sheets and an immaculate bathroom done in blue and yellow tile. George slowly stood up, his bulk shrinking the room.

Ron and Steve and Jerry all stood in the doorway, staring, unable to move. George reached up and took off his half-glasses, then set them on the table. He looked the picture of health, and maybe'd even lost a few unwanted pounds. No cuts on him, no bruises, no bullet wounds.

"Please tell me you're here against your will," I said, my voice on the verge of cracking. My hands holding the rifle started to quiver.

"What, are you an idiot?" he demanded gruffly. "I was kidnapped!" He blinked. "What the hell are you guys doing here?"

Ron let out a strangled sob and tackled his father in a bear hug. George stood there, still dumbfounded.

"Ron, we've gotta fucking **go**," I said. I looked at George over his son's embrace. "Unless you've got any objections?"

"I'm ready to leave," he said. "We just gonna walk out?"

"Hopefully," I said. I pushed my way through the gawkers at the door to the hallway. They were all so mesmerized at the sight of George that no one was watching the corridor or the nearby stairwell.

"You two check that door," I instructed Steve and Jerry, pointing them down the hall. If the hallway on the other side of the door was clear all the way back to the circular stairwell we'd descended I wanted to head out that way. I turned the other direction and jogged toward the unfamiliar stairwell with the bloody handprint, wanting to see if any of the people I'd heard before had started our way.

I rounded the corner and collided headfirst into someone. He bounced backward and nearly fell, hand grabbing the wall for support. Out of a lifetime of politeness I nearly apologized. Then I saw the automatic in his hand.

"GUN!!!" I bellowed, reflexively shoving the M4 forward and pulling the trigger. The rifle's muzzle was buried in the man's stomach when the gun went off. He jackknifed backward, his eyes huge. Past him I saw several pairs of feet appear on the staircase, racing down toward us. I threw my rifle up and began pulling the trigger, aiming at legs.

The long gun bucked twice and then stopped working. I looked stupidly at it, seeing the bolt locked back on an empty magazine. I'd hit one man, who was careening down the steps. Four more uninjured legs were propelling their owners toward me at breakneck speed.

"I'm out!" I screamed, backing up. I turned to dive around the corner, out of harm's way, and almost collided with Ron. He roughly shoved me aside and shotgunned the first guy to reach bottom. Ron worked the pump, his hand a blur, nailed the second guy before the first had even started falling. Half a second between his shots, maybe less. The man's revolver flew sideways at the impact. Ron racked the Mossberg again, moved forward, and finished off the guy I'd hit in the legs.

"Let's get the fuck out of here!" I yelled at Ron. I looked left, and saw Steve and Jerry frozen in the middle of the hallway, halfway toward the far door. "Go!" I told them, waving my arm. George started jogging toward them, and they broke from their trance.

Bodies covered the floor at the bottom of the stairs. I

could hear people running and yelling above us. A lot of people. Ron moved to the bottom of the stairs, pointed his shotgun up past where I could see, and fired two rounds to keep their heads down.

I dumped my empty mag and dug out a full one. It took me three tries before I got it into the mag well the right way.

"C'mon!" I entreated Ron, hit the M4's bolt release, and began running down the hall. I heard him close on my heels.

Up ahead I could see Steve and Jerry had opened the hallway door, and paused just past it. The corridor was empty all the way to the far end of the basement. Jerry watched us run toward him with a wide-eyed look on his face, while Steve dug around in his backpack. Just as George reached them I saw Steve produce the Uzi. He handed it off to George, who continued down the hallway at a fast jog, unfolding the stock as he went. He seemed familiar with the little weapon. Somehow I wasn't surprised.

Steve and Jerry were standing just in front of the 'T' intersection, watching our panicked approach. I checked behind me to make sure Ron was still coming. He was jogging toward me, but slowly, as he stuffed fresh shells into his Mossberg. Beyond him, at the end of the hall, two men rounded the corner with submachineguns in their hands.

"Watch out!" I yelled. I threw myself past Steve and Jerry, rolling into the side corridor. Ron dived in on top of me just as the air filled with hot metal. The two men opened up on full-auto, the rounds whizzing past my head like supersonic bees.

Jerry dodged out of the way in time, but Steve was a half step too slow. He cried out, dropping his rifle and falling sideways into our arms. We dragged him to safety. Bullets chewed up the walls and carpet in the main hallway.

Jerry leaned out past the corner and fired three times, then hopped back. Ron popped out low and fired once, then scrambled back under cover. The return fire slacked off dramatically as our opponents learned just how good shotguns were for clearing hallways. While they grabbed fresh shells and reloaded I checked Steve out.

Both his hands were covered in so much blood I couldn't find the wound at first. He was lying on the floor in front of the open gameroom door, soaking the grey carpet. Then I realized he was missing his left ring finger.

"It doesn't hurt, it doesn't hurt," he kept saying in disbelief. He couldn't stop staring at the place his finger used to be. I dug around in the pack on his back and found one of the military compresses Bob had insisted we bring along. I unrolled it and wrapped it around his hand as tight as I could in an effort to stop the bleeding. The gauze immediately turned red.

Ron and Jerry took turns firing rounds around the corner to keep our opponents' heads down, reloading as they went. I found Steve's rifle and dragged it over to him. He grabbed at it eagerly. I picked my own rifle up off the floor and was moving to help Ron and Jerry when I saw movement out of the corner of my eye. I pivoted left and fired half a dozen shots at the guard running across the gameroom floor toward us, a shotgun in his hands. He'd entered through the far door, thinking he'd surprise us in a flanking maneuver. He skidded sideways as the rounds hit him and landed facedown between the pool tables.

I kept my sights trained on the far end of the gameroom in case anyone else tried that strategy. "We've got to get out of here!" I yelled. Sudden fear struck me. "Where the fuck is George?" I belatedly thought to ask. The last time I'd seen him, he'd been nearing the circular staircase. As if in response to my question, I heard the chainsaw sound of the Micro Uzi echoing off the walls. Apparently he'd also run into some unfriendlies.

"How many guys you got down there?" I asked Ron.

"Three or four," he yelled back, his hearing destroyed by the gunfire. "They're at the end of the hall, keep popping out to spray rounds down this way." He fired another round of buckshot to keep their heads down.

I looked to the right, saw the door to the furnace room. I pointed at it. "Is there any back way out of there that'll get us closer to the circular staircase?" I asked them. Jerry shook his head. He traded places with Ron and fired twice down the hallway, the Remington booming hugely in the confined space. The ceiling panels bulged upward from the concussion every time he fired.

"Earplugs," I said to myself. "Earplugs would have been a good idea. Moron."

"WHAT?" Jerry yelled at me. I just shook my head, then grabbed him and pulled him back around the corner.

"Save your ammo," I yelled. "We're a long way from home." The walls were cracked and cratered from incoming fire, but whatever the builders had used for soundproofing was doing a good job of stopping the submachinegun rounds. I quickpeeked around the corner and saw two bodies lying at the far end of the corridor. There was movement and I jerked back as someone sent a four-round burst my way. They were serious, but not suicidal. They wouldn't come charging down the hallway, not when they had all the time in the world.

"We've got to get to your dad," I said to Ron.

After that first long burst from the Uzi I hadn't heard a thing. I refused to believe George'd been killed. Not after all we'd gone through to get him out.

"You go. I'll cover you," Ron said. I thought about it for a second, then grabbed Steve.

"You first," I told Steve. "As soon as we start shooting, you tear ass down that hall." From the look on his face a cartoon bubble should have popped into existence over his head with the word "Gulp" in huge letters inside it, but he nodded his head. I couldn't blame him. If we didn't want to charge the guys with submachineguns, we'd all have to run down fifty feet of exposed hallway with no cover if we wanted to get out of the basement.

"Covering fire," I told Ron. I gave him a three count, then we popped out high and low around the corner. I emptied the rest of my magazine at the far end of the hall, pulling the trigger as fast as I could. The hallway filled with gunsmoke as well as dust falling from the acoustic ceiling panels. When the M4's bolt locked back I spun into the side hallway, looking down toward the circular stairway as I did. Steve was just disappearing around the corner.

I leaned back against the wall, panting, a big smile on my face. At least Steve'd made it. Ron stood beside me, reloading his empty shotgun. I'd never heard him firing right beside me, so intent was I on the task at hand.

"You're next," Ron told me. Either his voice warbled, or my hearing was cutting in and out. I nodded, dropping my empty mag and shoving in a fresh one. I fired two rounds blindly around the corner to keep heads down while I waited for Ron to finish reloading. A responding burst sent rounds whining past my ear, and I ducked my head. The floor was littered with spent twelve-gauge hulls.

"Okay," Ron said finally. He and Jerry moved into position near the corner. I heard yells, but I couldn't tell which end of the hallway they were coming from.

"You ready?" Ron asked Jerry. They stepped out into

the hallway, not even attempting to make use of cover, and opened fire. I kicked into gear and sprinted down the corridor, rifle high at port arms. The two shotguns behind me firing in tandem thundered like meteors hitting the earth.

I flew past the corner, bouncing off the wall. With one hand George caught me before I fell and jerked me upright. Steve crouched on the stairway, rifle trained on the floor above us. The gauze around his left hand was totally red. I saw three bodies piled nearby, apparent victims of the Uzi.

"This going the way you planned?" George asked me sarcastically. The Uzi looked like a toy in his huge fist, even with its stock extended.

"What, aren't you having fun?" I shot back. I peeked around the corner in time to see one of the bad guys break from cover and dart for the open door at the far end of the gameroom. He made it without incident, but a few seconds later I heard two booming blasts from a shotgun as either Ron or Jerry spotted him and took care of business. I didn't want to fire down the corridor, because with my luck Ron or Jerry would step out into the bullet. All I could do was cower behind the corner and sneak quick glances.

I jerked in surprise as someone fired a pistol down the circular stairway. Steel warbled as the rounds ricocheted off the steps, and I felt my cheek burn. Steve fired three times, the rifle brass glinting as it tumbled to the floor. He moved up the steps, and fired again. His rifle in the close confines of the stairwell was so loud it was short-circuiting my eardrums. I couldn't hear the gunshots for some reason, but I could feel the pressure wave of the blasts. George moved to back him up. Everyone in the damn mansion had to know right where we were, and I could sense we were rapidly running out of time.

Flinching in anticipation, I snuck a peek around the

corner. Just as my eye cleared the wall I saw Jerry step out into the hall and begin firing his shotgun. As the first smoking hull ejected from the Remington's receiver Ron tore into view, heading my way. He slipped and fell as shotgun hulls rolled underfoot, then was up and running again. Jerry continued firing, the red shells flipping and twirling as they bounced off the walls. The fluorescent light panel above him flickered and then went out as the concussive blasts fractured the bulbs.

Ron was tearing down the hall fifteen feet away from me, still in the open, when Jerry's shotgun ran dry. Without a pause he dropped it on its sling, trapped it under his left elbow, and drew his .45. He was halfway through the magazine when Ron flew past me. I caught him as he bounced breathlessly off the wall and pushed him out of the way.

Jerry's pistol had fallen silent and I peeked back around the corner. He was out of sight, probably furiously trying to reload his two dry weapons.

Hoping Jer wouldn't pop out unexpectedly, I shouldered the M4, braced myself against the wall, and fired ten aimed rounds at the far end of the hall. Someone edged out and fired a burst my way. Against all reason I remained perfectly calm as the rounds whipped down the hall, peppering me with plaster dust. Without even a flinch I carefully squeezed off an eleventh shot.

"Got you, motherfucker!" I crowed. Arterial spray didn't look like anything but. Maybe they'd be more cautious about sticking their heads out. But just in case I emptied the rest of the magazine down the hall as fast as I could pull the trigger, empty cases bouncing off the walls at odd angles, then stuffed another 30-round magazine into the rifle, smoke seeping out from under its handguard as the oil on the barrel started to burn off. Jesus, how many magazines was that? How many did I have left? Ten had seemed way too many back in the motel.

The T-intersection was all lines and shadows once the fluorescent panel above it was blown out. I sensed movement, then the dim hallway was lit up with the booming flash of Jerry's shotgun. A second set of lights, closer to my end of the hall, disappeared under a shower of buckshot. A pause, then he shot out a third fixture. Half the space between me and Jerry was now dark, but he couldn't shoot out any more of the lights without leaning out into the hallway.

"Ron!" I yelled. He was beside me at once, and I pointed. "Shoot out the lights."

"What—?"

"Just do it!"

He mounted the Mossberg and blew out both the remaining lights between us and Jerry. Half of the main hallway, from the 'T' all the way back to us, was in darkness. At the far end of the corridor, I saw a shadow as our opponents began to get restless. I fired half a dozen times to keep their heads down.

"Well, come on already if you're gonna do it!" I yelled.

No answering yell, just suddenly there he was, a black silhouette tearing down the middle of the hall, arms and legs pumping wildly. Jerry was backlit and easy for me to see, but hopefully the guys on the far side of the hall wouldn't even notice he was gone.

He was almost to us when they opened up with their subguns. Jerry tripped and rolled into the wall, and we dragged him back under cover as chunks of drywall peppered us. Ron sent a hail of buckshot down the corridor.

"They're too far away," I said. "Try slugs."

"Christ," Jerry spat, panting hard from the run. He

struggled to his feet, a dim outline in the light shining down from the circular staircase. "Uh-oh." I watched him lift his arm and pull at his shirt.

"You okay?" I said.

"I got tagged," he said. "Fucking round slid right up the armhole of the goddamn vest. Ow." He worked his arm, wincing, then moved toward the stairs, shuffling like an old man. Energy seemed to be draining out of him as I watched.

"Is it bad?" I asked worriedly. It was too dark with the lights out to see how bad he was bleeding, not that any of us had the skills or the equipment—or the time—to treat a serious chest wound

"Can I call a time out if it is?" was his reply through clenched teeth. "Feels like someone's sitting on my chest, I can hardly breathe. I'm no doctor, but I don't think that's good." His breath was ragged.

With Ron firing intermittently down the basement corridor to keep us from getting overrun, the rest of us moved up the stairs. I reloaded, stuffing the partially-used mag back into the pouch on my belt. At the rate we were all burning through ammo I'd need every round.

"I haven't heard anybody nearby for a minute or two, but I think there's a bunch of them on the second floor," Steve whispered to me, crouched three stairs down from the marble of the first-floor hallway. A body missing half its head lay on the stairs to our left, leading up to the second floor.

"You don't have to whisper, I think they know where we are," I told him. "You look?" He shook his head.

I moved into the lead, and crouched before the corner. To our left I could see the glass doors leading into the garden room, less than thirty feet away. I didn't want to go up, try to get out the way we got in. Not only could I hear voices upstairs, I didn't want to get trapped on the second floor. The garden room was our way out, as long as... Cheek pressed against the textured plaster of the wall, I edged my head out into the white on white hallway until my left eye cleared the corner.

For the first time I got a good look at the entire first floor main hallway. Twelve feet wide, and so many chandeliers on full power it looked like a runway. Big wide doorways to either side, with an occasional piece of tiny furniture pressed up against the wall. A rosewood table here, a velvet-covered bench there. And, down at the end of the hallway, fifty yards away, near the big front door, those guys...what were they doing?

I jerked my head back as the world around me exploded. The chandelier just above our heads shattered into a thousand shards of crystal, the wall I was leaning against shook, the glass doors leading into the garden room disintegrated in their frames.

"Jesus Christ!" I stumbled down a step, and turned and looked at my companions. "They've got a belt-fed machinegun set up down near the front door!" A half-second longer peering down the hall, trying to make sense of what I was seeing, and I would have caught a round in the face. The machinegunner was on the floor, prone behind his gun, and there'd been guys to either side of him, hugging the walls and doorways, maybe half a dozen of them, all with rifles.

Rounds skipped across the marble floor and whined by my head. The big slab right in front of me cracked as a skipping bullet hit it just right, the dry sound loud even against the backdrop of full-auto bursts. Every third round seemed to be a tracer, the ruby red laserbeams only visible when the bullets struck something hard and veered off. There was one of those tiny rosewood tables just across the hall from the staircase. A stray round ripped off a leg and it slowly toppled to the floor, the vase on it shattering.

"What the hell's going on up there?" I heard Ron yell from down below.

"Anybody bring an RPG?" Jerry asked with a wincing, wry smile, hunched over against the pain.

"Shut up and watch our back!" George bellowed down to his son.

After a few long bursts the machinegunner was using his ammo more sparingly, but in-between long bursts from the belt-fed were cascades of shots from everyone else at the end of the hall, intended to keep us pinned in place. Across the hall to the left was a wide doorway. From the floorplans I knew it led into a big library which looked out onto the front lawn, although from my vantage point all I could see of the room were lines and shadows.

What the hell, nobody lives forever. I pointed the doorway out to Steve. "You see that?" I asked him.

"Yeah?"

I was up and running. Something tugged at my hair, then I was across the hall and through the doorway as the belt-fed opened up with one long ferocious burst. My eyes searched the library frantically, but I was alone. Directly in front of me were two tall windows that I knew looked out onto the front lawn, but all I could see in the closest one was my silhouetted reflection. I shifted the rifle to my left hand, grabbed a delicate-looking end table, and whipped it across the room at the window. The belt-fed had stopped firing and I heard the sharp crack of the table on impact just as Steve came flying into the room. He couldn't stop in time and somersaulted over a loveseat, landing hard. I pulled him up with a grin, only to see he was badly favoring his left leg.

"Twisted my knee," he said, cursing. He seemed to have forgotten he'd had a finger shot off only a few minutes before. The crimson bandage around his hand was dark and weighty with blood. I turned back to the window, expecting to see it fractured, and instead saw only the spindly end-table in pieces on the floor. The window looked undamaged.

"Shit," I swore. Steve was watching me and I jabbed my finger past him. "Watch our backs!" I admonished him as Jerry unleashed a load of buckshot down the hall at the men clustered at the far end. Jerry ducked back down the stairway as they answered with shots that sang off the marble floor and rattled the chandeliers.

I faced the troublesome window, shouldered my rifle, and quickly fired half a dozen rounds into the lower pane, walking them across the glass.

"What the...?" Steve said, staring at the window and the large white pockmarks in it where it looked like someone had thrown small snowballs against the glass.

"Armored," I told him. "We're not getting out that way."

Ron's shotgun boomed three times, the shots close together. I looked across the hallway and saw George start down the stairs with the Uzi, looking grim. They were trying to box us in. Jerry gritted his teeth, his face pale, leaned out slightly, and carefully fired three left-handed shots down the main hall just to keep the guys down there honest. He ducked back as the MG operator fired more long bursts at him. Which were followed by more subgun bursts from somewhere down near the belt-feds, and additional rifle fire. The air started to fill with dust and splinters from all the bullets hitting…everything. The noise was incredible. Jerry stared across the hall at us expectantly, hunched over against the pain, one arm wrapped around his chest. He looked open to suggestions.

Past the library Steve and I were in was a huge dining room, which led to a short access hall on the far side that came out pretty near where the machineguns were set up. I wanted to avoid the belt-fed at all cost. And preferably everybody else with a gun. In-between the library and the dining room should be a small foyer, and in there….

"C'mon," I said to Steve. I'd spotted the door we wanted and headed through it. The foyer was about ten by twenty and nearly pitch black. I hooked left and was almost on top of the door I was looking for before I could see it in the low light. We'd labeled it Door 1 on our surveillance logs, and it exited the north side of the mansion onto the beautiful broad lawn. It would have been the perfect way out but for the four-inch-thick security crossbolt running through the steel lockbox on the door. The ends of the crossbolt were set deeply into the metal doorframe and looked strong enough to stop a runaway locomotive. I tried the handle, ever the optimist, but it was locked. I could see no way to unlock the crossbolt.

"Not getting out that way," I told Steve, kicking the door in frustration.

From the access hall on the far side of the dining room I'd be able to get a bead on the belt-fed, a mere thirty or so feet further down the hall, right in front of the main door. That now appeared to be our only sure way out. I didn't like it, but I didn't see any other option. If we tried to make it out through the garden room at the end of the main hall the belt-fed operator and his posse would turn us into bloody hamburger.

I spotted the door leading to the dining room and we headed quickly for it, Steve limping badly. I kicked open the swinging door and rushed in, abandoning any attempt at finesse. The only illumination in the room was a small table lamp, but this time we were lucky—nobody was lurking in the shadows.

The dining table was huge, twenty people could've sat at it comfortably. Beyond it I saw the door leading to the short access hallway. The door was cracked an inch, the hallway beyond brightly lit. Steve and I had just started moving towards it when the door burst open and a man wearing a blue guard's uniform shirt and boxer shorts charged in with an M-16 in his hands. We were black figures in a dark room, and riddled him with rounds before his eyes had a chance to adjust to the dim light. He never saw who killed him.

Maybe the half-dressed guard had seen us dart across the hall and planned to intercept us, or maybe he was just trying to get a different angle on the rest of our group at the stairwell. Either way, the fire from the belt-fed and his friends had dropped off enough that they were sure to have heard our volley of shots. Any attempt at stealth forgotten, I ran through the open doorway into the short corridor. To the left it was dark and empty. I moved ten feet right and hugged the wall.

The machinegun rounds whiz-cracked by me on their way down the cavernous main hall. Eight-to-ten round bursts, the guy making no attempt to conserve ammo, shooting to keep the rest of our group pinned down. With additional full-auto rifle and subgun fire creating a near-physical wall of noise. I guessed we couldn't be more than thirty feet from the guns' position, but I was loathe to stick my head out into the line of fire. Too bad Bob hadn't thought to bring along any grenades. Directly across from us was the mansion's main staircase. Majestic ten-foot-wide steps made of marble and figured granite rose up out of sight, mostly covered by a blood-red carpet runner that looked Persian in design.

We'd advanced far enough forward that I couldn't see back down the main hall to the circular staircase, not without physically moving into the hallway. I jumped to the opposite wall of my little alcove and edged forward. The full-auto fire had fallen off to only occasional short bursts from what sounded like a single weapon. I also heard shouts. None of the rounds were aimed my way, so I raised my rifle, gritted my teeth, and leaned out as soon as the last burst flew down the hall.

Two guys were hunched over the belt-fed, a SAW, its top cover open as they hurriedly tried to reload it. Which meant they'd burned through an entire 200-round belt trying to keep us pinned down. The floor was covered in spent brass and belt links. Two more guys were behind them with rifles in their hands, staring far down the hall past me. I fired two rounds at the machinegunner, too quickly. Both missed. He jerked as the rounds tugged at his hair, turned my way, and started to hunker into the gun to loose a burst my way when I nailed him with my third shot. The bullet hit him in the shoulder and he rolled away from the SAW, screaming.

The other man by the SAW stopped working and rolled away as I twisted and fired at one of the riflemen hugging the wall behind him. Another guard dove and landed beside the belt-fed, its top cover now closed, scrambling to find its trigger. I pivoted fractionally and tried to find him with my Aimpoint before he got the MG back into play, before the men past him could raise their rifles...

"Grenade!" Steve screamed. I jerked back and saw a man standing on the main staircase, a dark object bouncing across the hall toward us. Without thinking I kicked at it. The side of my foot connected with the heavy grenade and immediately went numb, but the grenade went bouncing lazily away from me, angling into the main hallway toward the belt-fed. I pulled back around the corner and the world shook as the grenade exploded. There was a flash and an overpressure wave that was followed by a cloud of grit. I stumbled backward and looked up, only to see another grenade rolling my way across the hall. Steve grabbed me by the collar with his wounded hand and threw me back through the doorway into the dining room. He landed on top of me just as the second grenade went off.

My brain turned to static as the concussion physically lifted me off the carpet. Smoke billowed in through the doorway and I could hear marble chunks bouncing off walls nearby. Coughing, Steve rolled off me and struggled to his feet, his hair covered with white dust. My brain felt like it was about to short out. Strange spots of color floated before my eyes.

I'd barely lifted my head off the floor when I heard a metallic clank and saw another grenade bounce past the dining room's shattered doorframe.

"Fuck!" I bellyflopped onto my face, covering my head, as the third grenade exploded. The wall between the dining room and the access hall ruptured with a flash. Big chunks of plaster rained down on us and I heard shrapnel zinging around the room.

I had no feeling left in any of my limbs but somehow was able to roll over onto my left elbow. So much dust was swirling around I could barely see anything. Steve was on his face beside me, covered in white plaster dust, not moving.

A figure appeared in the fractured doorway, perhaps the

grenade tosser, and he squinted into the dark dining room. I looked around frantically for my rifle but it was nowhere to be found. Just as the man spotted me on the floor, and raised the subgun he held in his hands, Jerry appeared at my side, screaming and firing his shotgun. The surprised defender went down under a fusillade of double-ought buckshot without firing a shot.

I was trying to get off the floor but was having a hard time because my right arm wasn't working. Jerry stopped shooting the guard just as I reached my feet, and he saw Steve lying on the floor facedown. "*Motherfuckers!*", he yelled, and charged toward the main hallway. Wild gunfire echoed off the walls.

I found my rifle half-buried under rubble. I had to grab it with my left hand as my right was still totally numb. So was my right foot, which I'd used to kick the grenade. Rapid staccato semi-auto shots rolled around the mansion, punctuated by shouts. I grabbed Steve by the shoulder and rolled him over. He was breathing, but unconscious.

The second grenade had exploded in the middle of the main hall. Two chandeliers had been destroyed, leaving the area dark. There were big divots in the walls and floor, and I couldn't even find the door that'd separated the dining room from the access hallway.

I laid my rifle on Steve's chest. With my good hand I grabbed him by his webgear and dragged him through the dust and debris toward the main hall. Stopping a few feet back, I laid Steve down and poked my head around the corner. Jerry was standing in front of the mansion's main door, firing his pistol down the narrow stairwell, emptying the magazine as fast as he could pull the trigger. At least four bodies lay crumpled around the SAW, which appeared to be soaking in spreading pools of blood. It looked like the

Splashback

grenade I'd kicked had gone off just a few feet from their position. Two other bodies lay crumpled against the walls, huge shotgun wounds in their chests. Grabbing my rifle off Steve's chest I stepped into the hall and started toward Jerry. My right arm bounced awkwardly and my right foot flopped as I jogged spasmodically toward him. A burning ache began to materialize behind my bicep. I started to suspect my arm was broken.

Jerry ran his Colt dry and looked my way as he fished out a fresh magazine for it. Bits of plaster and wood were tangled in Jerry's hair. His face was splashed with blood, not his own, and his eyes were tiny dark circles surrounded by oceans of white. "Come on!" he roared, staring past me. I looked behind me and saw the rest of our group step out at the far end of the hall.

"Let's go, let's go!" I yelled, waving my rifle for them to hurry up. Our end of the building, at least for the moment, was free of adversaries, and I wanted to take the opportunity to get the hell out.

Jerry was sweaty and panting, his hands shaking as he pointed his reloaded pistol down the steep staircase beside the front door. A body lay on the steps, face down, but I didn't see anybody moving below.

"How many of them are down there?" I asked him, yelling as I was partially deaf. I aimed my rifle awkwardly down the steps with my left hand.

"Fuck if I know," he yelled back, his hearing just as destroyed, and fired three quick rounds down the stairs to make whoever was in the basement want to stay there. He looked at his M4 in my hands, then at the pistol in his. He stuck the Colt back in its holster and hurriedly began reloading his empty shotgun. "Cover me!" he shouted.

I glanced over my shoulder briefly just to make sure the

pounding steps I heard approaching belonged to our group, then pointed to the side hall with my rifle. "Somebody get Steve!" I told them, and went back to covering the stairs. Nobody was getting left behind. When Jerry got his Remington gassed up I pointed him at the stairs and turned to look at the rest of them.

Ron was on one knee behind the remains of an expensive love seat, covering the main hall to our rear, nervously glancing over his shoulder at us. There was a grunt from somewhere, then George stepped into view, Steve draped over his shoulder in a fireman's carry. He jogged toward me, the Uzi in his free hand.

"You okay?" he asked me. Both Steve and I looked like zombies, covered in blood and dust and pieces of the building. Jerry was bloody as a horror movie. George glanced at my strangely hanging arm.

Ron's shotgun boomed. "We're gonna have company!" he yelled. He stood and began backing toward us. "Circling around to the side, like you did!" There was a burst of full-auto fire from somewhere and I could hear the rounds thudding into the walls all around us. I couldn't see the shooter.

"Where is he?" Ron shouted. "Anybody see him?" He fired two shots down the middle of the main hallway just to keep them honest.

"Somebody open that fucking door!" I yelled, jerking my head at the big front door. A drop of blood flew from my nose.

"John?" George asked worriedly.

I looked at him with what I'm sure were crazy eyes. "I kicked a grenade!" I shouted into his face. "And I think my arm's broken. How's your day been?"

4:04 a.m.

Jerry undid the big sliding dead-bolt on the ancient door and pried it open. It was a good five inches thick and swung open slowly. We crouched in the hallway, but no rounds whipped through the doorway.

I saw movement at the far end of the hall, near the stairs we'd come up, and stepped forward. I pulled the M4 awkwardly up to my cheek with my left hand and fired half a dozen poorly aimed shots past Ron's shoulder. Ron went back down onto one knee and sighted down the Mossberg, waiting for a target.

"Let's go!" Jerry and George charged outside. I grabbed Ron and we moved toward the door, Ron covering the hall and stairway as we backed up. I caught a glimpse of something in the side hall and Ron swung the Mossberg that way, firing twice.

I stumbled backward through the doorway and let go of Ron's collar. "Come on!" I yelled at him.

Ron emptied his shotgun as fast as he could work the pump, firing indiscriminately at anything and everything, hoping to discourage anyone from pursuing us. When the Mossberg was dry he jumped backward through the doorway, grabbed the big brass knocker on the door, and pulled it closed after us. It thunked solidly into its wooden frame.

We turned from the house, not sure what to expect. The air was cool, stars just visible above our heads. Our group was spread in a ragged semicircle, staring out into the darkness. No gunfire broke the stillness, no yells or shouts disturbed the night. All I could hear was my harsh panting.

"No way," Jerry said, staring around wildly. His voice sounded weird. Ron furiously began shoving shells into his scattergun.

The garage stood fifty feet away across the fountain and

the driveway circle, all of its doors open. I saw the front end of one white van at the far end of the long building, but no sign of the others. To our left, the blacktop driveway slid away toward the front gate, empty of people or vehicles. The brown yard stretched away in all directions, flat and featureless. We were the only people in sight. No yelling, no shooting, no van engines turning over, nothing. Just the cool night air ruffling the hair on my forehead, one small cloud scudding across the sky. An owl hooted.

"Let's get the fuck out of here," Ron said, shoving fresh shells into his shotgun.

Our group ran madly down the drive toward the front gate. Jerry and I soon fell from the pack, him limping badly, gasping like a fish out of water, and between my useless arm and numb foot I wasn't much better. George dropped back and started helping Jerry with one massive arm around his chest. Steve still hung limply over his shoulder but George moved like he weighed nothing at all. I stopped and slung the M4 over my shoulder, then cradled my right arm in my left. I found I could move a lot faster if I kept my arm pinned against my side. My foot started to not be so numb, and that was bad.

At any moment I expected a hail of bullets to rend me in two. The guards still left alive would get another belt-fed up onto the roof and slay us all as we ran down the driveway. Some enterprising individual would hop into the van I'd seen and run us all over.

Somehow, we remained untouched.

As I lurched up the driveway toward the road and the promise of another dawn, the popping sound of a pistol echoed in the distance. A short, full-auto burst from something loud, probably a rifle from the sound of it, answered quickly.

"Shit, shit," I heard Ron say, and he put on a burst of speed. We were still too far from the gate and couldn't see anything.

More hollow pops, definitely from a pistol, reverberated in the cool night air. Two quick bursts, much louder, from the unseen rifle. Ron was in full sprint now, the shotgun at port arms, heading right for the gate. The rest of us tried to keep up.

"Bob," I said, finally remembering the radio. "Bob, you there? Bob!" I noticed the gate was open. I was a hundred yards out, breathing hard through clenched teeth, when I saw that the gate hadn't rolled open. A fleeing van had hit it dead center, buckling the wrought iron and tossing it into the middle of the road. The white rear of the van stuck out of the far ditch, the vehicle lying on its side.

"Bob, we're coming out," I panted into my radio. No response. God only knew if it still worked. "Bob, heads up, what's your status? Bob?"

We were fifty yards away from the road, and I looked over my shoulder as I painfully hobbled along. My arm was really starting to ache, and it felt like I was stepping on a nail every time I put my foot on the ground. Every jarring step sent a spike of pain through the entire right side of my body.

No vehicles were bearing down on us from the house, no people in sight, no tracers flicking out at us from the rooftop. I couldn't seem to get enough air, and as hard as I was working, I could barely keep up with George, who was carrying Steve and nearly carrying Jerry, who was fading fast and looking lost. Ron was nearly to where the gate had been and he finally got some sense and slowed down. His shotgun came up and he slid left, into the shadow of the perimeter wall.

A hoarse, scratching pant filled my ears. "Clear," I heard Bob gasp. The relief I felt upon hearing his voice was almost erased because of how horrible he sounded.

Ron heard Bob's voice in his radio headset and it calmed him down enough to get him thinking. He waited in the shadows as the rest of our pitiful group staggered onward. George, with his burdens, hung back and let me get ahead of him. I swung wide, across the blacktop lane, to get a better angle on the street, swaying on my feet.

Bob came into view, hunched over but on his own two feet. They were planted on the double yellow in the center of the road. He'd pulled his balaclava off and wasn't looking in our direction but rather east, down the road to our left. The wall blocked my view of whatever he was looking at. The stock of a rifle—not his MP5—was tucked into his shoulder, muzzle angled downward. "Then again…" I heard Bob in my ear, so hoarse he was almost whispering.

At first my eyes couldn't decipher the information they were receiving in the feeble illumination of the streetlight towering above Bob. There were piles of laundry scattered all around him, and he was standing behind an entertainment cabinet someone had abandoned in the street. The piles of laundry soon resolved themselves to be bodies, and what first looked like a glass-fronted cabinet turned out to be the windshield of one of the white vans, on its side in the middle of the road. As I got closer I saw the gatehouse was now in a ruin, the back end of another van sprouting from its crumpled bricks. Beyond that a car came into view, in the middle of the street, a sedan with two doors hanging open. Most of the windshield on the driver's side had been shot out. Bodies lay in and around the car, one hanging upside down halfway out the rear driver's side door, a pistol still in his hands. Spent brass littered the blacktop like popcorn on a movie theater floor.

The brick wall was less than twenty yards away. Bob turned toward the sound of our running feet just as Jerry called his name. He peered into the darkness outside the reach of the lone streetlight. As he squinted in our direction his face became mottled, and I heard a sound I couldn't identify.

Weird colors ran around his face and body, and for a brief second I thought the grenade had given me a concussion, then I heard the sound again and Bob turned slowly to look down the road once more. The weird light was everywhere, on the trees and the side of the ditched van and the shiny black asphalt of the road. I passed the spot where the gate used to be and finally I was out, away from the charnel house that had been Wellesley-Grange.

"...put down your weapon and put your hands above your head!" I heard the frightened young voice half yelling, half pleading over the PA as I passed the estate wall. Bob was staring at a police cruiser slung diagonally across the road, still rocking from its skidding stop, its rollers going and spotlight on. Bob didn't act worried, but I couldn't help but notice he was using the engine compartment of the overturned van as cover just in case. "Put your weapon down NOW or I'm gonna—Oh **FUCK!**" the cop exclaimed involuntarily as he saw Ron, Jerry, George, and I. I couldn't see the officer, but I knew he'd be crouched down behind the open driver's door of his car, gun out. With our dark raid clothing and painted faces he hadn't seen us until we'd moved into the pool of light below the old-fashioned streetlamp.

Everyone else stopped at the end of the driveway and looked at the cop car, then at Bob. I waved frantically at them to Go, *GO!*, then walked painfully toward Bob. Bob began backing up toward me, keeping the van between himself and the cop, who had no plans to come out from behind his cruiser door. There was a large pool of oil at the corner of the van where Bob had been standing.

"I've called for backup! Other units are on their way here right now. Nobody move or I'll fucking shoot all of you. Put your guns down and put your hands up!" The cop was back on the PA, and sounded all of twenty years old. Out of the corner of my eye I saw the boys spread out across the road. Nobody shouldered a weapon, but none of them exactly looked relaxed, either. Ron peered up the driveway at the house worriedly.

The closer I got to him, the worse Bob looked. He was weaving as much as walking, and breathing rapidly. The hair at his temples and the back of his neck was soaked, and the sweat had painted streaks in his blackface. His nostrils were flaring as he tried to control his pain. "Bob," I spoke to him, not even sure he could hear me. "Time to go."

"We complete the mission?" he said distantly, nearly croaking, still backing up, not taking his eyes off the cop car.

Bob could've just let the vans drive off, but he couldn't take the chance George was inside one of them, and so he'd had to deal with everyone who hadn't wanted to take us on inside the mansion. I looked around. Half a dozen bodies littered the asphalt from one side of the road to the other, and I saw several more in the ditch by the van. The one closest to me had fallen face-down, half on top of his M4. The man had been using the sedan as cover, and empty cases from his rifle were strewn across the trunk of the car. Pools of blood glittered blackly in the streetlight; guns, spent magazines, and empty cases were everywhere. I counted at least three empty MP5 magazines lying on the pavement, and wondered how close Bob had been to running out of ammo before he'd grabbed the M4 now in his hands. The MP5 was slung across his back. In the crisp night air the gunfire would have echoed over and around the rolling hills and sounded like a small war, which I guess, in a way, was exactly what it had been.

"Yes," I told him. "We've got George. He's alive. Time to go." Bob panted shallowly a few times, still shuffling backward, then slowly turned his head to look at me. Under the paint he was pale as a ghost, deep circles under his eyes.

"Good," he panted. "I'm about whipped."

I turned and looked toward the cop car. It was out of sight beyond the wrecked van, but between its spotlight, the alternating headlights, and the flashing reds and blues on the roof, we might as well have been naked for all the good the black clothes and facepaint did.

"We're leaving now," I yelled to the cop. With a hand on his shoulder I turned Bob around and we began to limp away from the scene. We stepped over and around bodies, being careful not to slip on the blood-slick asphalt. No sound came from the cruiser's PA, but I thought I heard a faint voice. I realized a few seconds later it had to be the cop on his radio, calling for backup.

George was standing impassively next to the gatehouse, Steve still over his shoulder. The rest of the guys were strung out across the road in an uneven line. I waved at them to go, and they hesitantly started drifting down the road. The sound of big V8's being pushed to their limits drifted over the trees toward us. More cops.

"They're coming out of the house," Ron announced ominously, peering up the dark driveway. "I've got five, shit, maybe seven guys? Heading this way. We gotta go." He waved quickly at us to get moving.

"Can you move any faster?" I asked Bob. I didn't know how he was still conscious, much less functioning, but we didn't have a lot of time. The Suburban was only a quarter mile or so away, but the engines I was hearing were a lot closer. The only consolation I had was that they seemed to coming from the far side of the cruiser that had already arrived, so at least we weren't running toward them.

In response Bob broke into a halting trot and we started down the dark road after the boys. I pinned my bad arm to my side and moved as fast as I could, passing Ron who waited for us to stagger by before moving. I looked back as I passed the gatehouse and saw the squad car's door was closed, but the vehicle stayed in place. I doubted he'd come after us, unless he was willing to drive over bodies. Between the sedan abandoned in the middle of the street, the two vans, and the bodies, there wasn't a clear piece of pavement more than three feet across. Not enough for a car, and it appeared he didn't want to take after us on foot. Smart man.

Bob and I followed the pack into the darkness, moving along as fast as we could, and Ron kept an even distance behind us, walking backward. They were spread out, jogging along either shoulder. Actually, jogging was too generous a term; what we were doing was stumbling and shuffling. If the Suburban had been any farther away I don't know if we'd have all made it. The moon ducked behind a cloud, and I really had to look where I was going to keep from falling into the ditch. As black as the road was, the blacktop was still shinier than the gravel shoulder, and I used that as my reference.

We rounded the gentle curve and the gatehouse dropped from sight. Another hundred and fifty, two hundred yards and the Suburban would be on the left, pulled off into the bushes at a wide spot we'd noticed the day before.

I felt myself fading fast. "You gonna make it, you pussy?" I shot at Bob as he staggered along doing what could only be called a shuffle-gasp. His panting was wet and syrupy. It felt like someone was jabbing my foot with a red-hot knife blade every time I put weight on it, and the pain ran in waves up and down my body. It felt like someone was trying to set me on fire, and having occasional success.

"Or die trying, old man," he spat between clenched teeth, his eyes focused ahead of him at something only he could see. Long dark strings hung from his lips.

The Suburban was running by the time I reached it. I threw my M4 inside and roughly shoved Jerry out of the driver's seat. He clambered into the back next to Steve, who was awake and looking around in confusion. Bob painfully maneuvered into the back seat as I rolled down the rear window. Ron showed up half a second later. He tossed his shotgun in then dived headfirst over the tailgate. George climbed into the passenger seat beside me and I slammed the Chevy into reverse with my left hand.

Once the front bumper cleared the bushes I slewed the truck around and awkwardly tossed it into Drive with my left hand. I pressed my nose against the windshield glass and floored the truck with my broken foot. Staggering down the dark road had been tough enough. Flying down it at sixty miles an hour without headlights or a moon was an entirely different experience. George reached over and rolled up the back window to cut the wind.

"You got an escape route planned out?" George asked me, arms braced against the dashboard.

The road in front of us exploded in light and sound as a police car with its lights and siren going careened around a curve a quarter mile ahead. He must have been doing a hundred miles an hour as he flew by us. A second later I heard the squeal as his brakes locked up when he realized what he'd just passed on the road. White smoke from his tires began fuzzing his brake lights in my rearview mirror as I hurtled around the curve.

"Shit. I knew there was something we forgot." I flipped on my lights, switched to my brights, and tried not to roll the truck as I took the sharp curves at double the speed limit. I heard the curses behind me and exclamations of pain as they were tossed against the sides of the truck. Maybe trying to outrun the police while driving with only one arm wasn't the best idea I've ever had, but I couldn't exactly pull over and let someone else take the wheel.

"This thing's got great pickup, but it corners like a pregnant cow!" I yelled to them. Flashing lights appeared behind me and caught up far too quickly for comfort. Between the siren and our racing engine and the wind whistling around the windows I could barely hear myself think.

"Roll down the back window!" Ron yelled. I saw the outline of a long gun against the rear glass.

"Put that fucking thing down!" I yelled back. "Nobody's shooting at any cops!"

"I was gonna go after the tires," he yelled back, sounding like I'd hurt his feelings.

"Yeah, right," I mumbled. At the speed we were going, a blowout would kill that cop just as neatly as shooting him.

We hit a straightaway and I floored it. The Suburban had a hell of a lot of horsepower, but it was also carrying over eleven hundred pounds of people. Plus gear. The cruiser had no trouble staying right on my ass, lights and siren going, spotlight illuminating the inside of our car as well as it could through the tinted back window. I tapped my brakes and he backed off about ten feet, but there was no way I was going to outrun or outmaneuver him.

"Why were you grabbed, anyway?" I asked George.

"What?" he said.

"Why were you fucking grabbed, Dad?" Ron yelled from the back.

George looked back and forth between us, blinking in disbelief. "What? The shit that just happened, and you don't know? You're kidding me, right?" He saw my expression. "You're not? Then how'd you find me? Why'd you come after me?"

"Because you were fucking kidnapped!" I snapped.

"This isn't getting us anywhere," George said disgustedly. He was turned in his seat, looking out the back window.

"I'm open to suggestions," I told him as I began slewing the Suburban through a series of S curves. Expletives erupted from the back of the truck as they bounced off the walls, and I nearly rolled the thing twice. The cruiser backed off my rear as I came out of the last curve, falling back about a hundred feet. I soon found out why. You can't outrun a radio.

The road did a long, slow curve to the left into a tiny valley. Trees lined the shoulders on either side of the road, covering gentle slopes that stretched upward fifty feet or more. The six police cars blocking the road ahead had all their lights going and lit up the trees nicely. Reminded me a little of Christmas.

I stomped on the brakes and skidded to a stop fifty feet from the closest cruiser. The cop behind me slowed down and pulled his car across both lanes about a hundred feet from my back bumper. I'd be able to ram him out of the way, but then where would I go? There might be a two-track or dirt road somewhere behind me that'd get me out, but I didn't know where it was and wouldn't be given the opportunity to find it, either.

In front of us the officers were hunched down behind their cars, shotguns and pistols pointed in our direction. Somebody got on a loudspeaker and began ordering us around. Put down your weapons, place your hands on the dashboard in front of you, blah, blah, blah. I stared at the flashing lights, mind blank.

"With a little luck we could take them," Ron said. "Get one or two of us into the woods…"

"That is **NOT** an option," George told his son, jabbing a cucumber-sized finger at him.

"No, it's not," I affirmed. I wasn't exactly hot to get handcuffs thrown on me again, but I wouldn't stand for them shooting at cops. I could tell myself the guards at the estate were on the wrong team, but there was no way I could let them start shooting at uniformed police officers who were just trying to do their jobs. Even I couldn't rationalize that. Besides, most of our group required immediate medical attention. As I'd whipped the Suburban around the curves, I'd felt bone scraping against bone in my arm, orange and green sparklers going off in my head. I wasn't doing any more fighting.

"You want us to just give up?" Ron asked. I turned and looked back into the Suburban. Steve was slumped in the seat, technically conscious, but looking around like he didn't know where he was. Bob was arched over beside him, hyperventilating, the tendons in his neck twitching. Fresh blood was dripping off his chin, a lot of it. Jerry was hugging his chest, hunched over, wheezing wetly, eyes squeezed shut against the pain.

"We've got no choice," I said. "And you know it. We're done. It's time to pay the tab we've been working on all week."

The cop on the loudspeaker kept yelling for us to put our hands in sight, and for the driver to exit the vehicle.

"Don't touch your guns or make any sudden moves," I told them without turning around. I rolled down my window, shut off the truck, and slowly tossed the keys out the window.

"What's going to happen with you?" I asked George tiredly. "Somebody grabbed you for something, and we killed a lot of fucking people to find you and get you out."

"I have no idea," he said. "Depends on what's happened since I've been gone."

"Swell." I leaned my head out the window. "I'm coming out!" I told the assembled multitudes. "We've got serious wounded, you're gonna need some ambulances! And my right arm is broken, I can't raise it."

The cop on the PA started giving me directions. He had me stick my left arm out the window and open the door using the outside handle. I slowly stepped out, and put my left hand on my head.

"See you when I see you," I told them through the open door. I carefully turned around and, at the direction of the officer, began backing up toward the cop cars in a clumsy step-hop. After about a dozen steps they had me kneel down. I barely managed to do it without falling over.

"Nobody says a fucking word," I heard George tell the rest of them. "Not to the locals. I've got some calls to make, if it's not too late. What day is it, anyway?"

I heard a sound I couldn't identify from inside the Suburban. "Bob?" I heard Jerry say weakly. "Bob?" The cop on the PA behind me was giving me some more directions but I all I could hear was the fear in Jerry's voice. There was a pause of a few seconds, and then the Suburban rocked violently.

"Shit! He doesn't have a pulse. Get him out, grab him!"

The officer on the PA realized something else was going on as well. "Stay in the vehicle!" he warned in a commanding voice, as the passenger side door of the Suburban flew open. "Make no sudden moves!" He didn't sound so sure of himself anymore.

His injuries forgotten with a new surge of adrenaline, I watched Jerry wrestle Bob's limp body out of the open door and lay him on the pavement. He began tearing at Bob's webgear as the cop on the PA began to freak out and I could sense the other police officers not too far behind me get nervous.

"DO NOT MOVE!" the PA user nearly screamed at Jerry. Jerry screamed back at him.

"Man down!" Jerry yelled at them, and me. He tore like a man possessed at Bob's clothes. He finally got Bob's gear out of the way and ripped open his BDU shirt. He immediately started doing CPR. And then Jerry did something. I don't know if it was because he'd watched too many war movies or had a sudden inspiration, but it was genius. Maybe the only word in the English language he could have said to change the dynamic.

He screamed out, "Corpsman! We need a corpsman over here!"

There were enough cops present that I was willing to bet at least one of them was a Marine Corps veteran, and if there was a single word in the English language that struck a deeper chord with them than *Corpsman!*, their version of "Medic!" I didn't know what it was. I turned my head and looked back over my shoulder. They were close, a lot closer than I thought they'd be, and in spite of the flashing lights and spots I was able to see some faces. At least one of them showed what could be doubt, or confusion.

"***Corpsman!***" Jerry screamed again, nearly sobbing, still frantically working over Bob. Even in the poor light I could see his hands were covered with blood. George slowly stepped down out of the Suburban and knelt next to Bob. His big hands took over on Bob's chest and Jerry slid up and began trying to breathe life back into his friend. "Suck it up, soldier!" he yelled into Bob's slack face between breaths. "Don't you fucking die on me!"

"Goddammit!" I yelled at the cops I could see, none of whom had yet moved. I could feel the tears streaming down my cheeks. "Do we look like gangbangers or Taliban to you? This was a rescue mission. Either shoot us or help us, but someone make a fucking decision!"

Epilogue

I can't say I was treated badly. Once they transferred me from the jail cell to the safehouse it was almost like I was staying at a nice Bed and Breakfast. Except I couldn't leave, and my door was locked at night.

I was driven away from the Suburban alone in the back of a squad car. They took me to the stationhouse lockup first, in handcuffs, until they realized that I really did have a broken arm. I think it was the screaming when they pulled me from the car by my arms that convinced them. Four heavily armed officers escorted me to the hospital where I was X-rayed and examined in record time. Because it was my upper arm that was broken they couldn't use a traditional cast, and for almost two weeks I'd had my arm strapped to my body like a bad joke. The cast on my foot was more traditional. All the gunfire had ruptured my left eardrum, for the second time. I hoped it was the last.

I only spent six hours in the jail cell. Then the frowning men arrived, dressed in rumpled suits and looking harried. Alone, I was taken by windowless van to a medium size, two-story colonial. The van pulled into the garage and I wasn't taken out until the outer door closed, so I had no idea where I was. Somewhere within an hour's drive of Columbia. Nothing to see out the ground floor windows of the house but half a dozen nearly identical houses.

My room was nice, if somewhat sparsely furnished. I had a bed, and a dresser, and a bathroom all to myself. My hosts brought in several sets of casual clothes for me to wear as all I had with me were my raid clothes. The small TV in the room was not wired for cable, and had no antenna, but there was an ancient VCR connected. I had my choice of any of a dozen comedies from the 1980s. The small library on the ground floor had a good selection of Ludlum and Stephen King.

Every day was the same for me. A knock on the door to wake me up. A long, one-handed shower and extended dressing period which involved sweatpants large enough to fit over the cast on my foot, which I had to wrap in a plastic bag in the shower. Then, downstairs to meet with my hosts for another eight- to twelve-hour Question & Answer session. The four of them lived in the house with me, and all of them sat in on what they liked to call my 'interviews.' I never asked them what agency they worked for, and they never volunteered the information. I figured it didn't really matter.

I didn't really need the knock on my door every morning. Usually I was awake by four a.m., drenched in sweat and shaking from the nightmares. I'd lie there for hours, staring blindly into the darkness, unable to relax, much less fall back asleep, mind and heart racing. I'm not sure if I ever cried out, so I don't think my hosts knew about the nightmares, but every once in a while during the interviews I'd suddenly come down with an uncontrollable case of the shakes. There was no way they could miss those. They'd wait until the tremors had passed, ask me if I'd like something to drink, then go on with the questioning like nothing had happened.

I had no idea what was happening with George or the boys. Where they were, what was happening to them. I assumed they were being questioned at length, as I was, but my captors wouldn't say. I had to threaten perpetual silence before they would even tell me what happened to Bob, if he was alive.

I began my tale at the phone call from Ron and detailed the entire episode, leaving nothing out. That alone took two days. Since then we'd gone over and over every single minute of my life since that fateful call, the four of them questioning and probing and burrowing for ever more information. I could tell they didn't believe my story at first. I could hardly believe it myself. But after a couple of days they stopped trying to get 'the truth' out of me and just listened to what I had to say.

Twelve days I'd been with them. I knew their first names: Robert, Phillip, Jim and Peter. Probably their real names, but who knew? Guys about my age, amazingly dogged in their single-minded pursuit of answers. They learned everything about me, while they gave me nothing. They were polite, but kept their distance. I got the impression that they were almost as much in the dark about certain things as I was. My guess was that they were mid-level intelligence analysts. From the way they worded several of their questions I gleaned that they had practically zero field experience.

No TV connection, which meant no TV news. No newspapers, no matter how much I begged. There was only one phone in the house that I knew of, and I couldn't get to it. Even the window in my room was fake, just curtains around a blank frame. I'm sure the house looked normal from the street, the window panes tinted so the neighbors couldn't see there was nothing but wall behind the glass. The only pleasant part of the whole experience was the food. One of them—I never knew which—was an excellent cook, and I ate like a king the entire time. I gained back all the weight I'd lost and more. My bruises faded, my scabs disappeared. A doctor came in, examined me, told me the reason I was having all the headaches was that I had a minor concussion. At some point I realized that I'd missed Christmas, but that fact didn't seem to register wholly on my brain.

On the thirteenth day of my captivity, I was awakened by the usual knock on my door. I showered slowly and clumsily, then one-handedly put on the freshly laundered clothes and headed downstairs. The four of them were sitting in the living room, as usual, two on the couch and two in chairs. The ever-present tape recorders sat on the table, the video camera was on its tripod, and each one of them had a thick sheaf of papers in front of him.

I sat in the chair of honor, a leather La-Z-Boy recliner, and tried to find a comfortable position for my arm. It was then I noticed the expressions on their faces.

"What?" I said. It was the first time I could remember them having expressions on their faces.

Peter squirmed a little on the couch. "We've got some news," he said slowly. "About your wife."

I froze for a second, then leaned forward. He pursed his lips, looked at Robert briefly, then back at me.

"She's in the hospital," he said. "Apparently she was involved in an automobile accident six days ago. We just found out about it."

When I still didn't speak he rubbed his chin and looked down at the papers in front of him.

"I told you this was a bad idea," Robert said.

"She's fine," Peter reassured me. "However, it appears, due to the accident, that…she lost the baby she was carrying." He finally got it all out, and sat back in the couch, relieved.

I sat in the chair and stared at them, blinking slowly, not saying anything. My silence apparently unnerved Phillip, for he bent down to his papers and began shuffling through them.

"Now," he said, getting back to a subject he was more comfortable with, "during the time you were being interrogated by these unknown operatives, did the drugs—"

"No," I said.

Phillip looked up. "What?"

"No more questions," I told them. "Not one. I'm done answering questions. You know it all already anyway."

Peter smiled warmly. "Mr. Phault—" he began.

"What day is it?" I demanded. "What day of the week?"

"Uh, Sunday," Jim said.

"You've got until nine a.m. Tuesday," I told them. "Talk to your supervisor, let him know. Figure out what the hell your plans are. But come nine o'clock Tuesday morning?" I pointed with my good arm in the direction of the front door. "If I'm not in a real jail that door better be unlocked. Because if it's not, you're going to have to kill me to keep me here." After interrogating me for nearly two weeks, I'm pretty sure they could tell I meant every word.

I stood up. "This interview is over," I said, and walked from the room, the rage-fueled adrenaline killing the pain in my foot more effectively than morphine.

Splashback

The first car arrived late the next afternoon. Through the shatterproof library window I saw it pull up to the curb in front of the house. Jerry got out of the back seat accompanied by two burly guys in polo shirts. He moved stiffly but looked healthy, if a bit uncertain about just what was going on. He wasn't the only one. My hosts had spent much of the last twenty-four hours arguing loudly, yelling at people on the phone, and running in and out of the house. Then, three hours before the first car pulled up to the curb, the house once again became quiet. The two guys walked Jerry up to the front door and rang the bell. When Phillip let them in I was in the front hall, waiting.

"John!" Jerry cried. He looked like he wanted to run up and hug me, but between our injuries and the roomful of strangers he was able to restrain himself. "So you're behind this."

"Behind what?"

"There's supposed to be some sort of big meeting."

"News to me," I said, glaring at Phillip. He went into the kitchen to talk with the two newly arrived guards.

Steve arrived next, about twenty minutes later, also escorted by two musclebound guys in plain suits. He was still limping, but otherwise didn't seem the worse for wear. The three of us commandeered the living room couch and quizzed each other. They'd had similar experiences to mine, penned up in some house or apartment somewhere, answering questions for days on end. Steve peeled off the bandage and showed us the stitches where his ring finger used to be attached to his hand.

"Guess I can't get married now," he said, trying to make a joke. None of us felt like laughing. "It's weird. I can still feel it, even though it's not there anymore." He stared at his hand. After a while he looked up at us and asked, "So what happened after I got knocked out? These pricks wouldn't tell me a fucking thing other than none of you died, and that you were cooperating. I wouldn't tell them shit until they showed me a video of you answering their questions," he nodded at me, "then I figured it was okay."

Jerry himself had been more than lucky. The bullet had gone in under his left arm, between two ribs, missed his heart, lungs, and every major blood vessel before exiting under his right arm.

"But it punched two holes in my plural, or whatever the hell the thing's called," he said.

"Pleura," I corrected him.

"What?"

"Pleura. It's the lining of your chest."

"Yeah, that's what I said," he went on, giving me a dirty look. "Anyway, since it had two holes in it it fucked up my lungs, and they were both partially collapsed. That's why I couldn't breathe for shit." When they'd peeled his vest off in the hospital the spent bullet had fallen into one of the nurse's hands. "And the bullet cracked a few ribs. I actually shouldn't be walking around, but I was damned if I was going to let them roll me up in a wheelchair." He looked at me. "What's Tramadol?"

"A painkiller. Why?"

"That's what they've got me on. It's not doing shit. Still hurts to breathe. Is it like Tylenol?"

"Not exactly."

Ron showed up a few minutes later as the sun was setting. He joined us in the living room while his two minders hung out in the kitchen with the rest of the muscle, eating all the leftovers.

"You talk to your dad?" I asked him. He shook his head.

"Haven't seen him since they drove him away in the

squad car," Ron said. He looked toward the kitchen doorway where we could hear all the hired help gossiping. "What's going on here?"

"Beats me," I said. "They don't need us all together to kill us, though, so that's a good sign. Anybody seen Bob?"

Nobody had, but Jerry had heard two nurses talking about someone he figured had to be Bob.

"Paramedics did CPR on him in the ambulance all the way back to the hospital," Jerry repeated what he'd heard. "His heart wouldn't keep going on its own. They finally figured out it was because he'd lost so much blood; his blood pressure was like twenty over two or something. That lung already had him fucked up, and then he had to fight everybody that ran away from us. He got beat to shit while we were inside trying to get past the belt-fed. I started asking questions about him but nobody would tell me a fucking thing."

"How you feeling?" Steve asked him.

Jerry shook his head and smiled ruefully. "It feels like I got hit by a car. Buncha cracked ribs, plus a bullet hole running from one side all the way out the other. They stitched up the entrance and exit wounds but the rest of it they're just gonna let heal up on its own. I had a drainage tube in me for a couple of days, that was weird." He made a face. "I still can't put my clothes on by myself."

"My guys were all running around like chickens with their heads cut off this morning," Ron said. "Anyone know what the big rush is?"

I told them about my wife. And child. They sat in silence for a few seconds, their faces going flat.

"They didn't cover the car windows on the way here," Ron said quietly. "I will be able to find the place again. They don't whack us all here in a couple minutes, trust me, you'll be leaving here tomorrow. Whether they want you to or not." He looked around at all the muscle in the house, and I could tell he was planning moves.

"I caught Peter Jennings by accident about four days after we got nabbed," Steve said. "We were still the lead story."

"They use our names?" I asked.

"No, no way. I'm just talking about the shootout. They're saying two or three domestic al-Qaida sleeper cells attacked a CIA language school."

"Al-Qaida," I said.

"Al-Qaida?" Ron said disbelievingly.

"Language school? What do you make of that?" Jerry asked me.

The front door opened and a huge black guy stepped into the house. He looked around, then went back outside to drag a wheelchair through the doorway.

"Grandpa Fucking Grinnand!" Jerry shouted, levering himself up off the couch. "I knew you were too stubborn to die!" He winced and put an arm around himself but the pain couldn't keep the smile off his face.

Bob held up a hand to stop Jerry from grabbing him. "Don't fucking touch me," he said bitterly, his voice weak and raspy. He sounded eighty. "About the only thing on me that doesn't hurt is my eyelids."

"As lovable as ever," Ron said with a grin, not put off in the least. I studied Bob carefully. After losing so much blood he was white as an albino. He was slumped, almost collapsed inside the wheelchair, and looked anything but healthy, but he was alive. That was all that mattered. As usual, his expression was unreadable. The beard was finally gone, and his head was shaved to stubble.

"What painkillers are you on?" I asked him.

"All of them," Bob told me.

With Bob's arrival there were so many stone-faced men in the house they couldn't all fit inside the kitchen. The crowd spilled out into the living room, but the five of us did our best to ignore them. While the boys talked amongst themselves, mostly comparing wounds, I studied the help. They seemed nervous, and I caught more than one of them checking his watch.

"You know, I had grenade shrapnel in my back," Steve said. "I never even knew it was there until they had me lay down so they could work on my hand. They were more worried about the concussion, but I haven't even had a headache. They can't figure that out."

"They found two nine-millimeters in my vest," I felt obliged to chime in. "I don't remember them hitting me. Sure felt the bruises the next day, though. It felt like they cracked ribs, but all the x-rays came back negative."

"Your ear looks better," Jerry said to Ron. Rows of black stitches encircled his ear like ants on the march.

"They pulled it apart, cleaned out all the pus and restitched it. I'm on about a zillion milligrams of Zithromax a day." He peered at Bob's eyebrow, which had also been professionally restitched, and nodded. Then he looked at the rest of us. "At least I wasn't the only one who caught rounds this time."

"You got off easy," Steve told him. "Your face was already ugly. I'll trade your ear for my finger."

They were talking loud and fast and brave because they were scared. Nobody knew what the hell was going on, and I couldn't give them any reassurances. Bob and I stayed quiet. We slouched next to each other, him in his wheelchair, me on the couch, and watched all the hired help. They were checking their watches ever more frequently, and conversations were starting to fade. When the knock on the front door came they all immediately fell silent.

Jim opened the door and two clean cut white guys in dark suits entered the house. They looked around silently, at the five of us sitting down, at all the muscle standing around eating, and then one of them moved back to the door and gave a little wave.

A minute later I heard a faint mechanical rumbling hum that lasted five or so seconds and it took me a second to place it. About ten seconds later the hum came again, and that confirmed in my mind it had been the overhead garage door on the house's attached two-car garage. I heard car doors close, then a door into the house open. There were murmurs, and the scrape of shoes on linoleum, then four men walked through the doorway of the kitchen into the room where we sat. All the help moved aside for them. Two of the visitors were in their forties, another bodyguard type and a guy that looked like a harried accountant. The other two were older, one of whom I recognized from TV. And newspapers. And magazines. And…everything.

"Holy shit," I heard Jerry mutter. One of the dark suits motioned that we should stay in our seats.

"Is that—?" Steve began, looking frantically back and forth at all of us, then fell silent and began shaking his head.

"Jesus, what the fuck did we get into?" Ron asked incredulously. He stared openmouthed at our visitors.

The guy I recognized looked around the house and frowned at all the muscle spilling out of the kitchen. While taking off his coat he bent to the bodyguard and spoke quietly to him.

"Everybody out," the suit said, waving at all the guards. They filed out the front door, talking quietly, nobody protesting or even apparently upset at being asked to leave. My four questioners left as well.

The three dark suits spread themselves around the room, standing silently in the corners. The accountant-looking guy, who I figured was an aide, moved the La-Z-Boy so that it was across from and facing all of us. He had a thick stack of papers under his arm, and kept almost dropping them. After he'd moved the chair, the aide slid the coffee table up to the La-Z-Boy and placed the stack of papers on it.

"Gentlemen," the guy I recognized said to us by way of greeting. He settled into the La-Z-Boy with a sigh. The aide stood on one side of the chair, and the older man stood on the opposite side. The man in the chair bent to the stack of papers and began flipping rapidly through them, skimming.

The past two weeks of my life seemed so much like a dream to me that seeing this famous man, someone I'd only known from TV and newspapers, sitting in a La-Z-Boy recliner not ten feet from me, hardly raised my pulse rate. He seemed just one more unbelievable facet of a story I myself was finding harder and harder to believe as the days passed.

"Where's my father?" Ron demanded. The man in the chair raised one eyebrow, and tilted his head to look up at the sixtyish man standing beside his chair. It might have been my imagination, but I thought I saw a hint of amusement on his face.

The sixtyish man standing beside the chair had blindingly white hair, receding slightly, cut in a perfect flattop. He huffed through his nose, then shook his head. "He's in Syria," he told us, "trying to clean up this mess." His voice was gruff, his speech clipped.

"What the hell was this all about, anyway?" I asked.

The man in the chair looked at me. "You know, when George Kelly told us that you pulled him out of Wellesley-Grange without ever knowing why he was taken, I just plain didn't believe him. None of us did. Of course, when I told him what you had to do just to find him, much less get him out, he didn't believe me. So I guess we were even."

"Will you tell us?" Bob asked quietly.

"Sarin and half a dozen other nerve agents. Anthrax. Ricin. Yellowcake uranium. A few other things too sensitive to go into here." He sighed. "Pretty much Saddam Hussein's entire inventory of weapons of mass destruction. The assistant to the DDO—that's Deputy Director of Operations, CIA—saw an opportunity with the war brewing, reached out to Saddam, and arranged to secretly transport it all to Syria. Using United States assets. Without our knowledge. For a hefty shipping and storage fee. We're still not exactly sure how much he's been paid, or been promised, but we believe it's over a billion dollars. That's with a 'B'. Your father found out about it."

"Holy crap," Jerry said.

"Why didn't he just kill George?" I asked.

"Stupidity and sentimentalism," Flattop said, leaning his arm on the back of the chair. "Mostly stupidity. Kelly saved his life in Saigon in seventy-two. Still has a scar. Hoped George would change his mind once he thought through just how much money he was being offered. That disk you had? It was a list of what materials were in which locations, plus a few access codes for certain facilities. Temporarily valuable, but after a certain point in time, it'd be useless. The ADDO planned to retire to a country where we couldn't touch him unless we wanted to start a war, and by then they'd have nerve gas or the makings of a hundred dirty bombs, compliments of him. Your father," he nodded toward Ron, "is busy tracking down the materiel."

"Why him?" Jerry asked.

Flattop told us, "Too many people already know about those storage sites, and Kelly spent a year and a half in Syria, he knows the country. He's coordinating the Delta teams."

George and I were going to have to sit down sometime and really talk. I realized I hardly knew the man. No wonder he'd barely blinked the second time we met, when he discovered his son and I torturing someone at his house.

I wasn't sure I wanted to hear the answer, but I had to ask the question. "So there were never any plans to kill George?"

The man paused before answering. "We're not sure. When the ADDO was unsuccessful in buying him off, he just snatched him and locked him up. Figured George would change his mind about the bribe, eventually, and if he didn't… We've been told that he would have been released about a week after you found him, after the ADDO was all done moving material around and had skipped the country. It might be true."

The five of us looked at each other, somehow unsurprised.

"Who are you?" I asked Flattop. I already knew who the guy sitting in the chair was, all of us did. It was the old guy with the ramrod stiff posture that had me puzzled.

"This is General William Alexander, Chief of Staff of the Army." The President of the United States, sitting relaxed in the La-Z-Boy, looked at Bob. "Catherine Alexander was his daughter."

The name meant nothing to me, but when I saw Bob jerk I realized that they were talking about his fiancée. Bob and the General stared at each other, neither of them speaking.

"Oh, man," Jerry said. He'd caught the connection immediately.

"You're her father?" Bob said. "*You're* her father?" He didn't seem to know how to react. His posture improved, but I suspected that under normal circumstances he'd have jerked to his feet, at attention, and begun and ended every response with a shouted "Sir, Yes Sir!".

I remembered Bob saying how his fiancée had been protective of her father's identity, unsure at first if Bob was really interested in her or sucking up to her father. Bob had figured he was just some mid-level paper pusher doing a stint in the Pentagon.

"Bill and I have known each other for over thirty years," the President said. "He's also friends with my father, been friends since before my father was President. When I heard about his daughter's death all I could think about was the day I went to her confirmation straight after a red eye flight. She was twelve years old, looked like a princess in that white dress. She asked me why my suit was so wrinkled, was I poor?" He smiled faintly. "She was so darn cute. Pigtails. And such a pistol." His eyes roamed around the room, finally settling on one of the ugly paintings. "Funeral was the twenty-first. Closed casket, of course, no media allowed."

Bob lowered his head and I could see his jaw muscles spring into focus. The General stared at a wall, blinking rapidly.

The President began to sort through the papers in front of him again, clearing his throat. "Did you ever find out who, specifically, put the grenade in the car?" he asked lightly, still shuffling papers.

"No," I said. "One of the flunkies, that I may or may not have ended up killing. Probably never know for sure. But I know who ordered it. Met him once."

"This the person?" He turned the paperwork around and slid it across the table. I found myself looking at an outdated photo of Sundance.

"Yeah."

He pulled the file back and looked it over. "Russell Mulcahy, a workgroup supervisor. George Kelly's supervisor."

"Was he in on it?"

We got a nod in response. "He was going to get a nice big hefty percentage. All he had to do was follow the ADDO's orders, which were to snag Kelly, keep an eye on the local investigation into his disappearance, and make sure everything was under control, and he'd earn seven figures. Maybe eight."

"The man wasn't up to the job," the General said with disapproval. "He wanted to kill Kelly, just to be on the safe side, but the ADDO didn't want that, and he was the money man. When Mulcahy found out that you had the disk," he said to me, "he panicked. Saw all his millions floating away. He figured this was going to be the only shot he'd ever have of making the big time, and threw everything he had east of the Rockies at you, even though the ADDO had told him to keep a low profile. Kept telling him, but apparently Mulcahy had selective hearing. They kept going back and forth about you gentlemen, which is why your opposition's behavior was so bi-polar, if you will, trying to kidnap you," he said to me, "and kill you," he finished, nodding at Bob.

"The first thing they did was try to kill me," I corrected him. "While I was out jogging."

The General shook his head. "They never tried to kill you," he said to me. "They only ever tried to kidnap you, find out what you know, and recover that disk."

I frowned. "That's not right. What makes you think that?"

"Emails. Transcripts of captured phone calls." He paused. "Enhanced interrogations."

My frown grew deeper. What he was saying wasn't true. How could it be? Those three guys who'd tried to grab me while I was out running—I jerked back in my chair. The thought had triggered a memory, something somebody had said while I was a prisoner. Johnson, the guy who'd had the OC in the elevator, while I was tied up someone else brought up the idea of maybe trying to snatch Bob instead of kill him, and Johnson'd said that was what they'd tried with me the first time. With three guys. Which had to be when I was out jogging, it had been two guys in the car following me, and the third guy had gotten impatient and gone into my house.

But they hadn't tried grabbing me, they'd shot me. I could see it clearly, looking over my shoulder, seeing the car sliding to a quick stop, the passenger door flying open, someone cursing, and the flashing cough of the Ingram MAC-10 firing. The burn across my back from the hit, then I was falling down the slope.

But…that MAC-10 was a select-fire weapon, with an insanely high RPM on full-auto. If they'd been trying to kill me, wouldn't they have just hosed me down on full-auto? It'd been just one shot. And then they'd never tried to hose me down with the subgun while I was in the ditch, when I would have been an easy kill.

Jesus, had the sudden stop caused the guy with the Ingram to have a negligent discharge? Did he shoot me by *accident*? And then the third guy, losing patience, goes into my house and gets charged by Oscar, he shoots the dog in self-defense, and Kelly shot him?

"Jesus Christ," I swore, feeling all the blood leave my face. It all fit. The fact it had all been an accident somehow made it even worse. I looked at the General. "They screwed up the first snatch on me, then they went after Bob, and ended up killing your daughter. I don't even..."

"If those people that Mulcahy and the ADDO sent after us are the best the CIA has to offer," Bob said quietly, "this country's in serious trouble. I thought they were borderline incompetent before all this, but dear God, sir."

"You talk to Sundance? Mulcahy?" I asked.

"Killed last week in London," the President told us. "Mugging gone wrong, apparently. Stabbed several times. Police are investigating, but there don't appear to be any leads." He closed Mulcahy's file and tossed it contemptuously aside. "Hard as it might be for you to believe, he still had a few operators in the area that you didn't kill. From what they've told us, and what we've been hearing from you in your debriefings, we were able to connect all the dots."

"What about the ADDO, the guy who started all this shit?" I asked.

"He's assigned to desk duty at Langley, doing non-classified work."

"What?" Ron's forehead creased in confusion.

"The ironic thing is," the President said, "we can't touch him."

"It's not just the weapons, the uranium and nerve agents," the General said. "Although if word ever got out that Saddam's toys are outside his borders open to the highest bidder half the free world would shut down in a panic. It's the people involved."

The President sighed. "Saddam Hussein himself was on a first-name basis with this asshole. Who planned to double-cross Saddam and sell his stuff to whoever had the cash, did I mention that? The Russian President wasn't involved," he told us, "but several members of his administration were apparently avid capitalists and looking to buy some WMDs. Add to that list the President of Kazakhstan, over a dozen disillusioned former Red Army generals, half the Uzbekistani government, couple of African thug-kings...." The President waved his hand like it was a list he'd already grown tired of repeating. "The Russian Mafia had big dreams, and were bribing, blackmailing, or butchering anyone they had to to make them a reality. Those involved are going to be taken care of by their own governments, in ways I've been assured will not draw attention to them or to what almost happened. I expect to see a lot of early retirements, but then again we're talking about countries where problem people have a habit of just disappearing. We, however, have a more civilized history. Not to mention the fact that the ADDO has already promised to air a lot more dirty laundry than just that if we ever try to touch him. And you wouldn't believe the dirty laundry we've got."

"What about another mugging?" Jerry said. He'd made the same assumption about the stabby London death of Sundance I had.

The President shook his head. "There are other political considerations involved," he told us, "that I'm sure you would find Byzantine. He's scheduled to testify before the Senate Select Committee on Intelligence in two weeks. To spill his guts, more or less, after some of my less-than-esteemed friends in the Senate offered him immunity. Secret closed-door session." He shook his head. "Twenty-four hours after the ADDO testifies the New York Times is going to know more about this than I do, and print it all, damn the consequences. But we can't touch him, and not just because I gave my word that I wouldn't give the order, and I will not break my word. If I ordered it, or even looked into the possibility, word would get back to people. The previous administration packed every government office it could find or create with people sympathetic to their point of view. I can't sneeze without someone leaking it to the media. Nobody in the Senate on either side of the aisle would return my calls, not if they suspected I killed off someone they'd given immunity to. They'd consider it a personal affront. Every bill I'd want passed would die in committee, and that would just be for starters."

"The ADDO just wants to finish out his last year and a half before retirement and fade away somewhere on his pension. We tracked down a lot of the money Saddam gave him, and froze it, but figure he's got at least fifty million more tucked away somewhere. He'll buy a nice chateau on the Riviera, get himself a mistress, and never be heard from again, which is just as well."

"You've got to be fucking kidding me!" Jerry exploded in disbelief. "You know what that asshole did." Suddenly Jerry remembered who he was talking to. He shut his mouth but continued to glare, one hand wrapped around his ribs.

I leaned forward, shaking my head. Ron's face was deep red, and I could see a vein pulsing in his forehead. The looks on the other guys' faces were just as upset and disbelieving. Bob never moved, he just sat alone in his chair, not really looking at anything.

Jerry opened and closed his mouth twice before asking, "Well, at least you guys got to the uranium and nerve gas and whatever else before this asshole sold them off." He was looking for some good news. "That's what Ron's dad is doing, right?"

"I really can't say," the President told us. "That is classified, you know."

That was it. Ron exploded. "Who are we gonna tell?" he yelled. The Secret Service agents all took a step closer, but nobody reached into their coat or dived on top of him. "My dad was kidnapped because he was trying to get that information to you guys! You know how many fucking people we had to kill to get him out?"

"Yes, I do," was the quiet reply. The President seemed unperturbed by the profanity. "Do you?"

Ron paused for a moment, blinking three times. "No, I don't," he admitted. "Not a fucking clue." And it didn't sound like he cared, either. His dad was alive. That was all that mattered to him.

The President put on a pair of half glasses, looked down at the papers in front of him and moved a few pages around. He found what he was looking for and ran his finger down the page, stopping near the bottom. He then glanced at the General, who leaned over and read the indicated item. The two of them looked at the piece of paper, then at us.

"Fifty-eight," the General said, in a General's voice. "That we know about. Two of whom were unarmed GS-11 computer operators down from Langley on a working holiday, two more who were domestic help at the estate. And currently there are nine more people in the hospital suffering from gunshot wounds, some of whom are not expected to survive. The estate security officers we've talked to at length, and all they knew was what they'd been told by Mulcahy, that George Kelly was a suspected terrorist that needed to be held incommunicado." The President looked over his glasses at us, but if he was expecting a big display of shock and horror, he was disappointed. We'd heard *that* bad news already. And I can't say it was unexpected.

Fifty-eight. It was a hell of a number. It seemed important to them that we know how many it had been. Did it matter what the number was, though? I tried to remember if I'd shot anyone in that gameroom that hadn't first shot at me. I couldn't, nor could I figure how many of that number I was responsible for. A lot. I'd been seeing their faces in my dreams. Nightmares. Whatever.

"You know," the President was saying, "I've stayed overnight at Wellesley-Grange on several occasions. The food was remarkable. I've been told that the security at that facility is top notch. Yet you, all of you, managed to enter the building. Undetected. Retrieve George Kelly from a padlocked cell in the basement. And escape."

"Getting in was easy," I told him. "Getting out took a bit more work."

The President frowned and stared at us, his eyes moving back and forth. The Secret Service agents positioned throughout the room were looking at all of us very curiously as well. They were probably still trying to figure out how the kids in front of them could have done what they did. I was there and I didn't know. We should all be dead several times over.

The President leaned back, and his hand brushed a lever on the side of the chair. He pulled it out of curiosity, and a footrest popped out as the chair tilted. He leaned back, stretched out.

"This is nice," he said, amazed. "I can't believe I don't have one somewhere. See if you can find me one," he told his aide, then looked back at us, lowering the footrest. "You know," he went on, "when I sat down with Bill and we reviewed all the reports and finally learned what happened, and why, and how your actions were related to his daughter's death, we couldn't believe it. I've seen the photos and still have a hard time believing it. The five of you withheld evidence from the authorities, obstructed an investigation, assaulted an FBI agent and a police officer," he was ticking them off on his fingers as he went, "deliberately ran over someone else, for the love of *Christ* beheaded a wounded man on the network news, killed over four dozen other people in two states and, I'm told, pretty much destroyed a historic Maryland mansion in a gunfight with CIA-trained security personnel. Whom you bested, according to reports, mostly using personal weapons including shotguns and pistols. All solely because you believed George Kelly had been kidnapped. Is that correct?"

"They started it," Ron said angrily. He wasn't sure whether or not he should be proud of his stats.

"We weren't the ones with the grenades," Jerry mumbled.

"All the people trying to kill us sort of confirmed our suspicions," I said tersely.

The President ignored my sarcasm. "Nobody knows we're here," the President said after a long pause. "My wife doesn't even know where I am, and I tell her everything. Bill and I came here because we wanted to see for ourselves just who you really are, what kind of people. And to try to figure out what to do with you."

"I figured the courts would handle that for you." I said. "Have they finished fighting over who's got jurisdiction? Or haven't they even started yet?"

He appeared to be thinking about the question, hands laced together on top of his stomach.

"You've been the guests of the FBI's Counterintelligence Division," the President told us. "WMDs aren't their normal cup of tea, but we couldn't exactly have the CIA people debrief you, could we? We're still not sure how many people under the ADDO were involved. So far, we only know about three for sure. Jeffers the ADDO, Mulcahy, and Phil Enterman, the station chief in Turkey who was first approached by one of Saddam's generals and made the introductions. He arranged the transport during blind windows—when we didn't have surveillance satellites overhead," he explained to us, "and found storage sites for the stuff while the deals were being made. Everybody else, including the man that ran the Wellesley-Grange Estate, was just following orders from higher up and wasn't aware anything illegal was going on. Well, this *is* the CIA," he corrected himself. "Anything more illegal than usual." The President looked at Ron. "Apparently Enterman fell down a flight of stairs and broke his neck soon after your father arrived to talk to him."

The news apparently hadn't been too upsetting to the White House. The President sounded like he was reciting a recipe for shortbread. Ron nodded his head, apparently unsurprised at the effect his father could have on people. He looked a little more relaxed now that he had some kind of update on his dad.

The President said, "I'm told you were all yanked out of the locals' hands pretty quickly after the debacle at Wellesley-Grange."

"Within hours," I said.

"Say anything to them?" Alexander asked gruffly.

I stared at him. "Yeah. 'Please take me to a hospital, my arm is broken. And my foot.'" He stared back at me without responding.

"I had the FBI's CIU take charge of all the investigations concerning you, all the incidents you've been involved in since this began," the President told us, looking at me. "They've been classified Top Secret and codeword compartmentalized for reasons of national security. We still don't have all those WMDs under our control, and I'll be damned if I'm going to jeopardize that operation now, after what had to happen just for us to become aware of the problem. The media is throwing a fit, but they hate me just for breathing air. I could tell them that divulging certain information would compromise operatives in the field and all they'd hear is 'Violation of My First Amendment Rights'. The Iraq invasion's going to distract them in a few months, but until then you're going to be the number one story." He looked at Bob.

"Our Lord Jesus Christ Himself could've reappeared in Times Square and Peter Jennings would've preempted Him to show that clip of you. Not that any government agency has confirmed the identity of anyone in that video yet, so your name is not really getting mentioned, at least not by any reputable news outlets. But it's out there."

He looked at the rest of us. "Two Maryland police departments are still trying to find out what really happened and who the heck you are, even though they've been officially told by the United States Attorney General to cease and desist. The same holds true for at least one Michigan police department, I'm told. They know who all of you are and have been anxiously looking for you for several weeks and don't seem to want to stop. So far, nobody outside of us has connected the Michigan incidents with the Maryland ones, but it could happen."

"I can classify whatever our investigations turn up, but that's not going to stop the press from digging into this tooth and claw. Not to mention the fact that explaining away the decapitation of an American citizen on national TV, even if I wanted to do it, is something beyond my powers."

"Why aren't we in prison, then?" Steve said. "Someplace federal."

The President cleared his throat. "It's up to you to make peace with God. The death of innocents is a tragedy," he told us. "It's something you'll have on your consciences the rest of your lives. That said, we are a nation at war, and war is a terrible, ugly thing. It is because of you, and you alone, that we became aware of this situation in time and we'll soon have total control over every WMD that was in Saddam's arsenal. Those weapons would almost certainly have been used to kill Americans, on our soil and abroad. Tens of thousands of Americans or our allies, perhaps millions." He stared at us. "Millions," he said again, waiting for that to sink in. Then he sighed, snorted, and shook his head. "We'll have them…and we won't be able to tell anyone."

"No?" I said.

"It was a rogue CIA officer who smuggled them out of Iraq. Using a lot of our intelligence infrastructure. Now that we've shut him down, I'm actually surprised Saddam hasn't started shouting to our press about this in one way or another. He won't admit to actually having those weapons, but claiming CIA officers tried to trick or blackmail him or smuggle nukes into Iraq to make him look bad seems like an obvious opening move. And we are in this up to our eyeballs, which means we have to shut up and take it."

The President leaned back, frowned, and cleared his throat again, obviously uncomfortable. "That, gentlemen, is why you're not in jail. That, and other…extenuating circumstances." His mouth wrinkled in something that might have been displeasure.

"What?" I said.

"Catherine Alexander, for one," he said, steepling his fingers in front of his face. "Personal feelings shouldn't be a factor in this, and I know my faith teaches otherwise, but I find I am unable to summon up much emotion over the death of men who murdered an innocent girl." He looked down, then suddenly had to clear his throat. He blinked quickly, as if something had gotten in his eye, then straightened up, and fixed Ron with a rueful, almost admiring smile.

"Your father is the other," he said. "To a lesser extent, the same factors that deter us from touching Arnold Jeffers, the ADDO, apply to you five gentlemen. George Kelly went out of his way to assure me, personally, that if any of you is ever tried for any crime related in the slightest to his rescue, he'll appear in open court and testify on your behalf, with physical evidence to back him up, whether it violates his security clearance or not. I'm very familiar with his dossier—one thing he isn't is stupid. We could always put a gag order on him, and put him in a federal lockup as soon as he opened his mouth, but I'm sure he's planned for that as well. I'm not dumb enough to think he's bluffing—I'm sure he's got something embarrassing on us hidden somewhere too. With unimpeachable documentation. Probably with some sort of dead man's switch that will disseminate it if he somehow vanishes." He waved his hand, like George's threat wasn't of consequence.

"And the police?" I said.

The President shook his head dismissively. "They're no longer in charge of the investigations," he said. "There might be bad blood for a while, they never like having investigations taken out of their hands in the name of national security, but if I have to, all I'll need to do is call the Governor and explain the intricacies of reallocating federal tax money to the states."

"What about Iraq, Sir?" Bob asked quietly.

"What do you mean?" the President asked him.

"I mean, you sold the war on Saddam, Iraq, being a state sponsor of terrorism and possessing weapons of mass destruction. If we go in there, and find nothing…"

"Everyone knows Saddam Hussein has WMDs," General Alexander said dismissively. "And not because of that dog-and-pony show Colin Powell put on at the U.N., Saddam's already used them. Chemical weapons. On Iran during the Iran-Iraq War. On the Kurds in the north. When we go in, if we can't find them, the media will just assume we're incompetent, which is their default setting." He shrugged. "I'm sure there will be other things to catch the media's interest. The man has torture dungeons underneath his palaces for God's sake." He paused. "Sergeant," General Alexander said smartly.

"Yes Sir!"

"Are you happy in 3d Group, son? Do you like what you're doing?"

"Very much so, Sir."

"Your CO put you in for the Silver Star for that action last fall outside of Manila, were you aware of that?"

"He told me he was going to, Sir. I thought I'd convinced him otherwise. I didn't do anything any one of my teammates wouldn't have done."

"Maybe not, but you did it while on fire. That tends to make an impression."

Alexander peered at Bob from under his snowy brows. "Budding military career, already with distinguished service. You're intelligent, young, whole life ahead of you. Yet you were willing to throw your entire future, your freedom, maybe even your life away for revenge."

Bob shifted in the wheelchair. His discomfort wasn't just physical, and he cleared his throat. "Not…not just revenge, sir."

The General waved a hand. "Then to help one of your friends. Was it worth it?"

The question caught Bob by surprise. "I never thought of it in those terms, Sir," he said after a pause. "Beyond the revenge, beyond our friendship, I was doing what I thought had to be done. We all were. That was the mission. We completed the mission."

The General chewed on a lip and looked at Bob. "You know," he said slowly, "my daughter loved you. That's more of a recommendation than you'll ever know. I just wish I'd had the chance to see you two together, see if you really were right for her." He tilted his head back, looked at the ceiling. "I never brought her much happiness. When she called and told me she was in love and planning to get married, to a Ranger no less, I was at a loss for words. I hoped…well, for once in her life she sounded truly happy, full of joy. You gave her that, if only for a little while."

Bob stayed silent for a long while, then asked, "Did you pull my file right after she called?"

"What do you think, soldier?" He paused. "Why do you think you were the youngest person selected for the Q course since the Viet Nam war? They had to pick somebody to be first for the new accelerated SF expansion program.

But I had nothing to do with you passing, you did that yourself. Although I can't say I turned a blind eye to your progress."

The President leaned forward and began flipping once again through the papers in front of him. I could see what looked like medical forms.

"You lost a finger," he said to Steve. "Tore ligaments in your knee. Grenade shrapnel in the back. Ruptured eardrum. Concussion."

Steve didn't know what to say other than, "Yeah."

"You got shot in the head?" he read, looking at Ron quizzically.

Ron pointed. "In the ear," he explained. The President peered at what was left of Ron's ear and did his best to not look disgusted. Whoever had restitched it had done the best they could, but it would never look good. It barely looked like an ear.

"Cracked ribs, partial collapsed lung…lungs," he corrected himself as he read, "surgery and twenty-seven stitches to repair a bullet hole…holes?" was the question posed to Jerry. Jerry nodded.

"Three fractured ribs, a gunshot wound to the right leg, gunshot wound to the left buttock, superficial gunshot and gunshot ricochet wounds to the left shoulder, neck, and both arms, one punctured collapsed lung, pleurisy, massive blood loss…" He kept peering at the sheets in front of him, shaking his head in disbelief. "And apparently you *died* on the table? Twice?"

"So they tell me," Bob croaked.

"How many gunshot wounds?" I said stupidly, then remembered the spreading pool of what I thought had been oil Bob'd been standing in next to the overturned van when we'd come running down the driveway. And he'd kept up with me all the way to the Suburban. Jesus hell, Jerry'd been right. Too stubborn to die. At least until the mission was complete. Jerry should still be in a wheelchair, and Bob should be in a medically-induced coma.

"Cracked rib, minor concussion, ruptured eardrum, twelve stitches for head wounds, multiple blunt force trauma. Broken arm." The President stopped and peered at something before him, then looked up at me. "Fracture of the metatarsal bone of your foot from kicking a grenade? A live grenade." He looked at the General, then back at me.

I shrugged. "It seemed the thing to do at the time." Out of the corner of my eye I saw two Secret Service agents exchange a wide-eyed look.

A longer pause from him. "They killed your dog. And," he said quietly, "you lost a son."

I jerked as if I'd been shot. I hadn't known it was a boy. Bob whipped his head around to stare at me, eyes wide, the news fresh to him. I slumped down against the couch, staring at my knees.

"My wife might be lost to me too, I don't know," I said flatly.

"They tell me you all have the symptoms of Post-Traumatic Stress Disorder. Problems sleeping, flashbacks, the shakes, nightmares, anger, depression, everything on the list and then some. You've definitely earned it." He looked up from the folder at us. "And none of you thought to quit, to give up, to say that you'd had enough? Leave George Kelly to whatever fate had befallen him? Go home while you still could, while you still had homes, still had lives, still had your freedom?"

"We did try to surrender, in the middle of this," Ron reminded the President, biting back sharper words. "To the

FBI. At my house." He jabbed a finger at his ear. "Half of us ended up getting shot."

None of the rest of us had a response, and I don't know if he was really expecting one. We'd made our choices, and stuck by them. Everyone else could decide for themselves whether or not, in their minds, we'd done the right thing. It didn't matter anymore to me. I'd picked that fork in the road and traveled all the way down it, and there was no going back.

"The debriefing agents say in their reports that you've all been nothing but cooperative when answering their questions, except when it comes to the matter of the just over thirty-seven thousand dollars in cash recovered from your vehicle, which itself seems to have appeared out of thin air."

We stared at him with uniformly blank faces.

The President leaned forward. "That reminds me," he said, shuffling through the pile of folders in front of him. He waved his harried-looking aide over, and handed the man a pale grey folder. The aide took it and went around the room, handing out copies of an eighteen-page, single-spaced document to each of us. I looked at the first page, then up at the President.

"Non-disclosure agreements," he told me. "I'm sure you understand the necessity. Failure to adhere to the proscriptions detailed therein would be a violation of the National Security Act. The pertinent sections of the Act as well as applicable tracts of U.S. Code have been included on pages five through nine of the NDA. I highly recommend you sign them."

I glanced over at Jerry sitting next to me. He was on page 2, reading intently. I kicked him in the leg and shook my head when he looked at me.

"Just sign it," I told him.

"Initial each page, and sign the last, but don't date it," the aide told us. I looked at the President, then at Bob, who was looking back at me with the same curious expression that was probably on my face. One of the Secret Service agents had to hold the papers for Bob.

When the aide had all the signed copies back in the folder, he gathered all the paperwork off the coffee table and retreated into a corner.

"Sergeant."

Bob straightened up incrementally and turned to look at General Alexander. "Yes Sir."

"How long are you laid up for?"

"They tell me at least eight weeks before I can start working out, however lightly. Another eight weeks, minimum, to get back into any kind of shape. Probably more. Most likely six months or more until I'm combat effective. Apparently dying increases your recovery time." In any other situation that sentence would have sounded strange to me.

"Are you aware that that video of you is the most-watched film clip since the Kennedy assassination?"

"So I've heard," Bob said glumly.

"At our request the media is now blurring your face and the faces of the men you fought, and the NSA is doing everything it can to scrub that video from the internet, but it will never go away completely. And your name has been attached to it, although that's never been officially confirmed, but a lot of people are trying. Your whole life is under a microscope. There is nothing that I or anyone else you've met today can do that will change that. We can only deal with the situation as it exists. Do you understand me?"

"Yes, Sir."

Splashback

"Because of your public face on what is a now-classified situation, we can't allow you to be charged for that incident even though it is clearly worthy of a court martial. Hell, by just about any civilized standard it would be considered a war crime, but... But. But." He huffed. "The Army could give you a discharge. Honorable, Dishonorable, or Medical, the end result would be putting you outside of our control. We don't think that's wise at the present time." He glanced at the President, then continued.

"We're going to be hitting Iraq in a couple of months, and we sure could use a modern war hero. You've heard the Al-Qaida cover story for your raid? We can expand on that. We can take you public, say you were on a covert mission to stop a domestic terrorist cell that was trying to smuggle a nuke into the country, and parade you in front of the cameras. You could hit all the talk shows, talking up the military, become a celebrity. You've heard of Audie Murphy, right? How do you feel about that?" The General peered at Bob.

"Permission to speak freely, Sir?"

"Absolutely."

Bob made a face. "I'd enjoy a court martial more, Sir."

The General frowned. "Your enjoyment is irrelevant. Attempted nuke smuggling or not, and that's probably the story we're going to leak, you beheaded a man. An American citizen. On TV. We are all aware of the extenuating circumstances surrounding the incident, and can control the dissemination of information to a certain extent because of security issues, but the public eye is going to be on you and us no matter what story we feed the media. The military has a responsibility to clean up its own mess, and you're part of the mess, so we've been pushing back, citing national security. But that only goes so far. You're famous now, whether you or the Army wants you to be or not. Believe me, it doesn't—world-wide celebrity status is not a plus in your line of work. What to do with you is the question, and so far nobody's come up with an ideal answer. One idea was to use you as a 'deniable asset'. Some of my staff favor nominating you for the Medal of Honor as part of this bogus nuke story, and believe that would totally suck the wind out of the other side, and do all that is possible to tame the repercussions of that jackass headchopping stunt. And, honestly, that is the best idea we've come up with so far, not trying to cover up the beheading or hide you away but doubling down the other way." He glanced sideways at the President, then went on. "As a professional soldier it galls me." The muscles in his jaw bunched up, and he blinked quickly several times. "That said, as a grieving father, I can't say I would have behaved much…differently…better…were our situations reversed." He cleared his throat and looked down.

"Cathy would not have approved," Bob murmured. There was a look of almost unbearable sadness on Bob's face for a second, then he shoved it underneath a stony mask. Alexander raised his head and looked at Bob.

"No, she would not," the General agreed. He peered at Bob from beneath his bushy brows. "You get it out of your system?"

Bob looked up at him tiredly and seemed to know exactly what Alexander meant. It took him a while to answer. "I'll never get over it," Bob told him dully. "But I'm getting used to it." He looked at me and gave a very faint nod. "It makes it easier knowing the people who did it are dead." I nodded back at him.

At that, the General nodded, like it was the response he'd been expecting. "You look quite different with the haircut and the beard gone," he observed. He sighed. "At least that's something. Goodbye, Sergeant."

"Goodbye, Sir."

And it appeared that was it. The General and the President seemed to be done with us.

Goodbye? I could see from the expression on his face Jerry still wasn't sure this was actually happening. Neither was I, it seemed less believable than some of the PTSD-induced fever dreams I'd been having lately.

"How does it work for us?" Jerry suddenly said.

"Excuse me?" the President asked him.

"I mean, if you're not arresting me, in six months I'm going to be graduating from Michigan State with a Criminal Justice degree," Jerry said. "Good grades and everything. Dean's list. I was planning on applying to the DEA and the US Marshalls. I've never been convicted of any crime. I've never even had a ticket. But, last I heard, you need a Top Secret clearance for those jobs, which means a background check. Done by the FBI." He waved a hand around the house, provided by the FBI's Counterintelligence Division. "Those background checks, I know, I've heard, you accidentally put down that your third cousin's middle name was Arthur when it's Andrew, and you get denied as a security risk. I was already afraid I wouldn't be able to get a job in law enforcement because of what happened two years ago. They don't just want to know about convictions, they want to know if I've ever been arrested, and for what. I could have lied and said no, or said, 'Yes, in connection with an octuple homicide, but it was ruled justified.'" He had to laugh at his predicament. "I didn't know if anybody would be willing to take a chance on me because of that, and now there's *this*. I'm gonna have to go back to school, get a goddamn cooking degree. Start at Leftovers and work my way up."

"Weren't you going to Michigan State too?" the President asked Steve. "Criminal Justice degree, all that?"

"Both of us," Steve nodded.

"Were you hoping for the DEA too? I know Mr. Phault here worked for them."

"Actually," Steve said, "my dream job would've been the Secret Service. But my grades aren't good enough."

"I thought I read somewhere that you're getting decent grades."

"I am. But good grades don't cut it. Maybe if I was a handicapped black Chinese female fluent in six languages they'd get me in, but all I speak is Spanish. It's harder to get into the Secret Service than it is to get elected President. Sir." I heard a snort and looked across the room at the guy by the fireplace. He was doing his best to keep a straight face, but his best wasn't good enough.

"Yeah, I've heard that too," our host said with a wry smile.

"Maybe my dad can get me a spot on the line at Chrysler," Steve said. "They don't do background checks for that, do they?"

The President flexed his fingers, and I heard a few of them pop. He turned to his aide standing in the corner. "Michael, you want to weigh in here?"

The aide stepped forward. "There are never any guarantees in life," the man told the boys. "But I'm not sure you realize the highly sensitive nature of the information you're privy to. Even within the FBI, no one outside of the Director, Deputy Director, and the mandated Counterintelligence investigating teams will have access to the information contained in those case files. Most agents likely will not even be aware of the substance of these events outside of what they've seen on the news. Speaking about these events, even acknowledging their existence—and that includes this meeting here today—to anyone, for whatever reason, would be a violation of the non-disclosure agreements you just signed, unless they have a signed copy of that document in their possession at the time of questioning." I tilted my head at that, and looked over at Bob. He saw me looking at him and raised his eyebrows in my direction. Steve had his head cocked, thinking about what he'd just heard.

"Local and state police departments are a completely different matter, of course, but say, for example, you were going through a pre-employment background check at the FBI or any other federal law enforcement agency that included a polygraph. If, during that examination they ask you any questions that you are legally proscribed from answering because of the NDA you just signed, do not lie, just state that you cannot answer that question and refer the agents to the Director of the FBI's Counterintelligence Division."

Jerry and Steve looked at each other, but smartly kept their mouths shut.

After a few moments spent idly rubbing his thumb, the President pulled a new file folder from the bottom of the stack and opened it. "One more thing I'd like you to do for me," he told us. "Look at this. Tell me if you've ever seen him before." He tilted the folder forward and a small packet of papers stapled together slid out of it onto the table.

There was a five-by-seven color photo stapled on top of a sheet of paper. It was of a white male in his fifties, with wavy grey hair and a big nose, wearing what appeared by its cut to be a very expensive suit. I'd never seen him before. As Jerry scooted closer on the couch to read over my shoulder,

I flipped the picture up and looked at the typewritten page beneath. There was a lot of information printed there. Registered vehicles, phone numbers, a Social Security number, an address, height, weight, hair color, eye color, and a name. Arnold Jeffers. The CIA's Assistant Deputy Director of Operations. The man responsible for everything.

"Never seen him," I said. Jerry, peering over my shoulder, shook his head as well.

"It was a long shot," the President said. "When he testifies in front of the Senate committee in two weeks that's pretty much going to be it, the beginning of the end. At least politically, for my administration, and I fear for the long-term security of this nation as well. The Senators from across the aisle will start leaking this information as soon as they realize what they have. Short term political goals have always been more important to them than long-term intangibles like national security or cultural decay. I thought that maybe if you'd ever seen him before we could get some leverage on him, stop this disaster from happening. Maybe you had some ideas?" I slowly lifted my head and saw two pairs of eyes boring into mine. They waited for an answer.

"Ron?" I handed the papers past Jerry. Ron and Steve looked at them briefly, just long enough to realize what they had, then passed them back to me without saying a word. I held the packet up and looked at Bob. He just shook his head, not wanting to waste anybody's time. He probably should've still been in the hospital.

"We'll put our heads together," I told him. I slid the packet back toward the President, but he made no move to take it. "You'll hear from us." The President blinked once, slowly, then nodded. He handed the empty manila file folder to the aide, staring introspectively at the packet on

Splashback

the table. I realized then that he'd made sure not to touch it when handing it over, which meant, among other things, that he'd suspected all along what our answer would be. Then the President stood up, and one of the Secret Service agents handed him his coat.

The aide stepped up and plunked a bulky package wrapped in brown paper on the table. He slid a sheet of paper in front of me, handed me a pen, and pointed to where I should sign. As soon as I did the property receipt went into another folder.

"That's it?" I said, as the two of them started for the door, the aide in tow. Secret Service men were in front and behind. "I mean, that's it?"

"Happy New Year," the President said to me, and then they were gone. A minute later the muscle-men started filing back into the house. Peter entered the room and walked up to me, wearing his normal, expressionless face.

"You're free to go," he told us. "Drivers'll take you back to wherever you've been staying. You can take off tonight if you want, or you can wait until morning. No rush. At your convenience," he said to me, "some of us would like to come out to Michigan, interview you some more. Once we start digging, I'm sure some things are going to pop up that we have questions about."

"I believe some arrangements have been made for you," he said to Bob. "Once the doctors approve you for travel you're to call your contact and he'll drive you wherever you're going. Contact information should be in your hospital room by the time you get back." He gave Bob a nod, then he left the room.

"I guess that's it," Jerry said, looking dazed. I probably had a similar expression on my face. It was over, just like that? *Happy New Year?* After everything that'd happened?

Somehow, it seemed too unbelievable. I kept expecting the door to be booted in by cops or FBI agents yelling "Suckers!". I glanced over at the brown package on the table again.

"What is that?" Ron asked.

"Thirty-seven grand in cash," I told him.

"You're fucking kidding me." He stared at me, then at the wrapped block of cash, then back at me.

"Surreal," I heard Bob murmur.

"What about our guns?" Jerry asked.

"Buried as deep as the truth on this one," I told him. "Probably already destroyed."

"Shit. You going to head back to Michigan, see Kelly?" he asked me.

"In a while," I said. "If that's where she is. If she'll see me. I have no idea what…" I shook my head and looked down at my bound arm, then at Bob. The operation to fix his lung left him sitting as cockeyed as the fractured ribs had.

"How about you guys?" I asked, suddenly blinking back tears.

Jerry, Ron and Steve looked at each other, then at the packet sitting on the table. Ron was the first one to speak. He ran a hand through his hair, and spoke slowly. "I don't know about you guys, but I was gonna hang around town for a while," he picked his words carefully, "see the sights."

Jerry and Steve, after careful consideration, both nodded.

"You sure?" I asked them. "You can walk away, now, slate clean. Back through the looking glass. Trust me, you'll never get that opportunity again. Ever. Is it worth the risk to you? Something can always go wrong."

I looked around at the three of them, and they stared

back at me silently. I glanced at Bob, hunched over sideways in his wheelchair. He'd never been easy to read at the best of times, and was just sitting there, glowering at nothing in particular. My hands were in my lap, and I realized I was spinning my wedding ring around my finger. I stopped, and looked up from the gold band to see Jerry's eyes upon it. He spoke without looking up, his lips pressed into a thin line.

"Life's too short to ever forgive anybody anything," Jerry said.

Washington Post - January 20

STAFF REPORT

POLICE REMAIN FRUSTRATED IN CIA SLAYING

ARLINGTON, VA. Arlington police officers still have not made any arrests in connection with last week's slaying of a high-ranking Central Intelligence Agency employee, and the police department still refuses to comment on the apparent lack of a motive or suspects.

Arnold Jeffers, 52, was brutally shot to death January 14th as he drove through the streets of Arlington, Virginia. In a startling discovery, the **Post** has learned that Jeffers was scheduled to spend the next day testifying before a closed-door session of the Senate Select Committee on Intelligence. After several attempts to get a statement from the CIA concerning his duties there, the CIA did finally confirm that Jeffers was the Assistant Deputy Director of Operations, one of the highest positions within the Agency. Neither the CIA spokesperson nor several Congressional staffers could tell the **Post** exactly why Jeffers was scheduled to appear, or what he was supposed to be testifying about.

The CIA spokesperson, however, assured the Post that Jeffers' murder had nothing to do with his upcoming appearance before the Senate committee.

An officer inside the investigation, who would speak to the Post only on condition of anonymity, expressed serious doubts about the CIA's official position. "Several senators have told me this was an emergency session of the Intelligence Committee, called specifically to hear Jeffers' testimony."

When they learned of his death numerous senators on the committee expressed shock and outrage at Jeffers' murder, but would not discuss his scheduled appearance before them, stating it concerned classified material. Senator James Griggs (R-Ohio) privately expressed doubts that Jeffers' murder had anything to do with his testimony, but declined to provide any details.

Jeffers was stopped at a traffic light in suburban Arlington when, without warning, two men jumped from a nearby vehicle and shot him to death inside his car. The men exited the back of a van, fired into Jeffers' car, then fled on foot with a third man, the driver of the van. Witnesses stated that the suspects were all white males, and one of the suspects had a limp, but further identification has eluded police as all three of the assailants wore coveralls, painters' caps, and paper filter masks. Police state the van was stolen just hours earlier from a local painting company. The police are asking anyone with information about this crime to contact their anonymous tip line.

The remains of the gunmen's caps and masks were found in a nearby dumpster, doused with gasoline and lit on fire. The suspects have not yet been located, although several witnesses have come forward with descriptions of the car they fled the scene in, a black late-model four-door sedan. According to at least one witness this sedan was possibly following Jeffers' car at a distance, driven by yet another unidentified male. The murder weapons, two pump-action shotguns, were brazenly left by the murderers on the hood of Jeffers' still-running car. Our police source told us the guns' serial numbers had been removed, and no fingerprints have been recovered from either the van or the weapons. The medical examiner's autopsy report stated Jeffers had been struck by some 52 pellets of buckshot, and died instantly.

"This was no random drive-by," our source told us. "This was an assassination. Somebody wanted this guy dead, in a very public way, and so far all the CIA has given us is the run-around." In our own attempt to shed some light on Jeffers' activities just prior to his death, and attempt to learn just why he was scheduled to appear before the Senate Select Committee on Intelligence, the **Post**

—see CIA MURDER, page **A6**

Next in the James Tarr Conspiracy Thrillers series

vinci-books.com/splits

Murder, deception, and a past that won't stay buried.

Phault's wife files for divorce, a Detroit business icon is assassinated, and a new client is hiding his true intentions. As ghosts from his past resurface with deadly intent, Phault realizes in the Motor City, danger has become just another day at the office.

Splits and Transitions: Chapter One

JUNE 2003

"I told you, I don't want you calling. Anything you want to say, you can say to my lawyer."

Her voice in my ear, as usual, sent a riot of emotions wildly bouncing around my head and heart. I stared down at the cup of coffee in front of me, today's copy of the Detroit Free Press next to it, and tried to find the right words.

After a slow, deep breath, I said, "I just wanted to talk."

"We've got nothing to talk about. If you weren't doing everything you could to stop it, we'd already be divorced. And we'd never have to talk again." Her bitterness held an accusation, and in truth she wasn't wrong. Michigan was a no-fault state when it came to divorce, and whether I contested it or not I couldn't stop it, although I'd been dragging it out as long as possible in the hope I could get Kelly to change her mind. The only thing that could have significantly slowed the process would have been the presence of minor children. And, to be honest, the fact that we didn't, currently, have a child was the main reason for the divorce.

Splashback

I took another deep breath, trying to calm myself. "I've been...I'm...I did what you asked, I moved out—" I began.

"Only because I threatened to call the cops on you." Not that she was living in the house we'd shared either. She'd moved out less than a week after I had. Too many bad memories there. For both of us.

I blinked and tried to find my way back to that calm center I'd had before dialing the phone. "Why can't we just talk? I know you're hurting. I'm hurting too."

"I don't care if you're hurting!" she screamed in my ear. "You should be hurting! They're dead because of you."

"I didn't kill the dog or the baby!" I shouted back at her, then found I was talking to a dead line. And realized that a number of people sitting nearby were staring at me. Squeezing the phone hard enough for it to creak I glared at each one of them in turn until they looked away. Then I looked around the Starbucks, which was brand new and just half a mile from my office. Other than the two retirees I was the oldest person in the place. I was definitely the angriest, having caffeine and hate for lunch. As usual.

In a surprisingly adult move I resisted the urge to throw my cell phone across the room and instead tossed it onto the folded newspaper, atop the article I'd been reading, trying to slow my pulse. A glowing, feature-length front page obituary on Bernard Mitton, Detroit icon. Businessman and philanthropist, he got his start with a furniture store that he'd turned into a very successful Midwest chain—The Ottoman Empire. Always loved that name. Used the cash from that to start several other very successful businesses. Dead in the middle of a street, shot down during an attempted carjacking at age seventy-three. Both he and his aging trophy wife, who'd actually hired me once. What a waste. It didn't make my mood any better.

There were half a dozen emails in my inbox when I came back from lunch, and a fresh fax in the machine. After skimming everything I grabbed the office phone and called Jerry Phillips. He answered his cell on the second ring.

"Yeah, I got another case in," I told him. "You available to work a surveillance tomorrow?

I'd known him for two years—been initially hired by his parents to find him, actually, and since then I'd seen a lot of drama with him and his friends. More than most people would ever believe, not that we were allowed to tell anyone. He'd graduated from Michigan State not quite two months earlier and been working for me while waiting for the job he wanted. I was going to miss him when he headed to FLETC (pronounced flet-see), the Federal Law Enforcement Training Centers in Georgia, where just about every federal law enforcement agent other than the FBI and DEA cadre were trained. He'd put in his application for the U.S. Marshals Service. Luckily, for me, the government's hiring process was horribly slow and inefficient, taking months, sometimes years to complete. Oddly enough, the USMS didn't polygraph its applicants which, in his case, was helpful. Very helpful.

"Morning? Yeah. Who's it for?" I could tell from the background noise he was driving.

"Uhhhh." I re-checked the paperwork. "MHC. Work comp. Where are you on your way to?"

"The gym." He coughed into the phone, then snorted. "MHC. Another hospital case? So we're watching a nurse who's out on carpal tunnel or a latex allergy. Waitwaitwait, they give you a description?"

"Ummmmm. Yeah. She's—"

"Let me guess. Five-two, two hundred pounds?"

My eyes scanned the paperwork. "Pretty close. A bit taller." I read through the descriptors. "A bit heavier."

"Okay, I take it back, she's got back or leg problems."

"Aren't you too young to be this cynical?" I checked. "Yep. Hip and knee."

I could hear him sigh. "You know, I can't believe how many of these so-called health professionals are just big fat giant pigs. The people you'd *think* would know better. Who do know better."

"Well, they work a lot of hours, and don't get much exercise," I said in their defense.

"You don't get fat by not exercising," he said sharply, "you get it by eating too goddamn much for the calories you're burning. There, look, I could write my own diet book, make a million dollars. I'll call it Shut Your Pie Hole."

"Oprah'd love you," I told him. "You're so sensitive. They're splurging for a two-man, so I'll e-mail you the address, and see you there at six." First goal of a work comp surveillance was to make sure the claimant wasn't working a second job while off work for the insured, so we usually started the first day at six a.m.

He must have heard something in my voice. "How you doing?" His concern was real. He knew my situation.

"Great. Living the dream. See you tomorrow." I hung up on him.

Just before four I heard the front door open and the click of high heels on the fancy laminate floor of my office. I was out of my chair and coming out from behind my desk when I heard the tentative "Hello?"

"Hi, can I help you?" I said from my office doorway.

"Are you Mr. Phault?"

"That'd be me."

She looked about twenty-five, pretty and thin, with curly blonde hair in a pile atop her head. She wore a short-sleeved white blouse unbuttoned dangerously low in front and a tight skirt that didn't come anywhere near her knees. In one hand was a small black clasp-purse, and she glanced around the office automatically. In her heels she was about five eleven, and was probably the best-looking person I'd ever had in my office. Other than me, of course.

"I got your name from the deputies down at the courthouse. I don't know if you can help me, or if I've even got a problem," she looked uncertain and a bit flustered. She paused and frowned.

I waved her into my office. "Come on in and sit down," I told her with a smile. I got settled behind the desk and she took the client chair in front of me, crossing her legs tightly at the knee. She tugged at the skirt to make sure it didn't ride too far up. Not that I was looking.

"What do you think you need a PI for?" I asked her.

She took a deep breath. "That's just it, I'm not sure if I do or not. Here, let me start at the beginning. I just moved here six months ago, from California. L.A., actually."

"Welcome to America," I said with a smile.

She looked at me strangely, not getting it at first, then gave me a wry grin. "Yeah, we're a bit out there. Oh, I'm Kerrie, Kerrie Edwards." We got back up and shook hands over my desk.

"John," I told her.

"Anyway, one of the reasons I moved here..." She frowned. "I had a stalker," she told me. "An ex-boyfriend. I had to get a restraining order against him and everything."

"He hurt you?" I asked.

She shook her head quickly. "No, he never laid a finger

on me, but he just became...obsessed, you know? He couldn't get over me after we broke up. God, that sounds conceited." She made a face.

I shook my head. "Lot of problems in the world caused by dudes who won't take no for an answer."

"Anyway, he wouldn't leave me alone. He'd send me flowers two or three times a week, call me ten times a day. I'd change my phone number, and three weeks later he was calling again, somehow he'd find it out. I'm pretty sure he was following me, too. I caught glimpses of his car, I think, a couple of times, but I could never say for sure. We were really close at one time, serious, but I was going through a rough spot in my life and he... Sorry," she stopped herself. "You don't need to hear my problems. I got the restraining order, and everything was fine for a week or so, then I saw him one night out my window, watching my apartment. This was like three o'clock in the morning, and I just got up to use the bathroom. I have no idea how long he'd been out there or anything. He was just staring."

"Creepy," I agreed.

"I called the cops," she told me, "but by the time they showed up he was gone. I kept an eye out for him, and didn't see him the next night, or the night after that, but then I saw him again. I called 911, but he took off. A couple of officers talked to him at work and he denied everything, said I was just trying to get back at him for dumping me."

"Of course."

"The police asked if I wanted to pursue it, try and get him for violating the order, but there weren't any witnesses, and Mike's one hell of a liar. I figured there was a better than even chance that the judge would believe him over me. So I came out here. I'd been wanting to make a change anyway."

"Michigan from L.A.? Detroit? That's a hell of a change."

"My mom lives out here," she told me. "And I just had a crappy receptionist job, it's not like I couldn't find something similar here. I'm trying to get my CPA, and once I saw most of my credits would transfer over I moved. I just packed my stuff into my car one day and took off, you know? I didn't tell anyone but a couple friends where I was going, just in case."

"And now?"

She made a face. "About a month ago I thought I saw his car again, here, following me. He drives this electric blue Mustang, I don't know, about an '88. It's souped up, with a loud exhaust. A couple of times I tried to turn around and follow it, see if it was him, but it just disappeared."

"So you've seen it more than once?"

She nodded. "I think I've seen him once or maybe twice a week for the past month."

That made me sit up. "Oh."

She shrugged. "I still don't know if it's him, the windows are tinted, and I've never seen the plate. But I think it is. I called my friends in L.A., and they checked his apartment. It's empty, and he quit his job. Nobody at the shop knows where he's working now. That doesn't mean he came all the way to Michigan after me, I know, but…."

"But it's got you worried."

She nodded nervously. "That's why I was at the courthouse. I was trying to get a restraining order against him. That's not what they call them here, they're…." She frowned, thinking.

"Personal Protection Orders," I told her.

"That's it. I went in front of a judge, but she told me I didn't have enough to get one issued. I couldn't say for sure it was even his car, or if it was him inside it. Or, if he's in this state, even where he lives. She sent me across the street to the Sheriff's Department."

I nodded. "They check to see if he was a resident?"

"Yeah. He doesn't have a Michigan driver's license, or any license plates registered to him here. They had no record of him on their computer. The judge said that part of getting a restraining order issued was that it had to be served on the person. I've got no address for him, no license plate, nothing. I might even be imagining the whole thing. The whole thing really freaked me out the first time, and just when I was starting to forget about it…."

"Well, I sure wouldn't fault you after the track record you've had with this guy," I told her. "Better to be safe than sorry. If he had a brown Taurus or something common like that I might be a little hesitant to make the call, but an electric blue eighties Mustang is a little different. Did he know your mom lives out here?"

"Yes."

I grabbed a legal pad from a drawer and jotted down some notes. "What I can do," I told her, "is run him on the computer, see what I can dig up."

"The police couldn't find any record of him anywhere."

"Apples and oranges," I assured her. "They ran him through the Secretary of State and LEIN, the Law Enforcement Information Network. That's driver's licenses, vehicle registration, traffic tickets, and criminal records. Do you have a Social Security number for him?"

"Yes, I've got everything," she said, starting to dig through her small purse. "From the first time, in California, for the restraining order. I typed it all out." She handed me several sheets of paper and I began unfolding them as I talked.

"This will make it a lot easier," I told her. "I can run him through a number of databases and search engines. Tax records, employment, phone bills, even utilities. Day-to-day life stuff. Chances are, if he's in Michigan, he'll turn up." I looked at the Xerox of his driver's license. The photo was small and a bit blurry.

"How much will that cost?" she asked me.

"Hundred bucks," I told her. "But if I find him here, you're going to have some decisions to make."

"What do you mean?"

"Even if you confirm he's in Michigan, you can't say for sure it was him following you. Unless something else happens, you still don't have enough for a PPO."

"Wouldn't the fact that he followed me here be enough?"

I shrugged. "You said he's a fast talker. He could say he didn't know you were here, that's he's only here because of a job, any number of things. Free country."

"What about the restraining order? It's still in effect."

"Are California restraining orders valid in Michigan? That's an actual question, because I don't know." I could see she didn't either. It was one more thing I'd have to look into. "Has he ever laid a hand on you? Ever physically threatened you?" She shook her head. "You want the good news or the bad news? Say he was caught red-handed doing something the California order prohibited, like appearing within your sight. Or closer than fifty feet or whatever the proscribed distance is, and it's just as valid here as an out-of-state warrant. You think anybody from California is going to fly out to Michigan to take him back there just to be charged? Is violation a misdemeanor or a felony?" I asked her.

She squinched her eyes up. "I think it depends."

"*You* don't even live there anymore," I told her. "Forget California. If he's here, the quickest way for you to get a PPO issued against him is to document him stalking you."

"But I told you, I couldn't tell—"

I shook my head. "Let's wait to worry about that until after we know something," I said. "But I'm not talking about sitting around waiting for something bad to happen," I explained. "It depends on how much money you'd be willing or able to spend, but there are a couple ways to go about it. Simplest, I think, would be to do surveillance on him. You show a judge an hour of video of him staring at your house or workplace, or I testify that I observed him following you home, and you won't have any problem getting a PPO."

"Oh, okay." She dug through her little purse again and withdrew some cash. She counted out a hundred dollars and handed it to me. "How long will it take you to do the search for him?" she asked me.

"I'll call you tomorrow," I told her, as I wrote out a receipt for the money. She gave me all her info and well as her current address, her mother's house which was in Troy not too far from my office.

"And tomorrow after we talk," I told her, "whether I find a trace of him or not, go to the Troy Police Department, and file what they call an 'information report'."

"What's that?"

"It's to let them know that something is going on. You may not have enough for a PPO, but going on record that you've got a concern will go a long way if there ever is a problem. Gets you on the scoreboard first. If the cops get a 911 call from your house, this report will pop up on their system, give them a heads up. And if you do see him," I told her, "don't wait, call 911."

I leaned back in my chair and studied her long enough for her to start to get uncomfortable, then spoke. "Look, brutal honesty here. If this guy is so obsessed with you that he followed you all the way to Detroit from LA, in violation of one restraining order, one more piece of paper isn't going to make you any safer. Not in the real world. Keep a cell phone with you at all times, and get a can of pepper spray. Better yet, Michigan's a 'shall issue' state, and you've got a Michigan Driver's license, go get yourself a CCW and keep a gun in your car if you don't want to carry it on your person. You don't need a CCW if you keep it at the house."

She made a face and shook her head. "I don't like guns. I don't want to get a gun."

"Liking's got nothing to do with it," I told her. "It's a tool, same as a hammer or a screwdriver." I paused, and decided to make my point. I stood up. Even with the desk between us I towered over her. "I'm no freak of nature, and you're not a small woman, but I've got five inches and at least fifty pounds on you. I don't care if you're a black belt or have a can of pepper spray already in your hand, or even a knife, if I wanted to rape you or kill you, ninety-nine times out of a hundred there is no way you could stop me unless you had a gun. Period. And I'm old enough to be your father. Well, older brother." I sat back down, seeing from the look on her face that I'd scared the hell out of her.

"Sorry," I said, trying to sound like I meant it. "I've never been accused of subtlety or political correctness. It's just that I've seen too many bad things happen to good people, especially women. Bullies don't stop what they're doing if you ask them nicely."

She bit her lip. "I just don't think I could shoot him. He's never been violent."

I nodded. "And that's just fine. I wish there were more

people in the world who couldn't shoot other people. And until you're sure you could pull the trigger, if you felt your life was in danger, don't carry a gun, because it'll be just one more thing your attacker'll be able to use against you. But if he did follow you here from California, he's dangerous, even if he's never been violent. You need to be careful. Let me get you a receipt, and I'll call you tomorrow."

Splits and Transitions: Chapter Two

When we'd arrived at six a.m. the neighborhood had been dark, the sky just starting to lighten. By six-thirty it was daylight and details had begun to emerge. The claimant's house was a two-story brick and wood edifice probably constructed during the Baby Boom. It seemed in decent shape, with some bright flowers out front. If she'd planted them, they might provide me an opportunity to get video of her doing a little gardening. Probably nothing that would violate her medical restrictions, but enough to justify my paycheck.

Only a third of the block was vacant lots covered in knee-high, unmown grass, and only one house on the block was boarded up which, for Detroit, made it an unremarkable residential area. Jerry was a hundred yards past her house on the opposite side of the street, hunkered down in the back seat of his Ford Explorer behind tinted windows.

Morning surveillances were usually very peaceful, if not downright boring. Watch the squirrels run around, listen to the birds chirp. With school out for the summer, there just wasn't a lot of early morning activity in the depths of the city neighborhoods. Only two cars on the entire block took off before nine a.m., their drivers presumably heading to work. As for what the rest of the residents of the neighborhood did for money, I could only guess.

Jerry's voice popped out of the handheld Motorola radio in the cupholder of my Tahoe. Loud. "Hey, did you hear about that Glove guy?" The radios would only reach half a mile in the city, but that was just fine for stationary surveillances, and most of the time while following someone. Beyond that distance we had cell phones.

I turned the volume down on the handheld. "The who?"

"The old guy we did surveillance on last fall. Domestic case, not insurance. Rich Detroit OG."

"Please don't try to sound like a gangster rapper, you're not P. Puff Diddy Daddy. Or is there a Snoop in there somewhere? Snoop Diggity?" I smiled behind the radio.

"Oh my God." He was almost choking. "Please stop. And you think I sound white? You know the case I mean. You and Mike did most of it, but I did one day, I think. Maybe two. He got killed in a carjacking. Him and his wife."

"Mitton," I told him.

"That's it. I was close. Just a little too slow getting out of the Bentley and gets popped by some crackhead idiot. Probably by accident, too, seeing as how it sounded from a witness like the dude panicked after the shooting and ran away without robbing him or the wife. Or taking the car." According to news reports the car had been paused at a stop sign when one man approached on foot. "How much was he worth, millions?"

"You can't take it with you."

"No, but it'd be nice to have while you're here. If I had the money for a Bentley, I wouldn't buy a Bentley. But then again I'm not an old dude or a rapper. Now his business gets it all, I guess. Shareholders or whoever. Seeing as we never could spot a girlfriend."

"Presumably."

We sat in silence for another ten minutes, staring at the nurse's house. Waiting for something to happen. Apparently she was in no hurry to run errands. The house began to shimmer slightly as the summer sun baked the concrete. I was parked in the shade of a maple with the engine off and all my windows cracked, but the humidity was awful. I'd be starting the car and blasting the A/C before long. And peeing in a bottle. The joys and romance of surveillance. I shifted in the seat, feeling my pistol poking me in the side. A full-size SIG P226 in a hip holster—hard to conceal, and not comfortable to sit on, but what it lacked in physical comfort it more than made up for in peace of mind.

"Hey, how long does that take?" Jerry said suddenly over the Motorola.

"How long does what take?"

"Getting your money after someone dies. Inheritance or whatever."

He was so young he had no experience with wills or settling estates. "That depends if there's a will or not. With a will it should be a lot quicker...theoretically. But the rich are different, and the more money there is, the more hassle. Someone always challenges the will, a black sheep son or daughter who's not getting a big enough slice of the pie, a bastard child or mistress who shows up at the last minute, a business partner arguing about stocks. Paternity, DNA tests, lawsuits, courtroom drama. If he didn't have a will, which I can't imagine, it'll go to probate, which takes forever. Either way, at a minimum, it will be months. More likely years, the lawyers bleeding the estate for two hundred bucks an hour. Apiece."

"He have kids?"

I thought back to the Freep article I'd skimmed. "I don't think so."

"I guess that's better, right?" I didn't respond, and a few seconds later he got back on the radio, his voice hollow. "Oh, shit, John, I...."

"Forget about it."

Other than poking her head out the front door to check to see if the mail had arrived, our nurse claimant didn't do a thing before we had eight hours on the clock. I told Jerry to meet me back there at eight the next morning, and headed into the office, arriving by two-thirty. I called Kerrie Edwards' cell phone a little before four p.m., and she got back with me within the hour.

"Well, the bad news is that his name is Michael Sullivan."

I could hear my client frowning on the other end of the line. "I don't understand."

"It's a common name, unlike Kerrie with an I-E."

"Did you run me?" She sounded surprised.

"No, just giving you an example. But, luckily, you had his Social Security number. That helps a lot, especially with credit card companies. I ran a comp report on him, non-criminal court records, talked to my contacts at a few utility and credit card companies…Unfortunately, or fortunately, I can find no evidence that he's in the state. None. If he's living here, his name is not on the lease or the mortgage. He's not paying any bills with checks or a credit card. If he's staying in a cheap hotel, or with a friend, hasn't gotten a job locally, and is paying cash for everything, he can stay under the radar. For weeks. Or months. But that won't last forever." A general search online for 'Michael Sullivan' had been totally useless except to remind me that it was the name of the character played by Tom Hanks the year before in the movie *Road to Perdition*.

"Darn it. I know it's him."

"Does he have any friends or relatives living in the area?"

"Not that I know of."

"I ran the plate on the Mustang. It's still registered to him in California. Doesn't expire for a couple of months." She'd been right, it was a 1988 Mustang, a GT, back from when they still had corners instead of curves. He didn't have any other vehicles registered to him, but if he was following her, and truly crazy or obsessed, I wouldn't have been surprised if he was using several different vehicles, and she only noticed the Mustang because it stuck out. She'd told me he was an auto mechanic. If he was working somewhere, maybe under the table for cash, he might have access to other vehicles.

"So what should I do now?"

"Do what I said. Head over to the Troy Police Department and file that information report. Then we can talk about what other steps we can take, surveillance or whatever."

"I'm just getting off work, so I'll drive straight over there. I've got to work tomorrow, and I hate to take another day off... How early do you get in the office?"

"If you want to stop by my office tonight after you're done at the PD, I'll be here," I told her. I had nowhere else to be.

I grabbed a sandwich at a nearby deli and then returned to my office to wait for Ms. Edwards. I didn't have a TV in the office, and I couldn't decide whether that was a mistake or a blessing. In various drawers and shelves of my office over the years I'd stashed books I knew I should read but had never gotten around to. A disintegrating marriage was giving me all sorts of free time I'd never had before. Currently I was about a third of the way through Hemingway's Islands In The Stream—I was reaching the end of 'Bimini', the first book of three inside the novel, when Kerrie Edwards knocked on the door. I waved her to the seat across the desk and put the book away, and shoved the remains of my dinner into the trash.

"Any problems at the PD?"

"No." She seemed in a better mood. "They said they'd have officers do some drive-bys of the house and keep a lookout for his car."

"Maybe they'll get lucky and he'll do something stupid, and they catch him in the act. But chances are you'll have one, maybe two cars a day drive by your house looking for his car. For maybe a week, before they move on to other pressing matters."

"So what can you do?" she asked me pointedly.

"Surveillance," I told her. "Sit on you and wait to see if he shows up. But you can invest a lot of time in a surveillance without anything to show for it. Meanwhile, you're paying me by the hour."

"How much?"

I told her, and she made a face.

"I'm worth it," I assured her with a smile. "But I don't want you to waste your money. You're pretty sure he knows where your mother lives, but he doesn't come to the house, you've only seen him while driving?"

"Right."

"Heading to work from home, to home from work, to school? You said you're working toward a CPA, right?"

"Yes, taking accounting classes at OCC. Night classes twice a week." She thought for a bit. "I know I've seen him twice on my way to work, two or three times on the way home. Maybe once at the college, at the far end of the parking lot, I'm not sure."

"Well, maybe it's all your imagination. Or somebody who lives in your mom's neighborhood has a car that looks like his. Hope springs eternal. But just in case…I think following you from home to work and back for a few days, also to school, would be the best bang for your buck. He's not coming to your home or workplace. If it is him, he's hanging back, and just following you in his car. From a distance. So I'll tail you, and see if I spot him. I've got a lot of experience doing that. And that way you're not paying me to sit for hours and hours when you're at work or sleeping."

"Okay, I guess." Her good mood after leaving the police department had evaporated. "How much would that cost?"

I'd punched her mother's address up on Mapquest. I practically had to drive past it to get from my current apartment accommodations to my office, and told her so. "You're barely out of my way. Pay me for four hours in advance, and that should cover a week of slight detours. I've got a full day surveillance scheduled tomorrow, but other than that I don't have anything else that should conflict." I was giving her a bargain because I felt sorry for her. Plus, if she wasn't crazy, and her ex had followed her from L.A. to Detroit, in violation of a restraining order, he could be real trouble. "Why don't you write out your schedule for me, and the address of your job." I looked at her and smiled. "And we can hope for the best. I sincerely hope you're wasting your money, but hope is not a strategy. You're doing the right thing. Do you have a better photo of him? That driver's license photo is pretty small."

She chewed at her lip. It would have been sexy if she hadn't obviously been so worried. "Yeah, I think so. I'll look for it when I get home."

Grab your copy...
vinci-books.com/splits

Author's Note

It was the third week of November, 1989. I was in Maryland for the wedding of my best friend, Jeff Barratt. I was a senior in college; he'd just gotten out of the 82nd Airborne.

The week before, I'd finished the very rough draft of my first novel, the first in this series, *Failure Drill*.

The week before, the Berlin Wall had come down.

The week before, my parents had been murdered in a crime that garnered national attention, had news crews broadcasting live from my front yard, and FBI agents answering the phone in our kitchen when my friends called wondering just what the fuck was going on, because they were watching my house on TV.

The week before had been a hell of a week.

It was in that highly charged, emotional, surreal, mind racing a-mile-a-minute state that I looked around the Columbia Inn in Columbia, Maryland (a hotel that no longer exists as it was, currently that site is occupied by the Sheraton Columbia Town Center. The nearby Bennigan's is

Author's Note

gone as well). As a young man who loved action movies and who aspired to be an author, looking around the hotel lobby/atrium, which was as it is described in this book, I had a thought—this would be a great place for a gunfight. During high-stress periods you either remember everything in crystal clear detail or forget seemingly impossible-to-forget things. The décor and setup of that hotel stuck in my mind, and hopefully you found the gunfight I set there as fun to read as I did to write.

The friends I had then are still my friends, even though we don't see each other much or talk as often as we should. However, when I use the word "friend" I'm using this definition:

Acquaintances help you move. Friends help you move a body.

This book is dedicated to those few true friends I have, both old and new.

While this book is fiction, there's a lot of the real world in it, both settings and people. Some of the characters in this novel (and *Failure Drill*) were inspired by people I know. People with whom I went through a lot. The phrase "the truth is stranger than fiction" is very very true.

About the Author

James Tarr is a regular contributor to numerous firearms/outdoor publications and has appeared on or hosted numerous shows on The Sportsman Channel cable network including *Handguns and Defensive Weapons* and *Guns & Ammo TV*. He is also the author of fourteen books (and counting), including the critically-acclaimed *Dogsoldiers*, *Whorl*, *Bestiarii*, and *Carnivore* (with Dillard Johnson), which was featured on The O'Reilly Factor. He lives in Michigan with his fiancée, two sons and three dogs.